R.D. BRADY

THE

BELIAL

RING

BOOKS

By R.D. Brady

The Belial Series

The Belial Stone

The Belial Library

The Belial Ring

The Belial Recruit

The Belial Children

The Belial Origins

The Belial Search

The Belial Guard

The Belial Warrior

The Belial Plan

The Belial Witches

The Belial War

The Belial Fall

The Belial Sacrifice

Vinci Books

vinci-books.com

Published by Vinci Books Ltd in 2025

1

A CIP catalogue record for this book is available from the British Library.

Paperback ISBN: 9781036702403

Printed and bound in Great Britain by Clays Ltd, Elcograf S.p.A.

Take, O Solomon, king, son of David,
the gift which the Lord God has sent thee,
the highest Sabbath. With it, thou shalt lock up
all demons of the earth, male and female.

The Testament of Solomon

Prologue

AD 642

THE SOUNDS of the mob worked their way through the thick stone walls of the Library of Alexandria. Hundreds of people, maybe even a thousand, were demanding the library denounce its heretical teachings—the same demand they had made for the last three days. But to Hypatia, inside the walls, their cries were just an undecipherable roar.

Hypatia's leather sandals slapped against the cool tile floor as she hastened down the hall. She passed the exhibits of the Sumerians and the rooms filled with the ancient Sanskrit writings from India. The library, she knew, held over seven hundred thousand of the world's most treasured intellectual works. It had been erected in the third century BC under Ptolemy's rule and had withstood the onslaughts of the Romans, the Christians, and other enemies of knowledge.

But the library would not withstand this latest onslaught. If the mobs didn't destroy it, the Muslim army of Amr ibn al 'Aas — which was now only a few days outside the city — would.

A torch suddenly flew through a window opening to Hypatia's right. She raised a hand to block the flaming embers from striking her face, feeling the sting as one made its mark on her cheek.

She quickly stomped out the dangerous flame, then quickened her pace, hurrying past the acquisitions room, one of the many translation rooms, and the gardens that led the back part of the library, a section which held mainly low-level staff.

Today that section was empty, most of the staff too terrified to come in. In fact, the whole back quarter of the library seemed to be empty. Those few who were present were all gathered in the records rooms, trying to save what they could.

Hypatia reached the small, dark room in the northwest corner. It held extra papyrus scrolls, rags, oils, and ink. To everyone but Hypatia, it was one of the least important rooms in the entire series of buildings that made up the great library. Few paid it any attention at all.

Hypatia glanced behind her at the empty hall before slipping through the doorway, careful to leave the door ajar. It was a risk to leave it open, but she had no other source of light for the dark room. She strode to the far wall and began to count the stones.

"Seven, eight." She paused, placing her hand on the eighth stone so she didn't lose her place.

She counted down from the ceiling. Twenty-seven. Crouching down to the stone where the row and column met, she slipped her knife from her sheath. Carefully, she worked the knife around the edge of the stone and edged it out until three inches protruded from the wall.

A wail from the mob cut through the room. And it sounded close. Hypatia's heart pounded. *They've gotten in.*

Need now overriding stealth, Hypatia yanked the stone from the wall and let it crash to the ground.

She reached her trembling hand inside the newly formed gap.

There was nothing but empty space.

Frantic now, she reached in farther, and her hand brushed a piece of heavy burlap. Releasing a breath, she pulled her prize from the wall.

She knew it was important to move quickly, but first, Hypatia had to make sure it was secure. Leaning back against the wall, she unwrapped the burlap. Inside the coarse fabric was a layer of silk, soft as a baby's skin. She marveled at its luxury. Pulling back the pale, silk leaves, she stared at the object. *So tiny - and so dangerous.*

Footsteps moved rapidly toward her, bringing her back to the present. She quickly re-wrapped the object and glanced at the door. A small face peered in at her. Hypatia swallowed down a small yelp.

"Teacher, are you all right?"

Hand on her chest, Hypatia willed her heart to slow down. "Yes, yes, Amaris. I'm fine. I thought we were meeting by the back stairwell."

Amaris looked away. "I saw you head this way."

And you didn't want to be alone, Hypatia thought, looking fondly at her young charge.

She had known Amaris since the girl was three years old. Amaris was now fourteen, but small for her age, making her appear much younger. Her pale skin and light hair only added to her youthful look. But her clear cobalt eyes told the true story. They shone with an intelligence and maturity far beyond that of a child.

As Hypatia gazed at her student, she knew this was the last time she would ever see her. Grief and tears threatened to choke her. She willed them back. Her mission was more important than her own feelings of loss.

Hypatia took Amaris's hand in hers and led her down the hallway. They turned a corner, climbed up a staircase, then wound down yet another long hallway before stopping at a stout door that led to an outside staircase.

The screams of the mob could barely be heard here. The angry crowd was congregated mainly at the front of the library; they had not yet worked their way around to the back.

Hypatia waited, hoping she was not too late. Three knocks sounded from outside the door, then, after a pause, two more.

"Thank God," Hypatia breathed as she moved aside the heavy piece of wood barring the door.

The door swung open, revealing a man. At the sight, Amaris tried to pull away, no doubt frightened by the man's appearance.

He towered over the two women, and a scar ran down the left side of his face, from his temple to his mouth, giving him a perpetual scowl. His bald head highlighted his missing left ear. Leather covered most of his legs and chest, and his bare arms and neck bore the marks of hundreds of battles.

Hypatia hoped Amaris could read the gentleness in the man's eyes.

In a soft voice, the man asked, "Is everything ready, Teacher?"

Hypatia nodded and turned Amaris to face her. "Amaris, I need you to go with Gaius. He will protect you. You can trust him."

She pressed her treasure into the young girl's hands. "And you must hide this where it cannot be found. Gaius has a letter for you that will explain what must be done. I need you to leave now. There is no time to waste."

Amaris looked from the package in her hand to Hypatia's face. Her bottom lip trembled. "You're not coming with us, are you?"

Hypatia ran her hands over her charge's hair before pulling her close. "It wouldn't be safe for you if I were to accompany you." She pulled back and stared into Amaris's eyes. "But know that I am always with you. You carry me in here." She touched Amaris's chest. "And in here." She touched the girl's head.

Amaris threw herself at Hypatia, clinging to her, her small body shaking as she sobbed quietly.

Hypatia knew she should pull Amaris off and send her away. But, God forgive her, she needed this moment as much as Amaris did.

Finally, Amaris's tears stopped. She pulled back. "I will not forget you and what you have taught me."

"I know, my child. I know." With a final embrace, Hypatia gently pushed Amaris into Gaius's arms, and closed the door behind them.

Sliding the bolt back into place, Hypatia leaned against the wall, her head down. But the sound of running feet and screaming from the halls below cut through her quiet moment. She straightened. There was no time to lose.

Running down the hall, she turned into the first hallway, the hall of the great exhibits. Just as she entered, the doors at the far side of the hall crashed in, and men came pouring through, armed with torches, swords, and clubs. The mob tore through the hall, setting the curtains ablaze and tumbling ancient statues without concern.

Scholars of the library rushed out of offices, their arms laden with scrolls and books, trying to save what they could. But when the mob spied them, they leapt upon these men of knowledge. Their loads marked them for death.

Hypatia, her arms empty, managed to slip past them.

At the end of the hall, she dodged under an ax aimed for a scholar's apprentice—just a boy, no more than seven years old. Hypatia shoved the apprentice out of the way, then whirled as the ax fell.

Grabbing her dagger from the sheath at her belt, she stabbed the assailant's neck. He clutched his throat and dropped to the ground, a pool of blood spreading around him.

The apprentice's brown eyes were wide under long dirty blond hair that had come free of its binding. Hypatia yanked the boy by the arm, pulling him out of the hall. Taking cover in an alcove, she ripped off the tunic that identified him as a member of the Library.

She peered down into the boy's terror-filled eyes. "You are a street boy, do you hear me? You are not an apprentice. You are a street rat." The boy stared behind her, his eyes riveted by the carnage.

Hypatia slapped him hard. His hand moved to cover the reddening spot on his cheek, and his eyes welled with tears —but also with understanding.

"Lucius, you must run. If anyone asks, you never worked here. You are a street rat, do you understand me?"

Lucius nodded, his large eyes swimming with tears. Hypatia's heart plummeted at the look of fear on his face. He was too young for this burden.

But she knew gentleness was not what he needed now. She pushed him down the hall, her voice fierce. "Run. Run!"

With a stumble, the boy ran down the hall. She didn't wait to see if he made it. She couldn't help him anymore.

Sprinting in the opposite direction, she ran for the exit at the back of the library. She tugged on the giant door, wrenched it open, and slipped out.

Flattening herself against a column, she held her breath as a group of five men ran past with torches. Her eyes followed the bright flames as they disappeared around the corner. Her chest was heavy with thoughts of what those flames would consume.

Hypatia glanced around, unsure which way to go. A whistle drew her attention to the right. There, a man with salt-and-pepper hair beckoned. He wore a leather vest and pants over a well-toned body, and led a pair of horses attached to a cart.

Hypatia ran for him. He quickly boosted her into the seat of the cart, then pulled himself up next to her.

"No, Antonius, no," she protested, pushing against him. She might as well have been pushing granite. "You cannot come. It is too dangerous."

He gave her a sideways glance and a snort. Then he quietly pointed, in succession, to himself, to Hypatia, and to the chariot—and then off into the distance.

Hypatia shook her head. "No. You must save yourself."

Antonius stared into her eyes, willing her to understand him. His tongue had been burned out by a group of marauders long ago, when he was a teen. Hypatia had been the one to find him, and she had nursed him back to health, keeping him hidden and safe. At the time, she had been only six years old. Antonius had refused to leave her side ever since.

Hypatia stared into his eyes and read all of that commitment there. She knew it was useless to argue with him. He would not abandon her.

Her hand caressed the side of his face. "All right, my friend, all right. We go together."

He nodded and spurred the horses on. Hypatia wanted to bring them to a gallop, but she knew that would draw attention, and with the mobs roaming the streets, they could easily crash. No—slow was safer.

They worked their way through the city, heading for the outskirts. Hypatia grew cold as she surveyed the damage from the mobs. Everywhere she looked, homes lay in ruins, reduced to smoking embers. Others still shone brightly, wrapped in devouring flames.

Whole families had been strung up in the streets—an undecipherable warning for some perceived crime. The wails of despair from unseen victims fought with the screams of irrational anger from the mobs.

Antonius turned the cart toward the market, which was usually full of life. But today, stalls burned on either side, and bodies littered the way.

Antonius tried to steer around them, but occasionally he would have to go over. Hypatia's stomach rolled with each bump.

At the end of the road, a barricade of debris and bodies blocked the way. Hypatia was struck with fear. *Could they have known we were coming this way?*

Antonius halted the horses and began the slow process of turning them around.

Feeling eyes upon her, Hypatia looked over her shoulder. A group of ten men had come up behind them, blocking their retreat. All stood silent. Hypatia recognized them for who they were. And who had sent them.

This group was no irrational mob. They were here for her.

Antonius caught sight of the men and leapt from the chariot, his battle axe in hand. With a scream from the back of his throat, he charged the men.

The first man ducked, but Antonius's axe buried itself in the shoulder of the second, who screeched in pain. Another man grabbed Antonius by the hair and stabbed him in the side. "No!"

Hypatia yelled as she jumped from the chariot and raced for him.

One of the men charged at her. She ducked his spear, caught its shaft as he swung it back, and kicked him in the chest. The man lost his breath.

Hypatia wrenched the spear from his grasp and slammed the end into his face. She then flung the spear— and her aim proved true. It plunged right into the chest of the man holding Antonius.

Strong arms wrapped around Hypatia from behind, yanking her off her feet. She was pressed up against her assailant, unable to move her arms, uselessly kicking her legs.

"Where is it, librarian? Where have you put it?" a voice snarled in her ear. It was a voice she recognized: Brutus.

"It's gone. You'll never find it."

Brutus dropped her and whipped her around. He wrapped his fist in the front of her tunic and pulled her close. "You'll tell us where it is. " He glanced down at her. "And even if you don't, there's still something he wants."

Hypatia went cold. *He knows.*

A yell from behind her drew her attention. A mob of at least two dozen men, their clothes and bodies stained with blood, charged down the road, blood in their eyes. The frenzied group wouldn't care who they killed. With demonic screams echoing from their lips, the mob fell on the men like ravenous beasts.

Brutus dragged Hypatia back, trying to get them both away from the carnage.

Hypatia dug her heels into the hard ground, tearing her skin but slowing his progress. She screamed as loud as she could.

Brutus screeched at her. "Shut up! Shut up! Or they'll come for us."

But his words were too late. The mob had seen them. As a wave, they surged toward the two of them.

"That was the idea," Hypatia murmured, as she snapped her head back, catching Brutus in the nose.

He cried out and his grip loosened. Hypatia slipped free, threw herself to the ground, and rolled. The mob flew right past her and pounced on Brutus. She lost sight of him under the mass of writhing bodies.

Getting to her knees, she braced herself to stand—when a spear lanced her chest. She fell back, the pain stealing even her ability to scream. With trembling hands, she pushed the spear out; blood poured from the wound, soaking the dry ground below.

Fearful, she looked around. Antonius lay on the ground, twenty feet to her right. She turned herself onto her side and pulled herself toward him, crying out with the effort. Exhausted and shaking, she reached his side.

He lay on his back, not moving; blood covered his chest. Hypatia lowered herself into the crook of his shoulder, whimpering with the pain. She pulled Antonius's arm around her.

Laying her head on his chest, she felt the unsteady beat of his heart. And then it went still.

Tears streamed down Hypatia's cheeks. Pulling his arm tighter around her, she whispered, "Until we meet again, my friend."

The mob howled, a few of its members catching sight of her. They advanced, but she knew they would be too late. Death would claim her before they could.

Hypatia thought of Amaris as she felt the last drops of blood drain from her body. She prayed she had escaped.

Mankind's freedom depended upon it.

Chapter One

Present Day

DR. DELANEY MCPHEARSON pulled the packing materials from the crate and carefully lifted out the metal folio. She braced her legs as she lowered the book onto the lab table in front of her. A white cotton blanket on the lab table kept it from making any noise as she set it down. It also reduced the likelihood of injury to the ancient tome.

Her auburn hair pulled back in a ponytail to keep it out of her way, Laney ran a gloved hand over the cover. Symbols were etched into the corners, and a trim had been added: it looked like vines. In the center was a title written in Enochian. Alone, it was an astounding find.

Her green eyes roamed over the other ten crates in the back of the room waiting to be unpacked. And they formed only a small portion of the crates still to be examined. They literally had hundreds of them.

Although Laney was excited about the opportunity to examine these books, the way in which their discovery came about had been brutal, causing the death of more than a hundred people. Those deaths always tempered the excitement she felt.

But awe still filled her, as it always did whenever she looked at one of the relics from the advanced civilization that pre-dated 10,000 BC. The very words of that ancient society were now right in front of her. *The find of a century.*

Today, she'd scan each page of this book. Some of the analysts at the Chandler Group had developed a translation program that worked pretty well. She'd send them the photos and they'd begin the translation.

But the words were only part of the story. Each tome was intricately carved with pictures that sometimes provided even more knowledge than the words.

She glanced at the cover longingly, wishing she could read Enochian. The program was good, but it still took a while to capture each of the pages, isolate the words, and translate them. And she was always impatient when she began.

But sadly, she didn't have any natural ability with languages. Luckily, she knew someone who did.

She glanced over her shoulder. "Hey, Henry. Can you come look at this?"

Henry Chandler, founder and head of the Chandler Group, an international think tank with a net worth just shy of a billion dollars, looked over at her. With dark, almost black hair and unusual violet eyes, Henry was a handsome man . . . and an intimidating one.

When Laney had first met him a year ago, she'd been nervous about meeting this man who was known as a titan in multiple spheres, even having been dubbed this generation's "most analytical thinker" by Forbes magazine. The fact that he also stood almost two feet taller than her modest five-four didn't help either.

But she quickly realized that all of his professional accomplishments were merely window dressing. At his core, Henry was a good man. One she could trust with her life. One she *had* trusted with her life.

Henry came to stand next to her, an eyebrow raised.

Laney gestured toward the book. "What's the title of this one?"

Henry's pupils constricted and almost wavered before he spoke. "Hard to translate into English. The closest word would be Alchemy."

They were working from a lab at the Smithsonian. The entire collection, the Shuar collection, was being housed there until its formal home down in Ecuador could be built. The Smithsonian was the safest place any of them could think of to house the ancient library.

Jake Rogan, the Chandler Group's head of security, had insisted, though, on adding some Chandler guards round the clock—in addition to the Smithsonian's already impressive security detail. Not a bad call, being that one of the books had been stolen from the collection prior to its move to the Smithsonian.

"Alchemy? Really?" Jake walked into the room and Laney's heart did a little flip.

Standing at six foot four, Jake had the broad shoulders of a football player and the V-shaped torso of a gymnast. Dark brown hair and eyes, and a nose just a little crooked, made for one beautiful, masculine man, in Laney's opinion. And he was all hers.

Jake leaned over and kissed her cheek before looking over her shoulder at the book. "Wonder if they ever figured out how to do it."

"It's not that hard," Danny Wartowski said from a desk at the other side of the room. The fourth member of their team was also the youngest. At age thirteen, Danny was the powerhouse thinker behind many of the Chandler Group's incredible projects.

Henry, Laney, and Jake all stopped and stared at him.

Danny must have felt them looking because after a minute he turned around. His deep brown eyes stared out at them from under a shaggy mane of brown hair. "What?"

"Alchemy isn't that hard?" Laney said. "Rulers for hundreds of years struggled to find the secret combination that would change metals into gold. Without any success."

Danny shrugged. "Yeah, but then there was Dr. Hantaro Nagaoka."

Laney glanced at Henry and Jake, who just shook their heads. She smiled. "Okay Danny, share with the rest of the class."

"In 1924, Dr. Hantaro Nagaoka discovered that if you place an isotope of mercury under paraffin oil and then bombard it with one hundred fifty thousand volts of electricity, you get gold," Danny said, surprise in his tone.

Danny often forgot that not everyone had a genius-level IQ. And seeing as Danny also bore more than a passing resemblance to the boy Elliot from the movie *E.T.*, it was also easy for others to forget that he was by far the smartest person in any room.

In fact, Danny was considered a genius even among geniuses. His IQ was greater than 200, while an average intelligence hovered around 100. Only two percent of the world population had an IQ above 175. Danny's IQ outdistanced even theirs.

"Really?" Jake asked.

"Really." Danny turned back to his screen, obviously done with the conversation.

Laney shook her head. *Danny, the king of obscure facts. What must it be like to have a brain that works like that?*

Shaking her head, she turned back to the book. What would this book reveal? The same thing that Dr. Nagaoka had discovered in 1924—or another way to create gold?

In the last few centuries, man always seemed to be "discovering" facts that other civilizations had already known hundreds, if not thousands, of years ago. An image of the Dogon people of Mali flashed through her mind.

In western Africa, the Dogon people claim to have known about Jupiter's four moons and the rings of Saturn for thousands of years. They even knew about the star Sirius and the two stars, Sirius B and C, that circled it. Modern man didn't verify these facts until the last century, with the invention of high-powered telescopes. The Dogon, by contrast, knew about Sirius as far back as 3,200 BC.

"I think I've found something," Danny said, interrupting Laney's thoughts.

Laney walked over to the other side of the room, joined by Henry and Jake. Danny had been working on the resolution of the book that was stolen two months ago from the Shuar collection. They'd been unable to clean up the security film image, but just this morning they had finally identified the book from the inventory.

"What have you got?" Henry asked.

"Hold on. I'll put it on the big screen." Danny hit a couple of buttons on his keyboard.

The four of them walked over to the ultra-high-definition seventy-inch screen on the right side of the room. The picture was beyond crisp. It was almost as if the book were lying right there in front of them.

"Where did this picture come from?" Jake asked.

"It was part of the inventory that Flourent did when they stole the Shuar collection," Laney said, her focus still on the screen.

Before Sebastian Flourent started any work on the collection that he'd stolen from the Shuar people, he had the people working for him document the find. The notes and accompanying documentation had been found when Jake recovered the collection.

Flourent and his people might have been complete monsters, but they were meticulous in their documentation.

The book on the screen was about a foot and a half by two feet. It was covered in what looked like gold leaf. Laney's hands itched to touch it.

The thieves who'd stolen the book had clearly been looking for this specific book—they had disregarded all the others. And they could have easily made off with a dozen of them, if not more.

Dread spread through Laney. She didn't know why the two who had stolen it wanted this particular book. But whatever the reason, it didn't bode well for the rest of mankind that the book was now in the hands of a Fallen.

And that was the real fear that nestled deep within her chest whenever she thought about this book. Not just that it was stolen. But that it was stolen by two of *them*.

Last year, Laney, Jake and Henry discovered that the world included beings other than humans. It also included fallen angels, who were reborn time and again, although most had no knowledge of their previous lives. As a result, they were usually alone, never even having knowledge of their brethren. They did, however, retain their abilities.

But two of them had worked together to steal this book.

Laney felt her familiar terror rise up, like it did whenever she thought of the Fallen.

She'd fought two together once. She never wanted to do that again. And she worried about what it meant that they now seemed to be teaming up with greater frequency. Because from what she and her friends knew, the Fallen working together was supposed to be a rare occurrence.

Henry clapped Danny on the shoulder. "Great work, Danny. Why don't you go get a milkshake to celebrate?"

Laney could tell that Danny was trying hard not to roll his eyes. "Right," he said. "Because you guys want to discuss this thing without me."

"No, of course not," Henry said. "I just thought you could use a little break."

Danny handed the control to Laney. "Okay. I'm going. What do you need, thirty minutes?"

Laney tried not to smile. "That should do it."

Danny nodded. "I'll go take Moxy for a walk." Danny's chow-shepherd, Moxy, would sit outside the lab room when they were examining the books. Even though she was well trained, the Smithsonian balked at the idea of a dog being in the room with the ancient books. So she stayed in an office right outside. "See you."

When the door closed behind Danny, Laney and Jake turned to stare at Henry.

"What?" Henry demanded.

Jake laughed. "You just tried to lie, very badly, to a super-genius. I know he's technically thirteen, but even a seven-year-old with average intelligence could have seen through that."

Henry grimaced. "I know. It's just, after Las Vegas, I want to keep him safe. And keep him away from all of this as much as I can."

"You know that's going to be all but impossible," Jake said. "Danny's as curious as the rest of us about what's going on."

"I know. But it doesn't mean I'm not going to try. He's been through enough. Whatever this book says, it's for the biological adults to deal with, not just the legal adults."

Laney patted his shoulder. Henry had taken Danny in when he was ten. Danny's own family had been unkind, to say the least, about Danny's intelligence. Henry had offered Danny a safe haven and a place to belong. He'd even helped emancipate him. In every way, Henry had become Danny's father.

"You're right," Laney said. "We'll keep him out of this as much as we can."

"Is that a Star of David?" Jake asked, directing their attention back to the screen. He pointed to a symbol in the bottom left.

Laney moved to stand next to him. Sure enough, in the corner of the book were two triangles overlapping to create a star. "It looks like it, but Judaism only dates to around 2,000 BC. Of course, the Star of David isn't only a Judaic symbol; it's also mentioned in both the Quran and Talmud as well. But it still doesn't make any sense."

Henry shook his head. "Technically, I suppose the Star could be dated to Abraham, which puts it at maybe 5,000 BC. But this text is still much older. It dates to at least 10,000 BC, if not earlier."

Laney traced the symbol. "It's also known as the seal of Solomon."

The seal of Solomon was two interlaced triangles, which was supposed to be inscribed with the name of God. In the Judaic tradition, the wearer was said to be protected by the symbol from fire, wounds, and other harms.

Laney's eyes roamed over the other shapes on the cover. "In fact, one could argue that a bunch of these other symbols are also related to Solomon."

She traced the picture of a beast that looked like a cross between a lion and a bear. "Solomon was alleged to have the ability to control the animals."

Henry pointed to a few wavy lines. "This might be water or wind."

"And Solomon could control that as well?" Jake asked.

Laney shrugged. "Allegedly he could."

"This is Solomon of 'split the baby in two' fame, right?" Jake asked.

Laney nodded. "But Solomon was more than that. He was supposed to have been the wisest ruler of ancient Israel. Israel went through a time of unprecedented peace and prosperity under his rule. Well, at least, until he became corrupted and started disobeying God's rules."

"What rules?" Jake asked.

Laney smiled. "He is alleged to have had over seven hundred wives and three hundred concubines."

Jake let out a low whistle. "Man was busy."

Laney elbowed him in the ribs.

Jake put his hands up. "Not that I would ever want that. I'm more than happy with my one woman."

She snorted. "Nice save."

Henry ignored their banter. "He also built the greatest temple: the first Temple."

Laney shook her head. "Actually, according to legend, *he* didn't build it. Demons did. Demons under his control."

Jake looked sharply at Laney. "He could control demons? As in—fallen angels? Could this book explain how?"

"I don't know, but if it does, it would explain why the Fallen wanted it," Henry said.

Laney stared at the images on the screen. "But that doesn't make any sense. Solomon lived around 1,000 BC. This book is much, much older than that. So this can't be depicting Solomon's reign."

Jake turned to look at Henry. "What's the title of the book?"

Henry examined the title, his pupils once again contracting. After a moment he turned to them, his mouth hanging open slightly.

Dread welled up in Laney. "Henry?"

"It's called *The Army of the Belial.*"

"Oh shit," Jake said.

Laney looked at the two of them but didn't speak. Her mind raced. *The Army of the Belial.* She'd heard that phrase before—but where? She gasped, grabbing Jake's arm.

"Laney?" He looked down at her, concern in his eyes.

"I just realized where I've heard that phrase before." She went silent, staring off into space. *It couldn't be, could it?*

"Laney?" Henry's voice cut through her thoughts. "Where did you hear it?"

"The War Scroll."

"Wait," Jake said, "that's one of the Dead Sea Scrolls, right?"

"Yeah. It's the one that talks about the final battle between the forces of good and the Army of the Belial."

Laney stared at the screen. The two Fallen from Vegas had gone to a lot of trouble to get this book.

"Oh, that's not good," Henry mumbled.

"No. That's not good at all." Laney agreed.

Chapter Two

JOHNSON CITY, TENNESSEE

AMAR PATEL SAT in his office, his pale green eyes focused on the monitor in front of him. Two boys, both seventeen, circled one another on a dirt floor. Yells could be heard from others in the room, but they were off camera. The camera remained fixed on the two combatants.

One of the boys was very muscular, his arms well defined. He outweighed his opponent by at least fifty pounds and was six inches taller. His opponent, by contrast, looked as if a stiff wind could blow him over.

In a normal fight, the smart money would be on the bigger opponent.

But this wasn't a normal fight.

The smaller teen had a look of complete confidence on his face as he watched his opponent. He smirked as the bigger boy circled him; at one point, he even turned his back on his towering friend. Sensing an opening, the larger boy charged from behind.

At the last second, the smaller boy moved, lightning fast.

He jumped straight up in the air. The taller boy fell forward, arms outstretched, sliding in the dirt.

The smaller boy landed, one leg on either side of the sprawled boy's waist. He grabbed the larger boy by the hair and looked up, his eyes focused on someone out of camera range. With a nod, he placed his hands on either side of the boy's head—then twisted so fast no human eye would be able to even see the motion.

Letting the larger boy's head drop limply to the ground, he stood with a grin, and bowed at the waist.

Amar smiled as well, wishing he had audio. He was sure the echo of the snapping of the dead boy's neck must have been impressive.

Amar leaned back. The kid was a little bit of a show-boat, but that could be beaten out of him. A little training, and the boy would be good. Very good. He texted a quick note to that effect into his phone before switching off the monitor.

Amar stood and stretched. His attention had only been half focused on the training module. He wanted to see how the translation was coming. But he knew it would take time, and it wouldn't do for anyone to see him anxious. A leader must at all times demonstrate control. Control was everything—especially with this group.

Amar walked down the hall. He felt a tingle of anticipation. Yesterday, the translator had said he was close, really close. Amar quickened his pace.

Taking the stairs at the end of the hall two at a time, he stepped into the wide hallway at the top. He strode down the hall toward the large door at the end, opened it, and nodded with satisfaction. Everyone was working, their focus on the tasks in front of them.

The room was large, with a giant picture window at the

other end. A large work table sat on the right-hand side and a wall of computers blanketed the left. Five individuals glanced up when he entered. All of them nodded respectfully before turning back to their tasks.

This room was the hub of his enterprise—at least, his more *important* enterprise. Of course he had managers overseeing his financial empire, but this room had nothing to do with that.

Amar walked over to the table. There, covered in glass, was the book. He stopped and gazed at it. *All that knowledge.*

He curled his hand into a fist and had to actively restrain himself from punching through the glass. He cursed silently. *The bane of their existence.*

Every time he saw it, his anger grew. If he could, he would kill the author over again. But seeing as he'd died over ten thousand years ago, it didn't look like that would be happening.

Amar glanced over at the translator, who was sitting at a monitor, muttering to himself. He'd found the man online— some recluse who was obsessed with Enochian. Heavyset, with a prominent chin and forehead, he was not an attractive man.

But Amar didn't need the man for his looks. He walked over, clapped the man on his shoulder. "So, Jeff, how's the translation coming?"

Jeff winced. "Fine, fine. Got that last section translated finally. Printed it out for you." Jeff nudged his chin toward the printer in the corner.

Amar made his way over, pulling the sheets from the tray. He read through them quickly. And then he read them again, more slowly this time, careful to keep his face expressionless.

Without a word, Amar made his way back out the

room, careful to keep his steps unhurried, to betray no reaction.

He closed the door softly behind him, gripping the papers tightly, pursing his lips. *Damn it. It is her.*

Chapter Three

LANEY AND JAKE walked up the stairs to Henry's office. He'd called them fifteen minutes ago and said he needed to meet with them immediately. Laney took Jake's hand as they reached the landing outside Henry's office.

They'd finished up at the Smithsonian a few hours earlier and headed home to the Chandler estate. The Chandler estate was the headquarters for the Chandler Group, as well as home to Henry, Laney, and Jake. Henry lived in a cottage a few hundred yards from the massive main house; Laney and Jake lived in cottages down on Sharecroppers Lane, a mix of business and residential cottages that previously had been sharecroppers' homes back in the late 1800s.

Laney had been packing for their first family trip when Henry had called and requested that she and Jake come to his office. Laney, Jake, Henry, Danny, and her Uncle Patrick were all heading to Hershey, Pennsylvania, along with Kati Simmons, Laney's housemate from Syracuse, and Kati's four-year-old son, Max.

A little weekend away filled with amusement parks, good

company, and lots and lots of chocolate. Heaven. And after the year they'd had, well overdue. Laney couldn't wait.

But although she was excited about the trip, she couldn't get the book out of her mind. *The Army of the Belial.* The images on the cover seemed to indicate Solomon, but also some type of battle.

"Hey, you with me?" Jake said.

Laney squeezed his hand. "Sorry. My mind's wandering."

Jake pulled her to a stop, stepping in front of her. He tilted her head up. "Laney, it's just a book. Don't go borrowing trouble."

She sighed. "I know, it's just—"

He kissed her, cutting off the rest of her statement. "It can wait. It's already waited ten thousand years. Let's meet with Henry, get everyone, and get out of here. The world won't collapse if we ignore the Fallen for one weekend. Okay?"

She leaned into him, her lips still warm from his kiss. "You're right. Let's go."

The double doors to Henry's office were closed. Laney could just make out the sound of voices beyond it, although the voices were too low to make out any words.

She glanced at Jake. "Any idea what this is about?"

They would be leaving for their trip in the morning and Laney knew Henry didn't have any meetings scheduled for tonight. Plus, he'd been very professional when he'd called, which told her that someone else had been nearby when he'd been speaking.

"There's one way to find out." Jake knocked.

"Come in," Henry called.

Jake opened the door, letting Laney go in first. Henry stood up from behind his desk. Standing across the desk from him was a man in a dark grey suit, dark tie, and white shirt: the standard uniform for a fed.

With surprise, Laney realized she'd seen this man before: once in Montana and once in Las Vegas. Both times in connection to Atlantis-related incidents. And now he was here. *This can't be good.*

With a sinking feeling, Laney crossed the room.

Henry gestured toward Laney and Jake. "Agent Matthew Clark, this is my chief of security, Jake Rogan, and this is Dr. Delaney McPhearson."

Dark blond hair, an athletic build—Laney guessed the agent was in his early forties. Crow's-feet were just beginning to form at the corners of his brown eyes. An easy smile spread across the man's face. "Matt, please."

Laney crossed the room and shook his hand. "Agent Clark. Exactly which branch of law enforcement are you with?"

Clark turned to shake Jake's hand while answering. "The SIA."

Jake loomed over the shorter agent. "The SIA? I'm not familiar with it."

"It stands for Special Investigative Agency," Henry said.

"We're a rather quiet offshoot of the Department of Defense," Clark offered.

"I see." Laney took a seat. *Department of Defense?* She darted a quick glance at Henry, who'd also taken his seat, but his face was unreadable.

She glanced at Jake, who was now leaning against the wall next to Henry's desk. He caught her eyes, giving a small shake of his head. He hadn't heard of it either.

"So, what can we do for you, Agent?" Jake's tone suggested that helping the agent was not exactly his top priority.

Clark looked between Laney and Jake, seemingly unconcerned with the rather lukewarm greeting he was receiving. "The government is aware of the situations in both Montana and Ecuador."

Laney shrugged, trying to keep her voice casual. "Lots of people are aware of the situations in Ecuador and Montana. It was pretty big news for a while."

Clark smiled. "Yes. Well, we're aware of the story behind the public story."

Both incidents had been in the public sphere. The finding of an ancient society's relics had made quite a stir. The media hounds had been all over both stories for weeks. But the truth behind the incidents, particularly the involvement of fallen angels, had not been made public.

"I'm not sure we know what you're referring to," Jake said, sounding bored.

Clark smiled again. "Look, I'm a 'lay all my cards' on the table kind of guy. And from what I've read on you three, you are as well."

Laney nodded, noticing Henry and Jake doing the same from the corner of her eye.

"Good," Clark said. "So. The SIA is aware that a fallen angel attempted to destroy the world in Montana and that you three stopped him. We also know that two fallen angels stole a book from the Shuar collection while it was housed in Las Vegas." Clark paused to glance at Henry. "And Henry, we know about your abilities as well."

You could have heard a pin drop. Laney scrambled for something to say, but her mind was an absolute blank. *How do they know? What is the government planning?* She forced herself not to look at Henry, not to reveal the fear she felt at someone else knowing what he could do.

Clark held up his hands. "We have no intention of

making any of this information public. In fact, the larger United States government is not aware of any of the facts I've just shared with you. That information is strictly in-house."

"How's that possible?" Jake asked, not having moved from his slouch against the wall, but Laney could read anger in the set of his jaw. Jake didn't like anyone coming in and dropping surprises on him. And she was pretty sure he was taking the information drop on Henry as a threat.

"We're an old agency that is given quite a bit of latitude," Clark replied.

"Why are you coming to us?" Henry asked.

Clark paused, then made eye contact with each of them. "Each of you has been intimately involved in these recoveries. You, in particular, Dr. McPhearson. The SIA decided that it was time for you to be aware of our existence."

"I'm still not exactly sure who 'you' are. What is your agency's agenda—" She corrected herself. "What are your objectives?"

Clark crossed his legs at the ankles, giving the appearance of being unconcerned. Laney was pretty sure the body language was intentional.

"We monitor the Fallen. When they're dangerous, we try to remove them. We're not always successful. But most of the time, we are. So if you're ever in need of help, you should call us." Clark leaned forward, placing three business cards on the desk.

Laney took one of the cards. It was a plain white business card with only a phone number and email. No identifying name, no affiliation, no insignia. "How long have you known about the Fallen?"

"Me? Personally?" Clark shrugged. "For quite some time. The SIA, however, has been around since 1776."

Laney started at the date. *Since the beginning of the United States*. The government, or at least a part of the government, knew that the Fallen were out there. And *had* known for over two hundred years. Laney wasn't sure if that was a good thing or a bad one.

How had the SIA managed to keep their existence a secret all this time, as well as their objectives? With oversight and computer leaks, how had information on this agency not been leaked? And what exactly had the SIA been doing with that knowledge?

A chill ran through her. She watched Clark, who was still seemingly at ease.

"So when you find one of these Fallen," Jake said, "what do you do?"

Clark leaned back in his chair. "Well, that depends. Some live normal lives, and no one knows anything about their abilities."

"How do you find them then?" Henry asked. "If they don't reveal what they can do, they'd be unremarkable. They'd look like everybody else."

Clark nodded. "True. But occasionally people slip. And when they do, we pay attention. Even your Dr. Radcliffe has a method of tracking them down. His method is very similar to ours."

Laney tried to look surprised, but she knew she failed. Too many surprises were coming at her too fast. Dr. Radcliffe, or Dom, was a brilliant agoraphobic who lived in a bomb shelter about a half-mile from where they now sat.

Dom was notoriously suspicious of the government. He would *not* be happy to know the government was aware of his data collection on the Fallen.

And Laney was awfully curious as to how they knew about that. The only way they could have that knowledge was if they had been monitoring their communications. And the Chandler Group's email had some pretty heavy security protocols in place.

"So what you're saying," Jake said, interrupting Laney's thoughts, "is that some of the Fallen live their lives without causing any problems?"

"Yes." Clark turned to Laney. "You're a criminologist, Dr. McPhearson. And from what I've read on you, your specialization is genetics and crime."

Laney nodded.

"So, you tell me: what's more important, a person's biology or their environment?"

Laney paused. It was a tricky question. People were born with biological predispositions for different personality characteristics. A penchant for risky behavior in the right environment could make for a great athlete. But in the wrong environment, it made a criminal. So it was the interaction between the two that was most critical. And according to recent discoveries, that interaction was proving to be more and more critical.

The research ran through Laney's head, along with all the explanations and caveats. But as she looked around the room, she realized that no one was interested in a lecture on genetics.

She shrugged. "That's a rather big question. To simplify the answer, I'd say people are born with biological predispositions, but the environment determines how those predispositions are realized. From that view, the environment is more important, because it's mutable. Biology is not."

Clark nodded. "Believe it or not, that applies to the Fallen as well. Some are actually good people trying to help."

Henry looked over the desk. "You have Fallen working with you."

Henry's words hadn't been a question, but Clark treated them like they were. He nodded. "Yes. They recognize their own kind. You are aware of that?"

Laney, Henry, and Jake all nodded. Over the course of the last year, they had learned that the Fallen feel an automatic connection to other Fallen when they are near one another. Fallen will also feel a connection to a nephilim, the child of a human and a Fallen, although that connection is weaker. And nephilim, like Henry, felt a connection to one another, but not to full-fledged Fallen.

Clark continued. "The Fallen working with us help us track down others of their kind. And sometimes, when the situation warrants it, they even help recruit them." He nodded at Henry. "Nephilim, too."

Henry gave the agent a smile that would have done a shark proud. "Well, if this is a recruitment pitch, I'm afraid I'll have to decline."

Clark gave an easy laugh. "Not at all."

"I'm not sure I like the idea of the Fallen being recruited," Jake said.

Clark nodded, his easygoing mask slipping just a little. "Well, being recruited by us is a good thing. The problem is —we're not the only ones doing it."

Chapter Four

LANEY STRUGGLED to keep her face expressionless. Someone—someone besides this government organization that they hadn't even heard of until two minutes ago—was recruiting the Fallen. *Shit* seemed too tame a curse for that kind of revelation.

"Who else is recruiting?" Jake asked.

Clark shrugged, although his tense posture made it clear he wasn't as nonchalant as he was trying to appear. "We're not sure exactly. We don't have any names—at least not any names of the big guys behind the recruitment."

Laney cut him off. "Big guys? So you think it's a group doing the recruiting, not just an individual?"

Clark nodded. "The Fallen have, throughout time, occasionally made their presence known. But usually they stick to the shadows, gathering power individually. Every once in a while, though, they begin to group. And when that happens, it never bodes well for humanity."

"What do you mean—in the past?" Laney asked.

Clark raised an eyebrow. "Hmm, I thought you would already know that."

Laney reined in her impatience. *No, I don't know that, jackass.*

"Well, there have been times in humanity's history when the Fallen have united," Clark said. "In those times, humanity has been on the edge of destruction."

"Atlantis and the world flood," Laney said.

Clark nodded. "That was one. The Trojan War was another. There have been other failed attempts as well, such as the Hundred Years War and World War II."

Now Jake interrupted. "World War II? Hitler was a Fallen?"

Clark shook his head. "No, although it's no secret he wished he was. He was part of a human group. But we believe some of his Übermensch may have been."

Laney knew the Übermensch were a later addition to Hitler's Lebensborn program. Members of the program had to be able to demonstrate their racial purity back to 1750 and be in perfect physical condition. The program resulted in the birth of forty-two thousand babies before its end in 1944.

In the final years of the program, though, Hitler added an additional membership requirement: each male member must be at least six feet tall. And members six feet six inches, or taller were regarded as Übermensch, the closest Germans to their warrior ancestors.

Laney's gaze strayed to Henry. One of the attributes that sometimes came with being a nephilim was extreme height. Laney had never thought of the Übermensch in relation to the Fallen. Had the Übermensch been nephilim? Had Hitler tapped into their unique abilities, or been trying to? It was a frightening thought.

Her head spinning, she shoved her curiosity into a corner of her mind, focusing on the issue at hand. "And you believe the Fallen are grouping again?"

Clark nodded. "Yes. And at the SIA, we don't like that. We thought you should be warned."

"But why us?" Laney asked.

Clark leaned back, his hands entwined across his flat stomach. "You three are interesting. For some reason, the Fallen seem to be swirling around you. You've been involved with at least four Fallen in less than a year. That's significant. And you're all still alive. That's remarkable. In the process, you've uncovered Atlantis artifacts that haven't seen the light of day in ten thousand years, if not longer. Whatever's coming, all our analysis suggests that you will be involved."

Laney felt her pit of fear—the fear that had been created in Ecuador, and had never entirely disappeared—get a little bit bigger. Whatever the Fallen had planned, she really hoped it left her and the ones she loved alone. They'd been through enough at the hands of the Fallen and those tracking down Atlantis artifacts to last a lifetime. Now it was someone else's turn to fight.

"Any idea why the Fallen seem to be swirling around us?" Jake asked.

Clark stood up. "Actually, I do. But I am not at liberty to say. Not yet."

"That's it?" Laney asked. The man walked in, told them the Fallen were recruiting for some evil purpose, most likely some form of world domination, and now he was just leaving?

Clark smiled. "For now. It was nice to meet all of you. And like I said, if you need us, call." Clark walked out of the room, closing the door behind him.

Silence settled over the room. Jake broke it. "What the hell was that all about?"

"I have no idea." Henry's eyes narrowed, still focused on the door where Clark had exited.

"Do we know if these guys are even legit?" Jake asked.

Henry looked over at him and nodded. "They are. I was skeptical when Clark first explained who he was. But he gave me the numbers of a few highly placed individuals within the government and military, most of whom I know personally. The SIA is real."

Laney glanced down at the business card in her hand. "So, do we think the SIA are the good guys . . . or the bad guys?"

Jake sat down next to her. "Jury's still out. For now, we stay suspicious. I'll tap some sources, see if anyone has any info on these guys. Henry, have you ever heard of them before?"

Henry shook his head. "No. Never."

Laney pulled out her phone and typed the name into a search engine. "Well, unsurprisingly, they have no official website. The only sources that do mention them seem to be conspiracy websites."

Jake leaned over to glance at her screen. "What do they say?"

Laney skimmed through the first few websites, her dread growing. "Nothing good. Apparently some consider the SIA to be the origin of the men in black myth. Others attribute multiple abductions and disappearances to them. And according to at least two sites, they aren't just an American group. They're multi-national."

Henry sighed. "Well, that's just great."

"How about your mom?" Jake asked. "Has she ever mentioned them?"

Henry shook his head. "No. But she does tend to keep things close to the vest. I'll ask her though."

Laney slumped down lower in her chair. "So, along with the knowledge that the Fallen are grouping together, which cannot bode well, we now have a shadowy government agency that seems interested in us. Fabulous."

Jake stood up, pulling Laney with him. "True. But the reality is that, as of this moment, nothing's changed. I say we put Agent Clark and his group out of our minds for now. We have a family vacation to take."

Henry smiled. "Danny's been practically bouncing off the walls all afternoon in anticipation."

Laney nodded, trying to smile. She knew Jake was right. Nothing had changed, but still. "Are we sure? Maybe we should cancel."

Jake shook his head. "No. Fact is, the only thing that's changed is our knowledge of this agency. There's no direct threat, no reason to put our lives on hold."

Henry nodded. "I agree. And besides, I think we've all earned a little fun."

Laney looked at both of them for a long moment and then blew out a breath, determined to make the best of it. "All right. Let's head to Hershey. A family vacation. What could go wrong?"

Henry and Jake went silent. Laney saw the concern that crossed both of their faces. They were no doubt thinking about the last few times this last year when peace had descended upon them. And then, of course, all hell had broken loose.

Laney sighed. "Well, let's just hope for the best, okay?"

Chapter Five

ATHENS, GREECE

1,500 BC

The wind pushed eleven-year-old Helen's short blond hair into her face. She swiped it back with an impatient gesture.

A crow let out a shriek as it flew overhead. Helen looked up with a shiver. She hated those birds, the harbingers of death.

"What's the matter, child?" Aethra sat only a few feet away in the garden, her embroidery in her lap, a basket of colorful threads beside her. Her hair had begun to turn to grey, but kindness shone in her brown eyes.

A kindness her son did not have. It wasn't Aethra's fault her son had kidnapped Helen. Helen tried to keep that in mind when dealing with the older woman.

Helen pointed up at the disappearing black shape. "The crows. They're a sign of death."

Aethra opened her arms and Helen walked into them. Helen sighed, enjoying the comfort. Aethra's arms weren't her mother's, but sometimes they were a good substitute. Like right now.

Aethra stroked Helen's hair. "You have nothing to fear. Theseus has made sure that you are well protected."

Helen glanced at the two guards who were always with them, but who never smiled. They were brutish men, both of them tall and battle-scarred. The two men had been her constant shadows for four months. But she was most definitely not comforted by their presence.

Theseus had dropped her in Athens with his mother after—

Helen buried her head in Aethra's chest. She didn't want to think about that night. About what he'd done.

Instead, Helen tried to just enjoy being outside, feeling the sun on her face. She was allowed outside for only short periods of time, after all. And although the courtyard was bordered by tall stone walls on all four sides, it was still large enough to allow her to run. It even had room for a small arbor of olive trees.

A familiar whistle sounded. Helen looked up in disbelief, stepping out of Aethra's arms. Hope bloomed in her chest. Could it be?

The guards stepped forward, pulling their swords from their sheaths. From over one of the walls, an arrow flew, lodging itself in the neck of one of the guards. The guard grabbed at his throat, but blood already gushed from the wound. He collapsed to the ground.

Helen's eyes flew to the top of the stone wall opposite the only guard who remained.

Two blond teenagers lay flat on the wall. One threw down a rope and quickly slid down. The other simply jumped from his high perch, landing with a nimble roll.

Together, the young men pulled their own swords free. Tall and muscular, they looked strikingly similar as they advanced on the remaining guard.

Aethra clutched Helen close, her arms trembling. "Oh no, child, you must run. You must escape." She tried to push Helen toward the door.

Helen sidestepped Aethra's hands before taking both of them in her own. Her eyes, though, never left the twins advancing on the remaining guard. She'd seen her brothers defeat men double this guard's size without breaking a sweat. This guard would be no match for them.

Helen glanced at the older woman with a smile. "Don't worry, Aethra. They won't hurt me. Or you, either. They've come to rescue me. That's Castor and Pollux."

Chapter Six

LANEY JOLTED AWAKE, still half in the dream, wanting to see Castor and Pollux defeat the guard. She stared at the ceiling, confused for a moment as to where the sky had gone. Looking around, she recognized the generic furnishings of the hotel room. With a shake of her head, she remembered she was in Hershey, Pennsylvania, not ancient Athens.

Unnerved, she rubbed her eyes. The dreams had become a constant of her sleeping life. It was taking longer each time she woke to remember where she was. *Who* she was.

A muscular male arm wrapped around her waist. Laney grasped Jake's hand and snuggled back into him.

"Another dream?" Jake's voice was husky from sleep.

"Yeah." The dreams had plagued her for the last two months; they'd started right after Ecuador. She was always a different woman or girl, from a different time and place.

"Who were you this time?" Jake asked.

"I'm not sure. Do you know who Castor and Pollux's sister was?"

"Yes, and so do you. They had two. The first one's name was Clytemnestra. And the second was Helen."

"Helen?" Laney rolled over to face Jake.

Jake leaned up on his elbow, his eyebrows raised. His finger traced a path down the side of her face. "Helen of Troy."

Surprise filtered through her. "Huh. I never knew they were related. In the dream, I was Helen. But young, maybe twelve years old. I'd been kidnapped. Castor and Pollux were coming to save me."

Jake nodded, and Laney could see the sparkle in his eyes. Myths always intrigued him. "Castor and Pollux were well-known heroes in the Age of Heroes. When Helen was approaching puberty, she was kidnapped by Theseus."

"Theseus? As in the minotaur and Crete?"

"Yes. He wanted to steal the virginity of a god's daughter. She was taken to Athens, where she was left with Theseus's mother, Aethra. The brothers, who were only teenagers at the time, saved her."

Laney felt cold. Jake's description matched her dream. "I don't know that story. How did I dream it?"

"You probably heard it in high school and just forgot."

"Is it in *The Iliad*?"

Jake's face clouded. "Actually, it's not. Her abduction is mentioned by a number of other authors, though, including Diodorus and Hellanicus of Lesbos."

"I've never heard of either of those people."

Jake brought her hand to his lips. "I'm sure one of your teachers mentioned Helen's back story when they taught *The Iliad*. Your subconscious probably just retained the information."

"I guess," Laney said, although she was far from convinced. She had, of course, heard about Helen and the Trojan War, but she couldn't remember ever having heard of Helen's early life.

And even if she had, why would she dream about it?

Jake took her face in his hands. "Helen was reputed to be the most beautiful woman in the world. I can see why you would dream you were her."

Laney smiled, chasing away her concerns. Jake was probably right. It was just a dream. She wrapped her arms around his neck. "You just earned a lot of brownie points with that comment."

Jake gave her a long, lingering kiss, until the phone interrupted them. With a groan, Jake let her go and reached for the phone. He picked up the receiver and let it drop. "Our wake-up call. Now, where were we?"

Laney rolled out of his reach. "Oh, no. We're meeting everybody for breakfast. We are not going to be late."

"A couple of minutes won't matter."

Laney gave him a pointed look. "Great. Then you can explain to my uncle, the priest, what we, an unmarried couple, were doing that caused us to be late."

Jake groaned, sitting up. "Fine. You want to shower first?"

"No. Go ahead."

Jake rolled out of bed. He stopped to kiss her on the forehead as he walked past, and then closed the bathroom door behind him.

Laney sat back down on the bed, clutching a pillow to her chest. The dream was beginning to fade. But she could still picture her brothers—

Laney shook her head. *Not my brothers. Helen's brothers.*

She looked around the room. The dreams were getting

harder and harder to shake. And a small part of Laney's brain was beginning to worry about the effect they were having. Why was she having these dreams? Was it some form of PTSD from Ecuador?

She sighed. Maybe she should go talk to someone. After everything she'd been through in the last year, she probably should be having regular weekly visits with a shrink. Maybe even daily.

She stood up and strode over to her suitcase to figure out what to wear. Whatever her subconscious was working through would have to wait. Today, she had a chocolate tour to take. Laney pulled out a navy blouse and her dark-wash jeans.

In the back of her mind, though, she had a feeling that she should pay attention to these dreams. They seemed to be trying to tell her something.

She just wasn't sure she wanted to hear it.

Chapter Seven

AMAR WALKED down the long drive to the barn. His estate sat on one hundred and twenty-three acres in the middle of nowhere. It had been an acquisition resulting from a particularly productive string of investments.

The former owners had not been as fortunate with their own investments, and had been desperate to get rid of the place. Amar got it for a steal.

He smiled. *A steal. What a great phrase.*

It had previously been a horse farm. The barn had housed over three dozen champion-level horses. When Amar took over, the first thing he did was have the barn converted for his pet project.

The barn itself was a work of art. The six-thousand-square-foot building had a grey rock face that matched some of the main house's exterior. Ahead, two barn doors loomed, each over twenty-five feet tall and almost as wide.

The screams of his cats wafted through the thick doors. He smiled. *Ah, my friends know I'm coming.*

Two guards saw him approach and quickly opened the

white barn doors. Each guard was a hulking man, fearsome looking, but only human.

Amar liked to have the humans around. Being reminded of their fragility did wonders for his ego.

He'd hired these two months ago. He knew they were spies for the Council. But he pretended he didn't. He liked controlling what information the Council received.

The Council. Humans scraping at my boot heels for whatever scraps I drop. His gaze flicked back to the guard. *But they do have their uses.*

The screech of the cats roared at him as he entered. He noticed one of the guards shiver at the sound. The guard had met his pets.

Amar smiled. *How horrible it must be to be human.*

Stepping into the giant space, he glanced around, nodding his approval. It was pristine. His humans might be weak, but they followed orders. He had about twenty Fallen and nephilim on the property as well, but he would never ask them to do something as menial as taking care of the barn. That's what humans were for.

All of the stalls in the barn had been removed, and in their place were eight giant steel cages, four lined up on each side. Amar smiled as he walked down the long corridor between them.

Only two of the cages were currently occupied. The beasts inside them were beautiful. Sleek, black, the Javan leopards prowled along the edges of their confines. Their skin rippled like water. At first glance, their coats appeared pure black. But each was actually spotted with marks of an even deeper black.

Amar was just shy of six feet tall, yet the leopards, when standing on all fours, were almost his height. The growth hormone they'd been given as cubs had turned them into nightmare beasts.

Amar stopped next to the cage with the larger of the two beasts. A giant paw, larger than Amar's head, swiped through the bars. With lightning speed, Amar ducked out of the way, chuckling.

Titus roared his displeasure at having missed.

"Don't worry, my friend. You'll have your chance."

Amar had decided they'd have a hunt soon. He'd been so preoccupied with the book that he hadn't had a chance to work with his pets. His bloodlust was building. He knew he needed to release it soon or . . .

He pictured the last time he'd gone too long without allowing his natural instincts to be indulged. It had taken weeks to get the bloodstains out of the house. And then, of course, he'd had to replace the whole staff.

It had been satisfying, but killing humans had become complicated. Laws, families. It was a nightmare.

He smiled at his pets. *Man against beast.* He chuckled again. *The perfect solution.*

Besides, killing humans offered very little challenge. They were too slow, too vulnerable, too weak. He'd been searching for a worthier foe when he'd come across a man doing some interesting research.

Amar had always been intrigued by science's almost limitless potential in this age. As a child, he'd seen pictures of the two-headed dog created by the Russian scientist Dr. Vladimir Demikhov. Although most of the world had been horrified by the doctor's creation, Amar had been fascinated. He'd always wanted to create a beast of his own imagining.

More recently, Chinese doctors had successfully merged human cells with rabbit eggs. Amar knew that combining his own cells with an animal would create a beast truly worthy of his skills. He'd convinced a scientist to add Amar's own blood to the cocktail given to the cubs in utero.

It had taken a few years to get the formula just right. The cats that had filled these cages, including the two that remained, were second-generation.

Enhanced speed. Healing. Now they were a worthy challenge. Finally, an opponent worthy of his time. Amar liked to think they were the feline version of himself.

The previous hunts had been exhilarating. Amar had almost been disemboweled. He smiled at the memory and then sighed. But now there were only two left. He would be sad when the hunts were over.

The new litter had twelve—but they were only a year old. He'd need to give them at least one more year, maybe even two, before they were ready.

Titus prowled his cage, easily the biggest of the cats Amar had created. His mate, Cleo, paced the cage next to him, agitated on behalf of her man. Amar had saved the best for last. These two were the strongest and fastest of the litter. They'd offer him the greatest chase yet.

Amar patted the cage. "Don't worry, Titus. It's you and me soon." He glanced at Cleo. "Looks like you'll have to get used to being alone."

Cleo just stared back at him, her silver-grey eyes almost human, her dark lips pulled back in a hiss.

Amar walked away from the cages and back out of the barn. His cell rang as he was heading to the house. He glanced at the screen before answering, then said, "Is it done?"

"No, sir. She's always with her group. She's never alone."

Amar sighed, staring up at the sky. He had hoped to

catch her alone. It reduced the possibility of her being harmed. But it seemed he'd have to chance it. "Fine. Take her anyway. I don't care who she's with. If Chandler and Rogan are there, though, make sure you bring enough men. Just do *not* let her be harmed. She doesn't heal quickly."

The statement brought him up short. Actually, maybe she did. They'd have to test that, once she was in his possession.

"Yes, sir. And the others?"

"Unimportant. Do not let anyone get in your way."

Chapter Eight

LANEY WALKED out of the theater at Chocolate World, holding tight to Max's hand. Not that she was worried he'd get carried away by the crowd. He was so hyped up on chocolate right at the moment, though, that there was a chance he might just bounce his way out of the place.

"Laney, can we go to the gift store?" Bright blue eyes from under a mop of wavy brown hair stared up at her. Two dimples winked at her from his cheeks. Max was four years old and cuter than any kid had the right to be.

Laney laughed, looking around. The people at Hershey sure knew how to market. The entire place was a gift store. "I'm pretty sure we can't avoid it."

She shared a smile with Max's mom, Kati, an adult version of Max, who was walking behind her.

Kati held out her hand to Max. "Come on, kiddo. Let's go see what we can find."

Max tugged on Danny's shirtsleeve. "Danny, want to come?"

Danny gave him a small smile before looking up at Henry Chandler. "Can I?"

Henry looked down. "Sure. Just stay where we can see you."

Danny took Max's other hand and Kati walked off with the two of them. Laney smiled at the friendship that had sprung up between Max and Danny. Danny was nine years older, but sometimes it almost seemed like Max was the older one, always making sure Danny was included.

Patrick cleared his throat from behind her. With bright blue eyes and red hair that still retained its color even as he approached sixty, Patrick Delaney was a Roman Catholic priest—and the man who had raised Laney since she was ten years old.

Laney glanced back at him, already knowing what he was going to say. "Yes, Uncle?"

Patrick nodded in the direction Kati and the boys had headed. "I should probably go keep an eye on them."

Laney tried to hide her smile. "Sure. That'd be real helpful."

Patrick gave her a grin before making a beeline for a display of giant candy bars.

Jake slipped his arm around Laney's waist. "Patrick has a sweet tooth?"

"Only for chocolate," Laney said.

Jake looked at his brochure. "Okay. So we've covered the 4-D movie, made our own candy bars, now all that's left is the chocolate tour."

Laney smiled. Jake had planned this weekend away like it was a military op. Seeing as he was a former Navy SEAL, she probably shouldn't have been surprised. But for a man who hadn't had a real family since he was a teenager, he'd done amazingly well on his first family trip. She leaned up to kiss his cheek. "Yes, sir."

"What's a chocolate tour?" Henry asked.

Laney linked arms with two of her favorite men. "I believe it involves singing cows."

She gave them both credit. The groans they let slip were very small.

Chapter Nine

THIRTY MINUTES LATER, Laney and the rest of the group were at the head of the line for the chocolate tour. They stepped off the stairs, Henry in the lead, waiting next to the teenage usher.

Distracted, the boy barely even glanced at them when he spoke. "How many in your group?"

"Seven," Henry answered.

The poor kid glanced back then, barely registering the rest of them before his head whipped back around and his eyes traveled up until they reached Henry's face.

He gawked for a full ten seconds before turning to look at the floats attached to the conveyor belt forty feet away. "Umm, you'll need to split into two boats."

Henry didn't even comment on the boy's rudeness. Laney knew Henry was used to people staring at him, but she wished he could just go *somewhere*, sometime, without having to suffer that reaction.

"How about Henry and I take the boys in one, and you guys take the other?" Kati suggested from behind.

"Sounds good to me." Laney stepped onto the moving platform, taking a moment to get her balance before walking to the first float and taking a seat in the front. Patrick followed her in, and Jake took the seat behind them.

Patrick took Laney's hand. "This reminds me of the trip we took to Disney. Do you remember?"

She smiled. She'd been eleven, and it was still one of her best vacation memories. She squeezed Patrick's hand. "How could I forget?" She settled in for an animated story of how chocolate gets made.

Jake leaned over the back as three singing cows sent them off on their trip. "I thought you were kidding about the dancing cows."

"I never joke about animatronics," Laney said.

A giant chocolate refining plant came into view on the sides of the float. Laney grinned. This was fun. She turned to Patrick. "What do you say after—"

The float jarred to a stop and the lights went out. A muffled shriek came from up ahead, followed by nervous laughter.

"Must be a power outage," Patrick said next to her in the dark.

Jake leaned forward, his hands resting on the back of the seat. "Odd that a place like this wouldn't have backup generators."

Emergency track lights in the floor came on, but they weren't strong enough to make much of a dent in the darkness.

Laney spied a shape walking toward them up ahead. "Someone's coming."

Jake flashed the flashlight he always kept on his key ring. Laney's breath hitched. The man walking toward them raised a weapon.

"Gun!" Jake and Patrick yelled in unison, just before the man opened fire.

Chapter Ten

LANEY GRUNTED as she slammed into the floor. Patrick leapt on top of her as gunfire raked their float.

When the barrage paused, Laney army-crawled out of the float, with Patrick right behind. Jake was already out, lying on his side, his gun pulled. When Laney had seen him slip it into his holster this morning under his jacket, she'd tried to talk him out of bringing it. Now she wished she had brought her own.

Gunfire sounded again, from behind them, but was quickly cut off with a yell.

"The kids and Kati," Laney said, fear coursing through her.

"Check on them." Jake returned fire with the gunman in front.

In the dim light, Laney could just make out Henry struggling with a man in the dark at the back of the second float. Henry lifted the man up and slammed him down to the ground. The man screamed and went quiet.

Laney stayed low, behind the floats, as she made her way

to where Kati and the kids should be. Patrick followed closely behind her. When they reached the float, she looked in and was relieved to see Kati and the boys huddled on the floor.

"Come on, Danny," Laney said. Danny quickly climbed out of the back. She gave him a hug while Patrick got Kati and Max out of the front seat.

"What's going on?" Kati asked. Even in the dim light, Laney could see that her friend was shaking. The words of Agent Clark floated through her mind: *Whatever's coming, all our analysis suggests that you will be involved.*

Laney reached over and squeezed Kati's hand. *Damn it. Is this what he meant? Is this attack part of what he feared?* She never should have let Kati and the kids come with them. What had she been thinking?

Laney put her arm around Max. "It'll be all right."

A yell from the direction of the first float told her that Jake had found his target. But gunfire was now directed at the floats from a different spot up ahead. The shooters had backup.

Henry came back around the float. He slid a gun along the floor toward Laney.

"Are you hit?" Kati asked.

Henry's voice was calm. "I'm fine."

But Laney could see the hole in Henry's shirt. He'd been shot. But she knew he was already as good as healed.

Jake duck-walked up to them. "I'm out."

"Here." Laney handed him the gun Henry had retrieved. She turned to Henry. "You need to get Kati and the boys out of here."

Henry took both boys in his arms. "I have two operatives in the parking lot. They should be heading here now.

I'll get Kati and the boys to them, and then I'll come back for you guys."

Henry looked down at Kati. "Kati, stay with me. Anyone steps out with a gun, you step behind me. I'm your shield."

"Henry, I can't—"

Laney grabbed Kati's arm. She didn't have time to explain about Henry's abilities, about how the bullets would hurt him but that he would heal almost instantly. She didn't have time to explain who Henry was. "Do it, Kati. He's your shield. Trust him. Now go."

Jake aimed the gun toward the remaining gunmen. "I'll cover you."

Laney squeezed Kati's hand. "Trust him."

Kati nodded.

"Now!" Jake yelled, leaping up and covering their escape.

Henry disappeared into the dark, Kati right behind him.

"Okay. Our turn to disappear," Patrick said.

Gunfire raked their float. "Any ideas?" Laney asked.

Jake nodded over the float toward the emergency exit across from them. "We're heading there. They may have more guys outside, but at least we'll have a better chance of seeing them. You guys ready?"

Laney nodded, but felt the familiar stirrings of fear. Why the hell did these things keep happening to her?

Jake leaned out and fired. The gunman dropped. But they could hear footsteps running toward them. "Don't know if that's the good guys or the bad. So let's get going."

The three of them bolted for the exit. Laney reached it first. She crashed through, Patrick right behind her. The door opened onto an alley lined with dumpsters.

Laney groaned. Even though she lacked her uncle's and Jake's military training, she recognized a perfect spot for an ambush.

A man popped up at the end of the lane from behind a dumpster. Bullets peppered the wall behind them.

"Laney!" Patrick pushed her to the ground.

Jake burst out of the door behind them, firing. The gunman dropped. Jake turned and grabbed a piece of wood, jamming it in the door.

"Uncle Patrick." Laney's eyes grew wide as she saw blood spreading across his sleeve.

He shook off her concern. "It's just a graze. Don't worry."

Gunfire crashed into the door behind them. Jake grabbed Laney and Patrick by the arms. "Let's move."

They reached the end of the alley. Jake grabbed the weapon from the man he'd shot. He slid out the magazine. "About ten left."

Behind them, the door to the factory blew open. "Go!" Jake yelled.

Together, they ran into the parking lot. A man appeared between some cars, and Jake took him down. Patrick made a beeline for the man, taking his weapon.

"Uncle Patrick, get down!" Laney yelled as a man appeared behind him. Patrick rolled to the ground, shooting. Bullets dotted the man's torso.

Arms wrapped around Laney, yanking her off her feet. Laney reared back and then dropped all her weight toward the ground, slamming the heel of her right boot into the man's instep.

He howled and released his grip just enough for her to take a step back and wrap her right arm around his neck. Dropping onto her knee, she yanked the man forward.

He flew over her shoulder with a yell. Laney kept hold of his arm as he dropped, and brought her heel down on his throat as he landed.

Laney looked up and saw Patrick and Jake were in hand-to-hand fights of their own. Scanning three-sixty, she saw three more men zeroing in on her. Fast.

Patrick looked over at her, sizing up the situation. "Laney! Run!"

She didn't pause. She ran.

Chapter Eleven

LANEY WEAVED between the parked cars, trying to put some distance between herself and her three pursuers.

A man stepped from behind a large panel truck ahead of her and smiled. "Going somewhere?"

Laney didn't stop. She ran full tilt, dropping her shoulder at the last minute and burrowing it into the man's hip. Grabbing his legs behind the knees, she yanked. With a yell, he slammed onto his back.

Laney landed three punches to his face before he could react. The last knocked him out cold. She detangled herself from him and looked behind her.

The men chasing her were still there, but closer. She took off again, trying to come up with a plan to lose these guys. She was outnumbered and outgunned.

She groaned. *Crap*. Why hadn't she at least checked the two guys she had taken down for weapons?

Guess that's what happens when you have two months of peace. Your survival skills get rusty.

Nearby, tourists and families had noticed the chase and

were either running for the factory or cowering behind cars. Good. She didn't want anyone hurt in the crossfire.

The thought gave her pause. She realized that her pursuers weren't actually *shooting* at her. They were all armed, but not one of them had taken a shot. *Why the hell not?*

Out of the corner of her eye she saw a blur of motion making its way toward her. She recognized that blur. *Thank God. Henry.*

The blur moved directly toward her. She came to an abrupt halt as the blur jolted to a stop right in front of her. She stopped so quickly, she lost her balance, and fell backward.

Her eyes traveled up the black boots, the black slacks, the black shirt, and finally came to rest on a chiseled face with pale blue eyes, mocha skin, and dark brown hair.

Her heart pounded. *Not Henry.*

Chapter Twelve

LANEY CRAB-WALKED BACKWARD, scrambling to get to her feet. The man reached down and grabbed her arm, pulling her up. "Been looking for you."

Laney stared into his face, terror leaving her paralyzed. He was a Fallen, or at least a nephilim. Either way, that meant superhuman speed and strength.

"We're going for a little ride." He picked her up, his hands squeezing her arms painfully. Over his shoulder she saw Jake running for her. And another blur.

She looked back at the man holding her. "I don't think so."

She headbutt him in the nose. He yelled, loosening his grip. She wrenched herself from his grasp. She quickly ran her right hand along the side of his neck while reaching around the other side with her left, pulling him into a choke.

Taking a step back, she twirled him around. Unable to get his balance, he fell back. But she miscalculated his weight and he dropped from her grasp.

With a yell, he fell onto his back, but nimbly jumped

back to his feet. Laney aimed a punch for his face, but he moved out of the way at the last minute and grabbed her fist. Laney shifted, avoiding the punch aimed for her own face.

The man wrapped his arms around her, trapping her against his chest. "Forgot about your little tricks. I won't give you that chance again."

He spun her around so her back was to his chest, then leapt to his feet. He pinned both arms with one of his own, and wrapped his other arm around her legs. She struggled but couldn't move against his strength.

From the corner of her eye she saw the blur of motion heading toward them. Her arms and legs might be trapped, but she could still move her head. She threw it back, catching him in the jaw.

"Bitch!" he screamed, releasing his grip slightly. Laney braced herself.

Henry slammed into the two of them, sending Laney airborne. She landed on the hood of an Altima ten feet away; momentum rolled her off the car, and she fell onto her back.

"Ow," she muttered, staring at the sky.

"Stop right there." A man stood two feet away. In blue jeans and a turtleneck, he obviously wasn't a cop. "Raise your hands."

Laney stayed on her back, putting her hands up. Keeping them in the air, she rolled back and then forward onto her knee. In the same motion, she wrapped her hands around the man's ankle, trapping his leg in place, and drove her shoulder into his knee. Hard.

The man screamed as he fell back, his skull slamming into a car's side mirror on his way down to the ground. Laney continued her forward momentum, landing a groin shot with her right knee followed by a right elbow to his chin. The man's eyes rolled back into his head.

"Night-night." Snatching the man's gun, she stood.

Patrick ran toward her from the left. He'd acquired a weapon somewhere along the way as well. Jake was slamming a guy onto the hood of a car one row over. No other gunmen were visible—except for Henry's.

Henry and his opponent rolled along the ground. The man picked Henry up and slammed him into a jeep. The windows exploded out with the force of the impact.

"Henry, get down!" Laney yelled.

Henry dove for the ground as Laney opened fire. Jake and Patrick joined in. Henry stayed low, crawling out of the circle of bullets.

Laney, Jake, and Patrick closed the circle around the Fallen, their bullets turning the man like a rag doll.

Jake reached him first. Grabbing the front of the man's shirt, he emptied his gun into the man's heart.

The man collapsed.

Laney dropped to the ground next to the assailant. "Who are you?"

Blood poured from the man's mouth. "One of many."

Chapter Thirteen

LANEY WATCHED the light leave the man's eyes. *One of many? What the hell does that mean?*

Patrick grabbed her arm and pulled her up. "You need to go."

"You mean *we* need to go," Laney said.

Patrick shook his head. "Laney, they weren't after all of us. They were after you." He pushed her toward Jake. "Get her out of here."

Jake took her arm. "Let's go."

Laney shook Jake free. "Wait just a minute. They weren't after me. They were after all of us. We *all* need to get to safety."

"Patrick's right." Henry stepped next to her. "The rest of us were just in the way. For some reason, they were trying to get to *you*. They didn't shoot at you, Laney. They were trying to *take* you."

Laney stopped moving, picturing the attack, the men running after her in the lot. The Fallen who'd grabbed her could have killed her. But he didn't. He'd tried to leave with her instead. Was it possible? "But why?"

"We need to get you to safety," Henry said.

Laney shook her head. "No. You need to stay with the boys and Kati."

"He should go with you," Patrick argued. "I'll take care of Kati and the boys."

Laney looked at his shirtsleeve, now soaked in blood. "Uncle Patrick, you've been shot. We need to get you to a hospital."

Patrick shook his head. "I told you it's just a graze. I'll take care of the boys and Kati."

Henry nodded. "Patrick should stay with them, but we need to go. I left Kati and the boys with my operatives. They're fine. And they're not the ones these guys were after."

Laney looked around, trying to wrap her mind around everything. "But why would anyone be after me?"

Jake took her arm, pulling her way. "We'll figure that out later. Right now, we need to move."

Chapter Fourteen

JOHNSON CITY, TENNESSEE

AMAR WALKED DOWN THE HALL, his footsteps echoing off the heavy wood floor. The architect of this home had designed it to look like a farmhouse, but it was really a king's farmhouse. Everything was overdone just a little.

The marble floor was imported Italian. The chandeliers were dripping in crystals. The fireplace mantelpieces had been taken from a castle in Austria. Everything was just a little more than it should be.

Just like me, thought Amar.

This house was so different from where he'd grown up. He curled his lip in distaste when he pictured the squalor his parents had lived in. They'd sold him when he was seven. He'd been one of a legion of child beggars on the streets of India.

And one day, when he was nine, his owner had decided he needed a new eunuch. Amar had disagreed.

He smiled. That day had been the beginning of his awareness of what he could do. The beginning of his empire.

Amar entered his dining room. His throne chair stood at the end of the table, his lunch covered by a silver lid.

His cell phone rang and he pulled it from his pocket, stepping toward the large windows overlooking the yard.

"Sir, they escaped us at the park. They're heading to Chandler's car. Should we give chase?"

Amar paused for a moment, trying to place the voice. It wasn't Zeke— it was Zeke's second in command. "Why are you calling me? Where's Zeke?

A pause. "Zeke's dead, sir. Jake Rogan killed him."

Amar went quiet, his mind flashing on his son. They didn't have a close bond—at least, not one based on emotion. But there was a connection there. Zeke had been made from him. And Zeke, therefore, *belonged* to him. Amar was the only one allowed to take his life.

His anger boiled up, but he kept a lid on it. Their goal was too close. He couldn't let it cloud his judgment, but his rage was making that hard to remember. "Chase them down. I want them dead."

"Including the McPhearson woman? I thought you wanted her alive."

"*Dead.* I want all of them dead." He simmered, letting the rage wash over him. But then common sense warred with his thirst for revenge and won. He growled. "No. Never mind that. Get McPhearson. She's your priority. Once we have her, we'll take care of the rest."

He paused, picturing his son. He'd had so much potential. His anger warmed him. "But hurt her. A lot."

Chapter Fifteen

LANEY, Jake, and Henry ran across the parking lot. They reached Henry's Escalade just as two Tahoes squealed into the lot.

Jake all but threw Laney into the back seat. "I don't think those are the good guys."

Henry jammed the key into the ignition and gunned it. "Time to go." He careened around the other cars waiting to exit.

A bunch of people honked their horns in irritation. Apparently they had missed the life-and-death gun battle in the parking lot.

Laney held on in the back as Henry swerved from side to side, weaving through the slower traffic. "You sure this is necessary?"

Henry's eyes flipped to the rearview mirror. "Yup."

Laney glanced back. The two Tahoes from the parking lot were behind them and moving fast. "Plan?"

Henry just pushed down on the gas pedal as they broke out of the park and into a residential area.

Jake looked around the car. "This the new one?"

Henry smiled. "Yup."

"New one?" Laney asked. "New what?"

"Car. I had a few improvements made to the manufac-turer's standard model."

"Like what?"

"Bulletproof windows, doors, and roof. And some extra toys." Henry hit two buttons on the dash. The back of the driver's seat slid open, revealing a small arsenal. A similar tray appeared in the dashboard in front of Jake.

"My kind of toys." Jake grabbed a Beretta and two magazines.

"This is the car you chose to bring on a family vaca-tion?" Laney asked.

Henry caught her eyes in the rearview. "Kind of a good thing I did, isn't it?"

Laney turned to watch the trees rush by them on the side of the road. *Okay. Good point.*

Henry made a sharp turn, putting them on the highway.

Jake slammed the magazine into place. "I, personally, would like to chat with these guys. Find out exactly what's going on."

Laney glanced back again. The SUVs were closer. "If they're anything like the parking lot guys, I don't think they're going to be too chatty. How about we just outrun them instead?"

"Working on it," Henry said. The Escalade accelerated.

They barreled down the highway. Other cars took notice and got out of the way. Henry sped toward a slow-moving Honda Civic that was matching the pace of the Toyota Corolla in the lane next to it.

Laney glanced back. The Tahoes were gaining. She

looked forward. Henry was almost on top of the Honda. "Henry!"

At the last second, Henry jerked the wheel, jumping them onto the shoulder. They flew past the slow-moving cars. On the service road, a cop car appeared, its lights flashing, siren roaring.

More lights appeared in the far distance behind them. Laney wasn't sure if that was a good thing. The cops had no idea what they were putting themselves in the middle of.

Laney turned around again. "Cops."

Henry gave a terse nod.

"We need to get off this highway." Jake pulled up a map of the area on his phone.

They rounded a turn. A half-mile ahead, two cop cars blocked the highway. Laney's stomach plummeted.

"Henry, turn left." Jake ordered.

"Left?" Henry asked.

"Now!" Jake yelled.

Henry wrenched the wheel. Laney felt the left side of the car lift off the ground for a few terrifying moments before it crashed back down. They bumped across the grass divider.

The oncoming traffic slammed to a stop as Henry cut across the other two lanes of the highway. Bumping onto the shoulder, they careened through the grass, before ending up on the service road. Henry pressed down on the gas pedal again.

They raced down a country road, which luckily was currently empty of traffic. As they rounded a blind curve, Laney let out a yell. Two deer darted into the road.

"Shit!" Henry yanked the wheel to the right. They plowed off the road and down a steep embankment. The

SUV bucked violently as it was lifted into the air by the uneven ground.

Oh God. The ground rushed up toward them. With a wrenching roar, the front of the car slammed into the ground.

The air bags exploded.

Laney fell forward, going headlong toward the windshield. At the last moment, two hands wrapped around her shoulders and pulled her back.

As the dust settled, Laney found herself sprawled across Henry's chest, with her legs still in the back seat. With a groan, she pushed herself up. "Thanks."

Henry nodded. A couple of cuts dotted his forehead, but they were already healing.

Laney sat on the divider between the two front seats and arched her back with a grimace. *Man, that hurt.*

"You okay, Lanes?" Jake asked

She turned and saw a deep gash in Jake's right arm. "Your arm," she cried.

"There's a first aid kit in the back, under the driver's seat," Henry said.

Laney scrambled to the back. Searching the floor, she found it and wrenched it free from its perch. She yanked the lid off, rummaging through for bandages and antiseptic.

Jake pushed against his door. "We don't have time for that. Henry, can you get your door open?"

"No. I'm dug in too deep. I think the back doors are our best bet."

Laney handed Henry the first aid supplies. "Wrap his arm. I'll try the doors." She turned to the door behind Henry. Tugging on the handle, she pushed. It moved, but not enough to let a person through. The frame must have bent.

She turned, and launched her feet at the door. With a groan, it opened a little more. A few more kicks, and she had it open wide enough to slide through.

"Got it." She crawled out.

Jake crawled into the back seat and out, his arm bandaged. "We need to move."

Henry appeared out of the car next. The three of them looked up the hill.

"Pretty steep," Jake said.

"And if those guys see the tracks, we'll be walking right at them," Laney said.

A squeal of brakes came from up top, followed by the slam of doors.

"Time to run." Henry grabbed Laney's arm. Together, the three of them sprinted into the trees.

Chapter Sixteen

LANEY RAN, ducking branches, leaping over brush. Her mind was moving as quickly as her feet. What were these guys after? Was her uncle right? Were they really after her?

She jumped over a downed tree and came down in a small divot. Her ankle turned. With a cry, she fell.

Jake dropped next to her. "Laney?"

Pain radiated up her leg. "It's my ankle."

Jake pulled her to her feet. "I'll carry you."

Henry jogged back. "Jake, let me."

Jake nodded.

Henry picked Laney up as if she weighed nothing. And then they were off again.

Henry kept pace with Jake, not even breathing hard. Laney knew that Henry could have sprinted away from them and gotten himself to safety easily. But he wouldn't leave them.

Behind them, they could hear the pursuit of many feet. Tendrils of fear crawled down Laney's spine. Their pursuers were getting closer.

Up ahead, the trees ended. Henry and Jake didn't stop, just burst through into the open grass. Fifty feet ahead, a thirty-foot-high chain-link fence stood in front of them. Cattle ate peacefully on the other side.

Laney looked to the right and left. A dirt road ran along the length of the fence, all two hundred feet. Signs hung on the fence every twenty-five feet. The signs had lightning bolts on them. The fence was electrified.

Chapter Seventeen

"HENRY, PUT ME DOWN," Laney ordered.

"What the hell do you think you're doing?" Jake asked as Laney placed most of her weight on her right foot, gingerly testing pressure on her left. She winced. Not as bad as it was, but not quite ready for her full weight.

She pulled the Beretta from the waist of her jeans and checked the magazine. "I guess I'm getting ready to make a stand. I don't suppose you guys would consider leaving me here? I'm the one they want. You two could still get away."

Both men just looked at her.

She sighed. "Yeah, that's what I thought."

With a lump in her throat, she raised her weapon. Henry and Jake did the same. If they were right, the men chasing them wanted her. Which meant she might survive this. But Jake and Henry . . .

She tightened her grip. *No. They would make it through, too.*

From the corner of her eye, Laney saw a car turn the corner of the fence to her right. Then another car appeared from the left. *Great. They brought reinforcements.*

The cattle behind them began to get anxious. They started mooing loudly, then running away from the oncoming cars.

Laney tensed, trying to figure out whom to aim for. From both sides, the cars barreled down the road toward them. She could hear the gunmen getting closer in the trees.

The cars were almost on top of them. Laney switched her aim from the trees to the car coming from her right. But then both cars steered off the road, aiming for the men just emerging from the trees.

Windows rolled down and the occupants of the cars simultaneously opened fire on the men pursuing on foot. The men tried to turn and run back to the relative safety of the trees, but were cut down in a barrage of bullets. A few were trampled under the wheels of the cars.

A minute later, all was silent, except for the moans of some of the dying men. Laney could only gape at the carnage in front of her.

Two men exited the cars and disappeared into the woods. What the hell was going on?

"Jake?" Laney asked.

"They're not ours," Jake said.

Laney tightened her grip.

The driver's-side door opened on one of the SUVs. A small woman with long wavy black hair stepped out. She walked over to Laney, Jake, and Henry.

Her deep brown eyes met Laney's. "You okay?"

Laney stared back at her in stunned disbelief. "Rocky?"

Chapter Eighteen

DETECTIVE ROCHELLE MARTINEZ of the Syracuse Police Department wrapped Laney in a fierce hug. "Thank God you're okay."

Laney hugged her back, but she was still reeling. She pulled back. "Rocky, what the hell are you doing here?"

Rocky glanced at Jake and Henry. "It's a long story. How about I tell it while we're on the move?"

Laney looked at Jake, who gave her a nod. "Uh, okay."

Jake slipped his arm around Laney's waist and helped her over to Rocky's car. Henry followed.

Rocky grabbed her radio from the driver's seat. "Mills, find any stragglers. I'm getting the VIPs out of here."

"Roger that. Safe trip."

"You, too." Rocky hopped into the driver's seat and buckled up. "Everybody good?"

Laney nodded from the back seat with Jake, but "good" was not what she was. She felt like she'd just stepped into an episode of *The Twilight Zone*. Where the hell had Rocky come from? And who were those guys with her? Granted,

Rocky was a cop, but that was in upstate New York. Her jurisdiction didn't extend into Pennsylvania.

Without another word, Rocky started the car and headed out of the field. No one said a word until they reached the highway.

"Detective Martinez, correct?" Henry asked.

Rocky nodded. "Call me Rocky."

"Okay, Rocky," Henry said, "you want to tell us exactly how you found us?"

Laney's head jerked up. There was anger in Henry's tone. Not something she was used to hearing.

"We had eyes on you in Hershey, but lost you on that ride," Rocky said. "And then everything went to shit. I've got people with Patrick, Kati, and the boys, by the way. They're safe. And luckily, the tracker on Laney's phone was still working."

Laney pulled her cell from her pocket. "You were tracking me?"

Rocky glanced back, guilt in her eyes. "Yes."

Something about Rocky's demeanor was off. Laney felt cold. She spoke slowly. "Rocky, how long have you been tracking me?"

Rocky took a deep breath. "For five years."

Chapter Nineteen

LANEY FELT as if she were in free-fall. Rocky had been watching her for five years. What on earth was going on? Laney spoke slowly. "Rocky, we've only know each other for four."

"I know. I'm sorry. I was sent to Syracuse to keep an eye on you."

Hurt and confusion fought for dominance inside Laney. Hurt won. "You befriended me... to keep an eye on me?"

Rocky's words rushed out. "No. It was never like that. I mean, I was supposed to keep an eye on you. I didn't need to become friends with you to accomplish that. But once we met, we had so much in common. Becoming friends was inevitable."

Laney sat back, dumbfounded. She couldn't form a thought.

But Jake could. "Who are you working for?"

Rocky shook her head. "I can't tell you that. Not yet. She wants to tell you herself. We're going to see her now."

"How did you end up working for her?" Henry asked.

Rocky glanced back at Laney. "You know my childhood wasn't easy. My current employer, she got me and my mom out of a bad situation. Found my mom a good job, sent me to college. Made me feel like I was worth something. That I could do something."

Disbelief spread through Laney. "And in exchange, you just had to lie to me."

Rocky winced like she'd been hit. "No. It wasn't like that. She explained to me what the stakes were—that there was more happening in this world than most people realized. I chose to help."

"And what exactly were you supposed to do?" Laney asked. "Watch me?"

"No. It was never like that," Rocky said. "I was just supposed to be around if you needed help. She told me that in all likelihood, I would never have to do anything. And then we became friends. And it became a moot point. If you needed help, of course I would help."

Rocky pulled off the road into a field. A helicopter was waiting. She put the car in park. "I know it's asking a lot. But I need you to trust me—just a little longer. Talk to my employer. Then you'll understand everything."

"And if we choose not to trust you?" Jake asked.

Rocky looked straight at Laney. "Then I've been instructed to give you my car and let you go."

Rocky's words hung in the air.

Laney took a deep breath. "Henry? What do you think?"

She could see the calculation in Henry's eyes. "I say we trust her just a little more. After we meet her employer, we can decide what to do."

"Jake?" Laney asked.

Jake took her hand. "I'd like to say let's take the car and run. But something's happening right now and we're completely in the dark. We need answers. This may be a way to get some."

Laney let out a breath. "Okay, Rocky. Let's go."

Chapter Twenty

TWENTY MINUTES LATER, they were flying over an undeveloped part of Pennsylvania. At least, Laney thought they were still in the state. She sat in the back of the chopper with Jake and Rocky. Henry sat up front with the pilot.

Laney stared out the window at the ground below. Jake sat between her and Rocky. She hadn't wanted to sit next to Rocky. She wasn't sure what to say to her, what to make of all of this.

"Laney?" Rocky's voice was nervous, her concern obvious.

Laney looked over. She knew Rocky was worried about their friendship, but honestly, she couldn't deal with that yet. She was still reeling from Rocky's unexpected arrival. The discussion about their friendship could wait. For now, there were some other issues she wanted to discuss.

"Last year, when I was attacked at my house, did you know about the Fallen?" Laney asked.

Rocky shook her head. "No. That was the first time I

heard about anyone with those abilities. And until I saw them and felt them, for myself, I didn't even believe what you had said, really. I figured it was adrenaline, or maybe you took a blow to the head."

Laney remembered dragging Rocky to the car, blood dripping down her side. She had almost lost Rocky that night.

Rocky met her eyes and Laney could tell she was reliving the same night. "Laney, I was asked to look out for you. That was all. I swear."

Laney nodded. She thought Rocky was being truthful with her, but she was no longer sure if she could trust her own judgment.

Laney grasped Jake's hand and looked back out the window. The helicopter began to reduce its altitude. Laney caught sight of a single road playing peek-a-boo through the trees below.

Up ahead was a clearing. The helicopter landed softly on the grass. When the rotors had turned down, Laney stepped out and stretched out her legs. Her ankle still smarted, but she could walk on it.

And once again, everything else ached. *I really should just accept constant aches as my new normal.*

Jake stepped up next to her. "You all right?"

Taking his hand, she gave him a little smile. "Not really."

He pulled her close, kissing her forehead. "Well, Dorothy, apparently there's another road to follow."

Laney nodded, but she couldn't help think of the cost of those other roads.

Rocky walked over to the tree line. "It's this way."

The rotors started up behind them. Laney looked back in alarm. A few seconds later the helicopter lifted off.

"It's okay," Jake whispered. "On the ground, the chopper would have been easy to spot. It's safer for it to take off."

Squeezing Jake's hand, Laney followed Rocky. But she wasn't sure she was convinced that everything was actually okay. She looked behind her.

Henry smiled. "I'm still here."

"My own guardian angel," Laney joked, but the truth was, she did feel better with him there.

The four of them followed the path through the woods. After about two hundred yards, Laney could just make out a little cottage tucked away between the trees. The stone and wood blended into the forest well. Large, leafy branches bowed over it, hiding it from the air. It would be easy to miss.

The little house was quiet, but Laney could see two dark SUVs parked around the back. A narrow dirt road led away through the trees.

Rocky climbed the short steps to the porch.

The door opened and Rocky disappeared through it. The shadows kept Laney from seeing who had opened the door. She took a deep breath and walked up the steps.

The boards of the porch creaked. The door stood open, but Laney stopped walking. It was only a few short feet, and an ordinary doorway, yet it seemed like a yawning cavern.

Laney didn't know why, but she was terrified to step into that house. Somewhere at the back of her mind, she knew that stepping over that threshold was going to change everything. And she just wasn't sure she was ready.

Jake slipped his hand into hers and squeezed.

She looked up at him and read the love there. She knew if she wanted to walk away right then, he'd be right there with her.

And if she walked in that door, he'd be next to her for that, too. She squeezed his hand back. "Okay. Let's do this."

Hand in hand, Laney and Jake walked into the cabin.

Victoria Chandler, Henry's mother, stood in front of the couch, waiting for them.

Chapter Twenty-One

"VICTORIA?" Jake said.

"Mom?" Henry said at the same time.

Laney just stared. As far as the world knew, Victoria Chandler had died almost twenty years ago when her car ran off a bridge. Laney knew that wasn't true, because Laney met Victoria Chandler in Baltimore, two months ago. But only that once, never before. *This* was the person who had hired Rocky to look out for her? Five years before they had even met?

"I don't understand," Laney said.

"I know." Victoria gestured to the dining table to her right. "Why don't we all sit down and I'll explain?"

Laney looked at Jake, who gave her a nod. She glanced at Henry's face as she walked over and took a seat. His jaw was taut. She could read the anger and confusion there.

Victoria turned to Rocky. "Rochelle, could you wait outside, please?"

Rocky nodded but looked at Laney for a second. Laney avoided her eyes.

Rocky left, leaving Laney, Jake, and Henry alone with Victoria—and the same bodyguard who Laney had seen with her in Baltimore stood by the door. Once everyone was seated, except the bodyguard, Laney said, "Victoria, you sent Rocky to watch me?"

Victoria nodded. "Yes."

"I don't understand." Laney looked between Victoria and Henry. "I never met Henry until a year ago. And you I only met two months ago."

Victoria paused. "Actually, we met thirty years ago. On January twenty-sixth."

Laney looked at Victoria in confusion. "You couldn't have met me. That's the day before I was born."

"No." Victoria's voice was soft. "That *is* the day you were born."

Victoria's words curled around Laney's mind and she tried to make sense of them. January twenty-seventh was her birthday, not the twenty-sixth. What on earth was Victoria talking about?

Henry's voice sounded just as confused as Laney's thoughts. "Mom, what's going on? Why did you send Rocky to watch Laney? And what do you mean her birthday isn't her actual birthday?"

Victoria placed her hands on the table and let out a pent-up breath. "I worried Laney would be in trouble one day. I wanted there to be someone nearby that could help her, should she need it. So I arranged for Rocky to get a position with the Syracuse Police Department. In exchange, she agreed to be there if Laney needed help."

Jake stared Victoria down. "Why would you think Laney would need help? And how did you even know who she was?"

Victoria clasped her hands in front of her. Laney saw a

small tremble in them. When Victoria spoke, her voice was soft. "I've rehearsed this speech a million times . . . and now I can't seem to find the words."

Tendrils of fear started to spread out from Laney's stomach. She didn't know what Victoria was going to say, but she was pretty sure she didn't want to hear it.

Jake's voice was steel. "Well, find them." Jake's arms were across his chest, his body tense. Henry had almost the exact same posture.

Victoria let out a shuddering breath. She glanced at Henry, her eyes apologetic. "You all know about how Henry's father died. What you don't know is that I was pregnant at the time. I had just found out a week before."

Laney stared at Victoria, her mind reeling at where this story could possibly be going. She glanced at Henry. His mouth was open, shock splashed across his face. He clearly knew nothing about any of this.

"You know about Henry's abilities, about who his father was," Victoria said. "I worried this second child would be targeted, especially when I found out she was a girl. I knew who she would become, what her destiny was. I knew I needed to protect her and I hoped that maybe, just maybe, if I sent her away, she could avoid her destiny altogether."

Laney shook her head. What the hell was Victoria talking about? "What does any of that have to do with me?"

Victoria looked at her. "I knew I had to keep my daughter's birth a secret. When she was born, I gave her to a family, and there was no record of her birth."

Confusion warred with doubt in Laney's mind. "And what? *I'm* supposed to be this daughter? Victoria, I'm not. My parents are Fiona and Derek McPhearson. I wasn't adopted. There *are* records of my birth. In a hospital. To my parents."

Victoria paused, her face fearful. Laney didn't know Victoria well, but what she did know was that Victoria was a strong woman. And whatever she was preparing to say was big.

Laney knew who her parents were, knew who she was, but Victoria's expression . . . Laney didn't like how it was making her feel.

Laney grasped Jake's hand under the table, trying to keep her face expressionless. She needed to borrow some of his strength, because she had a feeling that whatever Victoria was going to say next was going to shatter her.

Victoria shook her head, her voice soft. "No. The child of Fiona and Derek McPhearson, a little girl, born on January twenty-seventh, died. Your mother had complications, a lot of bleeding. She couldn't have children after that. Your father was so worried the day their child was born that he never left your mother's side, not even to see his child, not until the next day. And by then, their daughter had passed away—and you had taken her place."

Laney shook her head. "No. That's not true. Why would you say that?"

Jake squeezed Laney's hand. "If that were true, how did you accomplish that? You can't just switch babies."

Victoria shifted her gaze from Laney to Jake. "I have a lot of resources. There was a nurse at the hospital where Laney's mother gave birth. She was having financial problems. She agreed to help."

Laney sat back. It felt like she was trying to think through syrup. Her parents had always said she was a miracle baby. She wasn't supposed to survive and yet, there she was, all pink and perfect the day after her birth.

And her father had stayed away until that next day. He

had thought he was going to lose his wife, so he'd stayed by her mother's bedside.

"Why would you say all of this?" Laney asked.

Victoria stared into Laney's eyes. "Because it's true. I hid you away because I was trying to keep you from harm. But I couldn't hide you from your destiny. The world is reaching a critical point, and you are the only one who can save it."

"You don't have any proof," Laney said, ignoring the destiny remark. Maybe Victoria's daughter had a destiny, but she wasn't that daughter.

"Yes. I do." Victoria reached down to the chair next to her and pulled out a manila folder. She pushed it across the table toward Laney. "These are copies of your parents' hospital records, as well as your own. Look at the blood types."

Laney hesitated, not sure she wanted to see Victoria's proof. There couldn't be proof. It wasn't true. But she found herself reaching for the folder anyway.

She quickly scanned the documents inside. They were hospital records from when she was born: records for her and for her mother. There was also another record, for her father, from when he had been hospitalized for appendicitis a few years later. She scanned the documents for blood types.

Fiona McPhearson: Blood Type AB. Derek McPhearson: Blood Type A. Delaney McPhearson: Blood Type O.

The papers fell from her hand. The room seemed to tilt. A child whose parents had A and AB blood types couldn't be O. It was biologically impossible.

Laney looked around the table, shaking her head. "No. This is some sort of trick."

"Delaney, you can check the records for yourself. But the reality is, they are not your biological parents." Victoria's tone wasn't cruel, but she might as well have stabbed Laney with a knife. It would have been less painful.

Laney stared around the room. *It can't be true. Why was Victoria saying all this?*

Laney watched Victoria's face. There was no malice or cruelty there, only resignation, and sadness—sadness that she had to tell Laney at all.

An image of her parents flashed through her mind. Was it possible? Had her parents, who had died twenty years ago, never met their real daughter? What if other people thought she wasn't their daughter? If people were after her . . .

Laney went still. "Oh my god—my parents' car accident. It wasn't an accident, was it? They were killed. Because of me."

Victoria leaned across the table, trying to take Laney's hands. Laney pulled them out of her reach. "No, no, Laney. When I heard about the accident, I had it investigated. And it was just an accident. A horrible twist of fate."

Laney looked at Victoria, not sure she believed her. Who was this woman? Why did she know so much? Why did she think she had to give away her only daughter? It was too much.

Laney stood up. She could feel the tears wanting to break free, but she wouldn't let them. Not yet. "You're kidding, right? I'm your long-lost daughter and now I have a destiny? Oh sure, what do you need me to do? Save the world you said, right? How, exactly? I'm normal. I have no special abilities."

Victoria reached out her hands then drew them back. "No. You *are* special. You're like Henry."

Laney's gaze whipped to Henry, realization hitting her.

If everything Victoria said was true... Henry was her brother.

Henry stared back at her, his features frozen in shock.

Laney stumbled away from the table. "I need to go."

"Laney, please..." Victoria pleaded.

Laney ignored her. She turned to Jake. "Jake."

Jake stood up. "Let's go."

"Ralph, keys for the SUV," Henry ordered the bodyguard, his voice fierce.

Without a word, Ralph took the keys out of his pocket and tossed them at Jake, who caught them one-handed.

Laney had to keep herself from running. She needed air. She needed out. Yanking the door open, she bolted outside.

Rocky, who'd been sitting on the porch steps, jumped to her feet. "Laney, are you okay?"

"No." Laney ran down the steps to the SUVs in the back. The lights on one of them flashed as Jake unlocked it. Laney scrambled around to the passenger door.

She stumbled inside and slipped on her seat belt. She leaned her head back as Jake pulled away.

Visions of her parents flooded her mind. Tucking her in. Holding her hand. Pushing her on the swings. Tears ran down her cheeks.

It can't be true. It can't be.

Chapter Twenty-Two

HENRY WATCHED Laney all but sprint outside. The dual emotions of anger and sympathy warred inside him. He turned to the bodyguard. "Ralph, I need to speak with my mother alone."

Ralph nodded and headed for the door without a word.

As the door closed behind him, Henry paused to figure out what to say. He kept his back to his mother, trying to compose his thoughts. *What the hell just happened? Laney is my sister? And she's special?*

He'd seen no evidence of her having any abilities like his. And he hadn't felt any recognition with her, like he had with other nephilim. This made no sense. A million questions raced through his mind.

At last he turned to face his mother, his mind settling on a simple question. "Why?"

Victoria looked up at him, tears in her eyes. "I did what I thought best. To protect her."

Some of Henry's anger slipped into his voice. "She's my sister. And you gave her away? I've had a sister all these years and you never told me. I just—I don't understand how you could do that."

Victoria moved toward him, her hands in front of her, her tone pleading. "Henry, please. It was the only way I could think of to protect her—"

"Protect her from what, Mom? Who is she? She's not a nephilim. She's not like me. She doesn't have those powers."

"No. She's not like you. But she *is* a nephilim. A very unique one."

Henry groaned. "What the hell does that mean? Unique how? Does she fly? Have telekinesis? Why is she different? Why did you send her away to protect her? Why her and not—" *Me?*

Victoria walked over to him, took his hands in hers. "When you were born, I didn't know what the future would bring. Even when I got pregnant with her, I didn't know. It wasn't until I found out that my second child was a girl that I knew who she would become. What her destiny was."

"And what destiny is that? What is it exactly that Laney is supposed to do?"

Victoria let out a shaky breath. "I can't tell you that. Not yet. I owe it to her to tell her first."

Henry ran his hands over his face, wanting to hit something. "Mom, I don't understand you. I don't understand why you have to keep all these secrets. Why can't the world know you're alive?"

"Henry, I've told you. It's better if you don't know certain things. Safer."

Henry stared at his mother, his anger boiling back to the surface. "*Safer?* Have you heard about what's happened to me in the last year? How about what happened this morning? 'Safe' is not exactly part of my life these days."

"I know. But my life brings with it a whole other set of dangers."

Henry gritted his teeth. "Enough, Mom. Enough with the cryptic. What is going on? Who's after Laney? And who *are* you?"

"I'm no one."

"Goddamn it. That old tune doesn't carry anymore. You gave away your daughter to protect her from a destiny you knew about before her birth. You were married to one of the most powerful angels ever. Your son is a towering freak. And you're going to stand there and tell me that you're just a normal human being?"

Victoria's eyes flashed with anger. "You are *not a freak.*"

Henry tried to stay stalwart in his anger. But the fact that she chose to focus on that part of his little speech tore a laugh from him. She had always hated whenever he disparaged his height or his abilities. He groaned. "You're killing me, Mom. You are absolutely killing me."

She leaned up and took his face in her hands. "Henry, do you believe that I love you?"

Henry struggled against answering her question. He wanted answers to *his* questions first. But the answer to her question was a simple one, and he had the feeling that the answers to his questions were not.

He sighed. "Yes, Mother. No matter all this craziness, I've always known that you love me."

Tears sprang to her eyes then, and Henry realized that she had been uncertain. His forever strong mother had worried that he didn't believe she loved him.

When she spoke, her smile was a little wobbly. "And do you believe that I would never do anything to intentionally hurt you?"

"Yes, Mom." He worked on keeping the frustration out of his voice. "Where are you going with this?"

"I love your sister in the same way. So please, trust me a little more. Okay?"

Henry closed his eyes. Exasperation ran through him. His mother had always been like this: impossibly stubborn with her secrets.

He blew out a breath and opened his eyes. "Mom, after finding out the identity of my father, learning that I have a long-lost sister, and discovering that I'm part angel with superhuman skills, do you actually believe that your real identity could rock my world?"

Beckoning him to lean down, Victoria kissed him on the cheek.

"Yes."

Chapter Twenty-Three

JAKE DROVE down the unfamiliar roads, glancing every few seconds at Laney. She could feel his worried gaze but she couldn't work up the words to assure him she was fine.

Because she wasn't. She wasn't even close.

"When she was born, I gave her to a family."

"Your parents' child, a little girl, she died."

"But I couldn't hide you from your destiny."

Laney crushed her hands over her ears, trying to keep Victoria's words out. But they crept in. And then she was picturing each memory with her parents. Every memory was a lie. They thought she was their daughter, but she wasn't.

Laney wanted to deny it. She wanted to disbelieve everything Victoria said. But the story rang true. And even her own uncle had wondered about the events swirling around her for the last year.

Laney pulled her jacket tighter around her, trying to hold off the cold seeping through her. But she knew it wasn't simply cold. It was the truth. The truth seeping its way into her brain, into her body, into her heart.

She was Victoria's daughter. That was why Victoria had sent Rocky to watch her. That was why Henry had seemed familiar when she first met him. And maybe that was also why all of this violence had surrounded her lately.

She wrapped her hands around herself. *Oh God.* Her parents. Her thoughts stumbled over each other, a jumbled mess in her brain, heartache mixing with them.

"They were deceived, Jake. They were told that I was their child. But I wasn't. I was never theirs. Not really."

A dark thought crossed her mind. Her eyes flew to Jake. Concern was etched across every inch of his face as he watched her. A bone-deep cold settled within her. "Their child. They never got to mourn her. She died... and no one mourned her."

For some reason, the thought of that little body, her parents' child, entering the ground without anyone mourning her loss was the worst pain. *That poor innocent child.*

"Stop the car, Jake."

"Laney?"

"Stop the car!"

Jake pulled onto the shoulder, jerking the car to a stop.

Laney fumbled for the handle. Shoving the door open, she almost fell in her haste to escape. Stumbling to the edge of the trees, she crashed to her knees. Her stomach heaved.

Jake came up behind her, rubbing her back. "It'll be okay, Laney."

Laney vomited until there was nothing left. She felt weak, exhausted, shaky. "How could she do that to them? How could she do that to me?"

Jake pulled her into his arms, but Laney barely felt them around her, too lost in her own private hell.

Victoria is my mother. My whole life is a lie. And now I'm supposed to—what, embrace some unknown destiny? Save the world?

It was too much to ask of her. It was too much to tell her. "I can't do it, Jake. Whatever Victoria wants me to do, I can't."

Chapter Twenty-Four

JAKE HELD Laney by the side of the road as she alternated between crying and shaking. He didn't have a clue how to help her. So he just held her, murmuring into her ear that it would be okay.

After a time, she calmed, finally standing. Jake kept an arm around her as they made their way back to the car.

"I need to tell Uncle Patrick. He needs to——" Laney stopped short, and Jake felt her knees almost give out. He tightened his grip around her waist.

She stared up at Jake, looking so lost. "He's not my uncle. I'm not his niece. His niece is dead."

Laney looked as if her world had ended all over again.

"Laney, that's not——"

She stepped away from him, her voice edging toward hysteria. "He nearly gave up the priesthood for someone who isn't even related to him. He nearly got killed today for someone who's not even related to him." She stared off into space, but Jake knew she wasn't seeing what was right in front of her. She was reliving the past.

Jake grabbed her by the arms and yelled. "Laney!" It took three tries before her eyes met his.

"Laney, your uncle loves you. Yes, this is going to be a blow. But do you really, down deep, think this will change anything between you two? I've seen how much he loves you. He loves you not just like an uncle—he loves you like a father."

Tears streamed down her face. Her breaths came out in shudders. "But he's not, Jake. He's not my father. He's not my uncle. His niece is dead." She dissolved into tears.

Jake pulled her into his chest. *God damn you, Victoria.*

Chapter Twenty-Five

LANEY AND JAKE drove for an hour. Jake let Laney have her silence and she appreciated it. She needed time to think. She struggled to find any holes in Victoria's story, but she couldn't find any. Her father hadn't seen her until the day after her birth.

In utero, she, or rather her parents' daughter, had been diagnosed with a chromosomal disorder, Trisomy 13. Laney's parents always told her that the doctors had warned them she wouldn't survive a week. Yet she had survived—and the doctors had been astounded.

Laney leaned her head against the window, watching the scenery fly by but not really seeing it. From what she knew of Victoria, the woman wasn't a liar. She might omit, but when she spoke, it was the truth.

Laney wanted to bang her head against the window. She was Victoria's daughter. She turned to Jake. "How far are we from Baltimore?"

"About four hours."

Laney took a deep breath. It was too long. "Can we call the helicopter? I need to speak with Uncle Patrick."

Jake pulled onto the shoulder, pulled out his cell, and dialed. "Henry? Your mom's helicopter still around?" He paused and then rattled off their location.

Laney only half listened, trying to figure out what she was going to say to her uncle. When Jake disconnected the call, she turned to him.

"There's a field about twenty minutes from here," he said. "They'll meet us there."

Thirty minutes later, the helicopter landed. Laney could see Henry in the copilot's seat. Rocky stepped out of the back, her eyes searching Laney's face.

Laney didn't have the strength to be mad at her. She gripped Rocky's arm as she passed. "We're okay."

Relief poured over Rocky's face. She pulled Laney into a hug and whispered into her ear. "I swear I didn't know what Victoria was going to tell you. If I had known..." Her voice drifted off.

Laney buried her head in Rocky's shoulder, taking the comfort before getting into the chopper. She turned back when Rocky didn't follow her in.

Rocky gestured to the car. "I'll take the SUV. I'll meet you down in Baltimore."

Laney nodded, and a few minutes later, they were shooting through the air. Even by air, it took more time than Laney liked. She spent the trip trying to figure out what to say to her uncle. How did you even start a conversation like this?

Even though it seemed interminable, the ride also seemed to go too fast. Before she knew it, Laney was looking down at the lush rolling hills of the Chandler Estate. The helicopter touched down on the helipad behind the main house of the headquarters.

Kevin Chang, the head of estate security, stood waiting next to a golf cart. A dozen solar-powered golf carts were always available to help people move across the giant estate.

Kevin walked up as the helicopter shut down. "Everybody okay?"

Laney knew that he was asking about the incident at Hershey, not about what had been revealed in Pennsylvania.

"We're good," Henry said. "Do you know where Patrick is?"

Laney looked up in surprise. She hadn't even asked if everyone else was all right. Guilt added to all the other misery churning inside of her. The people she loved had been shot at, and she'd been too wrapped up in herself to even think of them.

"He's at Laney's cottage," Kevin said. "He got back with Kati and the boys about an hour ago. He's probably walking a hole in the floor waiting for you guys."

More guilt ate at Laney. She'd caused him so much worry over the last year, over her life.

Henry looked over at her and Jake. "Jake, why don't you and Laney take the cart? We'll walk."

Jake took Laney's arm. "Come on, Lanes."

Laney didn't say anything, just walked over to the cart and climbed in.

Jake drove the cart along the paths created for the estate. Flowers and bushes lined the paths. Normally, Laney loved riding across the estate. It was always so peaceful. But today, her mind was too chaotic to take in the scene. A lump formed in her throat as they pulled up in front of her cottage.

"You want me to come in?" Jake asked.

"Yes." She paused, looking at the stone cottage. "No. I think I need to do this alone."

He nodded. "I'll be out here, then. Just in case you need me, okay?"

She leaned over and kissed his cheek. "Thanks, Jake."

Jake took her hand. "He loves you. Remember that."

She nodded, climbing out of the cart. She walked slowly up the steps. Her legs felt like they had each gained twenty pounds. She opened the door.

Patrick was bounding down the hall before she even had the door completely opened. He pulled Laney through the doorway and into a fierce hug. "Thank God you're all right."

Laney hugged him back, trying to put all the love she felt for him into that one action.

Patrick pulled back, looking down at her. "Laney?" He paused searching her face. "What is it?"

She took a shuddering breath. "I need to talk to you."

Patrick gave her a long look. "Okay," he said, drawing out the word.

Laney took his arm and he winced.

"Your arm," Laney said. "Is it okay?"

He patted her arm. "It's fine. It's worrying about you that's going to put me in an early grave."

Laney couldn't laugh at his joke. But she managed to eke out a weak smile.

They walked into the living room and sat on the over-stuffed yellow couch. Laney normally loved this room, with its pale ivory walls and yellow and blue furniture. It was her favorite place to curl up. But the room offered her no comfort today.

Laney could see the concern on Patrick's face, the worry.

He took her hand. "Laney, whatever it is, you can tell me. We'll face it together, just like always."

She swallowed down the tears that threatened to break. *I hope so.*

"It's about—" She took a deep breath. "It's about Mom."

Chapter Twenty-Six

PATRICK WATCHED Laney struggle to find words. His dread grew, but also his confusion. After Hershey, he'd linked up with Kati and the boys and hustled them back to Baltimore with the help of a Chandler operative. But he hadn't been able to reach Henry, Jake, or Laney since the parking lot.

His imagination had gone into overdrive thinking of all the horrible possibilities.

Now he watched Laney sitting next to him, struggling to speak, and all he felt was confusion and worry. Why would Laney want to talk about her mom? Especially now?

Patrick had been extremely close to his sister, Fiona. When Laney had come into his sister's and her husband's life, Patrick had watched their joy increase exponentially.

And when Fiona and Derek had died, Patrick had been inconsolable. He'd let Derek's brother take custody of Laney, too lost in his own grief to notice what cruel people they were.

Later, when he learned of the abuse, he was angrier,

and guiltier, than he'd ever been before. Laney was the last link he had to his sister. He demanded that her custodians hand Laney over to him immediately and sign over custody —or he'd have them put away. They agreed.

Then he fought the church to allow him to raise her. He even threatened to leave—and he meant it.

He loved being a priest, loved the archaeological work he was able to do on their behalf. But Laney came before all of that.

From the moment he saw her swallowed up in that hospital bed, her arm in a cast, his sister's daughter had become his. At first, it was because Laney was all Patrick had left of Fiona. But then it was simply because she was Laney.

All that love he felt for his sister and all the grief he felt at her passing, though, now returned with Laney's words. Feeling shaky, he took Laney's hand. "That can wait. Are you all right? Where did you three go after the park?"

"After the attack, Henry, Jake, and I were chased down. We ended up crashing Henry's car and running through the woods. We were cornered, but Rocky showed up. She saved us."

"Rocky? What on earth was she doing there?"

Laney took a deep breath. "Apparently Victoria sent Rocky to Syracuse five years ago to keep an eye on me. To help me if I was ever in trouble."

Patrick stared at Laney, trying to understand what she was saying. Victoria sent someone to look after Laney? What on earth was going on? "Victoria? Henry's mother?"

Laney nodded.

"But I thought you just met her a couple of months ago."

"That's what I thought, too."

"Laney, I'm not understanding this. Why would Victoria send someone to look out for you? And when did you meet her before?"

Patrick could feel the tremble in Laney's hand. She looked at him, tears in her eyes. "Fiona McPhearson. Mom." She paused. "She wasn't my biological mother."

Patrick stared at her, waiting for more of an explanation.

But Laney stayed silent.

He reached his hand up to cup her cheek. Did she have a concussion? Had she been hurt worse than he knew during the attack? What was this nonsense? "Laney, honey, what are you talking about?"

Laney's words came out in a burst. "Victoria gave birth to me on January twenty-sixth. But she said she had to give me away to protect me. Mom and Dad's daughter, their biological daughter, your niece, she died. Victoria had me take her place."

Patrick paused, his concern growing. "Did you hit your head? Maybe we should take you to the hospital, get you checked out."

Laney stood up, her hands in fists, tears in her voice. "I'm not imagining this. I'm not hurt or delusional. I saw proof. I'm not their daughter. I'm not your—" Her voice broke. "I'm not your niece."

Patrick fell back on the couch. It couldn't be true. But as he looked at Laney's face, he knew that at least she believed it was. And Laney wasn't easy to convince. "Are you sure?"

Laney nodded, her voice shaky. "I am."

"Why are you sure?"

"I saw blood tests. There's no way I could be Fiona and Derek McPhearson's biological daughter."

Visions of Fiona ran through Patrick's mind. She'd been

younger than him, with red hair, just like Laney. And he remembered the heartache in her voice when she called to tell him that the baby she carried wouldn't survive. And then, the miracle: Laney was born, happy and healthy.

Laney had led a normal life, until this last year. Patrick had worried about how she seemed to keep getting caught up in these Atlantis situations. Was it possible that Laney really was someone else's daughter?

Patrick was glad he was sitting, because his legs felt weak. He felt like the rug had been pulled out from under them. It couldn't be true, though, could it?

Laney sat back down across from him. He knew she was trying to be strong, to hold back the emotions that were no doubt rushing through her.

Patrick leaned over and kissed her cheek, pulling her into a hug. "Even if it's true, it doesn't change anything, Laney. I love you."

He pulled her into his arms and hugged her tight. Laney wrapped her arms around his waist.

They stayed huddled together for a long time. Patrick knew Laney needed the comfort, the assurance. But his mind kept trying to figure out how any of what she said could be possible.

Finally, he pulled back, kissing her on the forehead. "I love you, honey. None of this, if it's true, changes that. But right now, I need to go. I'll be back."

Laney looked as if she'd been slapped. Patrick hugged her again before standing. He hated the hurt he was causing her, but he needed answers. He needed more.

He left the living room and strode down the hall to the front door before his resolve left him. The image of Laney's anguished face pulled at him.

Jerking open the front door, he was surprised to see

Henry sitting on the porch, Jake next to him. Patrick stepped onto the porch and nodded at Jake, who slipped into the cottage, closing the door behind him.

Henry stood, speaking quietly. "I have the helicopter standing by. Claude knows where to take you. There will be a car with directions waiting for you. I'm sorry, but I can't have Claude drop you right at her door."

Patrick hadn't even realized where he was going to go until Henry spoke. Victoria. He needed to see Victoria.

Patrick nodded, heading down the steps, but then stopped and turned to look at the tall man. "Take care of her, Henry. I love her—that hasn't changed. But I need some answers. I owe my sister that."

"I know," Henry said.

And Patrick realized, with a shock, that Henry really did. Because if all of this was true, Henry had a sister, too.

Patrick wanted to say more. But he couldn't form the words. So he just turned and walked down the path.

Laney's not Fiona's daughter. How can this be happening?

Chapter Twenty-Seven

THREE AND A HALF HOURS LATER, Patrick pulled up to the Maine home. It was a large two-story white colonial with black shutters, and flowers blooming along the front. A tree swing lay still under a towering willow twenty feet from the house.

The Chandler helicopter had dropped him forty miles away. As Henry had promised, a Jeep had been waiting for him, directions programmed into the GPS.

Patrick sat behind the steering wheel, watching the house. He'd noticed the electronic surveillance as he drove up the long drive, and he'd had to request access at the gate. So Victoria knew he was here—yet no one appeared. He was grateful. He needed a moment to prepare himself, to brace himself for the conversation to come.

His mind still reeled at everything Laney had told him—and at the heartbreak on her face. He knew he needed to be there for her, but first he needed answers. He owed Fiona that. He owed Laney that. She believed what she told him.

He needed to find out if it was true. Taking a deep breath, Patrick stepped out of the car.

He walked up the stone path. It was quiet, a slight wind blew, and the sun felt warm. It was a peaceful spot. It helped calm his emotions.

The front door opened when he was still five feet away.

A tall, muscular man, in his fifties, with dark brown hair, stepped back to allow him entrance. "Father Patrick, I'm Ralph. Victoria is expecting you. Follow me, please."

Patrick stepped in and Ralph closed the door behind him, then led him down the hall without a word. Ralph stopped at a door at the end and gestured for Patrick to enter.

The room Patrick stepped into was a large study. Two couches framed a brick fireplace on the right. On the left was an antique desk with a silver tea set. Victoria stood in front of a chaise lounge, her back to a bay window that looked out on an incredible garden.

"Victoria?" Ralph asked.

"That's all, Ralph. Thank you," she replied.

With a nod to Patrick, Ralph took himself back down the hall.

"Father Patrick, can I offer you some tea?" Victoria indicated the tea set on the desk.

The normality of the offer pushed Patrick's anger to the surface. This woman had brought all this drama and heartache to his family, and now she was offering tea?

He strode across the room. "Tea? No. I don't want any of your bloody tea. What I want are answers."

Victoria pursed her lips, her back going straight. "Of course. Could we at least sit?" She gestured to the couches.

Patrick gave an abrupt nod. He tried to swallow his

resentment. He needed answers, and his anger would only cloud the conversation.

"I take it Laney has spoken with you," Victoria said as she took a seat.

Patrick sat down across from her, leaning forward. "Yes. She's convinced you're her biological mother and that my sister was only her unofficial adopted mother. I don't see how any of that is possible."

Victoria took a breath. "It's true. Delaney is my biological daughter. Your sister's child died an hour after she was born."

Patrick stared at her. Who the hell *was* this woman? "Why should I believe you?"

Victoria took a folder off the table. "I showed these papers to Laney: the blood work." She pulled one sheet of paper from the folder. "I didn't have a chance to show her this one. It's a DNA test between her and Henry."

Patrick took the paper, checking the subjects' names. "This says John and Jane Doe."

Victoria nodded. "Yes. I didn't think it was wise to use their actual names."

Patrick scrolled to the bottom, According to the test results, their was a 99.9% chance the subjects were full brother and sister. Patrick felt shaken. "This could be anyone."

"The test can be re-done, but the result would be the same. And why would I lie about this? Why disrupt so many people's lives if it weren't true?"

Patrick decided to leave those questions alone for now. Right now, he just needed to know how and if this was really true. "How did you do it?"

Victoria's words were straightforward, but Patrick could hear the emotion underneath them. Victoria wasn't as calm as she would like him to believe. "I had a number of couples investigated. I knew that if I kept Laney, it would be too dangerous for her. I had a number of families lined up."

"Lined up?" Patrick was incredulous.

Victoria put up her hands. "Several couples that were expecting a child. A child with a slim to nonexistent chance of surviving birth. Like your sister and her husband. Your sister's child was diagnosed with Patau syndrome. The best-case scenario was that the child would survive a few days after birth. The worst case was that she would die in utero, which happens in most cases. The plan was only to replace a child who had died."

"Do you have any idea how cold you sound? 'Replace' a *child?* You can't replace a child."

Victoria's eyes snapped to him. "I know that. Do you think this was an easy decision for me? Do you think I happily handed over my child? This decision broke me apart. But I did it for Laney. I did it to keep her safe."

The room was charged with emotion and Patrick swallowed. "Where is my—" He paused, taking a breath. "Where is my niece buried?"

Victoria's violet eyes stared back at him for a moment. "Follow me."

Victoria walked out of the room, down the long hall, through the kitchen, and out the back door.

Patrick had to hurry to keep up with her. She walked down a path that cut through a riotous garden. A narrow path jutted off to the left a hundred yards from the house. Victoria turned down it and disappeared over a little rise.

Patrick followed the path, coming to a stop at the top of the little hill. Below him was a circular clearing, bordered by bushes and brightly colored flowers, daisies, black-eyed

Susans, roses, and a few more colorful flowers he couldn't identify.

A small wrought-iron bench sat off to the right of the clearing beneath a Rose-of-Sharon tree. And in the middle of the clearing was a white tombstone.

Patrick walked slowly toward the stone, his legs trembling. It was a beautiful spot. He had to give Victoria credit for that. And it was obviously well tended. He knelt at the tombstone and traced the carvings with his hand.

Sarah

She never had a chance to live,
But through her death helped save another.

In Hebrew, Sarah meant "princess." Touched, he turned to Victoria. "You named her?"

Victoria gave him an abrupt nod. "Sarah was—" She stopped, taking a breath. "That was supposed to be Laney's name. She was baptized as well."

Patrick was surprised at the comfort he took in Victoria's words. He turned back to the grave. Above the words, a stone angel was carved.

Tears sprang to his eyes. This was his niece, the last piece of his sister.

He knelt in front of the grave, bowed his head, and prayed for his little niece, who never had a chance to enjoy life. For his sister and her husband, taken too soon. And for Laney, who had been dealt this horrible twist of fate.

Victoria had given his niece her own daughter's name. He glanced around at the incredible flowers surrounding the grave. Victoria's doing, no doubt. She had mourned his niece as if she was her own. And the fact was, when

Victoria gave Laney away, it must have felt, to Victoria, as if her own daughter had died.

Patrick placed his hand on the top of the tombstone, using it to help him stand. He turned and looked at Victoria, who now sat on the bench. "It's a beautiful spot," he said softly.

Some of the defensiveness slipped from Victoria's posture. She gave him a sad smile. "It was an impossible decision. Your niece was never meant to be part of this world. But through Sarah's death, Laney had a chance at a normal life. A chance to be safe. And the only way for that to happen was for no one to know. No one, but me."

For the first time, Patrick didn't see Victoria as a cold woman who used people as chess pieces. He saw instead a terrified woman—one who made the heartbreaking decision to give up her only daughter in order to save her life. He still didn't understand why Victoria thought that it was necessary, but it was obvious that she believed it.

And the pain of that decision was etched across her face. Victoria's decision had given him decades of happiness —and had left Victoria with only decades of loss.

Patrick sat next to her on the bench. He took her hand, tears in his eyes. "I'm sorry for your loss, too. It couldn't have been easy giving her up."

Victoria nodded, but he saw her chin tremble. Her voice was barely above a whisper. "It wasn't."

They were silent for a moment. Patrick took a deep breath. "Laney's in trouble, isn't she?"

Victoria nodded. "Yes."

Patrick wrapped his arm around Victoria's shoulder.

Victoria let out a small sob before turning into his hug.

And Patrick hugged her back.

They sat there for a long time, sharing the pain of loss and the fear for the life of the child they both loved.

Chapter Twenty-Eight

HENRY BLEW out a breath as he stepped onto the landing in front of his office. He felt exhausted. Laney was safely home, but her world had been ripped apart. Patrick was off to confront Victoria. And as for him—he had no idea what to think, what to feel. And he was way too tired to even try to figure it out.

He knew his exhaustion wasn't physical. One of the side benefits of being a nephilim was that fatigue wasn't a part of his life. But emotional exhaustion? Well, his abilities didn't seem to be any help with that.

Henry pushed open the double doors to his office, a tingle running through his body. He glanced up sharply.

Jennifer Witt sat on his couch, flipping through a magazine. She looked up with a smile. "Hey."

Henry perked up at the sight of her. Standing six feet tall, with black hair and ebony, almond-shaped eyes, Jen was more than easy to look at. She was also a brilliant archaeologist and a nephilim as well.

They'd met last year, although he'd heard about her for

years from her brothers, Jordan and Mike. She was also one of Laney's best friends, and now one of his as well. He hadn't been handling the torture at the hands of Hugo as well as he wanted people to believe. Jen had been the person he'd been able to talk to. She understood.

"Hey," he said back to her.

Jen stood up, crossing the room to give him a hug. "I thought you guys would head up here as soon as you arrived. This *is* your guys' version of the Batcave, isn't it?" She paused. "Everybody okay?"

The heartbreak on Laney's and Patrick's faces flashed in his mind—as well as the anger on Jake's face, and his own feelings of confusion. "I'm not sure about 'all right.' But physically, no one got shot or broke anything. Oh wait, Patrick got shot, but it was only a graze."

Jen stepped forward, looking intently at Henry's face. "What about you? Are you all right?"

He gave her a small grin. "Not really. But it's good to see you."

Jen pulled him down to the couch. "More flashbacks?"

Since Vegas, Henry had suffered from insomnia and occasional flashbacks. Jen noticed something amiss one time when they were at dinner with Danny, and hadn't relented until he'd told her the whole story. And since then, she'd been the one he spoke with. His own personal counselor.

Henry shook his head. "No. No flashbacks, not for a week at least."

"Well, care to tell me what *is* going on?"

Henry had called Jen on the way back from the meeting with his mom. He'd explained about the attack in Hershey, but he hadn't been able to bring himself to explain about his mother's revelations. It was just too unbelievable, too fresh. He needed a little time to process it himself before he spoke of it to other people.

But even with all of that chaos, his priority was protecting Danny. He had a feeling the next couple of days were going to be intense. He needed to know Danny was safe, so he'd called Jen to see if she'd mind watching out for him. He had incredible security, but he wanted the best. And as far as he could tell, Jen was the best.

He blew out a breath. "It's been a rough day."

She gave a little laugh. "You do have a gift for understatement. I'm here as long as you need me. I spoke with Jordan and Mike as well. Jordan's cutting his vacation short. He'll be here in a few hours, and Mike's only in DC. He said if you need him, he can drop everything and be here in under an hour. Less, if he can nab a chopper."

Henry said a small prayer of thanks for the Witt family. Jordan was one of his security specialists, and his twin brother Mike was an FBI agent. Both were former Navy SEALs who'd trained with Jake, and having them around Danny eased his concern even more. "Thanks."

"That's why I'm here. But Kati called me from Hershey. Told me her version of the attack."

Henry cut her off. "How's she doing? How's Max?"

"Not going to lie. Kati's pretty shook up. Unlike the rest of us, that was her first gunfight. But she's strong. She'll be okay. And Max, luckily, didn't really understand what was going on."

"Well, I guess that's the best we can hope for."

"But I think there's more going on here."

"True."

Jen took his hand. "You don't have to keep it all in, you know. I know you're used to taking care of yourself, but it's okay to share the burden."

The idea of sharing this burden was more than a little appealing, but right now wasn't the time. "Maybe one day. I think Laney needs you more now."

Jen was quiet for moment. "It's okay for you to need someone, too, Henry."

A knock at the door grabbed Henry's attention. Agent Matt Clark walked in without waiting for an invitation.

Henry laid his head back against the couch, struggling not to groan. "Clark. How nice to see you."

Clark inclined his head, seeming to acknowledge the sarcasm in Henry's words. "Sorry to interrupt, but it's important, or I would have called."

Henry stood, his upbringing overriding his exhaustion. "Agent Matt Clark, this is Dr. Jennifer Witt."

"Ah, the archaeologist from Ecuador. An incredible find."

Jen shook his hand, her tone dry. "Actually, it was more of a theft."

Clark inclined his head. "True. But you and Dr. McPhearson did well by the Shuars."

"We could have done better," Jen said abruptly. She turned to Henry. "Well, I'll leave you to your unscheduled meeting. I'll go see Laney. I promised Danny dinner later. Join us?"

Henry managed to find a smile. "Best offer I've had in days. I'll find you when I'm done here."

Jen squeezed his arm before walking around Clark. She nodded her head stiffly. "Agent," she said before walking out of the room.

Clark watched her go. "You know, I don't think your friends like me very much."

Henry ignored the agent's accurate statement. He watched Jen leave instead, wishing he could go with her.

Whatever Clark had to say, Henry was pretty sure he didn't want to hear it. He'd had enough bombshells for one day.

Forcing the words past his teeth, Henry said. "All right, Clark what is it?"

"I realize this isn't a good time."

Henry raised an eyebrow.

"Yes. I know about Hershey. But I have some new information you need, especially after that attack. It was the Fallen, wasn't it?"

"Actually, there weren't any Fallen, but there was a nephilim. And a bunch of humans."

"I think I know who's behind the attack. They were after Laney, weren't they?"

Henry squinted at Clark. *Now what?* He spoke slowly. "We think so. But how did you know that?"

"We were worried that might happen."

"Well, thanks for the heads-up."

Clark put up his hands. "We had no concrete intel. It was really more of an educated guess. But what I have to tell you now is concrete."

Henry sank back into the couch, gesturing to the seat across from him. "Well, by all means, pull up a chair and lay it on me."

Clark pulled his seat toward Henry until he was only a foot away. "I know who's gathering the Fallen, the nephilim."

Henry's exhaustion disappeared immediately. "What? Who?"

"His name's Amar Patel." Clark pulled out his phone, hit a few buttons, and handed it over. On the small screen was a close-up of a man of Indian descent, probably in his late forties—dark hair, long nose, thin face, pale green eyes.

Henry handed the phone back. "Never seen him before. Do you guys have anything on him?"

"A bit. His formal title these days is venture capitalist. He makes most of his money through investments. And he's made a lot. But he has no criminal record—no formal ties at least. But there were rumors."

"Rumors?"

"Amar was born in a little village outside Trivandrum, India. He was on the streets by age seven."

Henry didn't like the sympathy that welled up in him. "Poor kid."

"Yeah, well, that 'poor kid' was apparently running those streets by the age of ten. He had a stable of kids working for him. As he got older, his reach extended until he controlled all the organized criminal activity in southwestern India. The authorities were just moving in when he closed up shop. They were never able to tie anything to him."

"He came to the States?"

Clark nodded. "He'd been diversifying for years. He had enough saved to start over, and start over well. He's worth millions now. But he's the guy we've been looking for. Since the very founding of the SIA, we have been—and are always—looking for him."

Well, that wasn't good. The agent looked awfully troubled, and while Henry didn't know Clark well, he was pretty sure not much fazed the guy. "Why? Which Fallen is he?"

"Samyaza."

Henry's eyes flew to Clark's face. Samyaza, the leader of the Fallen angels. The one who convinced them all to fall. "*The* Samyaza?"

Clark nodded. "Yes. He's the leader. And we believe he's the one trying to get to Laney."

"How'd you get this information?"

"I can't tell you that."

"Can't, or won't?

"Both."

Henry imagined himself strangling the answers out of the secretive agent. It wasn't an unpleasant thought. "How sure are you that it's Samyaza?"

"Pretty sure."

Henry raised an eyebrow. "Pretty sure?"

Clark shrugged. "Sometimes that's as good as you get."

Clark had referred to the Fallen as "Samyaza,"—which was the name given to him in the Book of Enoch. But Samyaza had been called by many other names over time. And one of those names had, for centuries, struck fear in even the strongest of men.

Henry's voice came out whisper-soft. "He's not known only as 'Samyaza,' is he?"

Clark shook his head. "No. Most people call him Satan."

Chapter Twenty-Nine

BALTIMORE, MARYLAND

JAKE WALKED up the stairs to Henry's office, his thoughts still on Laney. It had not been an easy night for her. One horrible dream had followed the next. Jake tried not to let it show, but the dreams were worrying him. They seemed to be getting more violent.

He shuddered as he remembered her screams during the latest dream. She'd been Joan of Arc, burning at the stake. From her screams, you would have thought Laney herself was actually being burned.

Jake took a sip of coffee from the travel mug in his hand. He rubbed his eyes, trying to make himself more awake. He hated leaving when she was sleeping, but Henry had called and it sounded urgent. And Jake knew Henry wouldn't call him away right now unless it was something incredibly important.

The doors to Henry's office were open, so Jake just walked in without knocking. Henry sat behind his desk, staring out the window at the hills beyond. Jake could see his profile, the worry on his face.

Henry turned as Jake approached. "Hey. Sorry for pulling you away from Laney."

Jake started to walk over toward him, but Henry waved him toward the big leather couch in the corner. Jake changed direction and took a seat on the couch. "Figured it had to important."

Henry took a seat in the matching leather club chair across from him. "It is. How's Laney?"

Jake paused, trying to put into words how Laney was. He finally shrugged. "Shell-shocked, destroyed, recovering. All at the same time."

Henry nodded.

Jake waited a beat before asking, "How are you?"

Henry sighed. "I'm used to my mother's secrets by now, but this one?" He shook his head. "This one took even me by surprise."

"You had no idea?"

"None. And I've been wracking my brain to see if I missed some clue. If there was something that I should have seen, that should have let me know that I had a sister. But there's nothing."

"And how do you feel about Laney?" Jake asked.

Henry looked surprised. "I love her. I think maybe part of me always knew who she was. From the moment I met her, we had this connection. I've always thought of her like my little sister."

Jake nodded. He'd noticed the connection between the two of them, and it had never made him jealous. He'd wondered why not, but the fact was, he'd never thought of Laney and Henry as anything but friends. And he didn't think either of them had either.

"Should I go talk to her?" Henry asked.

Jake pictured Laney as he'd left her, curled up in bed,

exhausted from the emotional whirlwind she'd been through. He shook his head. "She'll come to you when she's ready."

Henry nodded and blew out a breath. "Well, I didn't actually call you to talk about Laney. Not directly at least. Clark stopped by last night."

Jake's eyes flew to Henry. "What? Why?"

"He found out who was behind the attempt on Laney. The man's name is Amar Patel. He's a Fallen."

Jake took a sip of coffee, struggling to keep his voice calm. "Great. Where is he? I'd like to kill him."

Henry let out a short laugh. "Get in line. We don't have an address yet, but Clark's working on it. He does, however, know which Fallen Amar is."

Jake looked at Henry's face and couldn't help but notice the tension in Henry's jawline. Jake didn't really give a crap which Fallen this guy was, but dread began to settle in his stomach. He could read the fear in Henry's face. "Who is he?"

"Samyaza, the leader of the Fallen."

Jake nodded. "Okay. The leader. Great. I'll be sure to shoot him extra then."

A small smile flitted across Henry's mouth. "You never went to Sunday school, did you?"

Jake crossed his ankles. "It shows?"

"Just a little. Samyaza is the angel that convinced the rest to fall. He's the first Fallen."

Henry looked at Jake expectantly.

Jake looked back at him. "So?"

"He's Satan, Jake."

Jake looked at Henry, waiting for more, but Henry just sat there quietly. Jake shook his head. In his opinion, everybody put way too much stock in these ancient tales. Yes, the superhumans had extra abilities—but they could be killed. And Samyaza—Satan or whatever—could be killed just like the rest.

"Great. So we get to cut off the head of the beast."

"I don't think you realize—"

Jake cut him off. "Oh, I get it. He's the guy in charge. Doesn't change anything. He can be killed just like the rest of them. And as soon as we find the bastard, I'll make that happen."

Henry smiled. "Well all right then. Clark did have one other tidbit of info, too. It involves the Council."

Jake groaned. They'd found out about the Council during the Ecuador situation. The Council was a shadowy group of humans trying to track down Atlantis artifacts for their own benefit. "What about them?"

"Well, apparently, they're in cahoots with Samyaza and his friends."

Jake leaned forward, his chin in his hand. "Super. I'm guessing that's where all the humans we've been coming across are from?"

Henry nodded. "Clark thinks the Council is supplying them. In exchange for a piece of the pie when Amar achieves whatever the hell it is he's trying to achieve."

Jake would like to have been surprised that humans were helping, but he wasn't. He'd learned long ago that humans can and did do lots of things that were just plain crappy.

Jake sighed. "You know, I'm still not sure I trust Clark."

"Me either. But right now, he's all we've got."

"See, though, that's part of the problem. Clark walked in here, told us all of this, and then disappeared. But why tell us? He doesn't strike me as a particularly altruistic fellow."

"No. I don't think he is either. He's got an angle. I'm just not sure what it is yet."

Jake flashed on Laney, sleeping back in her bed. He didn't know what Clark wanted, but with everything focused on Laney these days, Jake had a sinking feeling that she was a big part of Clark's agenda, too.

Chapter Thirty

The Queen of Sheba lay back on the red and yellow cushions of the lounge out on the terrace. The white fabric draping the pergola waved slightly in the early evening air.

Her son, Menelik, only eighteen, stood opposite her. They shared the same coppery skin, but her son's hair was lighter than her pitch black tresses; his eyes as well.

His back to her, he watched the bustle of the city central three stories below. "I don't understand. You always said my father was a wise man. A good man."

Makeda sighed and walked over to her son. She put her hands on his bare shoulders and leaned into his back. "He was. When I met him, he was all that and more. But time has changed him. Power has changed him."

Menelik faced his mother. "It will not be easy."

She cupped his face in her hands as she had done every day since his birth. When had he gotten so big? She kissed his cheeks.

"No. It will not. You will meet your father. Spend time with him. Get to know him. Let him suspect nothing. But when you leave, you must take the Ark and the relic with you. They are no longer safe with him."

"And they will both stay here? They will be safe here?"

"The Ark will be. I have already begun preparations for its final resting place. But this will only be the first stop for the other relic. It has a long way to travel before it is home."

"Will you take it there?"

"Yes. It is my duty."

He took her hands. "Why then can't you go with me? Why can't you complete this task?"

She shook her head. "He would suspect me. And the fact is, I have aged. I will not hold his attention like I used to. You, however, are his son. You are strong, handsome, fast, and brave. He will be enamored of you. He will see himself in you."

Makeda stared at her son, and knew the truth in her words. Menelik had his father's blue eyes and strong cheekbones. Menelik's shoulders were as broad as his father's had once been, his stomach as flat. Unlike his father, though, Menelik's eyes stared with understanding and confidence, not arrogance. But Menelik's intelligence—that he had received from both of them.

Makeda held her son's hand to her cheek. Yes, *she thought,* Solomon will be very pleased with his son.

Chapter Thirty-One

BALTIMORE, MARYLAND

LANEY'S EYES FLEW OPEN. The dream started to fade. *The son of Solomon? Now I'm dreaming of the son of Solomon?*

The image of the stolen folio flashed through her mind. That must be why she was dreaming it. Of course, after the events of yesterday, she wasn't sure why Solomon would take the forefront in her subconscious.

And who the heck were Makeda and Menelik? Were they real, like with Helen, or just a product of her imagination?

Laney lay back heavily on the pillow. Was this all related to her destiny?

She pictured the seal of Solomon on the book the Fallen had stolen. Two intertwined triangles. Everything in her life seemed to be becoming intertwined. Is that why she'd had the dream?

Laney struggled to sit up, still exhausted despite the sleep. The Makeda dream had been relatively innocuous compared to some of the others she'd experienced earlier in the night. In each one, she felt everything the star of her dream felt.

Laney ran her hands over her arms, still picturing the flames dancing along her blackening skin.

She shoved the image from her mind, but reality wasn't any easier to face right now. After Patrick left, she'd dragged herself to her bedroom hoping that when she woke, all these truths would be easier to accept.

They weren't.

The door cracked open. Kati peered in. "You awake?"

Laney glanced at the clock. She'd been asleep, on and off, for over fourteen hours. "Barely."

"Want some company?"

Laney patted the bed, taking in Kati's pale face. Guilt washed over her. Laney had put Max and Kati in danger. Unintentionally, but nonetheless. "Are you okay?"

Kati sat down next to her, piling some pillows behind her back. "Yeah. A little shook up, though, if I'm being honest. I keep thinking that yesterday was just a small taste of what you've been going through for the last year. I don't know how you do it."

Henry, Jen, Jake, Yoni and everybody that had helped her floated through Laney's mind. "Well, I haven't had to do it alone."

Kati plucked at the blanket, letting silence fall between them. She glanced up. "Laney, how did Henry do all of that? He moves like the Flash, and can be shot like Superman."

"Not like Superman. Bullets hurt him. He just heals real fast."

"But how? How is he like that?" Kati paused. "The men you fought in our house and out in Montana... they were like that too, weren't they?"

Laney nodded slowly. "Yeah, they were."

Kati let out a breath. "How many are out there like them?"

Laney shrugged. "I'm not sure. At least two hundred, not including their children."

"Children? Their children have powers?"

"Some do. Henry does."

Kati nodded, and Laney noticed Kati's hand shaking. "Kati?"

Kati glanced over at her, giving her a small smile. "It's a little scary. What chance do us normal people have against people with those kinds of powers?"

Laney didn't know what to say. She sighed. "I know it's scary. But they can be defeated, you know."

Kati shook her head. "I think for right now, I'm going to leave you guys to figure that stuff out. I'm going to pretend I don't know."

Laney took her hand. "I understand. If that were an option for me, I'd do exactly the same thing. Do you know where Jake is?"

"He said he had something to take care of but he didn't want you to be alone, so he called me."

"Did he tell you what's going on?"

"No, but from the expression on his face, I could tell it was something big." Kati paused. "I saw Patrick flying off in the chopper yesterday."

"Has he come back?"

"No. Jake said he called last night, but Patrick didn't want Jake to wake you."

Laney nodded, her eyes straying to the French doors. How could everything have gotten so turned upside down? How was anything ever going to be normal again?

Kati reached out and touched Laney's shoulder. "Is everything okay?"

Laney swallowed down the hurt. Patrick was gone. She leaned her head back, tears clouding her vision. How sad was it that thinking about the threat of the Fallen was easier than focusing on her family drama?

Laney shook off the feelings and Kati's question. "How's Max?"

"He's okay. He didn't really understand what was happening in Hershey. He's with Danny and Jen. Danny's teaching him to play Skylanders."

Laney tried to give Kati a smile, but knew she wasn't convincing. "That's good."

Kati gave Laney a long look before taking her hand. "Laney, honey, tell me what's going on. I know this isn't just about the attack. Something else happened, didn't it?"

Laney looked over at her. "Oh Kati, it's all such a mess." And the story poured out of her. Rocky, everything Victoria had said, everything Laney had said to Patrick. The whole sordid mess.

"So, Henry's your brother?" Kati asked, her eyebrows raised.

Laney let out a breath, picturing Henry's face at the cabin. He'd been as shocked as she was. "Yeah. I guess that's the one good thing to come out of this mess. But how could Victoria do that? How could she just give me away? How could she do that to my parents?"

Kati stayed silent, picking at the blanket.

Laney looked over at her. "What?"

"It's just—" Kati stopped. "Do you think Victoria was telling you the truth about sending you away to protect you?"

Laney let her head fall back against the headboard.

"Yes. I think she thought she was doing it to protect me. But was that a reasonable thing to even suspect? I mean, why would she think I was in danger?"

Kati let out a strangled laugh. "You're kidding, right? In the last twelve months, you've nearly lost your life how many times? You've been kidnapped once and were nearly grabbed again down in Hershey. Lately, you are an absolute magnet for danger."

"Okay. That's all true. But it's also recent. Until now, my life has been pretty safe."

"Maybe. But maybe that's also because you didn't grow up with Victoria. I mean, look at Henry. His life hasn't exactly been normal."

"You're defending her?"

Kati put up her hands. "No. I'm just trying to help you determine if there are any good reasons why she did what she did."

"There aren't. You don't use people like pawn pieces."

"No, you don't. But she gave you two loving parents, who otherwise probably wouldn't have had a child. And she gave you your Uncle Patrick. Meanwhile, she had to live her life without you. And after Henry turned eighteen, largely without him too."

Resentment began to build in Laney. "You're taking her side. I can't believe it."

"No. I'm trying to understand her side. And as a mom, I don't know." Kati's voice drifted off.

"Don't know? Don't know what?"

Kati chewed her bottom lip. "Okay, don't get mad at me."

Laney glared at her.

"Or at least, don't get any madder. Just listen for a minute."

Laney nodded stiffly, leaning back against the pillows.

"I want you to think about Max. Picture him when we first brought him home from the hospital. Those first few months, and all the years that you've watched him grow up."

Laney did, a constant flow of memories. Laney had met Kati on the day of Max's birth. In fact, she had saved Kati's and Max's lives that day. And from that moment on, they had become a family.

"Okay," Laney said.

"Now, imagine someone was going to hurt Max. What would you do?"

Laney looked at Kati without blinking. "I'd kill them."

Kati let out a little laugh. She took Laney's hand and kissed it. "I know. And I am thankful every day that he has you in his life. But the fact is, we can't be there every moment of every day. What if you knew there were people who were after him? Or would be one day? What if you knew the only way to protect him was to give him up?"

Laney let Kati's words sink in, but she still wasn't ready to be on Victoria's side. "She couldn't have known that."

"She sent Rocky to look out for you five years ago. And look at everything that's happened to you. The fact is, she *did* know. Somehow she knew."

Laney wasn't ready to let Victoria off the hook. "But why not wait until danger appeared? Why send me away *before* it appeared?"

"You know, if she had done that, I wouldn't think too highly of her. She would have been putting her happiness before yours. If she had kept you for any amount of time, it would have been harder on you, harder on Henry, when you finally had to leave—but easier on her. She would have had the memories of those times to keep her going. Instead, she gave you away. She put your happiness before hers. To me, that sounds like a mom."

Kati leaned over and kissed Laney on the forehead before leaving.

Laney sat quietly, Kati's words flowing through her mind. She wasn't ready to forgive Victoria for what she had put her through.

But she had to admit, the only ones hurt here were her and Patrick. Her parents were beyond getting hurt.

No. Henry and Victoria were hurt too, a little voice whispered in the back of her mind.

Henry. When she'd first met him, she'd been bowled over by his intelligence, his kindness, his generosity in all things. The image of him risking his own life to save her uncle's was forever branded in her mind.

Laney kicked off her blankets. She needed to talk to her brother.

Chapter Thirty-Two

ABOUT EIGHT HUNDRED yards from the main building, Laney drove the golf cart over the rolling lawns to Henry's house. Ahead, a deep grouping of well-aged blue spruces guarded the way to Henry's home. The branches rubbed against the side of the cart as she passed through.

Most people who arrived at the expansive Chandler Group's Headquarters probably assumed that Henry's home was equally lavish. But actually, it was the exact opposite.

As she broke free of the towering evergreens, Henry's cottage came into view. A two-story home that had once been a caretaker's cottage, it was extremely modest by millionaire standards.

But Henry wasn't into the trappings of wealth. He knew that for the Chandler Group to be successful, he needed to present a wealthy image. Underneath the image, however, he preferred a simple existence.

There was no driveway, no noticeable wires. It was just a simple stone cottage, with a riot of wildflowers surrounding it, looking as if it could have been right at home at the turn of the nineteenth century.

Henry had added a second floor a decade ago and outfitted it with all the latest in electronics and security to allow him to work from home when necessary. Otherwise, though, it was minimalistic.

Inside, of course, the doorways and windows had been adapted to accommodate Henry's height. On the walls, there were a few simple sketches—bought because Henry liked them, not for their resale value. The furniture was chosen for the history he felt when he saw it, and of course, for its comfort.

Laney loved that about him. He could have lived in a huge mansion. Instead, he chose a simple cottage for him and Danny to call home.

Laney pulled to a stop next to the front stone path. The heavy oak door opened before she reached it.

Henry stood outlined in the frame. "Hey."

Laney climbed the three brick stairs. "Hey."

Henry stepped back to let her in. "I was about to get some sweet tea. Would you like a glass?"

Laney wasn't thirsty, but she said yes anyway. She followed Henry back to the kitchen. Pictures dotted the hall. Henry had added them in the last year. Pictures of Laney, Jake, Danny, Jen, Patrick, even some of Kati and Max, covered the space. At the end of the hall were even a few from when Henry was a child.

Just before the kitchen, a picture of Henry and Victoria made Laney pause. In the photo, Henry couldn't have been any older than four. Victoria stood behind him, her arms wrapped around him, giant smiles on both of their faces. The Victoria that Laney knew today had a head of pure white hair. But in the old shot, her hair had been a deep auburn—the exact same shade as Laney's.

Laney stepped into the kitchen. A giant farmhouse stove stood against the left wall, a brick archway above it. Large windows looked out onto a stone patio. The walls were a pale yellow, the cabinets a grey blue. Laney had always liked this kitchen. She always felt welcome in it.

She took a seat at the island, with its heavy oak counter. Henry got out two glasses and poured them each some tea.

"Thanks." Laney took the glass from Henry, taking a small sip.

Henry took a seat next to her. "So, how exactly do we start this conversation?"

Laney let out a shaky laugh. "I'm really not sure."

"Laney, I want you to know, I never knew any of what my mother—our mother—revealed. I didn't know . . ." His voice drifted off.

"You didn't know I was your sister?" Laney asked gently.

Henry nodded. "Yeah."

"You don't remember her being pregnant? Or anything?"

"I was only five. And Dad had just died."

Laney was jolted by his words. She'd forgotten about the timing. Henry's dad, her dad, had been killed just six months before her birth. Victoria had been pregnant when she watched her husband get killed for what he was.

Henry continued, unaware of Laney's thoughts. "I remember her going away for a few days, which was weird, because at that point, she barely ever let me be alone. That must have been when—"

"When I was born."

"Yeah."

"Henry, I don't understand Victoria. I don't get why she does what she does."

Henry gave a little laugh. "Well, you're in good company there, because I don't either. But what I've never doubted, no matter how many secrets she's kept, is that she loves me and that she's always doing what she thinks is in my best interest. And while this last revelation is incredible, I can't help but think she did it because she thought it was what was best for you, too."

"It's just hard to accept that. My whole life has been a lie."

"Not a lie. You had two parents who loved you. You have an uncle who loves you. You have other people in your life who love you. Who gave birth to you doesn't change any of that."

"Logically, I know you're right." Laney sighed. "But it feels different. It all feels different."

Silence settled between them. Thoughts of Victoria and James Chandler floated through Laney's mind. She shoved them away. When Henry had been abducted, they'd learned that James Chandler had actually been Enoch—or Metatron, if you called him by his angel name. Apparently, Enoch was reborn time and time again.

But Victoria... well, no one knew who Victoria really was. And despite Victoria's protestations, Laney was sure she wasn't just a normal human.

The fantastical identities of her biological parents, though, were too much for Laney to cope with right now. She needed to deal with the fact that she wasn't the biological child of Derek and Fiona McPhearson. That would be enough for today. Dealing with her supernatural parentage would have to wait until at least tomorrow—or, better yet, three years from now. Maybe then she'd be ready.

Laney glanced over at Henry. He looked so sad, so alone. She took his giant hand in both of hers. "The one good thing I can say about all this is that I get to have you as a brother. If I'm being honest, though, you've felt like my brother since we met. This news just makes it official."

Henry gently squeezed her hand. "I feel the same way."

Tears crested in Laney's eyes. *Henry's my brother.*

She stood, and Henry opened his arms. She walked into them and they folded around her. Tears ran down her cheeks. They held each other, sharing the loss of not getting to watch each other grow up, but also the joy of finally finding one another.

After a few moments, she pulled back and gave a small, embarrassed laugh, wiping away her tears. She'd been a crying mess lately. She wasn't ready to forgive Victoria yet, but having a brother—that she could get used to.

"Okay, enough with the waterworks," she said. "Any idea what this destiny thing is all about?"

"No, but I know someone who does."

Laney knew he was going to say that. She pictured Kati's face. Kati had been scared. And she had every right to be. If Clark was right, a lot of normal, everyday people were going to get hurt. And apparently, Laney was the one person who could prevent that.

She sighed, knowing her next action was inevitable. "Okay. Let's go talk to Victoria."

Chapter Thirty-Three

LANEY GLANCED down as Jake flew the Chandler helicopter over the fields surrounding Victoria's property. It was a beautiful piece of land, thirty acres near the sea. A house came into view, settled a couple hundred yards from the beach, a giant garden in the back.

Laney realized with shock that Victoria's house was incredibly similar to Henry's. Both had chosen simple little two-story cottages. *Like mother, like son.*

The helicopter started to descend and so did Laney's stomach. Victoria stood on the back patio, Patrick beside her.

When Henry had called Victoria to let her know they were coming, Laney learned that Patrick had stayed in Maine as Victoria's guest last night.

Laney had been shocked. Had Patrick *forgiven* Victoria? Was he okay with everything that she had done? What did that mean for Laney and Patrick's relationship?

Jake touched down the skids and began shutting down the chopper.

Henry turned to look back at Laney. "Ready?"

Heart racing, she put up a hand. "Just need a minute."

Jake looked at her over his shoulder. "Take as much time as you need."

Laney nodded, looking out the window at Victoria and Patrick. She searched Patrick's face. She didn't know what she expected to find. Happiness? Rejection? Anger? But she couldn't read it.

The rotors stopped spinning and Laney knew it was time. "Okay, let's go." She opened her door and stepped out.

Jake and Henry did the same.

Henry outpaced Laney and Jake, reaching the patio first. He walked over to his mother, murmured in her ear, and escorted her into the house.

Jake kissed Laney on the cheek. "I'll be right inside."

Laney watched Jake disappear into the house as well, leaving her alone on the patio with Patrick. Her eyes turned to him. "Hi."

Patrick didn't say anything. Just walked over to her and pulled her into his arms. "I love you, Laney. I always have and I always will."

Laney felt her knees go weak. She didn't realize how truly afraid she'd been that her uncle would leave her. That he'd turn his back. She held on to him.

His arms gripped her tighter. "Whatever happens, Laney, I'll be right here with you. Just like always."

Chapter Thirty-Four

LANEY WALKED with her uncle into the house, her arm wrapped around his. They stepped into the kitchen. It was beautiful. The cabinets were all white, with brown and white granite countertops. A giant farmhouse table stood in front of an old brick fireplace.

Laney realized, with a start, that it was also very similar to Henry's. *Genetics run deep in this family*, she thought, because honestly, it was the exact type of kitchen she would have chosen as well.

"Victoria's study is right down the hall," Patrick said.

Laney nodded, but her feet didn't seem to want to move. She wasn't sure how much more of this emotional roller coaster she could handle. It seemed like she was constantly being bounced from apprehension to joy to sadness and back again. And she had a feeling the next chat with Victoria was going to be yet another tumultuous ride.

Patrick stopped next to her. "It'll be okay." He looked down at her. "Laney, you've never been one to hide under the covers. If you do in fact have a destiny, it's coming whether you want it to or not. And I know you—you'd rather know what's coming."

Laney took a breath. She straightened her shoulders. Patrick was right. And she was done crying. Whatever Victoria revealed, she'd face it. "Okay. Let's go."

Patrick patted her hand and led her down the hall. They stopped at the last door on the right. Inside, Henry leaned back against a mantelpiece, a fire burning low next to him. Jake stood on the other side of the fireplace.

Two couches flanked the fireplace and Victoria sat on one, near Henry. She stood as she caught sight of Laney. "Laney, I—" She went silent and then said, "I'm glad you're here."

Laney nodded, walking in and taking a seat across from her.

Jake and Patrick sat down on either side of her.

Laney gave them each a quick glance before turning to face Victoria. "Okay. So let's hear about my destiny."

Chapter Thirty-Five

AMAR SAT on the couch in the living room, enjoying the peace. He took a sip of Merlot. *Delightful.* His mood dimmed, however, as he scanned the latest translation from the book.

He laid the papers on the oak coffee table in front of him and stared out the large picture window toward the barn. But he didn't register the sight; his mind was too full. *Could it be? After all this time?*

A knock at the door interrupted his thoughts.

Amar narrowed his eyes at the human guard who stepped in. "I said I was not to be disturbed."

The guard bowed his head. "I know, sir. I'm sorry. But a man arrived at the door. He insists on seeing you. He says his name is Gerard Thompson."

Amar cursed. Gerard. He was indebted to the man, he supposed, for finding the book in Las Vegas. And he had tied up the loose ends in the whole affair nicely. But still. The man took too many liberties. And the truth was, Gerard owed him much more than he owed Gerard.

Amar swallowed. Of course, it would not pay to make Gerard angry. Not with his connections. He darted a glance at the guard, but the man was staring at the floor. He could see nervousness in the man's frame. Not surprising. Gerard was always polite, and yet there was a tangible sense of menace around him.

"Very well. Send him in."

The guard nodded and disappeared back out the door. Only a few seconds later, the hairs on Amar's body tingled. Gerard walked in. Standing at six feet with blond hair and sharp cheekbones, Gerard had looks that would make a Scandinavian model jealous. Amar had never seen Gerard flustered, never seen him without confidence. The man was unflappable.

Amar strove for the same composure as he crossed the room, his hand extended. "Gerard. What a wonderful surprise. If you had let me know that you were coming, I would have had a lunch prepared."

Gerard grasped Amar's hand in a firm handshake. "A shame. Perhaps next time."

Amar gestured at his glass of wine. "I just opened a lovely Merlot. Can I get you a glass?"

Gerard followed Amar back to the couch. He sat in one of the large armchairs, his foot resting on his knee. "Thank you, no. I only stopped in for a quick update, and then I'll be out of your hair."

"There was no need to come all this way. I could have easily sent you the information." He gestured to the papers on the coffee table. "I was just reading the latest translation."

Gerard raised his hands, palms up. "Well, I just go where I'm told. And seeing as I'm here, why don't you just tell me what you've found?"

Amar paused for only a second, recognizing the order in Gerard's polite tone. Swallowing his resentment, he said, "The translation is about ninety percent complete."

"And what have you found out about Delaney McPhearson?"

"From what I've read, she is probably the one."

Gerard nodded, his hand on his chin. "Very well. And what of the rest?"

"Well, it's rather detailed," Amar hedged.

Gerard smiled, showing all his teeth. "Just hit the highlights for me."

"It echoes many of the same sentiments as the War Scroll."

"Does it mention the three?"

"Yes. Both of them."

Gerard nodded. "Good. What about the key?"

Amar smiled, careful to keep his expression neutral, his heart rate normal. "Nothing yet. But like I said, the translation isn't complete."

"Anything else of interest?"

"No, nothing stands out. I'll forward you a copy of the full translation when it's complete."

"Go ahead and send me what you have so far. I'll just get started with that."

Amar inclined his head. "Happy to."

Gerard stood with a smile. "Excellent progress. Perhaps if you send the results sooner next time, I won't need to intrude upon you."

Amar smiled in return, extending his hand. "Of course, Gerard. Although it is always wonderful seeing you."

Gerard shook Amar's hand. "No need to show me out. Enjoy your wine."

Amar narrowed his eyes as Gerard closed the door

behind him. *Bastard.* He glanced back at the hard copy on the side table. The key. So cleverly hidden.

Amar's eyes strayed back to the window, his anger only rising. So, they were checking up on him. He needed to work off some of his rage. If he didn't, he was likely to do something rash. And he didn't have time for the cleanup.

His eyes came to rest on the barn and he smiled. *And I know just the thing.*

Chapter Thirty-Six

LANEY WATCHED VICTORIA. Her hair was pure white but her skin had few wrinkles. Her eyes were the same deep violet as Henry's. Did that mean that James Chandler had green eyes? Was that where Laney had gotten hers?

Victoria's cheekbones were pronounced. Did Laney share those? It was hard to sit still when she wanted to run to a mirror. Laney pushed her curiosity out of her mind. There'd be time to play "who got what genetic traits from which parent" later. But it was still a struggle to rein in her thoughts and focus on what Victoria was saying.

Victoria glanced across the group. "You are all aware of the Fallen, of their existence." She waited until everyone nodded back at her. "Generally, they keep to themselves, they build their own power base, eventually die, and then start all over again."

"Why is that?" Patrick interrupted. "Why start from scratch each time? Why not start where they left off?"

"Because they have no memory of the life they lived before. At least, most of the time they don't. Every once in a while, though, one does—and he or she begins the next life right where they left off. When that happens, the Fallen begin to group. They begin to find one another; coordinate, organize."

Victoria sighed. "We're in one of those time periods now. I received word a few months ago that there were signs that the Fallen were grouping. I knew that meant that it was time for the Chosen to be called. I hoped that by hiding you away, not only would you be safe, but that maybe you could even avoid this. I was wrong."

Laney shook her head. "The Chosen? What, like *Buffy the Vampire Slayer*? Because I don't have any powers. I'm not like Henry, not like—" She almost said Jen's name, but caught herself at the last minute. "I'm not like any of them. I'm just a normal human."

Victoria shook her head. "No, Laney, you're not. You're the daughter of Enoch. Haven't you wondered why all these ancient sites are coming to light because of you?"

Laney flashed on the conversation she'd had with her uncle two months earlier. *Two Atlantis-related sites were discovered on two different continents, after being hidden for thousands of years. And you're the one constant between them.*

Patrick squeezed her hand, and she knew he was recalling the same conversation.

Laney shook her head. "This is crazy. I can't bench press a car or outrun a train. I don't have powers."

"No, you don't have the powers of a Fallen or of a nephilim. Your powers are different. Your powers come from the ring."

"The ring?" Laney asked.

Victoria looked each of them in the eye. "The ring of Solomon."

Laney struggled to keep her face blank. Her dream of

Menelik and Makeda took center stage in her mind. Makeda had wanted Menelik to get something from Solomon. Was it the ring? She pictured the folio the Fallen had stolen. The images associated with Solomon. Everything seemed to be circling back to him.

"You are familiar with the tales of the ring, aren't you?" Victoria asked.

Laney knew about the ring of Solomon. Her uncle had even taught a course on Solomon at Tel Aviv University one summer, and she'd been his teaching assistant. "During Solomon's reign, he was said to have come into possession of a ring that allowed him to control demons. He allegedly used the ring to have demons build the First Temple. The ring also allowed him to control the weather and animals."

"The folio that was stolen," Jake said quietly. "It was covered in images associated with Solomon."

Patrick frowned. "The seal predates Solomon by thousands of years, so how's that possible?"

Laney glanced over. "We think the symbols on the book were associated with Solomon, but that the seal of Solomon was an older creation, one which only later came to be associated with Solomon."

"To be honest, I thought the ring of Solomon was a myth," Jake said.

Victoria shook her head. "It's not a myth. It's very real. And Laney's right. Solomon wasn't the first owner. He was, however, the first and only owner whom the ring became associated with."

"Okay, but why is it important? Can't just anybody wear it?" Jake asked.

"Anybody can wear it—but only one person can wield its power." Victoria's eyes flashed back to Laney. "It's why they weren't trying to kill you yesterday. They need you alive. They need to test you."

"Test me?" Laney asked, hearing the squeak in her voice.

"To see if you really are the ring bearer," Victoria said.

Laney crossed her arms, feeling vulnerable. "Okay, well, let's just send them a memo detailing the fact that I'm not."

Victoria gave a little smile. "I'm afraid it's not that simple."

"Of course it's not," Laney mumbled.

"Do they have the ring?" Patrick asked.

Victoria shook her head. "No. To the best of my knowledge, it's still hidden."

"So then, why does any of this matter?" Jake asked. "If no one has the ring, it can't be worn and it can't be used. End of story."

"I wish it were that simple," Victoria said. "They're not going to stop just because they don't have the ring. The only way for them to be sure you and the ring are not a threat is to make sure you are the ring bearer and then..." Victoria's words died away.

"Kill me," Laney finished for her.

Victoria nodded.

Jake squeezed Laney's hand. "So where is the ring hidden? And who hid it?" Jake asked.

"The hiding place was created by one of the previous ring bearers."

Laney thought of her dreams. Were they related to this destiny? Were those people previous ring bearers?

"How many ring bearers have there been?"

Victoria paused, her words spoken slowly. "There's a ring bearer in existence at almost every point of humanity's existence."

Laney could feel her jaw drop. There were so many of them.

Patrick leaned forward. "Are the ring bearers always women?"

Victoria hesitated. "Since Solomon's time they have been."

"Why?" Jake asked.

"Solomon made the ring famous. He was not the first to wield its power, but he was the first to abuse it. The power of the ring is intense, consuming. It is given only to people who can handle that power. But with Solomon, it was too much."

Patrick nodded. "Solomon was not actually next in line for the throne. In fact, he was fourth in line. Two of his eldest brothers were killed. And his mother, Bathsheba, made Solomon's father, David, promise to place Solomon on the throne over his older brother, Adonijah. David did."

"And if he hadn't, the ring would have gone to a less powerful man," Victoria said. "A man who did not have nearly as much power to abuse."

Patrick continued. "When Solomon began his reign, he was the best of kings. Wise, compassionate, fair. He's revered as one of the greatest rulers in Israeli history, if not the greatest. But over time, he was tempted by his own power. Allegedly his wives turned him away from God, and he began to worship their foreign gods, even building temples to them. He was also, according to the tales, guilty of greed and, of course, polygamy."

"And he was the last male who was allowed to be a ring bearer," Victoria said.

Jake raised an eyebrow. "Because women are less corruptible?"

Victoria gave a small laugh. "Well, I wouldn't go that

far. I do have a theory, though. Since Solomon's time, the heads of nations have been almost exclusively males. The ring is incredibly powerful. I think it is simply too much power for a king to have that power as well. So, it has been given only to females, who, by gender, are always less politically powerful. Even the queens that live in infamy have generally been less powerful than their male counterparts."

"Like who?" Laney asked.

"Like Helen," Victoria replied.

Laney struggled to keep her face neutral as she remembered her dream from Hershey. "You mean Helen of Troy, the face that launched a thousand ships?"

Victoria nodded with a smile. "Now be honest: you never really thought thousands of men went to war over a pretty face, did you?"

Chapter Thirty-Seven

LANEY LOOKED AT VICTORIA, trying to understand once again how she knew all of this. "Helen of Troy was one of the ring bearers? So she wasn't just a woman who cheated on her husband and caused a bloody, decade-long war?"

Victoria gave Laney a small smile. "History has been very unfair to Helen. Now I ask you, what's more realistic: that countries went to war over a little bed-hopping, or that Helen was far more important than history acknowledges?"

Laney had always thought the rationale behind the Trojan War seemed a little far-fetched. But still, Helen was the heir to the Spartan throne. Whoever married her would be king of Sparta.

The thought brought her up short. Actually, that wasn't true. Helen was already married when she was abducted. The throne wouldn't have extended to someone who'd kidnapped her or whom she'd run away with, would it?

And why would all those other men join the fight? Even with the promise of the suitors to help Menelaus maintain his suit, it seemed odd.

Plus, the abduction had taken place nine years into Helen's marriage. If someone was going to grab Helen for her throne or for her beauty, wouldn't they have done it before her marriage, or just after it? Why wait nine years?

"Helen was the first ring bearer called to war," Victoria said. "Throughout time, the Fallen have gathered. The ring bearer is responsible for fighting them back. Helen has been unfairly maligned throughout time, by men who knew nothing of her and wrote about her hundreds of years after her death."

Laney knew that at least that part of Victoria's speech was correct. The main source people used when speaking of Helen—Homer's *Iliad*—was written at least five hundred years after she lived.

If, that is, she was an actual person, and not just a literary creation. Many ancient tales were actually oral tales, only written down years later. Who knew how much had been shifted, particularly by men when viewing a powerful woman?

"Helen is called Helen of Troy," Victoria continued, "but that's not who she was. She was Helen of Sparta, heir to the Spartan throne. In Sparta, the royal lineage ran through the daughters, not the sons. And while history has been inaccurately recorded many times, one thing they did get correct was the fighting prowess of the Spartan men. And do you really think that a society that put such an emphasis on the physicality of its men would allow its women to sit around? Spartan women were warriors as much as their men."

Patrick nodded, leaning forward. "There were actually warrior cults dedicated to Helen throughout Sparta. Young women trained in the art of war in the image of Helen. In fact, many cultures revered Helen. There were feasts and sacrifices honoring Helen and her brothers for centuries, right up until the end of Roman rule."

"That image is pretty hard to reconcile with her image as an adulteress who caused the deaths of thousands," Henry said.

"So Helen was alleged to have lived during the Bronze Age, right?" Laney asked. "Around 1,500 or so BC?"

Clark's statement about a gathering of the Fallen came back to her. He'd said one of the critical time periods had come during the Trojan War. Laney hadn't really focused on it at the time; she'd been too wrapped up in his casual reference to Hitler and superhumans.

Victoria nodded.

"How exactly were they supposed to fight the Fallen?" Jake interrupted. "Their weapons were axes, shields, spears —not exactly high-tech. They couldn't fight the Fallen with just that. They'd spring back up like Jack-in-the-boxes every time they were dropped."

"Well, they could fight them, they just couldn't kill them. At least not easily," Henry said.

Victoria gave Laney a small smile. "Helen was a brilliant woman. She knew if they couldn't kill the Fallen, she needed to find a way to contain them. So she created a prison."

"A prison? For the Fallen?" Laney asked, shocked. It was a great idea, but what on earth was strong enough to contain fallen angels?

Victoria nodded.

"Did it work?" Henry asked.

"Yes. And the prison is still there. It still exists."

Laney struggled to think of any ancient site that would fit the bill. Nothing came to mind. "Where is it?"

"Egypt."

Victoria leaned down and took a sip of water from one of the glasses on the coffee table. Her voice was almost casual. "So, tell me Laney; Have you started having the dreams yet?"

Chapter Thirty-Eight

"LANEY, ARE YOU HAVING THE DREAMS?" Victoria asked again, her gaze pinning Laney to her seat.

Laney thought about hedging, but one look at Victoria's face and she knew it would be a wasted effort. "I've had dreams where I'm a woman or girl from a different time. Helen, Makeda, Joan of Arc, others."

Victoria nodded. "The women you mention: they were all previous ring bearers."

Laney had known she was going to say that, but it still came as a shock. "Okay, even if they were, it doesn't mean I am. There have to be some requirements besides the dreams and being the daughter of Enoch."

Victoria nodded. "There are three trials. The first is the trial by fire. The second is the trial by greed, and the third is the trial by force. In the first, the ring bearer must save the innocent from fire. In the second, she must defeat the powers of greed and ambition. And in the third, she must overcome overwhelming force to bring the knowledge to light."

With each description, Laney felt her dread growing. In Montana, she had defeated a corrupt politician looking to use an Atlantis relic for his own political gain, as well as defeating an angel who was hell-bent on using that same relic for his own power. In other words, she had defeated both greed and ambition. In Ecuador, she had helped save a lost library of Atlantis: the knowledge brought to light.

But there was one problem, one possible fly in the ointment that left Laney with a small kernel of hope. "It can't be me. I mean, I give you that the incidents in Montana and Ecuador seem to fit the second two requirements. But I never went through the first, the trial by fire. I haven't been near a fire any time recently, other than one in a fireplace."

"You saved Elena and Eddie from fire in Ecuador," Henry said.

Laney felt her jaw pop open. She'd forgotten about that. She looked to Victoria, who shook her head.

"The trial by fire is the first trial. It has to predate the others."

Relief flowed through Laney. It wasn't her. She wasn't the ring bearer.

Patrick's voice was quiet. "You've been through the trial by fire."

Laney looked over at him, confused. "What are you talking about? No I haven't."

"Kati and Max," Patrick said.

Surprise filtered through Laney, followed by disbelief. "But that was four years ago. Way before any of this began. That can't be related."

"There's no time limit for when the trials must happen, only that they have to happen in order, and that the ring bearer must succeed," Victoria said.

"Why don't you tell us what happened with Kati and Max? Maybe you're right, and it doesn't fit," Henry said.

Laney looked around the room. Everyone looked back at her expectantly. "Okay, but I'm telling you, it doesn't fit." She took a breath. "It was the day I met Kati. The day Max was born, actually."

Chapter Thirty-Nine

Four Years Ago

LANEY HEADED DOWN ROUTE 92. It was late. The sun had already sunk beyond the horizon. It had been a stressful day. Laney had just completed two finals in graduate school: one in advance criminological theory and one in advanced statistical analysis.

Both had been mentally exhausting, and Laney, along with every other graduate student, had used all of the allotted four hours for each of the exams. And she'd still been writing when the four hours were up.

Laney flipped through channels on the radio, looking for something that fit her mood. "I can't believe I'm still keyed up," she murmured, finally settling on AC/DC's "Back in Black."

She turned right at the light. *How could they expect us to mention everything we learned in a semester in just four hours? It's not possible.*

But as was often the case in graduate school, the impossible became possible in the fourth and final year of classes. Laney had learned how to cram four months of material into a four-hour exam. It didn't make the process any less stressful, however.

So after a grueling day mentally, Laney had felt the need to be physically exhausted as well. To burn off her energy, she had headed to her martial arts school for a long strenuous workout. But it hadn't worked. She was still keyed up.

And she couldn't shake the edgy feeling. Every time a car's headlights appeared, she tensed.

What the heck is wrong with me tonight?

Headlights flashed over her car from behind, making her jump. Glancing in her rearview mirror, she watched the lights swerve to the right, then jerk back to the left. Then the car jerked even harder to the left, swerving across the median. The driver was moving way too fast for his apparent level of inebriation.

Oh God. That guy's going to get someone killed.

The driver drew closer, and Laney could tell he was going to try to pass her. Praying, Laney started moving as close to the edge of the road as possible. The driver pulled alongside her. Laney slowed, her hands gripping the steering wheel.

Come on, jerk, just get past, she urged, while hoping no car showed up in the oncoming lane.

He swerved, slamming into her on the driver's side.

Laney's car jerked to the right. "Shit!" She struggled to control the car, but he must have damaged the wheel. The car refused to go straight.

The drunk overcompensated, swinging wildly into the oncoming lane and speeding up. A small Subaru wagon came around the bend in the road. The Subaru driver tried to yank his car out of the way, but there wasn't time.

The front of the drunk's car crashed into the side of the wagon. Metal scraped along metal as the drunk's car continued forward, pushing the wagon over the metal divider and down the cliff below.

Laney hit her brakes, her heart racing. "Oh my God, oh my God!"

Scrambling for her cell phone, she struggled out of her seat belt. She vaulted from the car and dialed 911 as she sprinted across the road.

At the drunk's car, she slowed, sparing it only a glance. A male in his early fifties lay slumped over the steering wheel. He mumbled, turning his head toward her. The stench of beer drifted through his open window.

"Asshole." Laney ignored him. He wasn't her concern.

She ran to the divider, following the skid marks on the road. Her stomach clenched as she glanced down the cliff. The station wagon lay about a hundred feet down, right-side up. The driver's side was completely smashed in. Fire crept slowly across the rear of the car.

Heart pounding, Laney jumped over the divider, half skidding, half running down the hill toward the car as the dispatcher answered.

Cell phone to her ear, Laney yelled their location to the dispatcher. "The car's on fire. Hurry." She disconnected the call and shoved the phone in her pocket.

Flames had already engulfed the rear of the wagon, giving her plenty of light to see. As she made her way to the driver's door, her breath hitched. The door had been smashed halfway through the driver's seat. Adding insult to injury, a tree branch had crashed through the windshield, impaling the driver. No need to check for a pulse. The man was beyond anyone's help.

Breathing hard and shaking, Laney heard a moan from the backseat. *Someone else is in there.*

"I'm coming!" Laney yelled, rounding the hood. She fought the brush around the car to reach the passenger door, coughing as the smoke from the back of the car hit her, all the while keeping an eye on the flames at the rear of the car, which were steadily growing.

Eyes beginning to tear, Laney peered in. The woman appeared to be in her late twenties. And she was pregnant— very pregnant.

The woman's terrified eyes met hers. "Help us," she cried.

Her heart in her throat, Laney yanked on the door. It wouldn't budge.

The heat of the fire increased, and sweat beaded on Laney's forehead. She unrolled her turtleneck, pulling the fabric over her mouth. The smoke still got through, sending her into a fit of coughing.

Tears streaming down her cheeks, Laney yanked at the door. *Oh, come on. Come on!*

Planting her feet in the dirt, she pulled with all of her strength. The door swung back, throwing her to the ground. She scrambled on her hands and knees back to the door.

The wind shifted, and Laney took in a face full of smoke that almost set her convulsing. Coughing violently, she used the doorframe to pull herself up, and stood, swaying, in the open door.

Eyes stinging, she reached over the woman to loosen her seatbelt, feeling the heat of the encroaching flames. "You're going to be okay," Laney choked out.

The woman was barely conscious, her eyes closed. "Baby, save my baby," the woman mumbled.

"I'm getting you both out." Laney said, hoping she

wasn't lying. She darted another glance at the flames creeping over the back of the car. The fire was getting way too close to the gas tank for comfort.

The woman's seat belt miraculously came undone easily. Draping the woman's arms over her shoulders, Laney braced herself and pulled the woman from the seat. An extra tug and the woman's feet were free. Once she had the woman upright out of the car, Laney turned her so that she could drag her from under the arms.

With a groan, Laney pulled, continually darting glances toward the fast moving flames. She could hear sirens in the distance. But they wouldn't get here in time.

Laney struggled to move faster. Her chest ached from the smoke and she couldn't see for tears. Her legs backed into a fallen tree and she tripped over it, the woman landing heavily on top of her. With a grunt, Laney untangled herself and pulled the woman over the log, careful to protect the woman's stomach.

Wiping the tears from her eyes, she looked back at the burning car—just in time to see the flames reach the gas tank.

Laney threw herself over the woman as the car exploded.

Chapter Forty

"*THAT'S* HOW YOU MET KATI?" Henry asked, his eyes wide.

Laney nodded. "She and her husband had moved to town only a month before. She didn't really know anyone, and her parents lived across the country, and neither was in good health. I checked in on her every day, and before I knew it, I was helping raise Max."

Silence descended. Laney looked around. "What?"

Henry gave a little laugh. "You don't even see it, do you? You go above and beyond and think nothing of it."

Laney shook her head. "Anybody would have done what I did."

Patrick took her hand, giving her a kiss on the cheek. "No, honey, they wouldn't have. But I love that you think they would."

Laney could feel the blush spreading across her cheeks. "Okay. But that happened four years ago. The other two events were in the last year."

"It doesn't matter," Victoria said. "Saving Kati and

Max, that was the trial by fire. Your actions that night set everything else in motion."

Laney sat back, stunned, a chill running through her. Four years before she'd even met Jake or Henry, she'd already been on the path. For some reason, that thought terrified her.

"And you're sure that was the trial by fire?" Jake asked.

Victoria nodded. "Yes. Laney faced the fire and saved two innocent lives in the process. I'd say that meets the requirements. There's no doubt. Laney is the ring bearer."

Chapter Forty-One

LANEY RAN her hands through her hair as she walked through Victoria's house.

Victoria had decided to end their little chat about her destiny. Apparently, she thought that convincing Laney she was destined to bear the ring that would control the Fallen —and, by extension, make her a target for every single one of them—was enough of a bombshell for one afternoon.

She wasn't wrong.

Laney wandered into the kitchen and came to a stop. Ralph stood at the stove, stirring a large pot of sauce. The scent of something Italian and really good filled the room.

"That smells delicious," Laney said.

Ralph put down his spoon with a smile, wiping his hands on a towel. He walked toward her, his hand extended. "We haven't officially met. I'm Ralph."

Laney shook his hand, feeling the strength in his grip. "Hi Ralph."

He gestured to the island where a tray of antipasto stood. "Are you hungry?"

"Not really." Laney glanced out the French doors to the giant garden that stretched as far as she could see. That was her destination, yet somehow she found herself pulling out a chair at the island.

Ralph poured her a glass of iced tea before heading back to his sauce.

"Thanks. Um, how long have you worked for . . ." The words died in her mouth. What was she supposed to say? Victoria? Mom?

Ralph didn't seem to notice. "Thirty-two years."

Laney looked up in surprise. "That means . . ."

Ralph stopped stirring and looked at her. "Yes. I was here when your mother was pregnant with you. I was here when she made the decision to protect you."

Not "give you away"—protect you. Laney wanted to ask him questions. She just wasn't sure where to start.

"How— Did she—" she started and then stopped. "I don't even know what to ask."

Ralph gave her a smile, turning to lean back against the counter. "It wasn't an easy time for her. It was right after James died when she learned she was pregnant."

Laney struggled again against the rush of sympathy she felt for Victoria in that situation. Kati's words came back to her: *She put your happiness before hers. To me, that sounds like a mom.*

Unaware of Laney's thoughts, Ralph continued. "Laney, I know it's not my place. But you need to know: giving you away was the hardest thing she's ever done. And after all she's been through, that's saying something. I know you don't trust her, but if you could at least believe that, it might be a good start." He paused. "Can you wait here for a second?"

Laney nodded.

Ralph stood up, walking into the pantry just off the kitchen. He reappeared seconds later, a large album in his hands. "She'd be mad if she knew I was showing you this. But you need to know, she never forgot you." Handing Laney the album, he walked back to the stove.

Laney planned on taking it outside, but her curiosity had her flipping it open right away. On the first page was a baby picture; then a picture of Victoria holding a newborn. Below those was a picture of her and her parents in the hospital. Her eyes flew to Ralph in shock.

He nodded. "She had a nurse take the picture."

The next few pages were pictures of Laney over the first few years of her life, all taken from a distance. Victoria had watched her grow up from afar. As Laney turned each page, her incredulity grew.

When she flipped to the next page, she went still. There was Laney, no more than three, with her arms wrapped around the neck of boy who looked to be about eight years old. At first she didn't recognize him. But his violet eyes gave him away. "I met Henry?"

Ralph came to sit next to her. "After your third birthday, it was really tough for Victoria. She saw the pictures of you that the private investigator sent, but she needed to know you were okay. She arranged to be at the playground where your parents took you on Saturdays."

"The playground at the elementary school, down the street from my house," Laney said, remembering the spot. They had a giant slide, monkey bars, a big metal spider, and a ton of other toys. Laney had loved going there.

Ralph smiled. "I was with them. You and Henry ended up on the slide together. You tripped getting off. Henry helped you up. And that was it. You two were inseparable for the next few hours. Your parents and Victoria even laughed about how much you two took to one another. Your parents ended up inviting Victoria and Henry over for lunch. Your mother—I mean, Victoria—she looked like she was trying to memorize the day, so she didn't forget a moment."

Laney traced the picture. "I wish I could remember that."

"You were too young. But Victoria could see how much your parents loved you and how much you loved them."

"So it worked? She felt better?"

Ralph shrugged. "Yes and no. She knew you were fine. That eased her mind. But seeing you... it made it harder for her. You were sweet, feisty, and just plain happy. All in all, a pretty amazing kid. So she decided to stop having you followed. After being around you, it was too difficult for her to watch you and not be a part of your life."

Laney flipped to the next page, and there was a picture of Laney, ten years old. Her father's brother and wife were walking behind her. Laney gasped, her eyes flying to Ralph. "She knew about them?"

Ralph covered her hand with his. "No. She found out about your parents' death almost a full year after it. She just wanted to check, make sure you were okay. The private investigator told her about the hospital visits. Victoria was actually arranging to get you out of there when your uncle arrived. And then she didn't have to rescue you, because he did. When she found out he was petitioning the church to allow him to adopt you, she even exerted some pressure to make that happen."

Laney was astounded. "She did?"

Ralph nodded. "Victoria has a lot of influence. And she's always been there, Laney, behind the scenes, looking out for you where she could."

Laney flipped through the remaining pages. There were shots of her from age ten until just a few months ago.

Ralph nodded toward the album. "After the incident with your other uncle, she made sure she had constant updates on your well-being. Painful as it was for her, she wouldn't chance your safety again."

Laney flipped to the last page. A picture of Laney, Henry, and Jake from a month ago looked back at her. They had gone out to dinner. The three of them were laughing. Laney felt tears in her eyes. God, she'd turned into a leaky faucet.

She closed the album, pushing it toward Ralph. She felt shaky, not sure what to think of Victoria now. "Thank you for showing this to me. Is it okay if I wander through the garden?"

Ralph took the album and stood. "Sure. It's Victoria's pride and joy."

Laney wandered out the back door into Victoria's garden. Ralph's words and the pictures added to the rest of the noise in her mind. Victoria had kept tabs on her. She had cared.

Laney walked down the path, needing a little time to herself. Time to take in everything and assure herself that she wasn't going crazy. That everything was actually happening to her.

Spying a path cutting to the left, she followed it. She climbed a short hill and looked down. A grave sat in the middle of a beautiful garden, a garden even more beautiful than the one she'd just walked through.

In her heart, Laney knew this was her parents' daughter's grave. She felt a tug on her heart. What did that make her to Laney? A sister? A stranger?

Walking to the grave, Laney knelt down and read the

inscription. She traced the name. "Hi, Sarah. I'm Laney," she whispered.

Laney looked around. Victoria had taken care of the child. That made her feel better. The little girl who had never had a chance to live had been well taken care of for the last thirty years. Laney bowed her head, saying a prayer for the little girl's soul. She stood and turned. Her uncle stood only six feet away.

He gestured to the iron bench under the Rose-of-Sharon tree. "Is it okay if I join you?"

Laney nodded, not really sure what to say. She felt almost guilty for being here, as if she was intruding.

They sat down and an awkward silence descended between them. Laney struggled to figure out how to start the conversation. "So what do you—"

"How is—" Patrick said at the same time.

They both let out an embarrassed laugh.

Patrick took Laney's hand. He nodded toward the tombstone. "Laney, none of this changes how I feel about you. You have always been my child. And biologically, you never were. So as far as I'm concerned, you're still mine. And you always will be. I love you. Nothing can change that."

She leaned her head on his shoulder. "I love you too, Uncle Patrick."

They stayed like that for a few minutes, and Laney felt her world tilt a little closer to normal. Her uncle was still her rock.

"So," he said at last, "you want to tell me about these dreams?"

Laney sighed, pulling her head up from his shoulder. "It's been since Las Vegas, since we recovered the Shuars' treasure. I have these dreams about these women. All from different time periods."

"Do you know them?"

She shrugged. "Some of them. Joan of Arc, Helen of Troy. Just today, I had one about the Queen of Sheba and her son."

"Menelik?"

"You know him? Because I can't remember hearing about him before."

Patrick leaned back. "Menelik was the son of the Queen of Sheba and Solomon."

That fit with her dream. "So I guess you have heard of him."

Patrick smiled. "I wouldn't be much of a priest if I hadn't."

She shook her head. "I don't understand."

"According to legend, Solomon built the first temple in order to house a very critical object."

Laney nodded. "Right. The Ark of the Covenant."

"Menelik went to meet with his father for the first time when he was an adult. When he left, he allegedly took the Ark and brought it back to Ethiopia with him, where it's said to rest, even now."

Laney knew the Ark was alleged to be located in the Chapel of the Tablet in Aksum, Ethiopia. Although, now that she thought about it, no one but a single priest from the order was ever allowed near the Ark itself. "Do you believe that's true?"

Patrick shrugged. "Who knows? The Ethiopian Orthodox Church dates back to the time of Solomon, and they've claimed since then to have the Ark. Besides, they've been guarding something for over three thousand years."

Laney had seen pictures of the church. It was a very simple, non-elaborate church literally in the middle of nowhere. But the Ark was not the relic she was concerned with. "In my dream, Menelik brought two objects out with him."

"The ring?"

Laney shrugged. "I don't know. I never saw either object."

"Hm," Patrick murmured.

"Hm? What does that mean?"

"Well, there's an interesting conundrum regarding the Ark and Solomon. It's mentioned that the Ark was housed in the First Temple and then, all of a sudden, it's not mentioned. Not a word. No one says it disappeared, or that it was lost or stolen. It's simply never written about again—at least, not in any writings that I've ever seen. The Ark just disappeared from the history books without a mention."

"How come they think Menelik took it?"

"The rumors about it being housed in Ethiopia have been around forever. The original tale was written down in 1270 in the *Kebra Nagast*. Actually, Graham Hancock does a great job of tracking the tale of the Ark in *The Seat of the Soul*. You should read it. It's a great book."

"I'll get right on that," Laney said dryly.

Patrick gave a small laugh. "I suppose you won't be curling up with a good book any time soon."

"Probably not," Laney agreed. "But what about the ring? Where is that mentioned?"

"Actually, it's not. Not in the whole Bible. The only references to the ring of Solomon come from the Testament of Solomon, which people aren't even sure is accurate. The Testament is usually dated to sometime between the first and fifth century AD, although it's alleged to have been written by Solomon himself."

"But that was a thousand years after Solomon's death."

"Exactly."

Laney knew it wasn't unusual for works to be copied multiple times, and for one of those copies to later on be considered the original. Or for them to be handed down orally before being put to paper. So it's possible that the original was long lost to history, and only the copy dating to the first century still existed. "What does it say about the power of the ring?"

"It claims the wearer can control demons, as well as animals and the weather. But in the Testament, the demons are often grotesque animal-human hybrids."

Laney felt her jaw drop. "You're kidding, right?"

Patrick shook his head.

Laney closed her eyes and let out a breath. "Great. And we're taking all of this on Victoria's word?" She opened her eyes, glancing at Patrick. "How exactly does she know all these things? And why do we all believe her?"

"Well, she's been studying all of it much longer than we have. We've only known about the Fallen for a year. She is convincing, though, isn't she?"

Laney nodded.

He glanced over at her. "In your dream about Menelik, were you seeing the dream through his eyes?"

"No. The dream wasn't from Menelik's point of view. It was from Makeda's."

Patrick looked at Laney sharply, his eyes narrowing. "Your dreams—are they always from a woman's point of view?"

Laney thought back and realized with surprise they were. "Yes."

Patrick stroked his chin, his expression troubled.

"What is it? You look worried."

"I'm probably wrong," he began, and Laney felt a chill. The last time he said that, he'd been talking about his interpretation of Drew's paper on Atlantis. And he'd been right on the money.

Laney tried to keep her tone light. "Okay. You might be wrong. But tell me anyway."

Patrick hesitated. "These dreams you're having. I wonder if they're not dreams at all."

"Not dreams? Then what are they?"

"Memories."

Chapter Forty-Two

"MEMORIES? ARE YOU KIDDING?" Laney struggled not to groan. Seriously, she was at her tipping point for revelations.

Patrick put up his hands. "Just hear me out. All of this started because of Edgar Cayce's life readings on Atlantis, right?"

Laney nodded. A year ago, her friend Drew Masters had written a preliminary paper involving Cayce to pave the way for an archaeological dig he was working on. Drew's involvement in the dig resulted in his death by a Fallen. That loss still cut deep.

Laney shoved those feelings aside, focusing instead on what they had learned about the twentieth-century psychic Edgar Cayce.

According to Cayce, most people had lived multiple past lives. Over the course of his own life, Cayce performed numerous past life readings for people; and many of those past life readings involved the lives people lived in Atlantis.

Through his work, Cayce realized that humans had evolved on this planet as thought forms before taking bodies. These early humans had lived in complete peace, without violence or strife. Eventually, though, people had evolved into two groups: the Children of the Law of One, and the Sons of Belial. The good and the bad.

And although not mentioned in Cayce's work, Laney realized from reading the Book of Enoch that it was the fallen angels who were responsible for that division. They brought with them envy, strife, violence, and war. The Sons of Belial were eventually responsible for the destruction of Atlantis.

In his readings, Cayce said the Children, knowing the Sons would be their destruction, had sent three sets of emissaries to three separate locations across the globe, to hide the knowledge of Atlantis, save it from annihilation. One of those locations was the site Drew worked on. Laney found the other in Ecuador last year. And the third was still lost—although it was rumored to be located under the left paw of the Sphinx.

"Yes, Cayce's work is where all of this sprang from," Laney said. "But I don't think Cayce meant that you came back each lifetime as the exact same person, with the same goals, hobbies, and desires."

"I don't know about that. There have been readings that suggest that people come back very similar in each lifetime, right down to their career. Henry Ford, for example, was alleged to have been an inventor in Atlantis."

"So you think the subjects of my dreams are actually—what? My ancestors? Predecessors? Former selves? What am I supposed to call them?"

Patrick took her hand. "I think they might be you, in a past life."

Laney knew her jaw was hanging open, but she couldn't

seem to close it. "You're saying I was Helen of Troy, the Queen of Sheba, and Joan of Arc?"

"Is that really any crazier than being the daughter of a powerful angel?"

Laney snapped her mouth shut. She knew reincarnation was part of numerous belief systems across the world. The scientific research on reincarnation had also provided some incredible findings. She had read the case studies of children who seemed to be able to recount verifiable facts from their past lives. It was pretty convincing stuff.

In one set of studies, Dr. Ian Stevenson, of the University of Virginia, matched birthmarks with wounds received in a past life. All the cases had been medically documented.

And the list of highly intelligent individuals who supported the notion was quite astounding: Henry Ford, Mahatma Gandhi, Socrates, Napoleon, even Friedrich Nietzsche.

But recognizing the abstract possibility of reincarnation was one thing. Accepting that you yourself were the reincarnation of previous individuals, particularly historically important ones, was a little harder to accept.

"I mean, I guess it's not any more unbelievable than anything else I've heard or seen this last year," Laney said. "But these women we're talking about, they were incredibly powerful. I mean, Helen and Joan were warriors, the leaders of armies. They changed the world."

"You have that same strength, Laney. It's built in you. It's like that genetic research you told me about. You have this programmed into you. It just needs the right environment to bring it out."

"And you think I'm going to find myself in that environment?"

Patrick squeezed her hand, standing up. "I think you

already have. Look what you've done already. You saved Kati and Max, you uncovered that site in Montana, and then everything you did with the Shuar. And you've faced how many Fallen and nephilim at this point? And yet you're still here. There's something about you, Laney. Something special. We all see it. All of us but you." He kissed her on the forehead before heading back down the path.

Laney watched him walk away. Was it possible she actually was this ring bearer? Her mind whirled with everything she had learned, with everything people believed her to be.

Before she knew it, it had grown late. Looking up, she was startled to see the sun had begun to dip below the horizon.

She stood up and stretched, an ache forming in her lower back from sitting on the iron bench for so long. She hurried up the hill, her stomach growling. She hoped she hadn't missed Ralph's dinner. She rounded the top of the hill and came to a stop.

Victoria was in the garden, a basket beside her, down on her hands and knees, weeding. It was such a domestic sight that Laney was startled. Victoria always seemed so powerful, so all-knowing. Seeing her do something so normal was actually jarring.

Victoria must have felt eyes on her. She sat back on her heels, her eyes finding Laney's. She offered a tentative smile.

Laney gave a little wave and walked toward her, not knowing what to say. She had so many questions. She wasn't sure which one should come first. What was her father like? Did Victoria regret giving her away?

But those questions were too personal, and Laney wasn't sure she wanted the answers. Not yet, at least.

In fact, she really didn't want to know anything more

about her own past or her future. For now, she had more than enough to occupy her mind.

By the time Laney reached her, Victoria was standing next to a rose bush in full, pale pink bloom.

"It's beautiful," Laney said, and meant it. The flowers were huge, with over a hundred petals on each one.

"It's a Scepter'd Isle. The name comes from—"

"Shakespeare, Richard the Second."

Victoria's eyes went wide. "How'd you know that?"

"There was a priest at the rectory who kept a rose garden. I used to garden with him sometimes. His roses were beautiful. They're one of my favorite flowers."

"I've always loved them, too."

Silence descended between the two of them. And it was awkward. But Laney's mind was a complete blank.

Victoria took a step toward her. "How about we take a little walk? I'm guessing you have some questions for me."

Laney nodded, falling in step next to Victoria. But instead of waiting for Laney to ask anything, Victoria started rattling off information about her garden. Laney was relieved. She still wasn't sure what to say to her.

Victoria's love for the garden came through with each word, and Laney was glad to have the focus be on something other than her. By the time they had walked for fifteen minutes, Laney was actually at ease. They came to stop at the land's edge. Atop a tall cliff, the Atlantic Ocean spread out in front of them.

"This is incredible," Laney said. She breathed in deep, pulling in the peace of the scene.

"It's why I bought this property. When all the world goes crazy, I come here and I can feel at peace."

Laney nodded, understanding. She met Victoria's eyes,

and this time the smile came easily. "Thank you for showing it to me."

A flash of emotion crossed Victoria's face before she covered it. "You're very welcome." Victoria looked away. "We should probably get back. Ralph should have dinner about ready."

Laney nodded, turning to walk back to the house. Her arm grazed Victoria's, but Laney didn't pull away.

They walked for a few moments in silence. Then Laney realized she did have a question for Victoria. Not something about herself or Victoria, but something that had been bothering her since she'd learned of the Fallen.

"Victoria, when Edgar Cayce talks of humanity's beginnings, he says that at first we were all one group, no division. Then we split into two: the Children of the Law of One and the Sons of Belial. The good and the bad."

"Yes. Cayce got that right."

"Well, Cayce doesn't mention the Fallen, but I figured they were the reason humanity split."

Victoria nodded.

"Here's what I don't understand: why didn't we split before then? We were human, and humans come with desires. Not all of them good. So why didn't we act on those negative desires earlier?"

"Because there was no reason to."

"But why not? People must have coveted, envied, had all those motivations to do bad."

Victoria glanced at her, pausing before speaking. "How old was Enoch when he went to heaven?"

Laney wondered at the change in conversation. "Umm, three hundred fifty-six, I think."

Victoria nodded. "Do you remember any other ages mentioned in the Bible?"

"I remember something about humanity only living for one hundred and twenty years."

Victoria nodded with a smile. "Ah, yes. Genesis 6:3: *Then the Lord said, 'My Spirit will not contend with man forever, for he is mortal; his days will be a hundred and twenty years.'* But there are others mentioned: Noah, Adam, his son Seth, all lived for over nine hundred years. Others, too. Lamech is recorded as having lived for seven hundred seventy-seven years."

Laney recalled some of those references. "I've heard that, but to be perfectly honest, I always figured it was either exaggeration on the part of the writer, a legend that grew as time went on, or just a mistake in translation."

"It was none of those. In fact, those lifespans were short compared to early humans. In certain eastern cultures, individuals were alleged to have lived for thousands of years."

"Thousands of years? But that can't be right, can it?"

Laney knew Victoria's references, at least, were correct. The Sumerian King list contained dozens of kings, some of who had reigns lasting thousands of years. She remembered one that was supposed to have reigned for thirty-six thousand years.

Laney shook her head. But wasn't that supposed to be— She sighed. Actually, she had no idea what that was supposed to be. It was one of those archaeological facts that when you heard it, you said "Oh, okay" and didn't think too deeply about—because there was simply no logical explanation for it.

Victoria nodded, a small smile on her face. "Oh, those records are correct. You see, originally, humans were practically immortal."

Chapter Forty-Three

LANEY STOPPED WALKING. "Wait, *immortal* immortal? As in lived forever?"

"Almost. There was no violence, no disease. People could, and did, live for thousands of years."

Laney struggled to wrap her mind around the possibility.

"Think of all the great achievements of the far past. They were accomplished because people didn't have short lifespans. Archaeologists can't figure out Puma Punku or the Sphinx because they're looking at it through mortal eyes. In the modern world, those accomplishments are unimaginable. You have maybe a few decades of critical thinking before your faculties begin to slow. But originally, mankind didn't have that restriction. As a result, we had longer time periods to create, to think. The results were means and methods that, quite honestly, would be viewed as magic today."

Laney stared at Victoria. Was that the answer? Was that how humans had managed these incredible constructions at a time when traditional science argued we were no more than stone tool users?

Victoria's words left Laney feeling stunned. But even in that state of disbelief, she recalled reports of how some ancient sites were created. Puma Punku, the Luxor, and a bunch of others were created in areas where there were no trees to help roll these hundred-ton stones, no waterways to sail them down. So how did they do it?

Were incredible tales, like those of Merlin, true? Merlin was alleged to have used some form of telekinesis to erect Stonehenge, or magic that enabled him to turn the stones all but weightless. Even Solomon's incredible temple was supposed to have been erected in one day. Were those ancient tales true accountings rather than fanciful notions?

"I know it's a bit much to take in," Victoria said with a smile. "But I think you're beginning to realize that there's more out there than humanity currently understands. Every generation thinks it is the epitome of civilization. Civilization has grown, and been destroyed, many times over. And knowledge has been lost to the sands of time, sometimes never to be uncovered again."

Laney's thoughts were tripping over one another. Yet somewhere down deep, what Victoria was saying rang true. She decided, though, to focus on the beginning of this conversation. "But how do long lifespans relate to the split of humanity?"

"Before the Fallen, there was no need for greed, for envy. We lived forever. Anything you wanted, you could one day achieve. Nothing was out of the realm of possibility."

"How did that change?"

"With the Fallen came death, murder, human sacrifice even. And disease. They brought disease with them, like any conquering group. Human lifespans shortened dramatically.

All of a sudden, you didn't have forever to achieve what you wanted. You could be killed at any moment."

Laney wondered at the argument but also at the way in which Victoria was telling it. It was as if she had been there.

"And the Fallen? Why did they fall?" Laney asked.

"They wanted humans' freedom, our luxury of free will."

"All of them wanted it?"

Victoria smiled. "You're wondering how some could be good if they all chose to fall?"

Laney nodded.

"They had a very convincing leader."

"Samyaza."

Victoria nodded. "You met Azazyel. He was the warrior, but Samyaza was the general. He was the strategist. He recognized the weaknesses in humans and sent his troops to exploit them. And he was good at it. Machiavelli would have liked him. He made it appear that he was helping humans reach their own goals, when they were really working for him."

The description sounded chillingly familiar. "Like Satan. Tempting people into evil."

Victoria stopped walking. She looked Laney in the eye. "Satan, the red monster with a pitchfork and horns, is a literary device used to scare humans into behaving. But Samyaza was the real thing. He was the devil. And I'm guessing he still is."

Chapter Forty-Four

JOHNSON CITY, TENNESSEE

AMAR CROUCHED DOWN low on the branch, not moving. He scanned the area, his breath held, muscles taut. He turned his head to the right. *Was that a rustle?* He strained to listen.

Yes.

With a fluid grace, he swung down from the branch, landing in a crouch. He paused for only a second before sprinting toward the spot where he'd heard the sound.

Gerard's face stayed in the back of his mind. Amar pictured his presumptuous manner in daring to question him. Amar growled, his anger spiking.

He knew the landscape. A giant oak was thirty feet ahead, and smaller saplings covered the area before it, with a few dense yew scattered here and there. In the day, it wasn't much cover, but at night it gave Titus an advantage.

Up ahead, he could make out movement, but it was low to the ground. A cry came from the spot. Something was there. Something alive and hurt.

He slowed. The hair on the back of his neck signaled a danger he couldn't see. *Something's wrong.*

Amar whipped his head to the right just as Titus leapt from the shadows. Amar dodged out of the way, but Titus's claws raked his left thigh. Fire burned through Amar, but instead of screaming, he laughed.

"Well done." Amar circled around the beast.

Titus roared his disapproval. In the distance, Amar heard Titus's mate, Cleo, scream out her own displeasure. But Cleo couldn't help him. She was still locked in her cage.

Titus kept his eyes on Amar. Amar clenched his fists; the special gloves he had made glinted in the moonlight. Three sharp blades extended from the back of each hand: his own set of claws. It seemed only sporting that each of them came to the fight with the same weapons.

The pain in Amar's thigh disappeared. "Ready, my friend?"

Titus looked back at him with an intelligence not seen in other animals. Amar smiled. His cats truly were the top of the food chain—although still well below him, of course.

And this specimen was magnificent. It would be a shame to destroy him.

But I can always make more.

Amar leaped, landing on the tree limb above Titus, then swung to the next tree.

Titus prowled below. He ran for the tree and leapt, but couldn't make the branch himself.

Amar swung to the branch above the cat. Titus leapt again. As Titus's paws returned to the ground, Amar dropped onto the giant cat's back.

Raising his arms, Amar drove both of his claws into Titus's sides. The cat screamed, trying to shake Amar loose.

But Amar held on, twisting his claws in the feline's sides, his arms now slick with blood.

Titus lumbered to one side. Amar pulled out his claws and then plunged them in again, this time higher, into Titus's back. Titus made no sound, just fell heavily to the ground.

Amar climbed from the leopard's back, going eye to eye with the great cat. Titus stared back at him, and Amar could swear he saw hate in the leopard's eyes. Amused, Amar watched until the life drained from the cat's face.

Amar straightened with a smile, looking down at the majestic beast. *Nicely done. I think I'll have your head mounted on my wall.*

But he discounted the thought almost as soon as he had it. The beast was only doing what its nature encouraged. There was nothing special in the animal.

A noise, like a small whimper, pulled Amar's attention back to the spot where he'd been ambushed. Amar walked over, wondering what it was that had drawn him there. He came to a stop at the base of the tree and looked at the bloody mess below him.

It was one of the human guards—the one who had let Gerard in earlier. Both of the man's arms had been yanked off, the blood loss considerable. But he was still alive.

Amar followed the blood trail with his eyes; it led off to the right, disappearing into the bushes. Then he glanced back at Titus's carcass with a little laugh. *You little bastard. You laid a trap.*

Amar's admiration increased. Maybe he would mount the beast's head on his wall after all.

"Help me," the man croaked out, his voice barely above a whisper.

Amar knelt down. "Of course I'll help you."

The man's eyes grew large.

Amar smiled before burying his claws in the man's chest.

Chapter Forty-Five

BY THE TIME Victoria and Laney got back to the house, any good feelings Laney had had at the beginning of the walk had disappeared. Her thoughts were now of Samyaza, the devil incarnate.

That chilling thought warred with the tale of the Fallen's arrival. The story of the Fallen was the same as the story of Lucifer's fall from grace. She just hadn't put it together before—or maybe she had been intentionally ignoring the similarity.

In fact, no one had mentioned the similarity between the Book of Enoch's tale and the Bible tale. She was pretty sure they were all turning a blind eye. Going up against Fallen angels was difficult enough. Believing you were going up against the devil himself was a whole other world of terrifying.

Ahead of her, Victoria opened the door to the kitchen. Warmth flowed out into the night air. Laney breathed it in, along with the aroma of Italian spices.

As she stepped inside, the fireplace on the right was

roaring away. Ralph glanced up from the stove. He smiled at Laney, and then his eyes shifted to Victoria, concern in them. Victoria nodded ever so slightly at him.

For the first time, Laney realized there was more to Victoria and Ralph's relationship. Was it just a friendship? Or was there something else there?

Ralph placed a giant tray of garlic bread on the island, next to salad and the antipasto tray. Henry, Jake and Patrick stood around the island, drinks in hand, talking. It was a cheery scene, which warred with the dark thoughts of Samyaza still swirling around Laney's mind.

Laney couldn't miss the look of happiness on Henry's face at seeing Laney walk in with Victoria. She gave him a smile before she walked over to Jake and hugged him.

Jake whispered, "Nice talk?"

Laney struggled not to laugh. "Oh, sure. The nature of the Fallen and a fact-or-fiction chat about the existence of the devil. Real mother-daughter stuff."

Jake kissed her forehead. "Well, you have to start somewhere."

"Dinner is served." Ralph placed a large tray of lasagna on the island, next to the garlic bread. Laney nearly swooned. She hadn't realized how hungry she was.

Everyone loaded up a plate before taking a seat at the table. And by unwritten consent, no one mentioned rings, angels, or anything else having to do with their current predicament. Laney was relieved. She needed a little more time before they continued the conversation on her birthright.

While they ate, her uncle told more than one story about Laney when she was growing up. Victoria did the same for Henry. Laney noticed her uncle's attitude toward Victoria had softened. She wouldn't say they were the best of friends, but there definitely was a bond of some sort forming there now.

Laney sighed, thinking of how impersonal her conversation with Victoria had been. Maybe she, too, should cut Victoria a break. Letting go of her child couldn't have been an easy decision for her to make.

Jake leaned over, whispering in her ear. "You all right?"

Laney looked into his eyes, reading the love there. She took his hand with a gentle squeeze. "Yeah. I'm good."

Laney felt a gaze on her. She turned to catch Victoria watching her and Jake, a smile on her lips. Laney returned the smile.

"Well, I hate to break this up," Victoria said, "but there's more we need to discuss. How about we adjourn to the study for coffee?"

Oh, great. Time for more earth-shattering revelations from Mom, Laney thought as she stood.

Henry caught her eye and gave her a wink. Laney smiled, knowing Henry had been thinking the exact same thing.

He walked over, offering his arm. "Sis?"

She placed her hand on his forearm. "Let's go, big brother."

From the corner of her eye, she caught a tremble in Victoria's chin as she watched the scene. But Victoria turned away and headed toward the study before Laney could say anything.

Laney and Henry followed behind her, with Jake and Patrick bringing up the rear. Ralph stayed back in the kitchen. Apparently, along with being Victoria's bodyguard and chef, he also did the dishes. Poor man. Laney hoped he got paid a lot.

In the study, they each took their same spots, but Henry

sat next to Victoria this time, rather than leaning against the fireplace.

Victoria looked around at everyone. "I've told you about Laney's destiny. But she's not the only one with a destiny. No ring bearer goes into battle alone. Jake and Henry, you have a destiny, too."

Laney felt Jake jolt beside her. Obviously he hadn't expected this.

"What are you talking about?" Jake asked.

"Every ring bearer that emerges during a critical time is part of a triad. One human"—Victoria nodded toward Jake —"and one more-than-human. They are her protectors. Jake and Henry, you are Laney's."

"A triad?" Laney asked, looking at the shocked faces of Henry and Jake. She herself was also shocked, but comforted as well. It was nice to know she wasn't alone in this whole "fate has a plan for you" thing.

"Castor and Pollux," Jake said quietly. "They were Helen's."

Victoria nodded. "Yes. Throughout their lives, they protected her time and time again. They were always by her side and on her side."

"All ring bearers have protectors?" Patrick asked.

"Yes. But they are always different people in their lives. Family, friends, strangers. There's no hard and fast rule, it seems, as to who they are. But they appear when they are needed."

Laney looked between Jake and Henry. She'd met both last year when two Fallen were trying to kill her. Without their help, she wouldn't have survived.

"Why a triad?" Henry asked. "Why not an army?"

Victoria smiled. "There is an army, but the triad is the head of it. Three is always an important number. Right,

Patrick?"

Patrick nodded, his hand on his chin. Thinking-man mode. "Three is, of course, important in Catholicism, the trinity being composed of the Father, the Son, and the Holy Spirit. In Hinduism, there is an almost analogous concept with the trimurti, or the three deities. In other religions too, three is important: for example, the three jewels of Buddhism, or more generally in the three fates. The rule of three also underlies physics, and even consciousness: the id, the ego and the superego."

"Or the three stooges," Jake muttered, low enough for only Laney to hear.

Laney nudged his thigh.

Jake shrugged. "Look, I've never been a big fan of numerology. It seems you can find a number sequence that is relevant for anything as long as you look hard enough. How do we know the triad isn't just that—a convenient interpretation? Maybe there's nothing special or mystical about three for the ring bearer. Maybe it just happened to be, rather than being destined to be."

Victoria smiled. "There's always a skeptic in the group, someone who looks at a problem in a pragmatic way. That's your job. You're the present." She looked at Henry. "You're the past." Her eyes shifted to Laney. "And you're the future. The three sides of the triangle. The triad."

Laney could feel Jake stiffen beside her. She knew he didn't like the idea of a destiny being laid at his feet. Jake was independent. He wasn't going to like thinking that all his decisions up to this point had been irrelevant. That he would have ended up here no matter what he did.

But Victoria was right about three and about triangles. In building, a triangle could bear incredible weight without breaking. Did the same hold true for humans? Were three people an incredibly strong grouping, also able to bear incredible pressure?

"So—as a member of the Triad, what exactly is our job?" Henry asked.

"You keep her safe," Victoria said. "You protect her so she can do what she's supposed to do."

"And what exactly is that?" Laney asked. She knew she was supposed to fight the Fallen, but no one had really mentioned exactly how she was supposed to go about it.

"Lead the forces of good against the forces of dark in the final battle," Victoria said.

Dread and disbelief settled over Laney. "What? Like some sort of general?"

"Are we talking apocalypse, end of times?" Jake asked.

Victoria's tone was serious. "If the ring bearer is needed, it means the world has reached a critical time. An end-of-times tipping point. In the past, the ring bearers have managed to push the tide back." Her eyes found Laney's. "And now, it is your turn."

Chapter Forty-Six

"END OF DAYS? We're talking doomsday scenario, right?" Laney tried not to sound terrified, but she was pretty sure she failed. All she could picture was the stolen folio, the one about the army of Belial. Is that why they stole it? Were they getting ready for war?

Patrick took a look at Laney's face and seemed to realize this last little tidbit had pushed her over the proverbial edge. He grasped her hand and her eyes flew to his. He smiled. "It's all right."

Keeping her hand firmly clenched in his, Patrick turned to Victoria. "But all of this is a moot point without the ring. The ring bearer's power comes from the ring. How about we focus on finding it first?"

"Yes, of course." Victoria said, her voice conciliatory. "I'm sorry for laying all of this on you at once. I've been living with this for so long, it's no surprise to me. But to someone hearing it for the first time, it must come as quite a shock."

Laney nodded. *Quite a shock?* Victoria had a gift for understatement.

"How about you tell us a little more about one of the past ring bearers? Helen, perhaps," Patrick said, and Laney could have kissed him. Any topic other than her was a huge relief right now.

"You said Helen created the prison. But when?" Henry asked.

"During the Trojan War," Victoria said.

"When she was in captivity?" Jake asked. "How's that possible? Troy is in Turkey and you said the prison was in Egypt. How was she able to build a prison from there?"

Victoria inclined her head. "The Trojan War, as I mentioned before, is not quite what it seemed. During the war, Helen was actually in Egypt creating the prison for the Fallen."

Laney wasn't an expert on Helen, but that just didn't sound right. Next to her, though, had on his thinking-man's look again. "Uncle?"

He patted her hand. "It's actually possible. There were rumors that Helen was in fact in Egypt during the war. That she had been switched out for—I guess the closest term would be a doppelganger, who took her place with Paris in Troy."

Jake spoke up from the other side of her, his tone grudging. "And actually, Helen and Paris did stop in Egypt before continuing on to Troy. King Proteus was furious at Paris for what he had done, and Paris barely escaped. Some argue Helen stayed behind when Paris took off for Troy."

"So it's possible?" Henry asked.

Victoria nodded. "It's more than possible. Helen created a prison for the Fallen. It's known today as the Serapeum in Saqqara."

Laney fell back against the couch. The Serapeum. She'd actually visited it once with her uncle and Drew.

Located about thirty kilometers from the Great Pyramid in Giza, Saqqara is a City of the Dead: a city of cemeteries covering nine square kilometers. The Djoser Pyramid was usually the big draw in Saqqara, but the Serapeum had been the fascination for her. It had been undergoing renovations at the time, but her uncle had gotten them special permits to see the site.

"What's the Serapeum?" Jake asked, interrupting her ruminations.

"It's an underground necropolis that dates to the Bronze Age, when Helen lived," Laney said. "Inside, there are twenty-four huge granite sarcophagi and an older section with wooden coffins in small caves in the walls."

"Sarcophagi? For who?" Jake asked.

"Allegedly for the Apis bulls," Laney said.

The Apis bulls had been revered in ancient Egypt beginning sometime around 3,100 BC. When an Apis bull was born, Egyptians celebrated for three days. An Apis bull wasn't considered a mere animal, but the actual living embodiment of a god. The god changed over time, with some saying it was Ptah, others naming it Osiris.

The bull itself had a distinctive appearance: black with a white diamond on its forehead, an eagle on its back, and a scarab under its tongue. And when the bull died, it was given a royal funeral.

"But there has always been a mystery about the Serapeum," Laney said. "These giant granite coffins for the Apis bulls are all unmarked, except for three. Almost as if someone started putting hieroglyphs on them after they'd been uncovered. In fact, most of them have never been used."

"But surely the bones of the bulls demonstrate that that's what they were used for," Jake countered.

"That's the strange part," Laney said. "Bones have only been found in three of the sarcophagi. The rest remain empty. And the granite coffins are way too large for a bull."

"The wooden coffins in the caves of the Serapeum *have* been found with mummified bulls," Patrick interjected. "But no mummified bulls have been found in the granite Serapeum."

"So why do they think the giant sarcophagi are for the bulls?" Henry asked.

Laney shrugged. "Probably because they couldn't think of anything else that would fit in them."

"How big a sarcophagus are we talking?" Jake asked.

Laney pictured the giant sarcophagi in her mind. "You need a ladder to reach the top, and they're each about twelve feet long and six feet wide."

"Big enough for me," Henry said quietly.

All eyes flew to him. Henry was right. Even with his extraordinary height and strength, he wouldn't be able to move the thirty-five-ton lid.

"The sarcophagi weren't just coffins. They were jail cells," Victoria said.

"In Helen's time, they wouldn't have been able to kill the Fallen," Jake nodded, respect in his voice. "The weapons were rudimentary to say the least: swords, spears. We've only been able to kill them with an automatic to the heart. So they came up with the next best option."

Laney darted a glance to Henry and away. Actually, that wasn't entirely true. Henry had killed Gideon with a piece of metal. He'd shoved it into his chest with such force that the Fallen's heart had been all but obliterated.

"They can at times be killed without the aid of a gun," Henry said quietly.

Laney nodded at him before turning back to Victoria. "Were there any Fallen or nephilim working on Helen's side?"

"A few. Just like today."

"Her brother, Pollux," Jake said.

Laney looked over at him. "And Castor?"

Jake shook his head. "No. Just Pollux. Pollux was alleged to be the son of Zeus. Castor was mortal."

Patrick nodded. "You have to remember, the Bronze Age was the age of heroes and gods. There are tales of incredible strength and abilities. Maybe the gods and the heroes were more than human."

"Some were. Some weren't," Victoria said. "Some were simply figments of people's imagination. But it was much harder to kill the Fallen back then. In fact, they didn't know how to do it. They weren't even sure if it could be done."

"So how did they get the Fallen to Egypt?" Henry asked.

Victoria smiled. "Poison. It was Helen's idea. She knew they couldn't fight the Fallen the whole way to Egypt. Once they went down, she needed them to stay down. So she had them continually poisoned until they were in their coffins. Then they sealed them in tight. And they stayed there until they died. When they were reduced to only bone, their bones were smashed to dust."

"Achilles. The great hero. He was poisoned—brought down by an arrow to the heel," Patrick said.

Victoria nodded. "He was believed to be immortal. No weapon could take him down. He was the fiercest of fighters."

Jake jolted. "He was a Fallen?"

Victoria nodded. "Yes. There were many during that time that came together. Most on the opposite side of humanity."

"So if the war wasn't about Helen, what was it about?"

"Oh, it was about Helen, just not about her beauty. She was the general. She pushed back the Fallen."

A tremble ran through Laney. A general. "The Egyptian word for bull is *ka*. Which is pronounced exactly the same as another ka which is interpreted as a person's double and holds their creative energy."

Victoria nodded.

Laney continued. "So a tomb created for sacred bulls would be the perfect hiding place for the energy of a person's double. A perfect place for the ring."

Victoria nodded. "Yes. It's there."

Victoria said it with such confidence that Laney believed her.

"But . . ." Victoria drew out the word.

"But? But what?" Jake asked.

Victoria looked at Laney. "The ring *is* in the Serapeum. But I do not know where in the Serapeum it is located."

Laney pictured the archaeological site. It was huge, consisting of both the newer section and a much older section. And maybe there were even more sections that had never been uncovered.

Another thought struck Laney. "The renovations."

Her uncle nodded, concern on his face.

"What renovations?" Jake asked.

Patrick answered. "The Serapeum underwent an extensive renovation from 2001 to 2011. Radon gas had been found in the underground necropolis and walkways had collapsed. During the renovations, crews created walkways and metal skeletons for each of the granite sarcophagi. People were all over that place for over a decade."

Laney looked at Victoria. "Is it possible the ring isn't there? Could it have already been found?"

Victoria shook her head. "No. It's still there. It's hidden in a place known only to the ring bearer."

Laney swallowed as all eyes turned to her. She shook her head. "Well, I don't know where it is."

Victoria smiled. "Yes, you do. You just have to remember."

Laney's eyes flew to Victoria's. "Remember?" Her conversation with Patrick came back to her. "How can I remember something from someone else's life?"

Victoria's voice was gentle. "It wasn't someone else's life. It was yours. You do realize by now, the ring bearer is always the same person."

"No, I hadn't realized that," Laney countered.

Victoria's voice was gentle but insistent. "The dreams aren't dreams. They're memories. You just have to open yourself up to them and you'll know all you need to know."

"But I don't *want* to know." Laney realized with a shock that she had said the words out loud.

Victoria nodded. "You never do. But eventually, you always accept your destiny."

"Always?" Laney asked, still hoping there was a way to avoid what Victoria was telling her.

Victoria's voice was firm. "Always."

Chapter Forty-Seven

AFTER VICTORIA HAD FINISHED with her "you just have to remember where the ring is" speech, she'd told them she'd have the plane ready to leave early the next morning. Laney had wanted to leave immediately, and just get this over with.

But it would take at least twelve hours to reach Egypt. If they left right away, they would arrive in the morning and have to wait almost a full day before they could safely go to the Serapeum without detection.

So, they'd all trooped off to bed. Laney had slept a little, but every time she began to dream, she'd yanked herself out of sleep. She just couldn't handle another dream from her former selves.

Laney stared at the ceiling as Jake slept quietly next to her. Was this all possible? Was she the ring bearer? Had she been alive multiple times before? Or, from the way Victoria explained it, had she always been alive?

She rolled onto her side, crushing a pillow to her chest.

Shouldn't she be better prepared, then? If this were true, shouldn't it be less impossible to believe?

Her doubts assaulted her throughout the long night. At five, she crawled out of bed and headed to the airfield with everyone else. From the looks on everyone's faces as they boarded the plane, she didn't think anyone had gotten much sleep.

Laney stared out the window of Victoria's Gulfstream G550. It was a lot like Henry's jet. Idly, she wondered if Victoria and Henry had gotten a family discount.

Patrick was asleep a few rows behind her. Henry was sitting with his mother a few seats ahead, talking quietly. And Ralph was up with the pilot. Laney tried to sleep, but it eluded her. Her mind was simply too full of questions to shut down.

"What is it?" Jake mumbled from next to her.

She glanced over at him. His eyes were still closed, a blanket pulled over him. "I thought you were asleep," Laney said. It always amazed her how Jake seemed to be able to fall asleep at the drop of a hat.

"Nah, just resting my eyelids. So what's going through that pretty little head of yours?"

What wasn't? Destiny, Helen of Troy, the triad, the Fallen. You name it, she was thinking about it. But right now one thought was taking center stage: Victoria's comments about her previous lives. "Helen."

"Helen's always been a fascinating character," Jake said.

"You mean because of her beauty?" Laney asked.

Jake shook his head. "Not just that. From the very beginning her story is enigmatic. Even her birth."

"Her birth? How?"

"Well, according to the tales, Helen was the daughter of Zeus, as was Pollux. But in the story, Leda, Helen's mother, wasn't impregnated by a man, but by Zeus in the form of a swan."

"A swan? Seriously?"

He smiled. "Yup. And Pollux and Helen had company. Because Castor and Clytemnestra were also alleged to have been conceived that same night, but by Leda's actual husband, Tyndareus."

"Quadruplets?"

Jake shrugged. "According to the tales. And all of them were born from actual eggs. So I guess hatched is a better term."

"Huh," Laney said as she leaned back against the couch.

Jake squinted over at her. "Okay, I know that look. Your wheels are turning. What are you thinking?"

"I guess it's the question Clark asked a few days ago about the relationship between genetics and human development. Biology has been marinating in the back of my brain since then."

Jake smiled. "And?"

"Well, think about it. If someone asked you to explain the difference between identical and fraternal twins, what would you say?"

His eyes got larger. "I'd say fraternal twins came from different eggs, while identical twins came from the same egg."

Laney nodded. "Maybe the story of Helen and her siblings' birth just got confused by a storyteller who didn't understand science."

"So, what? They understood the science of reproduction thousands of years ago?"

Laney shrugged, thinking about what Victoria had said about civilizations being destroyed over and over again.

"Why not? After all, we know that civilization existed much earlier than we realize, probably predating 10,000 BC. And we think that those people may have even had aerial power. Is it really that crazy to think that they understood biology as well?"

"I never thought about that. Whenever you guys talk about earlier civilizations, it's always their advanced technology that you mention. I guess it stands to reason that if they were advanced in one area, they'd be advanced in other areas. But we're talking about the Bronze Age, right?"

Laney nodded. "Yes. The Bronze Age extended from around 3,300 BC to around 1,000 BC, give or take."

"And the ancient civilizations we're talking about predate that time period by at least seven thousand years. So is it really possible they were talking about the science of reproduction?"

"Who knows? Maybe someone who had already lived some previous lifetimes was there." She smiled. "Apparently that's a thing."

He took her hand. "So I hear."

"And maybe that someone explained the science to everyone else."

Jake leaned over and kissed her.

"What was that for?"

"I love how your mind works."

Laney snuggled into him, needing his warmth. "You know what Victoria said about me remembering?"

Jake nodded.

"My uncle said the same thing earlier. He thinks my dreams aren't just dreams. He thinks they're memories of my past lives."

"What do you think?"

All of her doubts crowded into her words. "I think if

that's true, they've got the wrong girl. If the women I'm dreaming about were previous ring bearers, they didn't just defend the ring; they led nations, armies. The world went to war. Is that what I'm supposed to do? Is that what's going to happen next?"

"I don't know, Laney."

She looked into his eyes, searching for something, anything to tell her it was going to be okay, but that comfort wasn't there. It couldn't be.

She leaned into his side. "Ever since I spoke with my uncle I've also been thinking about the War Scroll."

Jake raised an eyebrow. "Because of the stolen folio?"

"In part. The War Scroll was written by the Essenes. They were this apocryphal cult that existed around AD 30."

"Okay." Jake drew out the word. "So what about it has you thinking?"

She played with his hand, tracing his fingers with hers. "It tells of the final battle between the Children of the Light and the sons of Belial."

Jake glanced down at her, his eyebrows raised. "'The Children of Light' sounds awfully similar to Cayce's Children of the Law of One."

Laney nodded. "And from the description, they are the same. There are more religious overtones in the Scroll, followers of the rules of God, et cetera. But the concept is the same: the good versus the bad."

"Okay, so why is this scroll in your mind?"

Laney clutched Jake's hand to her chest, her head leaning into his shoulder. "Helen was part of a world war that lasted ten years. And in Homer's telling, that war involved gods, who were probably the Fallen or nephilim. Joan of Arc led an army in France, part of the Hundred

Years' War. What if another time of war is coming? What if I'm expected to lead an army of the Children of Light?"

"Then you'll lead it. And you'll defeat anyone who gets in your way. I've seen you take down every obstacle in your path when it comes to doing the right thing. Add in a little superpower, and you'll be unstoppable."

Laney nodded, looking away. There was no doubt in Jake's voice, but all she had was doubt. She closed her eyes, snuggling a little closer to Jake. But her thoughts were aimed a little further away.

God, if you're listening, and there's any chance you could, could you please pick someone else to do this?

Chapter Forty-Eight

CAIRO, EGYPT

AD 645

Amaris stood in the prow of the boat, looking for her first glimpse. The waves were rocking it from side to side, but she had gotten used to the motion. After three weeks at sea, the movement of the Nile was nothing. But she'd still be happy to have her feet on solid ground.

"Anything yet?" Gaius said as he came to stand next to her.

She smiled up at him, again amazed at how she had once feared this man. When Hypatia had handed her over, she had thought she was being sent to her death.

But Gaius had proved over and over again to be a good friend. In fact, he had become like the father she'd never had. Just as Hypatia...

Amaris shied away from that thought. It was too painful. Even now, three years later.

They had set sail that very night across the sea. Word of Hypatia's death had reached them almost as soon as they set ashore. She had cried for a week straight, barely eating.

Gaius had finally shaken her from her misery. "This is not what she wanted for you. She wanted you safe. She wanted you to live. Do not repay her kindness by tossing your life away."

His words had penetrated her cocoon of despair. Hypatia had taught her to focus on the good and to know that this was only one life. We lived many. She would see her teacher again.

And more importantly, her teacher had entrusted her with a mission. She would not fail at it.

She took Gaius's hand with a smile. "Just waiting for a glimpse."

Gaius gestured toward the shoreline. "There it is."

Amaris looked over, seeing the tip of the Great Pyramid cresting over the water. In no time, the Great Pyramid was joined by the lesser two. She let out a sigh. "We're almost there, Hypatia. It's almost safe."

Chapter Forty-Nine

CAIRO, EGYPT

THEY ARRIVED in Cairo just before dark, although after her dream about Amaris, Laney felt like she'd already been here. Out the car window, she watched the streets of Cairo fly by.

They were going to go to the Serapeum at dawn, when they were less likely to run into anyone. Which meant they needed to hole up someplace for the night.

Henry was driving, Patrick in the passenger seat, with Jake and Laney in the back of the Range Rover. Ralph and Victoria were in the Mercedes in front of them.

Laney glanced out the window. It had been years since she'd last been in Egypt. Something about the place always felt ancient. As if the whole country held the keys to an unknown knowledge.

People packed the sidewalks in the residential parts of the city. Some wore western clothes. Some were in traditional dress. Most women were modestly dressed, a few wearing full burkas—although colorful ones. Men wore long shirts over linen pants.

It was hard to make out any of the buildings out in the dwindling light, but Laney noticed when they started to be more spread out. And larger. They were entering Maadi, one of the more affluent areas of Cairo.

For a few minutes, Henry wound his way through the narrow streets, then they finally left the residential area behind and moved out into the desert. Up ahead, Laney could just make out some lights. It looked like a little town up on a hill.

As they drew closer, Laney realized it wasn't a town but a house—a very large one. It was three stories tall, with two large extended wings and a tall iron fence surrounding it. Balconies with curved archways lined each floor.

"It looks like something out of *Arabian Nights*," Patrick said. "Who lives here?"

"A friend of my mother's," Henry said.

"Friend?" Jake asked.

Henry shrugged. "That's what she said."

The Mercedes in front of them stopped. They waited for only a few seconds before the gates swung open. Then Ralph hit the gas and they followed him up the long windy drive, arriving at a large, round cobblestoned driveway in front of the mansion's massive front doors.

Laney stepped out of the car, wondering yet again who Victoria was. And how on earth she had made friends with whoever lived here.

Jake came to stand next to her. "You okay?"

She took his arm with a smile. "Yup. Just trying to keep my head from spinning off my shoulders."

Jake placed his hand at the small of her back as they walked toward the front door. "Well, please do. I rather like it perched up there."

They stepped through the front door and into a giant

foyer. The ceiling was three stories above them. A giant chandelier adorned with crystals of varying colors dominated the space.

"Wow," Laney murmured.

Victoria was up ahead, and looked back over her shoulder. "This way."

They all trooped behind her. Victoria stopped at the foot of the double staircase. "There are six bedrooms on the second floor. Everyone can pick one. Let's meet back down here"—she pointed to an immense sunken living room to their right—"in about fifteen minutes. There are still some things we need to discuss."

Laney hefted her backpack onto her shoulder, struggling not to sigh.

Twenty minutes later, she sat on the sleek, pale yellow couch in the large living room. She shifted, trying to get comfy. The couch looked soft and cushiony, but it turned out it wasn't very comfortable. Whoever lived here didn't seem to spend much time on it. It was stiff as a board.

Victoria had found them one heck of a safe house. The last safe house Laney had been in had had bowed walls and a couch that was a mouse hotel. This place had solid gold faucets and toilets that spoke to you. Above the couch was a painting by Salvador Dali—and Laney had no doubt it was an original.

Laney glanced around the room. "Living room" seemed too normal a name for it. The room was bigger than Henry's office. A full-sized grand piano—not a baby grand —sat in one corner, and it looked right at home. In fact, it was dwarfed by the space. Laney shook her head. How did people live like this?

The sound of male voices pulled her attention to the

arched entryway. Jake and Patrick walked in together. Laney smiled at the camaraderie between the two.

Jake took a seat next to her. "Man, this is not a comfortable couch."

Laney laughed. "I was just thinking the same thing."

Henry walked in, Victoria and Ralph behind him. He took a seat to Jake's right.

Victoria smiled. "Good. Everyone's here."

"Okay, so what exactly is the plan?" Jake asked. "The site is going to be guarded."

Ralph nodded. "Yes. But at night, there's only one guard who covers the entire necropolis. We have a better chance of running into thieves, or some tourists out for an illegal stroll, than guards. But don't worry about the guard —I'll take care of him."

Patrick leaned forward. "'Take care of'? What does that mean?"

Ralph put up his hands. "Nothing lethal. Hopefully, I'll just keep an eye on him. If he gets close, I'll just make him take a little nap."

Patrick's jaw tightened, but he nodded. Laney knew Patrick didn't like the idea of anyone getting hurt. She sighed. She supposed with her new role he was really going to have to get over that.

"And then the rest of us will head to the entrance of the Serapeum," Victoria said. "Patrick and I will wait outside while you three retrieve the ring."

"Right," Laney said, drawing out the word. "About that part. How exactly do we find the ring?"

"You're the ring bearer," Victoria said. "You already know where it is. You just have to think about it."

Laney stared back at her. "That's it? I just need to think

about it? I pretty much did that for the flight over here with no luck. Anything more specific?"

"The last ring bearer to touch the ring hid it in the necropolis. You need to focus on her, and then its location will be revealed to you."

Laney felt five pairs of eyes watching her. She swallowed. "Right. Just get in touch with my inner ring bearer and find a mythical artifact that's been hidden for nearly two thousand years."

Victoria nodded.

Laney felt her stomach bottom out. "Sure. No problem."

Chapter Fifty

DAWN WAS AN HOUR AWAY. The sun's light was just beginning to peek above the horizon. Laney stood on top of the hill, twenty-five kilometers from Giza, unable to believe she was here. Down below, Saqqara—the City of the Dead —lay still asleep.

The Serapeum of Saqqara was not the only Serapeum built in Egypt. Laney knew there was another one in Cairo. But the Serapeum here was much older, dating to at least 1,800 BC. As Laney had learned, the word "Serapeum" refers to any building dedicated to Serapis, a god invented in an effort to join the Greek and Egyptian gods together.

And this Serapeum, like some other important spots, had an avenue of one hundred sphinxes that heralded its entrance—although most of them were still buried. Laney imagined them covered in dirt, waiting to be awakened.

"You good?" Jake touched her shoulder.

She looked over at him. "Yeah. I'm just thinking about how this place was discovered."

Jake smiled. "Go ahead, professor. Tell me."

She laughed. "All right. It was the sphinxes that led to its discovery—by Auguste Mariette, back in 1850. He'd traveled to Egypt on behalf of the Louvre to find some Syrian and Coptic manuscripts. During his trip, he decided to search north of Saqqara."

"Why north?"

"He'd read Strabo's description of the Serapeum and had been intrigued. It took him very little time to find a small sphinx buried in the sand. Many of the descriptions of the Saqqara spoke of an avenue of sphinxes, reputed to be over a thousand meters long. A year of excavations later, he found the entrance."

Jake gestured to the landscape. "And the rest of it?"

Laney glanced around. "Saqqara is a city of cemeteries. It contains dozens of tombs and burial sites. It's a city of the dead."

"That an official title?"

"Actually, it kind of is. And Saqqara isn't even the only 'City of the Dead' in Egypt. There's another one in Cairo."

A shudder ran through her: *the City of the Dead.* What a horrible name. It sounded as if the dead rose at night, going about their business, only to be chased back to their graves at the first sign of light.

"It's going to be okay, Lanes," Jake said.

She nodded, but didn't say anything.

Side by side, she and Jake walked. Laney struggled to feel some sign of recognition. Helen of Troy had been here. Shouldn't she feel something?

Laney strained to feel some connection to that old life, something that would prove to her that what Victoria had said was true. But the only memories she could come up with were of the times she had been here with her uncle and Drew.

She knew the ancient sarcophagi lay down deep just ahead. She'd told Jake the site was discovered back in 1850, but it was more accurate to say it had been re-discovered. Back in AD 24, the historian Strabo mentioned the Serapeum, calling it the greatest discovery in all of Egyptology.

He claimed that a thirteen-hundred-meter-long avenue of Sphinxes led the way to the entrance. He also mentioned that sandstorms could whip up at a moment's notice and bury you before you reached the door. Even during Strabo's time, the door had been buried deep in the sand, no longer in use.

Laney glanced ahead to where signs pointed the way to the entrance. She knew that, as a result of the massive decade-long restoration, the site was now home to a temperature-controlled environment, and each sarcophagus was secured by a metal vaulted skeleton that kept the rock above it from crumbling. A wooden floor had also been added for the comfort and safety of the necropolis's visitors.

She followed Henry and Victoria through the sandy ground. Patrick and Jake were on either side of her, yet she felt alone. The burden of this outing was on her, and her alone.

Laney felt a chill despite the warmth of the air. Panic rose within her. Because she knew it wasn't just this outing that was her responsibility. If Victoria was right, nothing less than the entire future of humanity lay at her feet.

Laney took a couple of deep breaths. *Don't think about all that. One thing at a time.*

She could barely make out the entrance of the Serapeum in the dim light. Was Victoria right? Was this an ancient burial ground for the Fallen?

In her own fights with the Fallen, it was only through

modern weapons—automatic weapons no less—that they had been able to kill them. Laney knew that that was because those weapons had the power to shred the heart before the Fallen could heal.

In ancient times, there was no equivalent. There had been no weapon in existence that could harm a Fallen so quickly and so thoroughly that the Fallen could not recover from their injury. Weapons, no matter how strong, were simply too slow in delivering their injury. Helen had found a way around that.

And she had the ring, a voice whispered inside her mind. *A weapon more powerful than any gun.*

Laney watched Henry help Victoria over the uneven ground. Laney didn't think Victoria needed the help, not really. If there was one word she would use to describe Victoria, it was strong. Maybe not physically, but there was an inner strength that shone through her. Where did that come from?

Behind her, Laney could just make out the shadow of the step pyramid of Djoser, built by Imhotep. Reputed to be an incredible healer, able to coax medicines from plants and other natural remedies, Imhotep had been deified as a god, and you might believe it based on the grand structure he built.

The two-hundred-and-four-foot pyramid was alleged to have been the tallest building of its time back in 2041 BC. It was an incredible undertaking. What type of intelligence did it take to construct such a building? The world's first step pyramid.

Laney smiled. *At least, first that we know of.* Laney had learned that, if anything, more history was lost than was uncovered.

Her smile dimmed. *Was Imhotep a Fallen too?*

She glanced ahead to where the entrance of the Serapeum was just barely visible. Walls of packed sand towered over the sides of the path leading to its entrance. Laney knew that just beyond that entrance, the twenty-four sarcophagi lay quietly waiting.

The site continued to baffle archaeologists in multiple ways. First, no one knew how the granite necessary for the structures had been imported. Each coffin weighed an incredible seventy tons. Collectively, that meant that whoever had built it had to move sixteen hundred tons—over three *million* pounds—of granite. How on earth had they transported that much weight?

That wasn't the end of the bafflement, though. The passageways of the Serapeum were too narrow for the sarcophagi to have been moved through them using simple manpower. There simply wasn't enough room to fit all the people necessary to move it.

And they didn't have machines capable of moving them back then. In fact, even today, one of the twenty-four sarcophagi lay in the middle of one of the paths of the Serapeum below. That was as far as one team of scientists had been able to move it—with all of modern man's tools at his disposal.

Doubts flooded Laney. Her predecessor was brilliant, strong, and fierce. How was she ever going to measure up?

Her eyes drifted back to Victoria; they seemed to be drawn to the older woman time and time again. Who was she, really? Where did all her knowledge come from?

Laney shook her head. Her biological mother was obviously the keeper of many secrets. But now wasn't the time to push that issue. Maybe when this latest adventure was over, she could sit her down for some answers.

"This way." Victoria said, leading the way down the hill. Jake and Henry followed in her wake.

Patrick waited for Laney to catch up with him. He took Laney's hand when she came abreast of him. "Ready?"

She nodded, taking a breath. Time to see if all this destiny talk was real.

Chapter Fifty-One

THEY STOPPED a quarter of a mile from the path to the necropolis. Laney looked around. Not much had changed since she was last here. Up ahead was the path that wound down into the Serapeum. Nothing stirred, not even the air.

Patrick glanced at her and she nodded. "I'm good."

He started down the path. Henry followed behind with his mother, taking her hand when she stumbled. Laney watched the interaction from behind.

"What?" Jake asked.

"I didn't say anything," Laney said.

"No, but you thought something. What was it?"

Laney sighed. She never could seem to hide anything from Jake. "It's nothing. I just—" She paused. "Henry's a good son. And they seem to have a good relationship, despite everything she's put him through."

"And?" Jake prodded.

"And I can't help but wonder what my life would have been like if I had grown up with both of them. A big brother. A living mother. Don't get me wrong. I love Uncle

Patrick. I wouldn't trade him for anything. I just can't help but wonder if fate had twisted a different way, what I would have been like."

Jake pulled her to a stop, tipping her chin up to look in her eyes. "You would have been *you*. I don't think a different upbringing would have changed that. You would still be strong, defiant, stubborn—and amazing."

Laney felt a lump in her throat. She liked his words, but she knew it wasn't entirely true. A person's environment had a lot to do with the person they turned into. She leaned into Jake. "I don't know what I did to deserve you, but I am so glad I did it."

"Right back at you." Jake leaned down and kissed her on the lips.

Hand in hand, they continued forward to where Victoria and Henry had stopped twenty feet ahead.

Victoria met Laney's eyes as she and Jake joined them. Laney averted her eyes, though, looking instead at the walls of sand on either side of them. Somewhere under there the sphinxes lay sleeping. She glanced down toward the entrance. She could barely make it out even though it was only a hundred feet away.

Henry turned to Jake and Patrick. "Let's go make sure everything's clear. Laney, can you and Victoria wait here?"

Laney nodded as the three men set off down the path.

"You care about Jake a great deal," Victoria said, once they were alone.

Laney looked over at her and saw—actually, she wasn't sure what kind of expression it was. Hopeful, maybe.

But Laney didn't know how to respond. She wasn't sure she was ready to share anything personal with Victoria yet. But then she remembered her conversation with Kati and her promise.

She looked back at Victoria, who was still staring at her with those strange eyes. "He's everything," she said simply.

Victoria nodded. "I'm glad you have him. He's a good man. He reminds me of your father."

Surprised, Laney darted a glance at her. She was about to speak when Victoria nodded toward the path. "I think we're good."

Laney glanced over at where Patrick stepped out of the entrance, waving for them to come.

Laney and Victoria made their way over to them.

"All good?" Laney asked.

Patrick nodded. "Yes. Henry and Jake just went inside to check it out and turn on the lights."

As if summoned by their names, the two men reappeared.

"It's quiet." Jake looked at Laney. "Are you ready?"

Laney nodded, trying to put some enthusiasm in her voice. "Let's go find us a ring."

Chapter Fifty-Two

LANEY, Henry, and Jake watched as Patrick and Victoria made their way back up the path. The two of them had elected to stay outside, just in case their entrance had been noticed. Laney turned to the Serapeum, and flashed her light at the entrance only a few feet away.

She stopped right in front of it, her eyes looking for some sort of sign that they were in the right place. But there was nothing.

Not that there should be. Thousands of people had probably walked through this entrance over time.

Laney peered through the entryway. The lights in entryway were off but she could still make out a dim light further in.

"We kept the first bank of lights off. But about twenty feet in they're on," Jake said.

"Well, I guess it's time to go." Taking a deep breath, Laney stepped through the entrance. Immediately her foot got caught on the uneven ground, making her stumble. She landed unceremoniously on her butt.

"Ow," she said, getting to her feet. If she was the destined one, her destiny sure didn't seem to come with any grace. *I bet Helen of Troy was a lot more graceful.*

Henry followed her in, reaching down to help pull her up. "You okay?"

"Only hurt my pride," Laney said, dusting off her pants.

Twenty feet in, they all switched off their flashlights, not needing them with the exhibit lights. And what an exhibit. Pictures of the dig lined the walls. They were in only the front entryway and already Laney had goose bumps.

She knew up ahead the path turned to the right and that the resting place for the sarcophagi was actually split into two separate areas. There were twelve sarcophagi, six on each side, at the beginning of the path, followed by another small hallway, and then the remaining twelve sarcophagi.

They moved ahead, turning into the main area of the exhibit. Here, the floor was solid wood, and the first twelve sarcophagi lined the sides of the path, each in its own carved niche in the rock wall. Up ahead, the light illuminated the second portion of the path, which held the remaining sarcophagi.

"You weren't kidding about the size of these things." Jake stood next to one, gazing up. The sarcophagus was another four feet taller than him. Henry walked up to another one; the sarcophagus towered over him as well.

Seventy tons of hewn granite, placed within its own arched niche. The metal skeleton above each sarcophagus held the ancient ground at bay. It also gave the space an almost alien look, as if they were on some weird spaceship.

Laney knew the containers were perfectly constructed, with ninety-degree angles inside. The lids fit perfectly on top of the bases, not a whisper of air escaping. She shuddered, imagining being trapped inside, no air. Not an easy way to die.

Although Laney had been here before, it still felt eerie. She supposed it was the fact that it was night, but still, the light was the same regardless of the time of day: there was no natural sunlight in here.

"It's the stillness," Laney whispered.

"What's that?" Henry asked.

"I was trying to figure out why it's so creepy. It's the quiet. Last time I was here, there were workers, people milling about, lots of noise. Right now, it feels like we're the only people on earth."

Jake walked over to her and squeezed her hand. "So where do we start?"

Laney glanced up at him. "I'm not sure."

Henry's voice was low. "You know, Laney. You just have to remember."

You all make it sound so simple. She had been trying—the whole plane ride over here. And then again all through the night.

If Victoria was right and she was the ring bearer, shouldn't this be as easy as they all made it sound? Shouldn't she be able to tap into the memory with ease?

But that wasn't the case. She didn't even know whom to focus on. She'd dreamed of Joan of Arc, Helen of Troy, Makeda, and a half dozen other women. Who was the last one to hold the ring?

"Okay. I know I'm supposed have this great emotional connection to my past . . ."—Laney struggled for the right word—". . . selves. But how about if we start logically? Helen lived around 1,500 BC, and Solomon around 1,000 BC—which would be when Makeda took the ring from him. Amaris was the student of Hypatia, who was the last librarian of Alexandria, around AD 600."

"Wait—Hypatia?" Henry asked.

"Oh, right. It was actually one of my first dreams. Although I've had a few others since then about her. And the dreams weren't about Hypatia, exactly. They were about this young girl. She was a student of Hypatia and Hypatia wanted—"

Laney looked up, her eyes going wide. "Hypatia gave her something from the library to hide. A small something. She's the one."

"You're sure?" Henry asked.

Laney nodded. "Actually, I'm positive." *Amaris.* It had to be. It made the most sense. She smiled and looked over at Jake and Henry.

They looked back at her expectantly and her smile dimmed.

She sighed. "How about you two look somewhere else? You're making me feel awfully self-conscious."

Jake gave her a small smile, tapping Henry on the shoulder. "Come on, Henry. Let's go check out the pictures back at the entrance."

Laney waited until they'd disappeared down the pathway. She let out a breath, shaking out her arms, rolling her neck. "Okay. I'm the ring bearer, destined to find the ring, fight the Fallen, and save the world."

A wave of panic rolled through her. Laney shook her head. *Nope. Too much pressure.* She focused on reining in her breathing. *I'm just going to find a ring. That's it. Nothing important.*

She sat on the ground, her back against an ancient wall. She closed her eyes, trying to remember all the dreams of the young girl. "Okay, Amaris, show me where you put it."

Chapter Fifty-Three

GIZA, EGYPT

AD 650

Amaris held onto Gaius's big forearm. The crowds made her nervous. She could still picture the mobs at Alexandria. The poor people trampled under their anger.

Gaius leaned down, patting her arm. "It's all right, Amaris. This isn't an angry crowd. Look around. They're celebrating. They're happy."

People circled about them, some chatting, some rushing by, others talking excitedly. But Gaius was right: no one looked angry.

Fires were being lit as darkness had begun to fall. The fires brought up memories of Alexandria.

Amaris struggled to figure out why the crowds scared her. Finally she said, "It just—it looks different."

But that wasn't really it. Since Gaius and Amaris had escaped Alexandria, living in Rome until the situation in Egypt had calmed, the Muslims had cemented their rule.

Gaius shook his head. "It's no different—not for the people. One ruler or another, the only thing that truly changes for everyday people is the names."

She knew he was right. Rulers rarely concerned themselves with the plight of those under their control. Even before the Muslims took over, the life of everyday Egyptians was worth very little. It was no different now.

Amaris and Gaius continued through the crowd, skirting around a group of people that had gathered to watch two young men dance at the base of the Djoser pyramid. They stopped to watch for only a moment before continuing on their way.

Soon Amaris and Gaius left the crowds around the Djoser pyramid behind, heading southeast toward the Serapeum. Amaris imagined the ancient people who had built these towering monuments of Egypt. But then her mind focused on one. Helen, the creator of the prison. Gaius interrupted her thoughts. "Look, there it is."

Up ahead, two rows of sphinxes, twenty hundred in all, faced each other, creating a path that led to the Serapeum. Gaius and Amaris stopped at the beginning of the path. The sphinxes, although much smaller than the Great Sphinx, still towered above them. Already, though, the desert was beginning to reclaim them.

Years ago, Amaris would have felt frightened. But today, she felt empowered. This was where she was supposed to be. She could feel Hypatia urging her on. "Let's go. Will we be able to get in?"

"Yes. I had the entryway uncovered."

The Serapeum had been all but abandoned centuries earlier, when the animal cults died out. But still, some believers made their way through. Amaris noticed their footprints in the sand. Or perhaps those were the footprints of the merely curious.

Up ahead a faint light spilled through the ancient entryway. Amaris grabbed Gaius's arm. "Someone's here."

Gaius patted her arm. "It's all right. He's a friend."

Together they walked through the avenue of sphinxes. Amaris's dagger felt cool against her side. Her hand reached up and grabbed the leather satchel on the string around her neck. In contrast to the coolness of the dagger, the ring inside the pouch felt warm.

Up ahead, a small man appeared holding a torch. He had very little hair, but what he did have reached his shoulders. Most of his teeth were gone, but he grinned broadly, giving him the look of someone slightly deranged.

Gaius let go of Amaris's arm to greet him. "Dredgos. It is good to see you." Gaius wrapped the man in a hug, clapping him on the back. When Gaius released him, Dredgos gestured toward Amaris, saying something in a language she didn't recognize.

"What did he say?" Amaris asked.

Gaius grinned back at her. "He said he knew you were the one. He could feel it as you approached."

Dredgos stepped back with a bow.

Amaris stepped onto the sloping rock floor. Dredgos said something else to Gaius, and Gaius translated. "He says you should take his torch. He has lit the farther regions, but didn't want too much light at the opening in case it drew attention."

Taking the torch, Amaris nodded her thanks to the strange little man. She made her way into the cool earth, a refreshing change from the beating heat above.

At the end of the hall, she turned left and went still. The granite sarcophagi lined the rough-hewn hallway. Torchlight lit the way, the flames causing shadows to dance on the walls. She glanced to where the shadows stretched along the floor toward her. They looked like monsters, reaching for her as she passed.

Amaris gaped as she made her way down the hall. She had expected the graves to be big, but these were enormous. They towered above her. Which, she realized, was appropriate. They were the only structures that could contain the real monsters.

"Amaris? Are you all right?" Gaius called from behind her.

Amaris glanced over her shoulder at Gaius, who stood next to Dredgos back at the beginning of the path.

"I'm all right." She felt warmed by his concern. Until Gaius, she'd never felt a father's love.

"Do you want me to come with you?"

She shook her head. "No. This is my duty."

He nodded. "We'll wait back at the entrance for you." He disappeared back up the tunnel with Dredgos, leaving her alone.

Amaris looked around. Hypatia's note had said that she would be able to find the hiding spot, but as she looked around she wasn't so sure. The place was massive, and yet, there didn't seem to be any hiding spots, at least not any that wouldn't be readily discovered. Everything was out in the open. And she knew without even trying that she'd never be able to move one of the sarcophagi's lids.

Recalling Hypatia's letter to her, Amaris closed her eyes, calming her breathing, waiting for the knowledge to come to her.

Hypatia's voice drifted through her mind. "Focus, Amaris. Think of the ring. You'll know what to do."

It didn't take long. An image appeared in her mind.

Amaris smiled. "Got it."

Chapter Fifty-Four

LANEY'S EYES popped open and she sat still. *I can't believe that worked.*

Springing to her feet, she made her way halfway down the second set of sarcophagi. She stopped at the sarcophagus second from the back on the right-hand side, and walked around to the back of it. She traced the small cut marks at its base. They would be easily overlooked if you weren't looking for them. Two small interlaced triangles.

Laney then walked around the sarcophagus until she was at the midway point of the left side. Stepping up to the edge of the ancient cell, she ran her hands over its granite. Still smooth. Incredible.

Laney slid her hand over to the seam where the lid met the base. Not a single seam was visible.

Doubt crawled through her. Was she wrong?

Laney placed one hand just below the seam and another at the bottom of the sarcophagus. She had to really stretch. Her arms were barely long enough to cover the expanse. Whoever had thought of this hiding spot hadn't taken into consideration the smaller stature of those who might have to use it.

Grunting, she pushed. Nothing. Panic began to rise in her. *This is it. It has to be.*

Closing her eyes, she pictured what she'd seen in her memory. Not the full hand. Three fingers. Just like the triangle.

Repositioning her hands, she placed only three fingers on the same spots. She pushed all three fingers at the same time.

The granite moved.

Just an inch, but it moved. She heard a small sound from the back of the sarcophagus.

Heart pounding, Laney walked around. A little door, only four inches square, lay open. On trembling legs, she squatted down, swallowing hard.

Here goes nothing. Laney reached her hand in.

The space wasn't deep, only a few inches. Her fingers wrapped around a metal object. Trembling, she pulled it out.

Laney sank down to the earth and opened her hand. The ring was small, made of a dark, heavy metal. On its face were two interlaced triangles. Blowing off the dust, she noticed the four small jewels in each corner of the square ring's face. Each jewel represented one of the elements, which the ring bearer could allegedly control.

Laney stared at her find with both excitement and dread. *The Ring of Solomon. Not touched by human hands in almost fifteen hundred years.*

And she had found it.

As she closed her hand, the metal felt warm against her palm. She took a steadying breath. There was no doubt left.

Her whisper sounded like a yell in the still space. "I'm the ring bearer."

Chapter Fifty-Five

JAKE STOOD with Henry in the entryway of the exhibit. A multitude of footprints dotted the ground. Placards along the wall explained about the site's importance, and pictures documented the site's reconstruction.

Jake paced past the placards again. He had already read them. Twice. There was nothing here to hold his attention. Nothing, at least, that was more important than the woman in the next room. Time and again, he found his gaze straying back down the hall.

Henry leaned against the far wall, his legs crossed at the ankles, watching him. "She'll be all right, Jake. If there's any danger, it will have to get through us first. Or Patrick and Victoria."

"I know. I just—hell, I don't know. I just want to make sure she's all right."

Henry gave a deep chuckle.

"What?"

"You. You are well and truly whipped. And it's nice to see."

Jake wanted to argue, but the truth was, he probably was. And he didn't care. He was happy. She made him happy. "Maybe I am."

"So do I have to see what kind of shape my tux is in?"

Jake raised an eyebrow. Marrying Laney. It wasn't the first time he'd thought of it.

A feeling of warmth spread through him at the idea. Years ago, he never would have thought of himself as the marrying kind. And the idea of marriage still wasn't something he thought of as being for him. Except if he was marrying Laney. Then he knew there was nothing he wanted more.

Jake smiled. "Maybe."

Henry straightened away from the wall. "Laney."

Jake whirled around. "Did you find it? Are you all right?"

Laney walked toward them, her shadow growing larger behind her. She stopped in front of the two of them, and held out her hand.

A small, square metal ring lay there, with a jewel at each corner and two interlaced triangles adorning the face.

Henry smiled. "Knew you could do it."

Laney looked over at Jake. He could see she was proud to have found the ring, but also afraid because it confirmed who she was.

He shrugged, keeping his voice nonchalant. "That's what all the fuss is about? It's pretty ugly."

Laney laughed, and Jake saw some of the tension leave her shoulders. "I thought the same thing."

"All right, chosen one." Jake offered her his arm. "Let's blow this popsicle stand."

She smiled. "Absolutely."

Jake grasped her hand, but inside he was shaken.

Through all this craziness, he had hoped Victoria was wrong. He had hoped Laney wasn't the destined one, the ring bearer.

He wanted her safe, but how would he be able to keep her safe now?

Chapter Fifty-Six

JOHNSON CITY, TENNESSEE

AMAR PACED, waiting for the phone to ring. *Enough.* He grabbed his phone off the desk, punching in the numbers. His call was answered after the first ring.

Wind sounded in the background. "Sir."

"Where are you? Have you reached the target?"

"No, sir. We found the safe house, but they'd already left. We're trailing behind them now."

"Where have they gone?"

"According to our reports, they're heading to Saqqara."

Amar paused, picturing the ancient City of the Dead. He didn't doubt the intel. There were always hands stretched out who would happily sell their mother for a few coins. But Saqqara? Why there?

He pictured Djoser's pyramid. It couldn't be there, but the only other Saqqara site of any real relevance was—

He stood up straight. "The Serapeum. They're heading for the Serapeum."

There was a pause on the phone. "The Serapeum? Sir, I'm not sure I'm familiar—"

"Oh for God's sake, what do they teach you children in school these days? The Serapeum—the resting place for the Apis bulls. It's an underground necropolis. The ring must be there."

"Why is that, sir?"

Amar rolled his eyes. He needed to insist his people start reading. "Helen. She built it. She was a former ring bearer."

"Who is—"

"Enough," Amar barked, and the line went silent.

He stared out the window. If they were in fact going to the Serapeum, there could be no doubt. Delaney McPhearson was the ring bearer. And that meant she was too dangerous. They could not let her learn how to use the ring.

"How far from Saqqara are you?"

"Only a few miles away, sir."

Amar growled. "They could already be at the tomb by now. If she gets that ring..."

"I know, sir. What would you have us do?"

"Drive faster."

Chapter Fifty-Seven

LANEY PLACED the ring on the chain around her neck as she followed Henry to the exit. Since all of this started, a part of her had continued to believe that none of it was real. It was just a story—a story about someone else. And yet, the ring around her neck was very real. She couldn't deny that.

Still, that didn't mean that it worked, her rational side countered. It could all just be a legend. Maybe Solomon had a couple of lucky breaks in trying to control the weather. Maybe he was a charlatan and only called for wind and rain when a storm was starting up.

And the control of the animals? Her mind whispered. Maybe he just—

She shook her head. She had nothing to explain that ability, if Solomon actually had it. Maybe he just had a really loyal dog and the stories grew from there.

Jake touched her on the shoulder. "You all right?"

Laney gave him a small smile. "Slightly overwhelmed."

"Anything change when you found it?"

She sighed. "Not a thing. And I was expecting something. Maybe not a choir of angels, but a tingle or a feeling that told me it belonged to me. But it's just an old ugly ring."

"Well, did you try it on?"

She shook her head. "No. Not yet."

"Why not?"

She gave a little laugh. "Why not? Jake, do you realize all the surreal things we've found out about in the last year? For all I know, when I put this ring on I'll sprout wings, turn green, and start speaking in tongues."

Jake laughed. "Maybe. Or you could just shoot lightning bolts from your fingertips. That might actually come in handy."

Laney wrapped her hand around his arm. "I know my imagination is going into overdrive. But I think I'd like to try tapping into whatever power this thing has in a controlled environment."

"And you don't think hiding in a three-thousand-year-old necropolis, while on the run from Fallen angels, is a controlled environment? You have some pretty high standards, girl."

"Well, a girl's got to have standards."

He wrapped an arm around her with a little squeeze. "Standards and your own personal bodyguards. You have me and Henry to keep you safe and stay with you."

"At least there's that."

Jake stepped away as they reached the entrance. "Ready?"

"You go first," she said.

He looked at her for a moment. "Take your time."

She nodded, turning to look back down the necropolis. She knew she was stalling, but part of her knew that once she left the Serapeum, her life would be changed forever. She would be accepting her role as the ring bearer—and all that it entailed.

Laney rubbed the face of the ring. "Okay, former me's, any help you can give me would be greatly appreciated."

No answer came to her—not that she had really expected one. But a feeling of calm settled over her. She smiled, breathing deep. "Thank you," she whispered, then turned and stepped out onto the sandy path.

Up ahead, she could see Henry and Jake had reached Patrick and Victoria. They all waited for her. Above them, dawn had broken and the sky was a pale pink. Laney began the walk, feeling more confident as she neared them. When she came close, Jake reached back to take her hand.

The walls of packed sand on either side of them kept the City of the Dead from her view. But Laney felt the city coming to life in the morning light, rather than being chased back to sleep. She could feel the history, the ghosts of those long dead.

And yet she wasn't afraid. Instead of the feeling of creepiness that she had felt before they went into the Serapeum, she now felt a sense of communion with those that had been here before. The feel of those from long ago almost gave her a sense of peace.

Patrick smiled over at her. "Success?"

Laney gave a nod. "Yes."

Everyone seemed to realize that that was all she wanted to say right now. They didn't question her further.

Except for Jake. "What's the smile for?"

She linked arms with him. "I don't know. I just feel connected to this place now."

Victoria gave her a nod and a small smile. Laney smiled back.

Right now, she knew who she was; what she was meant to do. Maybe it was the ring. Maybe it was her former selves. Maybe it was fate. But whatever it was, she was in this fight now. She grasped Jake's hand.

They stepped out of the alleyway created by the packed sand.

"All right, let's get out to the airport," Henry said. "I'll feel better when we're—"

The sound of a rifle cut through the morning air. Jake yanked Laney back to the path, where she was hidden by the sand.

Laney slammed onto her back. She quickly rolled to her side. "Jake, we need—"

The words died in her throat.

Jake stared at her, but his eyes saw nothing. A bullet hole pierced his forehead.

Fear, stronger than any she'd ever felt, raced through her, chasing out any sense of purpose. She grabbed his shoulders while a part of her mind screamed that it was too late.

"Jake? Jake!"

Chapter Fifty-Eight

PATRICK PUSHED Victoria to the ground as the shot rang out. Henry pulled them both back into the relative safety of the pathway. Bullets continued to chip away at the sand that kept them from the shooter's view.

Laney's scream shook Patrick to his core. He got to his knees, staying low. Six feet away, Laney was crouched low over Jake, shaking him, trying to get him to respond.

Not Jake. Dear God, not Jake.

Patrick crawled over to her, his heart hammering in his chest. The bullet hole in Jake's forehead told the whole story. He was gone.

Patrick's breath left him and he struggled to get it back.

"Jake!" Laney yelled, over and over again.

Patrick wrapped his arms around her from behind.

She looked over her shoulder at him, her mouth moving, but no words coming out now. She shook like she was freezing, and tears streamed down her face.

Patrick felt the hole in his chest threaten to swallow him whole. "I'm so sorry, sweetheart."

Laney tried to push him off, but he held on. She collapsed, sobbing into his arms, her heart breaking. Patrick's own heart felt like it was going to break for her.

Next to him, Victoria grabbed Henry's arm. "Get her out of here."

"No." Laney threw Patrick off with a strength that shocked him. She sat in front of Jake's body, her arms out. "I won't leave him."

Patrick looked over to Henry for help, but Henry looked like he was in shock. His mouth gaped, his eyes fixed on Laney and Jake.

Patrick yelled. "Henry!"

Henry finally pulled his eyes from Jake to focus on Patrick.

Patrick gripped the tall man's arms. "Laney. You need to get her out of here. Get her to the plane and take off."

"But the rest of you—" Henry began to argue.

Victoria cut her son off. "Don't matter. *She* matters. Get her out of here."

Henry's eyes cleared. He gave an abrupt nod, grabbing Laney by the shoulders. "Laney. We have to go."

She shoved at him. "I'm not leaving him."

"He's gone, Laney," Henry said. "We have to go."

"No!" she screamed, shoving Henry away again.

Bullets continued to chip away at their cover.

"Get her out of here, Henry," Patrick yelled, leaning against the packed sand, trying to find a shot, but there was nothing. The shooter, or shooters, were too far away. And every time he popped his head out, he had to yank it back.

"Sorry, Laney," Henry said as he grabbed her, throwing her over his shoulder and sprinting away.

Patrick could feel his jaw drop as he watched the trail of dust race after them.

Victoria grabbed Patrick's arm. "Hurry. There isn't much time."

Chapter Fifty-Nine

HENRY RAN with Laney over his shoulder, the image of Jake a constant in the back of his mind. While he struggled to figure out where to go, part of his mind rebelled against what had just happened. Denied that he had just lost the man he loved like a brother.

The sand made it difficult to run fast. And Saqqara didn't offer much by way of cover. There was the Djoser pyramid and the smaller Userkaf pyramid; besides that, there were just a few scattered sand dunes. Hiding spots were in short supply.

Henry sprinted through the dusty ground, at times slowed by the sand to almost human speed. Images of Jake clouded his mind, but he shoved them out. He needed to focus on getting himself and Laney to safety.

The gunshots died away, and Henry knew that whoever had been shooting at them at the entrance had realized that their quarry had left. But why shoot now? They hadn't shot at Laney in Hershey. What changed?

The ring. Laney had found the ring. Before, they hadn't

been sure that she was the ring bearer. They had been waiting for proof. And her discovery of the ring provided that proof, confirmed her identity. And marked her for death.

The sound of engines behind him told him that he'd been spotted. Henry tried to increase his pace, but the sandy terrain was making that difficult. He glanced back. Two cars gave chase on the road parallel to him, and one blur trailed behind the cars but was catching up fast. A Fallen or a nephilim.

Henry swore silently, struggling to come up with a plan. He knew the City of the Dead was filled with ancient tombs and edifices. If he headed there, he could probably lose the cars, but not the man.

He veered left. There was no choice. Out in the open, he and Laney were sitting ducks. Henry sprinted toward Djoser's pyramid. The cars had to stop, the barricades keeping them out. He heard the slam of doors as men joined the footrace. He prayed they were mere mortals.

Laney hit him on the back. "Put me down."

"Laney, we have to—"

She cut him off. "I know. I have a plan."

Chapter Sixty

LANEY CROUCHED in the entrance of the Djoser pyramid, hidden by the shadows. She was still shaking, but she forced herself to not picture Jake.

Not now, not now, she thought over and over again as his image tried to worm its way in.

Henry had all but tossed her at the entryway as they'd turned the corner of the pyramid, hidden from their pursuers' view. She'd rolled, and her shoulder still stung from the impact.

Henry leapt up the side.

The blur was ten feet away.

Laney prayed he hadn't noticed Henry's throw.

The blur came closer, and then, without slowing, it leapt to the first level of the pyramid.

Laney slid out, using the side of the entry for cover. She fired round after round at the blurry pursuer.

The blur turned into a man. He crashed to the first level and rolled off, onto the ground below.

Laney stalked forward, peppering his torso with bullets, taking aim at the heart.

Henry jumped down next to her, grabbing her hand. "They're coming."

Laney looked past the Fallen and, sure enough, another seven men were sprinting toward them, all running at normal speed. *Thank God for that.*

Laney and Henry ran in the opposite direction. But once out of the pyramid's enclosure, it was all but impossible to maintain any speed. They were running on sand.

Henry turned around and grabbed Laney, once again throwing her over his shoulder. But even with his abilities, the sand was a struggle. He jumped over a sand dune, landing hard on the other side. His feet started to slide and Laney was thrown.

Laney tucked as she flew, rolling down to the bottom of the dune. She sat up, spitting out sand, feeling it in her clothes, hair, mouth.

Henry grabbed her hand. "We have to—"

A man flew over the sand dune, landing twenty feet away from them. The same Fallen who'd run them down.

Laney crab-walked backward before scrambling to her feet. Apparently she hadn't killed him—only slowed him down. And not much at that.

Yells from the top of the sand dune grabbed her attention. The seven men who'd been chasing them were now lined up. All of them with weapons pointed at Laney and Henry.

"Henry, get out of here," Laney ordered, but her voice shook. The image of Jake that she'd been struggling to keep out of her mind came back with the force of a train, nearly dropping her to her knees. She'd lost Jake, and now she was about to lose Henry, too.

Henry looked down into Laney's face. "I'm not leaving you, Laney."

Fear shot through her, setting her shaking. She grabbed Henry's hand. "Don't do this. Run. You can escape. Run," she begged.

He pressed a kiss to her forehead. "I'm sorry I wasn't a better protector."

"No!" Laney tried to step around him, to block him from the shooters. He wouldn't let her. "Henry, please go."

Her heart felt like it was going to split in two. She couldn't lose him, too. She knew she would never survive losing both of them.

A barrage of bullets thundered from above. Henry pushed Laney to the ground, covering her with his body, hugging her to himself.

Laney screamed, her whole body starting to shake. "No! No! No!"

Finally, the sounds died away. Laney's heart pounded, her voice disappeared. *No, not Henry, too. Please, not Henry, too.*

She stayed still, knowing that if she didn't move, didn't speak, she wouldn't have to know. It seemed like forever, but she knew it was only a few seconds.

Finally, Laney whispered: "Henry?"

"I'm okay."

Relief washed over her; if she'd been standing, she would have collapsed. She wanted to burst into tears and throw up at the same time. She struggled to calm her breathing. *He's alive. He's alive.*

Henry rolled off her and helped her sit up. Laney looked to the top of the sand dune.

The seven men that had been there had been replaced by five different men, all dressed in black. And instead of pointing their weapons at Laney and Henry, they had them directed at the seven men they'd just shot.

The Fallen was also down. Another man in black advanced on him. He had the dark complexion and hair of an Egyptian.

Laney was about to yell out a warning, when the Fallen sprang up from the ground. The man in black was ready for him. He emptied five shots into the man's chest, all at the heart.

The Fallen fell back. The man in black emptied the rest of his bullets into him.

Satisfied the Fallen was well and truly dead, the man in black turned to Laney and Henry. "Dr. McPhearson? Mr. Chandler? I'm Mustafa Massri. Agent Clark contacted us and said you might be in need of assistance."

Henry stepped in front of Laney. "And who do you work for?"

Mustafa bowed. "The Egyptian division of the SIA. We'll take you safely to your plane. If you'll follow me."

Laney looked at the Fallen and the seven dead men on the dune. The other men in black hadn't pointed their weapons at either Henry or her. They seemed completely focused on the men they'd shot. And obviously they knew about the Fallen.

Laney wasn't sure she trusted Mustafa or the SIA, but then, once again, they didn't have much of a choice.

Henry looked down at her. "Laney?"

She nodded at Mustafa. "Lead the way."

Chapter Sixty-One

HENRY SAT in the back seat of the Land Rover. Mustafa sat in the front passenger seat while another man in black, who hadn't been introduced, drove. Two other Range Rovers, one ahead and one behind, accompanied them as well.

Laney sat next to Henry. Henry knew adrenaline had kept her going at Saqqara, but now it had begun to fade. And the loss of Jake was hitting her, coupled with the close call of both of them nearly losing their lives.

She stared out the window, not saying anything, her face expressionless. But she held Henry's hand in a death grip. Henry knew his hand in hers was the only thing keeping her from falling apart.

Mustafa turned around in his seat. "I'm sorry we were so late. We received word only thirty minutes ago. It's a miracle we were able to reach you at all."

"We appreciate the assist," Henry said.

Mustafa nodded, his deep eyes conveying his sincerity as they passed over Laney before settling back on Henry. "And

I'm sorry for the loss of your colleague. I hear he was an incredible man."

A shudder ran through Laney. Henry gripped her hand harder. He saw the lights of the airfield up ahead. He squeezed her hand, silently telling her to hold on, that they were almost there.

"Thank you. He was—" Henry swallowed as a wave of grief hit him. When he spoke, his voice shook. "He was family."

Mustafa nodded. "I understand."

Henry looked at the plane up ahead. They were getting close, but it seemed to be taking forever. Henry knew he was close to losing it. To distract himself, he asked, "How exactly did Clark know we were in trouble?"

Mustafa shrugged. "That I do not know. You will have to ask him. And if you manage to get some answers from him, well, I hear miracles do happen."

Henry turned his head, clenching his teeth. Oh, he'd get answers. He didn't doubt that for a minute. If Clark knew about the attack, there was something he hadn't shared with them. Something that could, perhaps, have saved Jake.

The Range Rover pulled up to the Gulfstream. It was already running. Henry had called Claude as soon as they'd gotten in the SUV. He'd also texted Patrick, who had told him to go on without them. That he and Victoria would see to Jake.

What Patrick had meant was that they'd see to Jake's body.

Henry struggled to hold in his grief. He needed to be strong for Laney now.

The Range Rover pulled through the gates of the airport and drove onto the tarmac, coming to a stop next to his mother's jet. As soon as they stopped, Henry opened his door, coming around the other side to open Laney's.

Mustafa beat him to it. The agent gently helped her from her seat. "As salaam alaikum, Dr. McPhearson," he whispered.

Peace be upon you. In Arabic, it was a standard greeting, almost the equivalent of a "hi." But as Mustafa said it to Laney, Henry had the feeling that the sentiment was deeper. It was more of a wish. Mustafa was recognizing the loss Laney had suffered,

Henry took Laney from his arms. "Thank you again, Mustafa."

"I believe the thanks is mine. You and Dr. McPhearson are our hope. If you ever need us, we'll be there."

Mustafa bowed once more, then got back into the car and drove to the entrance of the airport, stopping next to the other two Range Rovers. Henry knew that Mustafa and the other agents would wait to make sure no one prevented the jet from taking off.

As soon as Mustafa's car drove off, Laney sagged against Henry, all the fight going out of her. Grief-stricken eyes turned up to him. "He's dead, Henry. Jake's dead."

As her breaths turned to sobs, Henry lifted her up and carried her gently into the plane. Laney's cries tore through him.

Jake's dead. Henry's eyes filled with tears, and he had trouble maneuvering up the steps. Henry was now Laney's only protector.

As he entered the cabin of the plane, Henry promised that no one would be allowed to get to her. No one.

A fierce need to keep her safe settled in the pit of his stomach. But he knew that without Jake, the fight was going to be that much harder.

His mother had been right: a triangle was strong. Now that they were only two points, how could they possibly win?

Chapter Sixty-Two

THE FLIGHT HOME from Egypt took close to twelve hours. Laney spent the first three sobbing. Henry felt helpless, not having a clue how to help her. Then she'd fallen into an exhausted sleep, only awakening as they landed.

The plane wheeled to a stop. Henry took off his seat belt. He glanced down at Laney, but she hadn't moved. "Laney? We're back."

She looked at him with vacant eyes. Slowly she reached down and undid her belt. She couldn't seem to focus.

Henry reached down and helped her stand. She didn't protest, just leaned against him. The pilot had already opened the plane's door and pushed out the steps. Henry helped Laney to the door.

At the bottom of the steps, Jen, Rocky, and Kati stood. They all looked devastated. But when they saw Laney, they were a flurry of movement. They rushed up the steps. Henry stepped back, letting them take her.

Laney looked at her three friends. "He's gone."

Kati ran a hand over Laney's hair. "We know, sweetheart. We know."

The women took Laney's arms, cooing soft phrases as they bundled her down the steps and into the waiting Town Car. Once she was settled in the back seat, with Kati and Rocky for support, Jen walked back to Henry.

She placed her hand on his cheek. "Henry?"

He looked at her and felt the loss crash down on him again.

Jen wrapped her arms around him.

Henry cried, feeling the pain of Jake's death, the emptiness that had taken up residence in his chest.

They stayed like that for a few minutes before Henry pulled away. He wiped his eyes. "You should take care of Laney. She's going to need you."

Jen wiped a tear from his cheek. "We will. But I'm here if you need me, too."

Henry nodded.

Jen leaned up, placing a soft kiss on his lips.

It wasn't a kiss of passion, but of love, support, and maybe the promise of something more some day.

Then she walked back to the car, climbing into the driver's seat.

Henry watched them drive away. The hole in his chest ached and he leaned against the bulkhead.

How can Jake be gone? How am I going to tell Danny? Oh God. I have to tell Tom, too.

He pictured Jake's foster brother. They'd just reconnected after years apart.

He crushed his hand in his fist. *God damn it. This isn't fair. It's not right. Those bastards are going to pay.*

Henry walked down the steps to his own car.

Kevin Chang, his security chief, got out of the driver's

side. Jake had hired everyone on security. In fact, he'd served with most of them.

Kevin's face was blank, but Henry read the grief in his eyes. "What do you need me to do, Henry?"

Henry paused, but he knew. He'd known all along what was coming next. "Call everyone. I need every operative we have."

Kevin nodded. "What should I tell them?"

"Tell them we're going after the bastards that killed Jake."

Chapter Sixty-Three

CAIRO, EGYPT

PATRICK CLOSED THE BEDROOM DOOR, leaning heavily against the wall behind him, his head bowed. He still couldn't believe everything that had happened since last night: flying to Egypt, finding the ring.

His breath hitched. *And then Jake.*

Patrick winced as he remembered Laney's screams of anguish, her shocked face as she looked at Jake. He closed his eyes, trying to shake the image from his mind.

With effort, he pushed off from the wall and headed down the tiled hall with its stucco walls. He rarely felt old, but right now, he felt every creak, every ache in his body. Walking down the hall felt like running a marathon.

At the end of the hall was the kitchen: Patrick's first destination. Idly, he acknowledged that it was a chef's dream kitchen. Sleek lines, lots of stainless steel.

But Patrick couldn't work up the energy to be impressed. Even the back wall, which opened into a large patio with an infinity pool, raised no enthusiasm.

He knew it was beautiful with the desert hills in the distance. But it was as if he was looking at the world through dimmed lenses. All the colors and sounds felt muted.

Turning his back on the landscape, Patrick filled a kettle with water and then rummaged through the cupboards for teacups and tea bags. Setting up a tray, he stared out the window, not really seeing anything, his mind all but shut down. The whistle of the kettle roused him.

Shaking his head, he pushed back from the counter. He added the teabags to the teapot and poured the water in. The familiarity of the ritual calmed him. Feeling more centered, he took the tray and headed out of the kitchen.

There was a solarium around the corner. At least, he thought it was this way. The place was so big, he'd already ended up lost a few times.

Turning right at the end of the hall, he saw the large double French doors he was looking for. He made his way toward them, hoping Victoria was there. He pushed them open and stepped into the room.

The glass ceiling and walls, as well as the fact that they were three stories up, gave one the impression of sitting in the sky. A large, white, leather couch wrapped around two thirds of the wall, with colorful rugs and pillows scattered about the room. Victoria was curled up in one corner of the couch, her feet tucked under her, her head resting on her hand as she stared out the windows.

Patrick crossed the room, placing the tea tray on the ottoman in front of her. "Victoria?"

She didn't move.

Patrick reached out a hand and gently touched her shoulder. "Victoria, are you all right?"

Victoria turned around from the window, her face looking drawn and tired. She gave him a small smile. "Sorry. I didn't hear you come in."

"I thought we could both use a cup of tea," Patrick said, pouring two cups. "Milk?"

She nodded. He added it to one of the cups before handing it to her.

Victoria nodded her thanks. "Laney and Henry are home now. I just spoke with Henry."

"How's Laney?"

Victoria's chin trembled. "Not good. Her friends met the plane. They're taking care of her."

Patrick nodded, his heart feeling heavy. He watched Victoria and, for the first time, he noticed the resemblance to Laney. They had the same cheekbones, the same full lips.

Their eyes were different, though. Laney must have gotten those from her father.

Victoria interrupted his inspection. "You were older, when you first became a priest, right?"

Patrick nodded. "Older than some. I'd been in Vietnam, done and seen some horrible things. I needed to feel like I was giving back. I needed to find goodness. The priesthood offered me that."

"Do you ever doubt that decision? Wonder if you should have done something else?"

Patrick leaned back on the couch. "I think everybody second-guesses their decisions at some point. Especially the important ones. For me, it was when I got custody of Laney. I worried that my being a priest would somehow take away from my being a parent to her."

"Did it?"

"No. It was no doubt different. But she grew up

knowing the importance of giving back, helping others, being strong. How can I say that was wrong?"

"But you did doubt sometimes?" Victoria pressed.

Patrick could tell his answer meant a lot to her. He nodded. "Of course. Kids can be cruel, and having a priest show up for all those events when parents are supposed to be there . . . I don't think it was easy. Never mind having her dates pick her up from the rectory."

Victoria smiled. "That must have been a sight."

Patrick returned the smile, knowing he was latching on to the memory to distract himself from his grief. "The priests all took a shine to her. For her first date, she was twelve. The boy's name was Michael Buffalino. He was a nice kid. He came to the door, and there were four of us waiting to greet him. Not sure I would have been able to stand up to four priests in order to date a girl, but he did."

"I missed all that," she said softly.

"Are you having doubts? About your decisions regarding Laney?"

Victoria sighed. "How can I not? I gave her away to try to protect her from all of this, and yet—here she is in the middle of it. And now Jake... "

Victoria took a sip before placing the cup on its saucer. "I just keep wondering if I did the right thing, sending her away. Would it have been better if I'd kept her with me? Could I have prepared her for what was to come?"

"Is there really any way you could have done that? Without making her hard? One of the parts of Laney I love the most is how much she cares for other people: strangers and friends alike. If you'd told her about her future when she was young, I can't help but wonder if she would have closed herself off from people."

Victoria nodded. "She probably would have. I've seen it before."

"You have? When?"

Victoria looked startled, as if she only just realized what she'd said. "Forgive me. I'm exhausted. I don't even know what I'm saying."

Patrick nodded, but he wondered if she was telling him the whole truth. "Victoria, how do you know all the stuff that you know? How do you have all of these resources?"

She smiled. "I may be tired, Patrick, but I'm not that tired. I know I'm asking a lot, but it's easier for everyone if they don't know too much about me. It keeps them safe. It keeps me safe."

"You can't think we'd bring you harm."

"No, not intentionally. But a small slip-up, and it would be..."—she paused as if struggling for the right word—"... problematic."

"I take it there have been problems before."

She nodded. "Once or twice. Now I play it safe."

"Except for reaching out to Laney and coming out of hiding for Henry."

She shrugged. "They are my kryptonite. I'd do anything to keep them safe, keep them happy."

"Can you tell me what happened back at the Serapeum?"

She shook her head. "No. I'm afraid that's one of the things it's not safe to tell you about."

"But how is it possible—"

Victoria took his hand. "Please, Patrick. I don't say these things to be unkind."

He placed his hand over hers. "Very well. For now."

She nodded. "For now."

A knock at the door caused Patrick to turn. Ralph stood

in the doorway. "The plane will be ready in an hour. We should leave in thirty minutes."

"Are we all going?" Patrick asked, not able to ask the question he really wanted to ask.

"Yes." Ralph's voice softened. "I'll bring Jake."

Chapter Sixty-Four

LANEY LEANED HER HEAD BACK, lulled by the movement of the car. Kati sat on one side of her, Rocky on the other. Jen was driving up front. Laney would occasionally catch Jen's worried gaze through the rearview mirror.

Kati held her hand, occasionally giving it a squeeze. But none of them tried to make her talk. *Thank God.* She wasn't ready for that yet.

Laney watched the trees pass by, blurry from the speed. It was like a dream image. Which was actually perfect. Because right now, she felt like she was in a dream: a really horrible dream. Nothing seemed real or solid. Her body was on automatic pilot, she felt so disconnected from it.

Jake. She took a shuddering breath. Her chest felt like it was in a vise.

She closed her eyes, felt the fresh wave of grief, the tears slipping down her cheeks. *It can't be true. Jake can't be dead. This is all some horrible mistake.*

Kati squeezed her hand. "What can we do for you?"

Laney opened her eyes. "Nothing. Just be here. That's enough."

Rocky nodded, resting her head on Laney's shoulder. Laney leaned into her, feeling the sorrow well up in her. It was threatening to swallow her whole.

Tears dripped onto her shirt. She didn't care. Kati leaned over, wrapping her arms around her. Laney held onto her like she was a life preserver. *How do people survive this?*

Jen glanced over her shoulder at them before whipping her head back to the road. She slammed on the brakes. "Shit."

Laney reached out to grab Kati before she could hit the floor.

"What the—" Rocky yelled, but the rest of the curse died in her throat.

Ahead, a car blocked the way. All Laney's feelings of being disconnected with her body disappeared and she was immediately slammed back into reality. Her head whipped around as Jen slammed the car into reverse.

Another car sped into view, pulling across the road, cutting off their escape.

Laney's gut clenched. They were trapped.

Chapter Sixty-Five

LANEY LOOKED AHEAD of her and behind, her grief-stricken mind taking precious seconds to recognize the danger.

It didn't take Jen nearly as long. "Call Henry," she ordered Rocky.

Turning to Laney and Kati, Jen said, "The car's bullet-proof. We're staying in it until the cavalry arrives."

Rocky closed her phone and pulled out her sidearm, checking the magazine. "Henry's on the way. And let's prepare just in case the 'wait and see' plan doesn't work."

Kati gripped Laney's hand, her face pale. With her other hand, she gripped her necklace, the one that spelled out *Max*.

The movement pierced Laney's heart. She pictured Max, his big eyes just like his dad's, his smile just like his mom's.

Laney turned Kati to face her. "It's going to be okay, Kati. I promise. Now I need you to do exactly what we say, okay?"

Kati nodded. Laney knew terror had taken her voice.

Laney turned to Jen. "This goes south, your job is to get Kati out of here."

"Laney, what are you—" Jen began.

Laney cut her off, refusing to let Jen look away from her. "She's all Max has left. You get her out of here. You promise me."

Laney knew Jen wanted to argue, but she gave Laney a terse nod instead.

Laney pulled the seat back in front of her down to reveal a handgun and magazine. She slammed the magazine into place.

"Two guys ahead, two behind," Rocky said.

Laney glanced out the windows. Both sets of men had exited their cars. One pulled out a machine gun. He blanketed the car with a round of fire.

Laney dove to the floor, pulling Kati with her. Rocky lay crouched next to them. The car's bulletproofing held.

Laney got up slowly, glancing over at Jen, who was still in the front seat. "Jen, you sensing anything?"

Jen nodded. "At least one is a nephilim. I don't know about the other two behind us. Too far away."

Laney looked at Rocky, who was scanning between the front and back of the car. "Aim for the heart."

Rocky's head stopped moving; she stared out the front windshield. "How's this thing proofed against grenades?"

"It's not," Laney answered, following Rocky's gaze. One of the men pulled a grenade launcher onto his shoulder.

"Oh my God." Laney reached around Kati, flinging open the door, her heart pounding.

Jen was already outside, pulling Kati from the car. "We need to move."

Laney's heart rate tripled as she saw the grenade launch, heading straight for them.

Chapter Sixty-Six

"GET OUT!" Rocky yelled.

Laney leapt out the door, pulling the trigger as she flew. Ahead, Jen disappeared into the woods with Kati. Laney said a quick prayer of thanks for that break.

Laney could hear Rocky returning fire. The men dove for cover on one side of the road; Laney ran for cover on the other side.

The car exploded as Laney dove into the ditch along the road. Metal shrapnel flew in all directions.

Laney raised her head to find a jagged piece of metal just two inches from her face. She imagined what would have happened if it had landed just a few inches over.

Shoving that image aside, she started to crawl along the ditch, hoping she could come up behind two of the men, give herself at least a fighting chance.

Laney peeked out in time to see two men converging on her. One had a cut in his forehead that wasn't healing. Good. She leaned up, aiming for his chest.

Pulling the trigger, she cursed: he'd caught sight of her

and jerked to the right. She quickly compensated and let off a volley of shots. One caught him in the neck. Not where she was aiming, but it would do. He dropped to the ground, a spray of blood following him down.

The other man sprinted at her, but he had no noticeable injuries. *Nephilim.*

Laney had no other choice. She yanked the chain off her neck and shoved the ring on her finger.

"Stop!" she screamed.

The man paused. From his face, she could tell he was as surprised as she was.

But whatever she was doing to him, he was fighting it. Slowly, he began to move his limbs—and smile.

A two-foot piece of metal erupted from his chest. His smile turned to a silent scream of agony. Jen's head appeared over his shoulder as she twisted the metal, throwing the man to the side.

Laney whirled around, catching sight of a blur sprinting toward them. She leveled her gun, pulling the trigger over and over again.

"He's mine," Jen growled, taking off at a run. She slammed into the blur, pounding him into the ground, her hand wrapped around the man's throat.

Laney didn't have time to watch; movement to her right caused her to turn. The fourth gunman. She'd lost him in all the commotion. He had already lined her up. There was nowhere for Laney to go. She raised her hands.

"It's too late for that," he said, and pulled the trigger.

Chapter Sixty-Seven

"LANEY!" Rocky yelled as she dove in front of Laney.

The bullet caught Rocky in the back. She fell onto Laney, pushing her backward against the ground.

Laney's eyes went wide. Her breath seemed to disappear.

Her head snapped upward again at the crack of another gunshot. Henry appeared behind the gunman, who slumped to the ground.

Frantic, Laney rolled Rocky off of her. "Rocky?"

The bullet had punched through Rocky's chest, leaving a gaping hole. Blood dribbled from Rocky's mouth.

"No, no, no, no," Laney moaned, putting her hands on the chest wound, trying her best to stanch the flow of blood. But the blood just swirled through her fingers, dripping to the ground below. "It'll be okay, Rocky. We'll get you fixed up."

"Liar," Rocky choked out, trying to smile. "'S'okay, Laney."

Tears swam in Laney's eyes. She grabbed Rocky's hand. "No, it's not okay. Why did you do that? You shouldn't have done that."

"Had to."

"Damn it, I don't care what Victoria told you to do. You didn't—"

"Not for her—"

Rocky's struggled breathing stopped. Her hand went limp in Laney's grip.

Laney pulled Rocky up, hugging her to her chest, rocking back and forth. "Rocky, no, no."

Jen knelt down next to her, wrapping her arms around the two of them. Laney's tears fell on Rocky's dark hair. *Not again. Rocky can't be gone, too.*

Jen released Laney as Henry knelt down next to them. "Laney," he said quietly.

Laney looked at him. She felt her world slipping away again.

Henry gently placed his hand on Rocky's shoulder. "Give her to me, Laney. I'll take care of her."

Laney shook her head, even as she let Henry take Rocky from her arms.

Tears trailed down Laney's cheeks, and sobs shook her frame. "This can't keep happening, Henry. It can't."

Henry gently lay Rocky down on the ground.

Laney stared at her friend. Memories assaulted her. *You can't be dead. You can't be.*

She reached over and touched Rocky's cheek. Already, it felt different. There was no spark of life. She closed Rocky's eyes.

Tremors worked their way down from her hand until her whole body was shaking.

Jen wrapped her arms around Laney from behind, helping her to stand, then pulling her away.

Laney didn't fight her. She didn't have the strength to.

Chapter Sixty-Eight

LANEY SAT in the back of Kevin Chang's car with Jen as Henry sped toward the estate. She replayed the gunfight in her mind.

She should have moved faster. Gotten out of the line of fire. Noticed the fourth shooter. If she'd done any of that, Rocky would still be alive.

The ache in her chest that had developed after Jake's death seemed to have gotten wider. It was now a bottomless pit in the middle of her chest. *Innocent people keep getting killed because of me.*

Panic surged through her and she sat straight up, grabbing Jen's hand. "Kati. Where's Kati?"

Jen squeezed her hand. "It's okay. She's safe. I hid her away, with a cell phone. She called security. Henry's men have already reached her. They're bringing her back to the estate."

The panic slowed, but didn't completely dissipate. As long as Kati was around her, she was in danger. "I want her,

Max, and Danny in Dom's shelter until this is over. My uncle too, as soon as he gets back."

"When we get there, we'll see—" Henry said.

Laney's voice whipped out. "No. We will not 'see.' They need to be protected."

She looked over at Jen and caught Henry's eyes in the rearview mirror. "The humans involved in this mess are dying. I need to know they're safe. These guys are going to keep coming for me, and no one else is going to die."

Even as the words left her mouth, Laney knew she had just crossed a line that couldn't be uncrossed. She'd just broken the world into two categories: humans and non-humans. And Henry and Jen were in the non-human category.

With a shock, though, she realized: so was she.

And right now, the humans needed to be protected.

Henry nodded. "Okay. I'll take care of it."

Laney turned to look out the window, her hands curled into fists. Rocky's blood was on her shirt, on her hands. The damn ring was covered too.

She swallowed down the bile that tried to rise. She didn't want this destiny. Not at this cost. It was too steep a price.

Henry drove through the gates and they closed behind him. It appeared that double the usual number of guards were on duty, and they were all armed to the teeth. Laney noticed the anti-aircraft Stinger missiles system had also been raised.

Henry had had the defense system installed after the helicopter attack last year.

It was illegal for any private citizen to have such a weapon system.

Apparently, Henry no longer gave a damn who knew about it. He wasn't taking any chances.

Laney struggled to rein in the emotions swirling inside of her. She took a deep breath. "Drop me at my cottage, please."

Henry glanced back at her. "Laney, I think it would be better—"

"Henry, I need some time. My cottage, please."

Henry nodded, and a minute later, he pulled up in front of her place. Jen started to get out of the car.

Laney shook her head. "I—" She swallowed. "I just need a little time alone."

Jen looked at Henry, who shook his head. She turned back to Laney. "I know. But you can't be alone right now. It's not safe. But I'll stay back."

Laney wanted to argue, but she knew it was futile. They were right. "Okay." She climbed out of the car.

Laney watched the car drive off and turn onto the main drive. She turned to look at her little house. She pictured Jake sitting on the porch. His spirit was everywhere.

Memories of Rocky warred with memories of Jake. Laney felt like she was choking on them.

Jen stood silent behind her, letting her have her moment.

Taking a deep breath, Laney looked at Jen. "Could you —Would you—" She sighed. "I'm going to go in alone, okay?"

Jen followed Laney up onto the porch. "I'll stay here. Do what you need to do."

Laney nodded and went inside. Closing the door behind her, she hurried down the hall and through the small kitchen to the back of the house.

She tensed as she eased the back door open. She didn't

like deceiving Jen, but she needed some space. She needed to be alone.

Silently, she slipped out the back door and down the steps. She crossed out the back gate, walking up the hill that bordered her yard.

At the top of the hill, Laney began to pick up the pace. Before she knew it, she was flat-out sprinting. She flew over the grass. Her feet pounded the ground.

Images of Jake and Rocky in death assaulted her with each step. Her breaths came out in pants; her legs and arms felt leaden.

Gasping, she came to the crest of the hill above the field of mammoth sunflowers. They were all dead. Giant fallen stalks lay on top of one another. Not a sign of life was left. Numb, Laney pushed her way among the tall plants on trembling legs.

She searched the field, looking for the center, the place where she and Jake had picnicked months ago.

Frantic, she pushed stalks aside. *Where is it? Where is it?*

Finally she found it, although the stalks had almost completely buried it. She raised her hand to her cheek, feeling Jake's touch. She pictured his eyes, his mouth.

She could have sworn she heard Rocky's laughter, felt her arm around her shoulder. Then the images of them in death returned.

And Laney screamed and screamed and screamed until her throat was raw and she had no breath.

Chapter Sixty-Nine

CAIRO, EGYPT

PATRICK COLLECTED Laney's and Jake's bags and carried them down to the foyer. They were leaving for the airport in a few minutes.

He was trying to keep himself busy by checking to make sure nothing had been left behind. He dropped the bags next to the front door.

Victoria walked down the stairs and gave him a small nod.

Her phone rang and she answered it. "Henry? How are you? How's Laney?" Victoria gasped, reaching out a trembling hand for the bannister.

Patrick moved toward her. His heart pounded. *Oh God no.*

Victoria sank heavily to the stairs, tears in her eyes. "Yes, I'll tell him." She disconnected the call.

Patrick knelt down in front of her, his chest tight, his legs on the edge of collapse. "Is it Laney?"

Victoria grasped his hand, shaking her head. "No, Patrick, no. She's fine."

Relief washed through him. *Thank God.*

Victoria squeezed his hand. Her chin trembled. "But there was another attack. Rochelle is dead."

Patrick sat down before his legs gave out. Rocky had been a constant fixture in Laney and Kati's home. She had such a strong spirit. It was impossible to believe she was gone, too. "What happened?"

Victoria's face was pale, her eyes empty. She sounded like a ghost. "They were ambushed on the way home from the airport. Rocky saved Laney."

Patrick closed his eyes, feeling the new grief wash over him. "Who else?" He cleared his throat. "Who else was there?"

Victoria looked up. "Laney, Rocky, Jen, and Kati."

"Oh dear God." Patrick's hand flew to his throat. "How are the rest of them?"

"Alive but shaken. Very shaken."

Patrick pictured Rocky sitting at Laney's table, beating him at Scrabble. He looked at Victoria, knowing this new grief on top of Jake's death would be Laney's undoing. "We have to tell Laney. Rocky's death on top of—" He cut off.

Grief rolled through him, stealing his voice. Getting his emotions under control, he said, "We have to tell her."

Victoria grabbed his hand, her eyes swimming in tears. "We can't. Not yet. It might not work. Please, Patrick."

Patrick grasped her shaking hand. He hesitated for only a moment before pulling her into a hug. He felt her sobs as she wept quietly into his shoulder.

Patrick stared up at the ceiling, tears swimming in his eyes as well. He prayed the same words he'd prayed when Laney was kidnapped, back when this all began.

Dear God, please keep her safe.

Chapter Seventy

BALTIMORE, MARYLAND

LANEY DIDN'T KNOW how long she'd stayed in the field. She remembered crashing to her knees at one point. The next thing she knew, she was waking up, and Jen was sitting next to her, waiting.

She looked up at Jen, her throat aching. "They're gone, Jen."

Jen pushed Laney's hair from her face. She reached down and gently pulled Laney to her feet. "I know, honey. Come on."

Laney didn't fight her. Jen slung Laney's arm around her shoulder and practically carried her back to the cottage.

At the house, she led Laney upstairs and turned on the shower for her. Before leaving her alone, she leaned over and kissed Laney on the forehead. "Get undressed and hop in. I'll go grab you some clothes."

Laney did as she was ordered, not having the strength to think for herself. She let the water run down her body. Closing her eyes, she allowed the heat to chase away some of the cold that had seeped into her bones.

It was a while before she realized the water had gone cold. She turned it off and stood staring at the wall, trying to figure out what she was supposed to do next. The simplest of tasks seemed incredibly complex right now.

Finally, she stepped out, drying herself off and pulling on the clothes Jen had left for her. When she opened the door, Jen was just outside. Jen opened her arms and Laney walked into them.

The wave of grief shattered over her again. Laney sobbed and sobbed, feeling like her heart had been smashed into pieces.

Grief stabbed at her like a weapon, slicing away her happiness, her comfort, her future. And guilt ate at her. Because she knew, down deep, that Jake and Rocky were dead because of her.

Me and my damn destiny. She as good as killed them herself.

Jen led her into her room, tucked Laney in bed, and then crawled onto the bed next to her. She rubbed Laney's back. "It'll be okay, Laney. It'll be okay."

Laney wanted to believe her. She wanted to cling to Jen's words. But she knew it was a lie. It was never going to be okay again.

Chapter Seventy-One

WHEN LANEY WOKE, daylight streamed in through the blinds. She stayed quiet, not wanting to let Jen know she was awake. Jen had been constantly by her side through the night, and Laney had needed her. But right now she needed to be alone.

Memories of Jake ran like a film through her mind. She slammed her fist into the pillow. How could he be gone? She remembered last year when she and Jake had taken a break, both of them unsure how to say what they really wanted.

How could she have been so stupid, taking time off from him? Why had she wasted their time together? Why hadn't she just told him how she felt?

It had been obvious to her from almost the moment she met him. She trusted him. She loved him.

But those feelings had been new and frightening.

And that was what had really led to their break. Fear. She'd been afraid of what she felt—so she had shied away from fighting for him, fighting for them. *So stupid.*

And now he was gone. There was no more time for them.

Rocky's face, her hand going limp, flashed through Laney's mind. Laney felt like it was happening all over again. She lowered her face into her pillow, thinking she was too exhausted to cry, but the tears came anyway.

The hole in her chest was still there. It felt like it was the size of a canyon.

She glanced at the clock. 8:47 a.m. She'd been home for less than twenty-four hours, yet it felt like it had been a lifetime. She sat up, feeling an ache in her back.

She immediately spotted the ring, sitting on her bedside table. Jen must have cleaned it and put it there.

Laney glared at the thing, hating the sight of it. Her damn destiny. Her being the destined one was what had gotten Jake killed, Rocky killed—hell, years ago it had even gotten Kati's husband killed.

Right now, she would be happy if she never saw the damn thing again.

There was a knock at her door. Jen peeked her head in. "Hey."

Laney swallowed, but her voice still sounded raspy. "Hey."

"I'd ask how you're doing, but I'm guessing that's a pretty stupid question right now."

Laney tried to smile but failed. "Yeah."

"Well, I thought you should know that Henry's meeting with that agent from the SIA this morning at nine."

Laney struggled to think through the molasses in her mind. "What? Clark? Why?"

Jen sat on the edge of Laney's bed. "We didn't tell you before. You had enough going on. Clark's the one who sent the Egyptian SIA to help you. Which meant he knew about the attack somehow. Henry wants to know how."

Laney couldn't believe her own stupidity. Why hadn't she wondered how the SIA had shown up just in time?

The bullet hole in Jake's forehead flashed through her mind. But this time it was anger that boiled up, not grief. "Clark *knew?* He knew we were going to be attacked?"

Jen nodded. "That's what it looks like."

Laney threw off the covers and yanked the ring off the side table. *That bastard.*

Chapter Seventy-Two

LANEY TOOK the stairs to Henry's office two at a time. It was 9:03. They were late.

Jen kept pace with her. "Laney, you need to calm down. I know you're angry, but it's not going to help you get any answers."

Laney whirled on her and Jen backed up a step. "He *knew*. Jake would be alive if he'd told us. Rocky would be alive. But he didn't. He's holding back and people are getting killed."

Laney continued up the stairs, Jen following her. Part of her brain knew Jen was right, but she couldn't hold back her anger. It was like a never-ending tide. Reaching the landing in front of Henry's office, she barely spared a glance at the woman who sat on the couch outside Henry's door.

Laney stopped at the double doors and took a deep breath. Rocky's and Jake's faces flashed through her mind. She pushed the doors open.

Clark sat in one of the leather chairs in front of Henry's desk. Henry shot to his feet as soon as Laney appeared. He came around the desk toward her, his eyes wide. "Laney? Are you all right?"

Laney held up her hand to stop Henry from reaching her. She walked around him and positioned herself directly in front of Clark.

Clark stood. "Dr. McPhearson, I am so sorry for the loss of Mr. Rogan and Ms. Martinez."

Laney narrowed her eyes. "Are you?"

"Of course. I only wished we'd been able to get—"

Laney threw a right cross at his face.

Clark dodged it with superhuman speed, leaping five feet away.

Laney went still. "You're a Fallen."

Chapter Seventy-Three

LANEY'S HEART raced as she studied Agent Clark by the windows. All this time, he'd never told them what he was. He'd leapt out of the way of Laney's punch with super-human speed. If he were a nephilim, Jen and Henry would have felt a connection to him. Which meant there was only one possibility: he was a Fallen.

In a blur, Jen and Henry were on either side of him, just out of his reach.

Clark looked over at Jen. "Interesting. We'd heard you didn't reveal your abilities."

"Only when someone I care about is threatened," Jen replied, her eyes cold.

Clark nodded, putting up his hands and looking at Laney. "I'm not a threat. I told you before that the SIA has Fallen working for them. I just failed to mention that I was one of them."

"I think it's time you placed all your cards on the table, Clark," Henry growled.

Clark nodded, his hands up. "Agreed. Can we all sit?"

Henry looked to Laney. "Your call."

Laney gave an abrupt nod, still reeling from learning of Clark's true nature. The surprise had taken the edge off her anger, but it was still there, boiling just beneath the surface.

Laney walked over to the couch, slipped the ring from her pocket, and placed it on her finger. At the ambush, when she put the ring on, she thought she'd been able to control that Fallen, at least a little. Although she really had no idea how she'd done that. Still, better safe than sorry.

Apparently, Jen and Henry had the same idea. They each pulled over a chair, positioning them so they were in front of Laney and slightly to the side. Enough space for Laney to see, but also close enough that they could guard her if necessary.

Clark didn't quite manage to hide his smile at the precautions. He turned his own chair around so it was facing them. "Okay. So where should we start?"

"How about with how a Fallen ends up working for the SIA?" Henry asked.

Clark nodded. "All right. I discovered my abilities when I was eleven. I was beyond amazed. My parents both knew I had them. They were worried about what would happen if someone found out, so they taught me to always be on guard. But one day—someone found out. I'm still not sure who or how."

"What happened?" Laney asked.

"I came home from college and there was a man sitting in my kitchen. My parents were still at work. He told me there were more people out there like me. And he showed me what he could do. He said he had a place where I could go, where I'd feel accepted for who I was. What he didn't realize was that I already had that place. My parents had always made me feel loved and accepted. I told him that.

He smiled and left." Clark paused. "Two days later, my parents were dead. The man showed up again two weeks after their funeral, and asked if I still had a place where I felt accepted."

The brutality of the act stunned Laney. Sympathy tried to overwhelm her rage. She kept it in check. "What did you do?"

Clark shrugged. "I tried to kill him. Of course, I failed. I didn't know much about my abilities, and I certainly didn't know how to kill someone else like me. Then the man disappeared. I spent the next few years looking into people like me, trying to find a way to kill that man, if I ever saw him again. SIA learned about my research and looked me up. The rest, as they say, is history."

In spite of herself, Laney felt compassion for him. But she hardened herself against it. Even if he'd had a rough time of it, that didn't mean he hadn't used the Egypt situation to his advantage. After all, she did have the ring.

"What about Egypt?" Henry asked.

Clark sighed. "What I'm about to tell you can't go beyond this room. Lives are at stake if any of this information leaks."

Laney nodded, and noticed Henry and Jen do the same.

Clark paused. "SIA has a mole inside Samyaza's group."

Chapter Seventy-Four

LANEY STARED AT CLARK, her anger returning full force. "You have a mole? Didn't you kind of bury the lead in this little conversation?"

Henry's response was equally heated. "Why the hell didn't you tell us sooner? We could have found Samyaza and ended this already."

Clark shook his head. "The mole has a very specific mission. And we weren't ready to take the fight to Samyaza. Not until Laney had the ring and knew how to use it. But our mole warned us about the attack, although he couldn't safely reach us until the last minute. I scrambled the SIA as soon as I heard."

Laney watched Clark's face through the whole re-telling. Her anger began to ebb. She realized she believed him.

But she wasn't sure if that was because Clark was telling the truth or because he was a good actor. She had a feeling it was the former and sighed. "I'm sorry for taking a swing at you."

Clark smiled, inclining his head. "Not the first time somebody has, and probably won't be the last."

"So, tell us more about this mole," Henry said, his arms across his chest. Apparently he wasn't as convinced of Clark's sincerity.

Clark stood. "Actually, I brought someone with me to do that. She's waiting outside."

Laney flashed on the woman they'd seen outside Henry's office.

Clark disappeared through Henry's doors and was back in a few seconds. Beside him was a small woman, shorter even than Laney's five foot four. With pale brown hair and light brown eyes, she gave off an air of fragility.

The woman glanced around the room nervously.

Laney realized she'd probably overheard the yelling earlier. Poor woman, she probably thought she was walking into a viper's den.

Laney stood, as did Jen and Henry.

Clark led the woman over to them. "Amanda Datson, this is Dr. Jennifer Witt, Dr. Laney McPhearson, and Henry Chandler."

As Amanda shook hands with each of them, Laney realized that her earlier impression of fragility had been off the mark; Laney could sense the strength in her.

And Amanda didn't even blink at Henry's height. Interesting.

Clark ushered Amanda to a chair next to him and they all re-took their seats. "Amanda here is an analyst with the SIA. She's been with us for about three years." He turned to her. "Amanda, I have agreed to share with these people the identity of the mole."

Amanda's eyes grew big. She shook her head. "No. You promised."

Clark gently took her hand. "Amanda, they can be trusted. I wouldn't do anything to put him at risk. Please. Tell them your story."

Amanda looked at him for a long moment before turning her attention to Laney, Jen, and Henry. "All right. Although, I'm not sure how to begin."

"How about starting with how you know the mole?" Jen asked.

Amanda gave a small smile. "Well, that's easy. I've known him all my life. He's my brother."

Chapter Seventy-Five

AMANDA TOLD her story without embellishment, without hesitation, but Laney could feel the woman's pain. It wasn't an easy story to tell.

Amanda sat on the chair next to Clark, her voice calm but her hands clasped tightly in her lap. "Maddox and I grew up like most kids, with a normal mom and dad—or so we thought. Then one day, Dad never came home."

She took a breath and Laney could feel the sadness, even years later. Her love for her father was obvious.

"I was eight. Maddox was ten." She looked away for a moment before continuing. "Maddox became my protector after that. I mean, he was always a good brother, taking care of me. But after Dad disappeared, we had to move to a not-so-great neighborhood. More than once we got hassled. But Maddox, he held everyone at bay. By the time he was twelve, he had a reputation, and most people left us alone.

"Every once in a while, though, some older kid would get it in his head that he could take Maddox. Maddox was big for his age." She gave Henry a small smile. "Not quite as big as you, but he's taller than most. I think he's about six-six or so now. Anyway, the big kids would come and the big kids would fall."

"So he became a hard case," Jen said.

Amanda shook her head. "Only to the outside world. To me, he was the brother who I watched cartoons with, made forts with. And who taught me how to fight. But I was never as good as him. Maddox has skills that I didn't have. He's gifted. He's like our dad."

Laney looked at Amanda but didn't see any fear or jealousy in her. She loved her brother, that was clear.

"Was your dad a Fallen?" Jen asked.

Amanda nodded. "I didn't realize it while he was with us. But my dad... he was fast, really fast. One time, we took a family vacation to Mount Rushmore. Maddox and Mom were asleep, but my dad saw I was awake. He asked if I wanted to go on an adventure."

Amanda smiled. "He took me to the park and we climbed the rock face. Or rather, Dad jumped up it with me on his back. We sat on top and watched the dawn. I was five. It's my best memory of him."

Her smile disappeared. "But when we reached the ground, he warned me not to say anything about our climb. At the time, I thought it was because we'd get in trouble with the police. But now I realize he was making sure I didn't mention his abilities."

Laney looked at Clark. "Was he actually a Fallen or a nephilim?"

"He was a Fallen," Clark said. "In fact, at the SIA we identified him as Baraqel."

"The teacher of astronomy," Amanda said with the ghost of a smile. "My dad loved the stars."

"So they can be good?" Surprise was written across Jen's face.

Laney knew Jen was asking out of more than idle curiosity. One of her parents was a Fallen, although Jen had no idea which one. But the idea that her parent could be good must be comforting. Especially considering the alternative.

And Laney hadn't had a chance to tell her about their previous conversation with Clark—about how he'd said that some Fallen spent their whole lives as good, decent people. In fact, she was having some trouble believing it herself. She knew they had discussed the possibility of Fallen being good, but it was still hard to believe.

Amanda shrugged. "Mine was. Maddox is, too. Anyway, when we were teenagers we were recruited by Samyaza's group. We didn't know at the time what their end goal was. We just thought it was somewhere safe."

Amanda went silent. And although her facial expression remained unchanged, her knuckles went white from gripping her hands together.

Laney knew this group was not warm and fuzzy but Amanda sitting here suggested they had let her go, which didn't make any sense.

"So, they just let you go when they realized you didn't have powers?" Laney asked.

Amanda shook her head. "No. To get out, my brother had to kill me."

Chapter Seventy-Six

AMANDA GLANCED AROUND THE ROOM, no doubt realizing the shock her words had caused. Taking a breath, she continued. "Maddox was sixteen when they first contacted us. I guess Maddox's reputation got to the wrong ears." She went quiet.

"They asked you to join them?" Henry prodded gently.

She shook her head. "No. First they killed our mom."

Laney gasped, her eyes flying to Clark. *Just like they did with Clark.*

Amanda pushed a stray hair out of her eyes and Laney caught the tremble in her hand. Her heart went out to her.

"Of course, at the time, we didn't know it was them," Amanda said. "But that's their M.O. They take people they think are nephilim or Fallen, and they isolate them. Make them want to belong to something. Maddox and I were in foster care for a year. It wasn't a good year. We went through three foster families. The last placement, they separated us. I think that was the last straw for Maddox. So when Amar's people came to him, he listened."

Amanda sighed. "He thought he was doing the right thing for both of us. They promised us a place to belong, with people who had the same powers. People who could teach him how to use his abilities."

"And what about you?" Jen asked.

"That was the icing on the cake for Maddox. They wanted me, too. After all, I was Maddox's full sister. There was a chance I had abilities, too."

"Where did they take you?" Laney asked.

"Actual location? I didn't know. It wasn't until later that I learned we were somewhere in Oregon. It was a compound. There were a bunch of us, maybe twenty."

Jen inched forward in her chair. "Did they all have powers?"

Amanda shook her head. "No. Only five did. The rest were like me. Normal. They gave us two weeks to demonstrate what we could do. Those that passed, lived. Those that didn't . . ." Amanda shrugged, letting her words hang in the air.

"So... how are you still here?" Laney asked.

"Maddox recognized the situation as soon as we arrived. He warned me that he was going to act like he didn't care about me. He knew he had to make it look like he was part of the program. So he became the star pupil, ruthless. He even"—she caught her breath—"he even hit me once, broke my arm. But it worked. They believed him."

Laney knew there was horror on her face.

Amanda glanced at her. "I know how it sounds. But he needed them to believe he was committed. If he didn't, he wouldn't have been able to save me."

"How did that come about?" Henry asked.

"Graduation Day. And one last test. The candidates with abilities had to kill the rest of us."

Amanda paused. "After my dad left, Maddox met this old vet on the streets. He'd been in Vietnam. He taught him this way of stopping blood from flowing through the carotid artery. It knocks a person out for hours. I could never figure out how he did it. It always seemed like something Spock would do. Anyway, he knocked me out. When I woke up, there were bodies piled on top of me. And it was dark. First thing in the morning, they were going to burn us. But Maddox got me out, hid me away. When I made my way to the police station, SIA showed up a couple hours later, before the police could haul me off to the loony bin."

"And Maddox?" Laney asked.

Amanda's jaw tightened. "He's still with them. It's been nine years."

Jen turned to Clark, her voice filled with indignation. "Couldn't you guys offer him protection? Get him out?"

"We could and we did," Clark said. "He refused. He gives us intel, but that's not why he stays. He's saved dozens of kids."

"But he's had to take a lot of lives to do that," Henry said.

Clark nodded. "Yes."

Laney wondered what that did to a person's soul. Did it rip it to shreds? Or did the saving of lives help balance out the scales?

"Maddox is how you knew we were in trouble in Egypt," Henry said.

Clark nodded. "Yes. And it was a huge risk for him to take." He turned to look at Laney. "But he knows how important you are."

Jen and Henry looked over at her as well. Laney felt the weight of their stares. Everyone kept telling her how important she was. Funny, though, she didn't feel important. She felt lost.

Clark stood up. "I'm sorry we couldn't get to you sooner. And I'm sorry about Rogan and Detective Martinez."

Amanda stood as well. "I'm sorry for your loss as well."

Laney nodded, but at the mention of Jake and Rocky, tears clogged her throat. A blanket of grief fell over her. She struggled to keep the tremble out of her limbs.

Henry stood in front of her, blocking her from their view and gestured to the door. "Let me walk you two out."

But Amanda moved around Henry to stand in front of Laney. Laney stood up, feeling a little wobbly.

Amanda looked in her eyes. "I *am* very sorry for your loss. But I need to ask you something."

"Go ahead."

"My brother was my protector for years. And for the last nine years, he's protected those he could. But now, there's going to be a fight. I know it. You know it."

Laney nodded.

Amanda pressed a piece of paper into Laney's hand. "And now *my* brother needs a protector. If Amar finds out he's the mole, Maddox will be in real trouble. Agent Clark has told me what you can do. So I'm asking you to be Maddox's protector. Will you do that?"

Laney felt the weight of Amanda's request. Laney was drowning in grief right now, and she wasn't sure she could even put one foot in front of the other without tripping herself. The additional burden of defending someone else felt like it would break her.

Yet the idea of saving someone when she kept losing those she cared about... it was like a light in the darkness. It was something to cling to and strive for.

She glanced down at the paper Amanda had given her. It was a photo of Amanda from years ago. Standing behind her was a very tall boy, his arms wrapped around Amanda, giant grins on both their faces. Maddox.

Laney grasped Amanda's hand. "Yes. If he needs it, I'll be his protector."

Chapter Seventy-Seven

LANEY AND JEN sat out on the veranda. Henry was walking Clark and Amanda to their car. Laney had needed to escape outside. The walls felt like they were closing in. The air had felt thin.

Laney lay on the lounge. She let out a breath, picturing Amanda's face. Why had she agreed? She could barely take care of herself; how was she going to protect someone who was in Amar's control?

She glanced over at Jen. "That was an incredibly sad story."

"It seems like everyone with a nephilim background has one," Jen said.

Laney reached over and squeezed Jen's hand, but didn't know what to say. Jen's own back story was pretty rough, too.

Abandoned by her mom when she was young, she'd bounced around foster care for a few years before ending up homeless at the age of nine. After a year on the streets, social services had caught up with her, and she'd ended up with the Witts, who'd adopted her only two years later.

"You sure that was wise? Agreeing to protect Maddox?" Jen asked.

"What else could I do? Are you telling me you could have looked in her face and said no?"

Jen sighed. "No. I don't suppose I could have. So. We now have a supercharged army hell-bent on world domination. Isn't that the plot line to every little boy's favorite comic?"

"So it would seem. Jake's favorite is—" The wave of grief blindsided her.

For a moment, she'd forgotten he was gone. And then she automatically felt guilty for forgetting. Leaning back, she took some shaky breaths.

Jen sat down next to her, wrapping an arm around her with a squeeze. "It's okay to cry, Laney."

Laney let herself be comforted for only a few moments before pushing back. "No, it's not. And that seems to be all I'm doing lately. Right now, we need to get the guys that did this to Jake and Rocky. Then I can mourn."

"Okay. So how can I help?"

Laney held up her hand with the ring on it. "Well, I guess I should try to use this thing." She glanced over at Jen. "I don't suppose you feel like doing my bidding right now?"

Jen smiled. "Not particularly."

"Didn't think so."

A family of deer munched quietly in the grass about fifty yards away. Laney picked out one deer and focused just on her. *Come over here.*

After a minute, the deer looked up, blinked, and scampered away. Laney sighed, sitting back. "Oh yeah, I'm the chosen one all right."

Jen stood up. "Why don't I leave you alone to concentrate?"

Laney nodded distractedly, staring at the ring. How could this little piece of metal possibly tap into some innate power? She shook her head, focusing now on a squirrel that had scampered up the magnolia tree.

For an hour, she switched between focusing on animals and the weather, with nothing to show for it. Finally she yanked the ring off her finger, ready to toss it as far as she could throw.

"So, I guess practice isn't going well?"

Laney's heart gave a little leap and she glanced over her shoulder. But it was only Henry. Jake always used to sneak up on her like that.

Disappointment and fresh grief rolled through her. "Are you here to tell me I should practice more?"

Henry walked over to her. "No. I'm here for whatever you need."

A stab of sorrow welled up, nearly choking her. She looked away from Henry, staring at the grass, trying to get her emotions under control. "They can't be dead, Henry. They can't be."

Henry's voice was quiet. "But they are. And the men that killed them have gotten away with it. No one can stop them but you."

Frustration poured out of her. "Stop them? Henry, I don't know how to use this thing. I have no special powers. I'm not like you, or Jen, or Amanda's brother. I'm not one of you, no matter what Victoria says. I'm not special or super. I'm just normal."

Henry was quiet for a moment. "I think that might be the problem. You don't believe you have the ability. You're not really trying, because you don't think it's of any use."

Laney wanted to argue with him, but she knew he was speaking at least part of the truth. She *was* trying—but at the same time, she really didn't believe it would work. "I don't know. Maybe."

Henry turned her to face him. "Laney, if my mother, our mother, is right, you are the ring bearer. How else could you have found the ring?"

Laney shrugged.

"And if Clark is right, Jake and Rocky are just the beginning. Amar and his army are going to rip through this world. And you are the only thing standing in their way."

"But Jake . . ."

"Jake believed in you. *I* believe in you."

"What if I fail?"

"What if you succeed?"

Laney expelled a breath. She placed the ring back on her finger. "Okay. Let me try again."

Chapter Seventy-Eight

LANEY SPENT the rest of the afternoon trying to get some sort of response from the ring. And all she had to show for it was a blinding headache.

Needing a break, she walked across the veranda, opened the French doors, and stepped into the kitchen. Rummaging through the cabinets, she found a bottle of water and some aspirin. She downed two pills, followed by a quick swallow of water, and leaned against the counter.

The lives of all those lost since she'd learned about the Fallen flashed through her mind. Most prominent were the images of Drew, Rocky, and Jake.

Drew, her best friend, whom she'd lost just before she'd learned about all of this.

Rocky, who'd saved Laney's life at the cost of her own.

And Jake. Laney shuddered, her breaths coming out in gasps. She turned around, grasping the counter tightly as her knees weakened. *How can they all be gone?*

The door to the kitchen opened behind her. She glanced over her shoulder.

Standing in the doorway was a short, heavily muscled bald man with just a trace of Israel in his voice. "Hey Lanes."

Laney practically ran across the room. "Yoni!"

Yoni's gorilla-like arms wrapped around her. "I'm so damn sorry, Laney."

Laney felt Yoni's tears fall onto her neck. Yoni had been one of Jake's closest friends. They'd been through SEAL training together, had shared years in the service, and then Yoni had followed Jake to the Chandler Group. Yoni had even made Jake his son's godfather.

Laney and Yoni stayed locked together for a few minutes, sharing their loss. Finally, they broke apart.

Laney grabbed some tissues from the box on the counter, offering Yoni some.

Unashamed, he took a handful, wiping at his tear-stained face. "Do you know who did it?"

Laney shook her head. "The person who took the shot? No. But we know who the guy is that ordered the hit. His name's Amar Patel. He's a Fallen."

Yoni swore. "When are we going after him?"

"We don't have any idea where he is. But there's a mole in his group. The SIA agent is going to push him to see if he can find out where Amar is."

"SIA?" Yoni asked.

Laney explained about Agent Clark and the group's objectives.

"Well, great. Nothing more trustworthy than some men in black."

Laney gave a little laugh. "Well, so far they seem to be on the up and up." She pictured Amanda's face as she spoke about her brother. "And they have a good reason to do what they're doing."

Henry appeared in the doorway. He nodded at Yoni. "We have a problem."

Laney straightened away from the counter. "What?"

"Agent Clark just called. They've lost contact with Maddox."

Chapter Seventy-Nine

LANEY PACED the length of Henry's long office. Yoni ran a similar track against the windows. Henry and Jen sat waiting. Clark was supposed to call them to fill them in on what was going on.

The wait was killing her. If they'd lost Maddox, it would make tracking down Amar that much harder.

Amanda's face flashed through Laney's mind. *And Amanda will have lost her brother.*

Laney slammed her fist into her hand. *God damn it. Too many good people are getting killed. This can't go on.*

The screen above the conference table flashed to life. Clark's face appeared.

About time. Laney strode over to the table. "What's going on?"

Clark glanced across the room, his eyes settling on Yoni. "Perhaps we should speak in private."

Laney cut him off. "This is Yoni Benjamin. He's one of us. So what happened to Maddox?"

"After Amanda and I left you, I contacted Maddox. I

asked him to see if he could find out where Amar was. In the past, he's told me that there's some big compound where they meet. But he hadn't been trusted with that information." Clark fell silent.

"And?" Henry urged.

"Maddox got me the location."

Relief flowed over Laney. Finally, they had a target. "That's great. Where is it?"

"Tennessee, just outside Johnson City, on the border of North Carolina. I've sent you the coordinates."

"Great," Laney said. "So let's get started on an assault plan."

Clark nodded. "I've already started calling in my agents, getting the gear and transports ready. We should be good to go in about twelve hours."

"I'll start pulling my resources as well. We'll be ready," Henry said.

Laney glanced at the screen. For someone who had been tracking down Amar for years, Clark didn't exactly seem excited about finally catching him. "What about Maddox?"

"He missed his check-in."

"Has that happened before?"

"By a few minutes maybe."

"How long has it been?" Henry asked.

Fear splashed across Clark's face for just a moment, but Laney caught it. "Two hours."

Chapter Eighty

JOHNSON CITY, TENNESSEE

AMAR SAT in his throne chair, at the heavy wood table that dominated the darkened dining room. The rest of the chairs were empty. Amar took a last bite of his Cornish game hen and placed his silverware on the plate.

Wiping his hands on the linen napkin, he pushed back a little from the table, his hands on his stomach. "Well, that was delicious."

He glanced over his shoulder at the two men standing guard at the door. Unlike the guards at the barn, these two were his brethren. "After we're finished here, you boys should go get yourself something to eat."

The dark-haired one nodded at him. "Thank you, sir. We will."

Amar waved away the words. "Well, I suppose that's it for the pleasant portion of the evening. Let's bring in our guest."

The dark-haired guard nodded again before disappearing through the doorway with his blond companion.

Amar inspected the tapestry that hung on the wall to his

right. It was one of the *Unicorn Tapestries*: "The Unicorn in Captivity." Most of the tapestries hung in the Metropolitan Museum of Art. This one depicted the death of the legendary animal.

Amar liked to keep it around to remind him of the fragility of his own existence. And of the importance of loyalty among his followers.

There was shouting from the hall. The two guards reappeared in the doorway, a man in shackles held between them.

They shoved the man inside, and he sprawled across the floor, landing right next to Amar's chair.

Amar held out his hand and one of the guards handed him a phone. Amar brought up the text messages. He clicked on the most recent, turning it around so his captive could see it:

Shady Creek Farm, Johnson City, Tennessee.

Amar glanced down at the man's bruised face and watched as it healed. "Hello, Maddox. I hear you've been a bad boy."

Chapter Eighty-One

BALTIMORE, MARYLAND

LANEY CLOSED her phone and walked back down to her cottage. She stopped at a bench on the path—she needed to sit down for a minute. Her uncle had tried to sound strong when she spoke with him, but she knew Rocky's death had hit him hard.

But there was something else in his voice, something more. She knew him so well. There was something he wasn't telling her. She shook her head. She simply didn't have the energy to figure out what it could be right now.

That was the last phone call she had to make for the time being. She'd already spoken with Jake's brother Tom, Rocky's mom, and Rocky's partner, Detective Mike Chapman. All of them had been shocked and demanded answers. Answers she couldn't give them.

Rocky's and Jake's images swam through her mind for the umpteenth time. And with them came the familiar punch to the gut. *Too many people are dying.* Laney took a breath, stood, and continued down the path toward her cottage.

She knew Henry and Clark were off making plans for uniting their two forces. Jen had stepped out to call her brothers. And Yoni—well, Laney wasn't sure where Yoni had disappeared to. Laney had used everyone else's distractions to slip out on her own.

Once again, all those who had died since this insanity began flashed through her mind. A never-ending tide of death. She pictured the Shuar and all they had lost last year, Kati's husband, King Julian, Drew, Jake, Rocky.

Glancing at her ring, she blew out a breath. "And you and I are supposed to defeat all the super-powered bad guys."

Amanda's face appeared in her mind. But this time she pictured what Amanda would look like after hearing of her brother's death. Maddox had risked his life time and time again to save others. And they were going to wait twelve hours before trying to save him.

In her gut, Laney knew he wouldn't still be alive then. He'd be one more name on the list of people killed because of this insanity.

Slipping her hand into her pocket, she fingered the piece of paper with the location of Amar's group. It was a large farm on the outskirts of Johnson City, Tennessee.

From aerial photos, they knew it was a hundred and twenty-three acres, but it didn't have any noticeable security. Of course, seeing as it was populated by super-beings, they probably weren't too concerned about random burglars.

The ring on Laney's hand felt heavy. She lifted it, watched the sunlight glint off of it. She'd found the ring. She'd been through the trials. Her Father was Enoch. She was supposed to be able to use the damn thing. Why wasn't it working?

Maybe Henry was right. She didn't believe she was the one.

She shook her head. Whether she believed it or not, she had to figure out how to make it work or this whole thing was going to be a waste of time. She was supposed to lead the army of good.

She walked up the three steps to her porch. Her legs felt heavy. She sank into the porch swing. *The General of the good.* This couldn't be real. And how was she supposed to do this without Jake?

Helen had succeeded—but her trio had remained intact. Joan of Arc's trio had been broken and things hadn't ended so well for her. Was Laney's success also doomed? Were they all doomed?

Laney dropped her head into her hands. Was she going to lead everyone to the slaughter? How on earth were they going to take on an army of nephilim and Fallen? Even with a few super-beings on their side, they were grossly outnumbered.

The picture of Amanda and Maddox drifted through her mind. Laney knew Maddox was a grown man now, but all she could picture was the tall lanky kid with the big grin, his arms wrapped around his little sister.

She stood. She couldn't let him die while she sat around and did nothing. She wouldn't let one more person die.

Laney strode to the front door and opened it. She could hear the ping from her computer. Someone was trying to call her. Frowning, she made her way to the kitchen.

Turning on the computer, she clicked on the Face Time link.

A man of Indian descent, in what looked to be his late forties, appeared on screen. "Dr. McPhearson, I thought it was time we met, so to speak."

Laney went still. "Amar Patel."

Chapter Eighty-Two

ON SCREEN, Amar nodded at her. "Ah, good. This would have been very awkward if you didn't know who I was."

Laney pulled out one of the island chairs before her legs gave out. Samyaza was calling her. Whatever he wanted, it couldn't be good.

Fear charged through her but she kept her tone gruff. "What do you want?"

"Politeness really is a dead art, isn't it?"

Laney crossed her arms and stared at the screen, saying nothing.

"Very well. Straight to business. I know you have the ring."

Laney struggled to keep her face unmoved. "And?"

"And I want you to think about all the people you've lost so far. Including Jake and your friend Rocky. Not a very feminine name, but you people do seem fond of boyish names for girls in this age."

Hearing Jake's and Rocky's names come from that bastard's lips nearly undid her. She gripped the sides of her chair, narrowing her eyes. "And why do you want me to think about them?"

Amar gave a little laugh. "Oh, I'm sorry. I misspoke. What I meant is that I want you to think about all the people I'm still going to kill. Henry. Your friends, Jen and Kati. And what are those two boys' names? Ah, yes. Danny and Max."

Laney nearly growled. "I won't let you near them."

Amar smiled. "Now that's the spirit I'm looking for. You ring bearers always live up to your reputations. Helen, now she was my favorite."

"Really? Because I heard she killed you."

Laney's guess paid off. Amar's face darkened. "But I went on to live another day, didn't I? You know, I've really never understood all the animosity humans have shown us. After all, we gave you medicine, power. You were meaningless bits of walking carbon before we came along. No goals, just existing. We gave you purpose."

"Really? Because the way I hear it, humanity didn't need medicine before you came along. And people were living rather long, healthy lives until you showed up, sowing dissent."

Amar paused, giving Laney a calculating look. "Let me guess. You've been chatting with a certain purple-eyed witch?" He shook his head. "She's always sticking her nose in where it doesn't belong. And she hasn't even told you the whole story. Why don't you ask her about her part in humanity's downfall? Now *that* is a really interesting tale. But I digress. We were chatting about how I'm going to kill all the people you care about."

"Not going to happen."

"Good, good. Love the spirit. So I thought I'd offer you a deal."

"A deal?" Laney couldn't help but recall the stories of the devil offering deals to people. It never worked out in their favor—always in the devil's.

"Yes. How about we take everyone else out of the equation? We meet, mano-a-mano, as they say."

"Meet?"

Amar laughed. "I misspoke again. I meant fight to the death. Me versus you and that little ring of yours. We'll see who the most powerful actually is."

Laney stared at him. "When and where?"

Amar smiled. "Wonderful. I'll call you with the coordinates once I set it up. And I promise, you meet me and I let all your little friends live."

Laney heard the actual promise in those words: And I'll kill you.

"Deal." Laney clicked off the screen and pushed back her chair. She wasn't going to let anyone get killed, not if she could help it.

"You are not actually going along with that." Yoni stepped out from the living room.

Laney sighed. "I wondered where you'd gotten to." She walked over to the refrigerator and pulled out a bottle of water. She tilted one toward Yoni. "Want one?"

He ignored it. "Well?" Yoni demanded.

Laney unscrewed the cap, taking a drink. "No, of course I'm not going along with whatever his little plan is. I'm not actually suicidal. But if it keeps him content, so be it."

"So what are you planning?"

Laney looked at Yoni, taking in his eyes, still red from grief. "You're my friend, right?"

Yoni nodded. "I'm a little hurt you even have to ask."

"Sorry. But I need a favor. Can you get me a helicopter, without anyone knowing?"

"Yeah," Yoni drew out the word. "But why would I do that?"

"I'm going after Maddox."

Yoni shook his head. "Absolutely not. That's crazy. You can't take them on. I don't really get all this crazy talk about abilities and that ring, but I know you're outmatched. You need to bring Jen's brothers, Henry—hell, everyone."

Laney shook her head. "No. No one with any abilities. They can sense one another. I'm not letting anyone else get killed." She held up her ring. "Besides, I have my own weapon."

"Laney—"

She cut him off. "Please, Yoni. No one else is going to die. No one else is going to put their life on the line for me. It's my turn now."

Yoni looked at her for a long minute, then turned and headed to the front door. "Fine. I'll call you when I have it."

Laney ran after him and grabbed his arm. "You can't tell anyone, Yoni."

"Laney—"

"I mean it. If you tell anyone, I'll find a way to go on my own. I won't put anyone else at risk."

"God damn it, Laney. You're going to get yourself killed."

"Better me than anyone else. I die, this all goes away."

"No, Laney. I understand that much. You die and all this begins."

"Promise me, Yoni. For Jake. Promise me."

He didn't speak for a long moment and Laney worried she'd lost him. "Fine," he growled. "But I'm going with you." He turned on his heel and stormed down the hall.

"Of course." Laney called after him. The front door slammed shut after him.

No chance in hell, Yoni. Laney returned to the kitchen and sank back onto the stool.

"I wish you were here, Jake," she whispered.

Jake had always had faith in her, no matter what. And his strength gave her strength. Now she had to be strong on her own.

No. Not on her own. She had Jen, Henry, and all the others that would stand by her side in this fight. She imagined those she cared about going against the Fallen and getting torn apart. She wouldn't let that happen. She couldn't.

She stood up. It was time to do what she apparently was born to do.

She headed up the stairs. She just needed a few supplies first.

Chapter Eighty-Three

JOHNSON CITY, TENNESSEE

AMAR CLICKED off the computer with a smile. *Well, that was fun.*

"Was taunting her really necessary?" Gerard asked.

Amar's good mood dimmed. The blond wonder had stopped by for another surprise progress report. It was as if the man didn't understand how to use a phone.

"Necessary? Probably not. Fun? Absolutely."

"We are not doing this for your amusement, Amar. You were warned not to bait her."

Amar's eyes narrowed. "You do not need to remind me about the goal, Gerard. I am well aware." He shook off his resentment. "Besides, enjoying one's work makes for a happy life. Don't forget who told you about the next stage. Without me, you two would know nothing about——"

Gerard raised his hand. "Quiet. There are people everywhere."

Amar smiled. "So there are. But sometimes you guys seem to forget my role in all of this."

"We don't yet know what your role *is* in all of this."

"But I'm guessing it's pretty important—or you wouldn't be here, would you?"

Gerard sighed. "Fine." He gestured toward Amar's tablet. "But you've just incited her."

Amar gave a bitter laugh. "Hardly. She just lost two people close to her and she just got the ring. Even if she has time to practice with it, she's got to be off her game. And now she's even more rattled by the threats to the rest of those she holds dear."

"Was it wise, though, to bluff that way?"

Amar smiled slowly. "Who said I was bluffing?"

Chapter Eighty-Four

HENRY PLACED his phone down and closed his eyes. He'd arranged everything he could think of that they might need for the coming battle.

He had all his operatives on the move to him or to Tennessee, depending on where they were coming in from. Most would be ready to go within the hour, although Clark wanted them to hold off until he could get all his own people into play.

Henry stared at the clock. Six p.m. Time had flown.

The door opened and Jen walked in.

Tall, strong, she was an incredible woman. Henry felt energy flow into him at the sight of her. He knew that part of that was their nephilim connection. But there was something else there. Something, he hoped, he'd one day be able to act upon.

"How's Danny?" Henry asked.

"Eating. He pulled up the schematics for Shady Creek and then I sent him downstairs for some food. Kevin's with him," Jen said.

Henry nodded. Good. Ever since Jake's death, he hadn't wanted Danny to be alone. Jake had been like a big brother, and Danny was taking his death hard. "I spoke with Dom. After Danny's finished, he and Moxy will head over to his place and stay until everything's over. Kati and Max are already there."

Jen sat on the edge of Henry's desk. "He'll be okay, Henry."

"I don't know, Jen. He's been exposed to more violence in his short life than any kid should have to deal with."

Jen covered Henry's hand with hers. "As long as he has you, he'll be fine. So just make sure you come back."

A spark went through him at her touch. For a moment, time seemed to stop.

A knock at his door broke the spell. Jen jumped off the desk and Henry yanked his hand back.

Jen's twin brothers, Jordan and Mike Witt, walked in. Both were six feet tall with sun-highlighted blond hair. They were almost perfectly identical, right down to their matching expressions of grief.

One look at their faces and reality came crashing back. Both Jen and Henry hurried over to them.

Jen reached Mike first. She pulled him into a hug. "I'm so sorry, Mike."

Mike hugged her back, a shudder running through him.

Henry walked up to Jordan, extended his hand and then pulled him into a hug.

After a few seconds, Jordan pulled back. "How are you doing?"

Henry sighed. "Honestly? It doesn't seem real yet. I keep waiting for Jake to walk in the door or call me. I don't know when it will sink in."

Mike nodded. "How about Laney? How's she holding up?"

"She's hurting, but she's trying to hide it, doing what needs to be done," Henry said. "You know how she is."

"Where is she?" Jordan asked.

"I don't know." Henry pulled out his phone, concerned. Actually, he hadn't seen her since the meeting with Clark. He dialed Laney's number, but it went straight to voicemail. "Jen, do you know where she is?"

Jen shook her head. "I haven't seen her since the conference call with Clark."

"Maybe she just needs a little alone time," Jordan offered.

"Maybe," Henry said, but he didn't think so.

Tendrils of doom crawled over him. When he'd first met Laney, she'd risked her life to save both those she cared about and complete strangers.

And he knew the death toll was getting to her. And then Amanda had elicited that promise from her.

Henry's head popped up. *No. She couldn't have.*

He strode across his room, reached for the phone on his desk, and punched the button for security.

"Henry?" Jen followed him over.

He shook his head as security answered. "Sean, have you seen Laney recently?"

"No, sir."

"Has anybody left the estate?"

"Only Yoni. He took off about two hours ago."

Chapter Eighty-Five

JOHNSON CITY, TENNESSEE

YONI HAD BEEN as good as his word. He'd gotten the chopper and flown him and Laney down to Tennessee. When they'd driven out of the Chandler Group's property, Laney kept waiting for a radio call to show that the alarm had sounded. But all had been quiet.

Yoni had arranged to rent a chopper a few miles from the estate. Laney held her breath until they were in the air, expecting someone to stop them. No one did.

But the whole flight, he'd tried to talk Laney out of her plan. She was resolute, though. This was ending tonight— one way or another.

Once they neared the Tennessee border, Laney directed Yoni to a field in the middle of nowhere just a few miles inside the state line.

Yoni landed the chopper and then shut it down.

He turned to Laney. "Are you sure about this?"

"No one else is getting hurt, Yoni. This is my fight."

"Yeah, yours and mine," he grumbled. "You keep forgetting that part."

Laney saw the car she'd arranged sitting only fifty feet away. "Right. Yours and mine."

As Yoni got out of the chopper, Laney pulled the syringe out of her pocket. She pulled off its cap, pressing the plunger slightly to release any air. She tried to still the shaking in her hands.

Laney quietly got out. *It's to keep him safe*, she reminded herself as she rounded the back of the chopper.

Heart hammering, she walked up behind Yoni, who was pulling a pack out of the back of the chopper. Before she could have second thoughts, Laney plunged the syringe into Yoni's neck.

Yoni yanked it out before she could empty all of its contents. But it was enough. His eyelids started to droop. "Laney, why?"

Laney wrapped her arms around him, stumbling under his weight. She lowered him to the ground. "I'm sorry, Yoni. But I won't let anyone else get hurt. And that includes you."

She checked his pulse. Strong. She patted down his jacket and found his cell phone. She pulled it out, removed the battery, and threw it as far as she could.

Climbing back into the chopper, she looked at the radio. *Okay, how do I disable this thing?*

Shaking her head, she finally pulled some pliers from her pack and snipped off a couple of wires.

Laney pocketed the keys, grabbed her pack, and hopped out.

With only a quick glance at Yoni, who still lay peacefully on the ground, Laney ran for the car. The keys were hidden in the wheel well, as she had arranged. She drove off before she could change her mind.

A stab of guilt pierced her as she caught sight of Yoni's crumpled body in the rearview mirror. She looked away, clenching the steering wheel, hardening her resolve. *No one else is getting killed.* Her eyes narrowed. *Except Samyaza.*

Forty minutes later, Laney drove down a quiet country road. It hadn't taken her as long as she'd feared to reach the estate.

She pulled over to the shoulder and turned the engine off. She pulled her iPad from the passenger seat and brought up the aerial view of the farm Clark had sent them.

There were only three structures on the property: a farmhouse, a barn, and a utility shed. The utility shed was set farther back on the property, but the barn and farmhouse looked like they were both about a mile from her current location.

Although "farmhouse" was probably the wrong word for the home. Laney had pulled up some photos from when the house had been on the market a few years before. The house was a good ten thousand square feet, and it was decorated to the nines. This was not a Ma and Pa Kettle farm. The place even had a ballroom, for God's sake.

The extravagance of the place reminded her of Gideon. She shook her head. *These Fallen sure like the good things in life.*

Laney zoomed in to get a better view of the land. The whole property was pretty densely covered with trees, but about a quarter of a mile from the house, all coverage stopped. They'd cleared the whole area except for a few artfully placed bushes in front of the house.

She zoomed in to the side of the house. It looked like the trees were a little closer there. That would be her way in.

Laney wasn't sure where Maddox would be held. To be honest, she wasn't even sure he was here. All she knew was that she had to try and find him. She needed one mark in the win column.

Laney shoved the iPad under the seat, grabbed her pack, and pulled out her Beretta. She checked the magazine. Full.

And this time she'd loaded it with hollow points. She needed as much stopping power as she could get.

She filled her pockets with extra ammo and a small remote, then zipped them shut. A pair of night vision goggles, on a strap around her neck, and she was ready to go.

She stepped out of the car and rubbed her arms. The body armor felt strange. Jake had bought her the suit a month ago.

At the time, she'd thought he was nuts, but now it gave her comfort. He was always looking after her, even now.

Rubbing her ring, Laney set off on foot.

She jogged at the edge of the road for a half-mile. No cars went by.

At the half-mile mark, she moved into the trees. Although the moon was bright, the trees blocked out almost all of its light. She put on the night vision goggles and immediately the night turned green.

Up ahead, she could see the fence for the property. It was a rancher's fence, just two horizontal posts between vertical ones every six feet or so. She could slip through easily.

But she waited, inspecting the posts and the trees around them. *There.* Up in one of the tall oaks, she could just make out the green light of a security camera.

Laney scrounged in her pack and pulled out a remote. Aiming it at the camera, she pushed a small button. The light dimmed and disappeared.

Laney smiled. Danny's little invention. A small, directed electro-magnetic pulse. If Danny was right, and he normally was, she had just taken out their security cameras but left the rest of their electricity up and running. Hopefully, she had bought herself enough time to get in, find Maddox, and get out.

Laney took a step forward, feeling more than a little confident. So far, everything was going according to plan.

A hand slipped over her mouth. "Don't make a sound."

Chapter Eighty-Six

AMAR WATCHED his two best fighters move in on Maddox. He'd decided to have a cage match, in Titus's old cage. He thought it would be entertaining.

Cleo hissed as a man flew into one of the metal rods of the cage. Amar rolled his eyes. *Oh, for God's sake.*

Maddox laughed, swiping his long hair from his eyes. "This the best you got, Amar? Tsk, tsk."

The other combatant ran at Maddox, landing a lucky punch on his ribs before circling out.

Maddox looked at the man with a grin, blood seeping between his teeth, one eye swollen shut but healing. "That all you got? My grandma hits harder."

"Oh, I got more." The man across from him raised his fist.

"Enough." Amar pushed himself from his chair. "Pick up Smith."

The man in the cage walked over to Smith, who was lying in an unconscious heap in the corner.

Amar shook his head. He'd sent two of his men into the

cage to take care of Maddox. It should have taken only a few minutes to finish off the nephilim.

And it was supposed to have been a nice stress reliever after Gerard's visit. The man had left a few minutes earlier, and Amar had kept Maddox hidden until then. He didn't need Gerard's probing questions.

But instead of watching his men wipe the floor with Maddox, he'd watched Maddox wipe the floor with both of them. Amar glared at his men. They were supposed to be two of his best fighters. How the hell was this possible?

Amar studied Maddox. The man was tall, standing around six foot six, with dark brown hair brushing his shoulders and almost-matching brown eyes.

But there was a savagery that surrounded him. He didn't just look intimidating. The air around him felt intimidating.

He was the opposite of Gerard, Amar realized. Whereas the layer of steel in Gerard was covered with a fine polish, Maddox was all primitive predator. He didn't even try to hide who he was. What he was.

If Amar could turn him, Maddox would be an incredible asset to his operation. The man was one hell of a fighter. He'd even killed his own sister to escape the—

Amar stopped in mid-thought. He strode up to the cage. "Amanda. That was your sister's name, wasn't it? Tell me, Maddox. How did you kill her again?"

Maddox spit out a mouthful of blood and said nothing.

"Broke her neck, if I recall," Amar said. "But now I'm beginning to wonder. Maybe I need to start a search for your little sis."

The change was slight, just a tightening of the jaw. But Amar caught it. He smiled wide. "So, she is alive and well.

I'll be sure to take care of that as soon as I finish some other business."

Amar turned to the three other men who'd come in with him. "Fit him with a collar."

"Sir?"

"A collar." Amar's voice whipped out, pointing at the collar hanging over Titus's now-empty cage. The collars kept the beasts from roaming past the boundaries of the property during the hunts.

Amar smiled. "I think it's time for another little hunt."

Chapter Eighty-Seven

AS SOON AS the man's hand slipped over Laney's mouth, Laney grabbed his arm, trapping it. Then she dropped to her knee and rolled her shoulder and hip forward, almost as if she were going to do a forward roll. The man flew right over her, landing on his back.

Laney drove forward with her knee, ready to make sure the man never had the option of reproducing, when he let out a strangled cry. "Aw crap, Laney."

Laney stopped. "Yoni? What the hell are you doing here?"

Yoni rolled onto his knees. "Apparently I'm getting my ass kicked."

"Sorry. Sorry." She helped him up. *Shit.* Apparently Yoni had needed the whole syringe to stay down. "How did you get here?"

"I put a tracker in your pack. And then I stole a car from some kid when you abandoned me. I'm not feeling real good about that part, by the way."

Laney groaned. She'd taken the battery out of her

phone and disconnected the GPS on the car. She hadn't thought to look for another tracker.

He nodded. "Yeah. I know you."

"Did you tell anyone else where I was?"

"Not yet. While I took a nap, someone stole my phone and disabled the radio in the helicopter. I would have stopped and made a call but I was pretty sure you were trying to get yourself killed. So I headed here instead."

She breathed a sigh of relief. "Great. Now it's time for you to go." She pushed at his shoulder. She might as well have been pushing an oak tree. He didn't even sway.

"No. I told you before, I'm going with you. I know what you're up to. If you're going after that guy Maddox, then so am I."

"No. I'm going alone."

"Yeah, well: alone plus one."

"No, Yoni. No way."

Yoni didn't budge. "Jake was my best friend. And he loved you. If he was alive, he'd be right here, where I am. And seeing as he can't be here, it's my job to be here."

Laney's heart broke. "No, Yoni. If anything were to happen to you... You have a son. Think about him."

"I am. I'm thinking about the world he's going to grow up in if these guys succeed. I'm thinking about the man he's going to become. It's my job to set an example. You don't let your friends face danger alone. So, I'm coming, Laney, or I tell everyone where you are. Your choice."

Laney stared at him. She knew he wasn't bluffing. "Okay. But don't you dare get yourself killed."

Yoni saluted. "You got it, boss. So what's the plan?"

Laney glanced over at him. "The farmhouse and barn are up ahead. Maddox is probably in one of them."

Yoni grabbed her arm. "Probably? As in maybe?"

"Yoni, you can leave at any time."

He put up his hands. "No, hey, this is great. We'll just walk up, face an unknown number of super-powered humans who each take a magazine to the heart to kill, and hopefully find the guy we're looking for. It's great. I hate plans that get bogged down in too many details."

Chapter Eighty-Eight

LANEY WALKED QUIETLY through the trees. Yoni was to her right, about six feet away. He moved soundlessly.

Laney had seen Yoni in soldier mode before. And although she had planned on making this little trip solo, she had to admit that she was glad he was here.

Yoni put up his hand.

Laney stopped and lowered herself to the ground. Together they crawled toward a large dense yew bush.

Laney looked over at Yoni, but he had a finger to his lips. He pointed ahead and to their right.

Laney strained to hear. Then the sound of a gunshot cut through the night.

Yoni grabbed Laney's arm. She knew he was getting ready for them to run.

She hunkered down, shaking her head. "Listen," she whispered.

Branches snapped from the direction of the gun blast. A wind blew toward them, and Laney could just make out the blur as it raced up the tree across from them.

Laney's heart began to gallop. Only a Fallen or nephilim could move that fast. Two more blurs moved into the clearing underneath the tree, pursuing, searching.

She knew the Fallen could sense one another, so the men in the clearing knew their quarry was nearby. But they might not know that she and Yoni were as well.

Laney wasn't sure what was going on. She didn't know if she should help somebody or just let them all just kill one another. So for the moment, she stayed silent.

The man in the tree leapt down, landing on one of the men. The movement was fast, but not so fast that Laney didn't catch a glimpse of his face in the moonlight. *Maddox?*

The man Maddox landed on let out a yell, and his partner turned.

But Maddox was faster. He pulled the first man up from the ground and used him as a shield. Bullets immediately dotted the man's torso.

Laney leapt to her feet and lit up his partner. The man collapsed to the ground.

Maddox's head whipped around toward her.

Laney moved from behind her cover, careful to keep from pointing her gun at Maddox. "Maddox, I'm with the SIA. I'm here to get you out."

From the corner of her eye, she noticed Yoni getting to his feet, keeping his weapon trained on Maddox. Apparently he wasn't yet convinced that Maddox was a good guy.

"You're human," Maddox said.

Laney nodded and then stopped. She shrugged. "Sort of. I've met your sister."

She reached the man whom she'd shot. His wounds were already beginning to heal. Laney pressed the muzzle of her weapon against his chest and pulled the trigger twice. The man's chest exploded in a burst of blood. Satisfied that his heart was now beyond repair, Laney stepped back.

Maddox watched her with a bemused expression on his face. "And who exactly are you?"

"My name's Delaney McPhearson."

Maddox jolted, but then the man he was holding began to stir. "Excuse me a sec."

He reached down, picked up the man's weapon, shot him point blank in the heart four times, then let him drop. He turned back to Laney. "I've heard a lot about you."

"Good things?" she asked.

"Well, that depends on the source. According to Amar, you're the end of us all. According to Clark, you're the savior."

Yoni interrupted. "Any chance we can save the meet-and-greet for later? We need to move."

Maddox raised an eyebrow.

"Yoni Benjamin, former Navy SEAL, current Chandler Group operative. All-around badass," Laney said.

Yoni nodded. "The woman don't lie."

"Come on, time to get you out of here," Laney said.

Maddox shook his head, pointing at his neck. "'Fraid not. This little thing will kill me if I step off the property."

Laney stepped closer, noticing for the first time the collar padlocked around his neck.

"Is that a dog collar?" Yoni asked.

"Technically it's a cat collar, but regardless, I need to get it off," Maddox said.

"Pretty big cat," Yoni mumbled.

"Okay, so where's the key?" Laney asked.

"Back in the barn." Maddox nodded his head in the direction from which he'd come.

"Of course it is," Laney muttered.

Chapter Eighty-Nine

OUTSIDE JOHNSON CITY, TENNESSEE

HENRY YELLED INTO THE PHONE. "How long?"

He was sitting in the copilot seat of the quiet, stealth-modified helicopter. He'd purchased it a few years ago, in case it was ever needed on one of the Chandler Group's projects in more contentious areas. He'd never imagined he'd be using it in the States.

Henry could tell Clark, who was on the other end of the line, didn't have such a fancy toy available. The agent was yelling into the phone to be heard above the noise of his own chopper. "Ten minutes away. We'll meet you outside the northwest gate."

"No. Laney's sure to be on the property by now. We're landing inside."

"Henry, that's suicide. We don't know how many men are in there. And you don't know she's there."

Henry pictured Laney's face as she realized that both Jake and Rocky were dead; her look of concern when she heard that Maddox was missing. He knew her. She was taking this risk to avoid anyone else getting hurt. She was inside the estate. He had no doubts.

"She's there. I'm willing to stake my life on it."

"You *are* staking your life on it. They'll see and hear us way before we can get close."

"Not me. They won't know I'm coming. My team and I will rappel in and create a landing zone for the rest of you."

Henry knew Clark was thinking of the dangers. Henry pressed his case. "It's Laney. You're the one who keeps saying she's the most important person in this mess. If we wait, we could be too late."

Clark's sigh was barely audible, but Henry caught it. "All right. How long until you're in place?"

Henry glanced at his watch. "Seven minutes."

"We'll be right behind you." Clark disconnected the call.

Henry put down the radio and glanced over his shoulder. The Witt siblings looked back at him, waiting. "We're going in as soon as we get there."

"We'll be ready," Jen said.

Henry nodded, taking in the head-to-toe body armor they each wore, the high-powered weapons in their hands. Mike and Jordan had been trained for this. But Jen? She was born for this.

He felt a flicker of hope. They'd get to Laney before it was too late.

Henry glanced behind him. Kevin Chang was in the second chopper, and had another three guys with him. He knew Clark had at least that many, maybe even a few more. And there were more still, speeding toward the area by air and by car.

"It'll be enough," Henry muttered as he turned his eyes forward again. *It has to be.*

Chapter Ninety

LANEY RAN through the trees behind Maddox. She could make out lights ahead, and as they moved closer, she saw the outline of the barn.

Maddox stopped at the edge of the trees.

Laney glanced up at him. "Maddox, do you feel anyone near?"

Maddox nodded. "Yes, but I don't think they're in the barn. The house, maybe the trees. But I can't tell about the Fallen."

"Well, I guess that's as good an assurance as we're going to get," Laney said.

Yoni slipped back to join them. He'd disappeared to do a little reconnaissance on his own. "I didn't see anyone. There's a tree over there that will give me a bird's-eye view. I should be able to cover you from there, at least as you cross the open space. Give me two minutes to get into position."

Laney nodded. "Okay."

Yoni disappeared. She and Maddox waited. Laney

counted down the seconds. At two minutes, she tapped Maddox. "Let's go."

Maddox sprinted across the open space. Laney could barely see him in the shadows. The night vision goggles were no use here, not with all the light; they would just blind her.

The barn door opened up ahead, and a shaft of light spilled into the yard. Laney sprinted for it, slipped through the door, and closed it behind her.

It took a moment for her eyes to adjust. Giant cages covered the space. But the area was completely wide open.

Laney felt exposed, vulnerable. She raised her gun, straining to hear any noise. She heard a scuffle to her right, and Maddox appeared from a doorway, holding up his hand. "Found it."

Laney rushed over. "Any problems?"

"No, the place is empty. I think they may be out looking for me."

Laney took the key from him, and Maddox turned around and kneeled so Laney could reach his neck. The guy was seriously tall.

One quick twist, and the lock clicked. Laney pulled the padlock off.

Maddox undid the collar. "Thanks."

"No problem. Now let's go."

Without a word, Maddox headed back for the large barn door. He flattened himself against it, listening for any noise outside.

Laney did the same, and as she did, her gaze roamed over the cages again. "What are the cages for?"

Maddox went still, his eyes darting back to the cages. "I can't believe I didn't notice."

Laney's voice was serious. "Maddox, what was in here?"

"Her name's Cleo. And I'm guessing she's out there, looking for me." He looked down at Laney. "And I'm guessing she's looking for you, too."

Chapter Ninety-One

THE CHOPPER FLEW through the night air, barely making a sound. In the back, Jordan and Mike attached themselves to ropes, ready to rappel down. Henry and Jen didn't have ropes. They wouldn't need any.

Henry looked everyone over. "Everyone good to go?"

They nodded.

Henry's eyes stayed on Jen.

She nodded again. "I'm ready. Let's do this."

Henry spoke into the radio. "Kevin, you good to go?"

"Affirmative. Ready to jump," came the reply.

"Follow us in," Henry said before ringing off.

The pilot skimmed the tree line, speeding to the south-west corner of the property. From the satellite image, he knew there was a good-sized clearing there where Clark could land his choppers.

"Thirty seconds," the pilot warned.

Henry nodded, looking out the open door to the ground below.

The pilot flew over a tall oak and the clearing appeared below them. He hovered in place. "Go!"

Henry didn't pause. He jumped from the helicopter, rolling when his feet touched the ground. He sprang back up, his weapon raised.

Jen was already on her feet. With her eyes glued to the trees, she covered her brother's descent. The Witt brothers disengaged themselves from their ropes and ran to set up a perimeter to cover the other chopper.

Henry strained to hear if there was anyone nearby, but all he could hear were the SIA choppers inbound.

"Henry!" Jen pulled her weapon to her shoulder and let off a burst into the trees. Henry felt a tingle along his skin. A nephilim was nearby, and it wasn't Jen.

Returning gunfire came from the trees.

"Take cover!" Henry yelled as he sprinted for the tree line.

Jen reached it just ahead of him. "Let's flank them," she said.

Henry nodded, and was moving into place when the gunfire cut off. With a quick glance at Jen, he ran to the sniper's nest, where he came to an abrupt halt.

Jordan was already there, a shooter at his feet. Jordan emptied his magazine into the man's chest. Michael had already taken a knife to the other shooter's heart.

Henry looked at them, dumbfounded, "How——?"

Jordan smiled. "You guys have a weakness. You're so focused on using your radar to figure out where the threat is, you forget that we humans can just sneak up on you."

Chapter Ninety-Two

LANEY SPRINTED through the trees toward the edge of the property, Yoni next to her and Maddox just ahead. She stopped short when she heard the gunfight.

"Henry. It has to be Henry." She looked at Maddox. "Go to them."

Maddox shook his head. "I'm not leaving you here."

Laney grabbed his sleeve. "Listen to me. Our guys need to know we're here. They need to know how many men there are, what the layout is. They need to know you're safe. You can tell them all that. And you can run a hell of a lot faster than we can. We may be able to get out of here without getting into much of a fight. So go. Tell them."

Maddox handed his weapon to Yoni, but his eyes stayed on Laney. "Once I reach them, I'm coming back for you."

Laney nodded. "We're counting on it. Now go."

Maddox disappeared into the night.

Yoni nudged Laney. "We need to move."

As she followed him into the dark, the roar of a giant cat cut through the air.

"What the hell was that?" Yoni asked.

Trembling at the sound, Laney pictured the giant cages in the barn. "I'm guessing that's Cleo."

As quietly as they could, they made their way through the underbrush. Up ahead, Laney could see where she'd cut through the trees on her way in.

She tapped Yoni on the shoulder. "We came in through there."

Yoni nodded, moving forward.

Laney jumped as another screech from the cat pierced the night air. It was closer this time.

"What kind of cat do you think that is?" Laney asked.

"Big," Yoni said, putting up a hand to stop her. Ahead of them was open space for about fifty feet. Yoni looked around, pausing to listen. Laney did the same. There didn't seem to be anyone around.

Yoni grabbed Laney's hand. "Let's go."

Together they sprinted into the clearing, their feet pounding the ground. The cover of the trees was only thirty feet away.

To Laney's right, the shadows moved, and fear lanced through her. She flashed her light across the shadow—and saw the cat for the first time.

It was a black leopard on steroids, full of fury.

And it was leaping right for her.

Chapter Ninety-Three

AMAR STOMPED UP THE STAIRS. He had wanted to be part of the hunt for Maddox. Maddox would be a truly worthy opponent.

Instead he stripped off his metal claws, flinging them on a side table as he passed. *Damned responsibilities.*

He climbed the stairway to his project hub. Only his translator was working there tonight; all the other humans had been sent home while the rest of his brethren gathered in the ballroom downstairs. They were making plans for the next stage—and for what to do about Delaney McPhearson.

Amar smiled. He knew *exactly* what he wanted to do with her.

He pushed open the door to the workroom. "This better be important, Jeff."

"It is, sir. It is." Jeff thrust a printout into Amar's hands.

Amar glanced down at the stack of papers. It was easily ten pages, single-spaced with very little white space.

He eyed Jeff, who still had remnants of dinner, or

maybe lunch, on his tie. Probably both. "How about you summarize so I can get back to my plans?"

"Uh, yes sir. Um." Jeff mopped his brow with the bottom of his shirt. "This is the last of the translation." He paused.

Amar circled his hand in the air. "And?"

"And that term you were looking for. It's there."

"The root race?"

"Yes."

Amar scanned the pages quickly. "Does it mention anything about the fifth root race?"

"Um, yes, page eight, at the bottom."

Amar quickly pulled out page eight, scanning it. *Finally.* Then his eyes narrowed and he looked up. "Has anyone else seen this?"

Jeff wouldn't meet his eyes. "No, sir. You said for your eyes only."

Amar stepped forward, crowding Jeff into the table. He could smell the man's sweat. "You're lying."

Jeff swallowed. "He said I had to. Said he was your boss."

"Who said?"

"Mr. Thompson."

Gerard. Of course. "And has he seen these translations?"

"Uh, yes, yes sir. I sent them to him right before I called you."

Amar trailed his fingers along the table. "You sent him the results *before* contacting me?"

Jeff's breaths came out in pants, and Amar was pretty sure the man was only a few seconds from a full-blown panic attack. "Um, I thought, I mean he said—"

Amar put his arm around Jeff's shoulder. "No worries,

my friend. You've done good work here. And now everything's been translated?"

Jeff nodded. "Yes. That's everything."

"Excellent." Amar slipped his arm around Jeff's neck and pulled tight. He used his other arm to lock the chokehold in place.

Jeff thrashed, grabbing at Amar's arm, his eyes wide.

Amar ignored his futile gestures, pulling his arms tighter. Soon, Jeff stopped moving. Amar held on a little longer to make sure the man was dead and not merely unconscious.

Finally satisfied, he let the man drop. Jeff hit the floor and rolled onto his side.

Amar turned and headed for the door. *Gerard knows. I need to move quickly.*

In the distance, he heard gunshots and smiled. Well, at least the Maddox problem was being handled. He wanted to go join the fun.

But there were plans to be made. Very important ones.

Chapter Ninety-Four

YONI EMPTIED his gun at the giant cat. It dodged out of the way. With an angry roar, it leapt again, swiping at Yoni.

Laney shoved Yoni to the ground, rolling him away. The giant cat landed silently on its feet precisely where Yoni had just been standing. It turned slowly toward them both.

Laney stared back at it, terrified. The cat was black, but somehow it had spots, like a leopard's, that were even darker than black. Yet it was bigger than any leopard she'd ever seen. It must have been at least eight feet from the tip of its nose to the end of its tail. And it stood almost five feet at the shoulders.

The giant cat stared at them and licked its lips.

"Oh my God," Yoni whispered. "Don't move, Laney."

Laney didn't think she could move even if she wanted to. She was literally scared stiff.

There was a rustling from behind the cat. Two men appeared, weapons in hand. The cat let out a roar.

"Shit!" one of the men yelled before they both opened fire.

The cat leapt out of the way with a feline grace. Laney and Yoni rolled to avoid getting shot.

"Move, Laney," Yoni yelled as he pushed her toward the trees.

Laney army-crawled as fast as her limbs would allow. Behind her, the cat howled in fury, and a man screamed.

Laney got to her feet, trembling, and sprinted into the trees. She could hear Yoni right behind her.

As fast as she dared, Laney raced through the trees. She struggled to hear if they were being pursued. But she couldn't hear anything over the pounding of her own heart.

Just ahead, the path split in two. Which way?

Yoni pushed her to the right.

Laney urged her legs to move faster down the path that cut through the trees. As she ran, she noticed the ground on either side of the path seemed to rise.

Forty yards farther down the path, and the ground on either side was above their heads. Her dread increased with each footfall. *Oh no. No, no.*

Up ahead, a structure loomed. Motion-sensor lights flashed on.

Laney tried to slow down, but still she slammed into it. The utility shed. The building was twenty feet tall, its sides sheer. There was no way to scale it.

She looked at the ground that loomed above them on either side. They might be able to pull themselves up the trees and bush.

"Laney, let's go." Yoni grabbed a tree to their right.

An ear-piercing screech made them both go still.

Slowly, Laney looked behind them. The cat stood only thirty feet away. It prowled along the edge of the lights, its hackles raised.

"You got any bullets left?" Yoni asked, quietly.

Laney shook her head. She had some in her pack, but she was pretty sure the cat wasn't going to let her reload. "No. I'm out. You?"

"No."

Laney rubbed the ring on her finger. "Yoni, get behind me."

"No chance."

"I'm not asking."

"Laney, what the hell do you think you're going to do?"

Laney realized that no one had explained to Yoni about the ring. He didn't know what she was supposed to be able to do.

She glanced down at the metal object. Of course, she hadn't actually been able to do anything yet. She shoved those doubts aside.

"I was thinking I might try to talk to it," Laney said.

"You're kidding, right?"

"Yoni, get behind me." Something in her tone must have gotten through, because Yoni stepped back.

"Everyone's gone crazy," he grumbled. "Henry thinks he's a superhero, and you think you're Dr. Doolittle."

Laney ignored his mutterings, focusing instead on the beast moving carefully toward them. The cat knew it had them trapped.

Yoni stopped beside her. "This is as far as I'm going. I'm not sure what you think that little ring is going to do, but it's not even shiny enough to blind that thing."

"Yeah, well I'm planning on trying something else. Now, get—behind—me."

With a growl, Yoni did. "You get yourself killed and I'm going to be really mad at you."

The leopard roared. Laney's heart skipped a beat.

The hair on Laney's arms stood straight up. She could barely see the black shape as it slunk toward them.

It crossed through a ray of moonlight and Laney's breath hitched. It really was a beast out of someone's nightmare.

"Do you see that thing?" Yoni asked, his voice shaking.

Laney had never heard Yoni sound afraid before. She really wished she didn't hear it now.

The leopard padded closer. It was now only twenty feet away.

"If you're going to do something, now would be the time," Yoni urged.

Laney swallowed. "Stop," she commanded, but even to her own ears the word sounded weak.

The leopard stalked closer.

Laney pictured Jake. She pictured Rocky. She pictured Amar getting away with their murders. Anger welled in her. *Not going to happen.*

"Stop."

Laney's voice rang with authority, with power. She barely recognized it as hers.

The leopard paused, her ears twitching. Laney stared into the animal's eyes, not really sure how this was supposed to work. *You don't want to hurt us. We're on the same side.*

The leopard moved closer until it was only a foot away. It sniffed at Laney—and then rubbed its head against her chest with a loud purr.

Tentatively Laney reached down and rubbed the cat's head. More purring.

Laney let out a breath. "You're just a big sweetheart, aren't you?"

Yoni gave a nervous laugh. "Okay Doc, now how about

we take your new pet and go get the rest of our guys? Oh, and maybe on the way, we can stop for a clean pair of shorts for me."

Chapter Ninety-Five

LANEY RAN THROUGH THE TREES. Yoni ran on one side of her, the leopard on the other.

She didn't know how to explain how she felt. It was as if every day of her life, every trial and tribulation she'd endured, was so that she could have this moment. So she could accept who she was.

Yoni's eyes strayed time and again to Cleo. He hadn't asked how Laney had managed to control the leopard, but he obviously wasn't convinced that the control was complete. He glanced over at Laney. "When we reach the mansion, we'll link up with Henry. We're not doing anything until we have more weapons."

Laney grinned. "That's where you're wrong. I have the ultimate weapon."

Yoni glanced over at the leopard again, but Laney didn't correct his assumption. As they ran, she'd been testing her abilities with the ring, reaching out farther and farther with her mind, feeling the animals nearby, feeling the weather, and knowing where the Fallen were.

No one had mentioned that power of the ring. She knew where they were. She could feel all the Fallen, all the nephilim within a mile.

And it was time to bring the fight to them.

Up ahead, Laney could make out the house. She stopped at the edge of the trees. Two armed men stood at the front door, but they didn't hear them approach. The men were humans. Laney glanced over her shoulder, and wasn't surprised when Henry, Jen, and Clark appeared.

Cleo gave a growl from deep in her throat—bringing the three super-humans to a stop.

Laney looked over at Cleo. *They're friends.*

Cleo's growls cut off immediately.

Laney looked at the three behind her. "It's okay. She's with me."

Henry looked between Laney and the giant cat. "Um, I guess this means you figured out how to get the ring to work?"

She nodded before turning back to watch the house. "It's time to finish this." She glanced at Clark. "Did Maddox find you?"

"He's gathering up strays." Clark stepped next to her. "What's the plan?"

Laney gestured to the cat with her chin. "Cleo and I are going in first. I need you guys to take out the guys on the porch, with silencers if you've got them, and then follow me in. I'd like a thirty-second head start."

"No way," Yoni argued.

"How many are in there?" Clark asked.

"Fallen and nephilim? About a dozen. They're all in one room. I'm guessing it's some kind of briefing."

"How do you know that?" Jen asked.

It was hard to explain. It was just a knowledge—one

that she had complete confidence in. She shrugged. "I don't know. I can feel them. I know exactly where they are."

Yoni looked at Henry. "You can't possibly be on board with this."

Henry looked at Laney for a long moment. "Actually, I am. Thirty seconds. No more."

Laney nodded, visions of Jake and Rocky in her mind. She rubbed the ring. She was going to make Amar regret coming after her friends.

Chapter Ninety-Six

WITH CLEO AT HER SIDE, Laney climbed the steps, barely glancing at the two downed guards. After Yoni and Clark had taken the two men out, Henry had had to hold Yoni back from going in with Laney.

Laney didn't let herself feel bad. She'd explain everything to Yoni later.

Right now, she needed to end this.

As she opened the door, she let the anger build, feeling the rage course through her. She walked down the hall, almost able to *see* her rage expand out from her. Even Cleo seemed to sense it, letting out a little whimper, but staying with her nonetheless.

Up ahead, the doors to the ballroom were closed. Laney narrowed her eyes and focused her energy on them. A gust of wind tore through the windows near the entrance. It crashed into the doors and blew them into the room.

Laney strode through the destroyed entrance.

Amar was at the front of the room, a comically shocked look on his face.

A man charged Laney from the right. She watched him out of the corner of her eye.

Laney's voice was calm, steady. "Shoot yourself in the heart."

The man placed his gun to his chest and pulled the trigger.

Another two Fallen ran at her from the other side of the room. Cleo leapt on one as he drew near.

Laney stared down the other one. "Stab yourself in the heart. A lot."

The man did, falling to the floor. A pool of blood grew around him.

Ahead, Laney saw Amar. For a moment he looked startled, then he covered it with a smirk. Ten of his Fallen surrounded him, and another ten humans as well. "You can only control us one at a time. You'll never get us all."

Laney's eyes flicked over Amar's group before returning to him. "I'm not trying to get you all. I'm only going to get you."

Laney heard the footsteps behind her. Moments later, Henry and Jen sprinted into the room and took positions at her side; Maddox came up right behind Laney, Clark at his side.

Slowly the room began to fill with more men from the government and from the Chandler group. The leopard let out a roar, prowling in front of Laney.

Amar's smile began to disappear. "You can't win."

"Yes, I can." Laney's eyes darted to the glass bordering the room. The windows shattered as gusts of wind tore through them, showering Amar and his minions.

"Take them," Laney ordered, leaping forward.

Gun blasts burst out. Fallen and humans alike leapt from their positions, clashing with Laney and her group.

Henry and Jen each took one Fallen, grappling with them hand to hand.

The SIA agents paired up to take down other Fallen, one aiming for the head to slow them down and the other aiming for the chest to finish them. Jordan and Mike followed the same approach.

The leopard took a graceful leap, landing on one of the Fallen. She raked a giant claw down his body and opened the man from chin to groin.

Laney ignored all of it. Her focus was only on Amar. Like a coward, he ran out the door in the back as soon as the fighting began. As Laney pursued, two humans tried to block her path. Without a thought, she shot them each in the head. They'd chosen the wrong side.

Laney knew that the door Amar had escaped through led to a long wide hallway, which in turn led to an outside door. She dodged the fighting around her and sprinted after him, crashing through the doors just a few seconds after he did.

Up ahead of her, Amar turned into a blur.

Laney narrowed her eyes. *Oh no you don't.*

Cleo! With me.

Without looking, Laney knew the leopard had left her snack and was sprinting toward her.

Laney's eyes flicked to a tall statue up ahead. With a thought, a wind blew through the door ahead of Amar, grabbing the statue and slamming it into him.

He collapsed to the floor. Laney ran up to him, her gun leveled at his heart, as she heard giant paws beating a path down the hall. She glanced back and saw Cleo bearing down on her.

Hold him.

Cleo leapt. Her giant paws landed on Amar's chest,

pinning him to the ground. With a single swipe, she disemboweled him. He let out an inhuman shriek.

Cleo roared in response.

"Call it off!" Amar ordered, although the gurgle of blood in his throat took some of the sting out of his command.

Laney stared at the man. The decent thing to do would be to take him into custody. Let the government study him, find out his weaknesses, see the extent of his network.

That would be the decent thing to do.

Cleo met Laney's eyes, awaiting her orders. In that moment, Cleo and Laney were of one mind.

Laney saw Jake's face, a bullet hole in his forehead. She felt Rocky's hand going limp in her own, her life slipping away. And Laney caught a fleeting glimpse of another leopard: Cleo's mate.

Anger, power, and need coursed through Laney. Her eyes drew to a squint. "Take his head," she ordered.

Laney turned away as Cleo's jaws closed around Amar's head. As she strode back down the hall, Amar began to shriek in terror.

The decent thing to do would be to let him live.

She heard the wet rip as the giant cat tore Amar's head from his neck.

But this is war.

Chapter Ninety-Seven

LANEY WALKED BACK down the hall to the ballroom. The sounds of the battle had all but died away. She stepped into the room and realized the fight was over.

The ballroom was a disaster. All the windows were smashed. Glass and blood littered the wooden floor. Bodies lay across it as well, some in pieces.

Laney quickly looked around, seeing Laney, Jen, Yoni, and the twins. She spotted Maddox in the back corner as well. She let out a breath. They were all right.

Jen walked up to her. "You okay?"

Laney glanced around, trying not to stare at the large pools of blood that dotted the room. "Did we lose anyone?"

Jen shook her head. "No good guys. Couple of injuries, nothing life threatening."

"And the bad guys?"

"Twelve were killed. Another three escaped. They're being chased down now."

Laney nodded. A gunshot pulled her attention to the right. "What's going on there?"

There was one gunman standing over each surviving Fallen. Any time they moved, they were shot. At the back of the room, a group of paramedics bustled in the back door with stretchers and medical cases.

"Clark's orders. The Fallen who aren't dead are to be kept immobilized until they can be drugged," Jen said, before bending down to help an SIA agent who was wounded.

Laney walked over to look as a paramedic inserted a needle into a Fallen's arm. Laney read the label on the IV bag: *amobarbital.* A strong sedative.

Clark had come prepared. And he had also borrowed a page from Helen's book.

Clark caught sight of Laney and walked over, a clipboard in his hand. The man had gone from warrior to bureaucrat in seconds.

"What's the plan with them?" Laney nodded at the Fallen.

"We have a facility set up in West Virginia. It's known only to the SIA. The captives will be held there, perpetually drugged, except for when we interrogate them. I'm hopeful they can tell us something."

"You're sure this site is secure?"

He nodded. "We've been preparing for this for a long time. The only people who know about it are completely trustworthy. We'll interrogate each of them, find out what they know, where the other cells are. We need the intel."

Laney knew he was right, but it was still a huge risk. "And you'll tell me what you find out?"

Clark nodded, and Laney could see a newfound respect in his eyes. "If this is war, you're the reason we're going to win it. So yes, my paycheck may come from the U.S. government, but as far as I'm concerned, you're in charge."

"And you'll tell me where this place is?"

"I've emailed you and Henry all the information you need to find it and access it. Like I said, you're the boss." He started to walk away before turning back. "Amar?"

Laney met his eyes without flinching. "Taken care of."

Clark nodded. "Good." He walked over to another sedated Fallen, making a mark on his clipboard.

Cleo slipped in the back door, licking her lips. She looked around the room before padding over to Laney. Laney rubbed her head. "Good girl. Sit."

The cat perched next to her and Laney leaned into her, surveying the scene. Another bloody battle—and once again, she'd survived. But each time the cost increased. This latest battle had cost her Rocky and Jake.

What would the next one cost? Because, regardless of Samyaza's death, Laney knew another battle would be coming. She could feel it in her bones. This wasn't over.

Henry walked up to her, giving Cleo a wide berth. "Samyaza's taken care of?"

"Yes." Laney looked up at Henry and then away. She should probably feel some guilt at how she'd killed the man. But she didn't. What did that mean?

Henry nodded. "You all right?"

Laney felt cold seep through her, despite the warmth radiating through the leopard's skin. The specter of the fight yet to come tempered any relief she might have felt at tonight's success, and the responsibility of the ring weighed her down. "What if Clark's right? What if we're at war?"

Henry took her hand. She looked up into his eyes, eyes like Victoria's, and read the commitment and confidence there. "If we're at war? Then we fight. And we win." He paused. "What's wrong?"

"Are we sure Amar was Samyaza?"

Henry gestured around the room. "Well, obviously he was planning something."

"Yeah but..."

"Yeah but what?"

She sighed. "It was too easy."

"Too easy?"

Laney nodded. "He's supposed to be *Samyaza*. The leader of the Fallen. It should have been... harder."

"We caught him unaware. And it wasn't that easy. You and Yoni did almost get eaten by a cat."

Laney rubbed Cleo head's. "Nah, not my little sweetheart."

"We got him, Laney. It's over."

Laney looked around, a chill creeping over her. "Then why do I feel like it isn't?"

Chapter Ninety-Eight

IT TOOK hours to secure the farm and get all of the Fallen ready for transport, all while holding off the local police. By the time they were done, the sun was up.

They were still hours from home, but Laney wasn't up for another helicopter ride, and she could tell no one else was either. She stood next to the Suburban they were borrowing from Amar. Cleo had already been loaded inside, and was dozing.

"Laney."

She turned to see Maddox striding up to her. She smiled, but her smile disappeared at his expression. "Maddox, what's wrong?"

Maddox nodded toward his cell. "I just spoke with Amanda."

Laney smiled, feeling confused. "She wasn't happy to hear you're okay?"

A smile replaced the frown. "No, she was. She said to tell you thanks. She's going to meet me in Baltimore."

"Good. But why Baltimore?"

The frown reappeared. "Amanda uncovered an email. There were plans in place to go after some friends of yours: Max Simmons and Danny Wartowski."

Laney felt her knees go weak. "How?"

"They were supposed to grab Max at his school, and Danny from some bookstore. If that didn't work—bomb."

Laney felt the ground shift underneath her. She pictured Amar and wanted to kill him all over again.

Maddox touched her shoulder. "It's okay. Amanda intercepted the message. It never got through."

Laney closed her eyes, sinking back against the SUV. "Thank God. But they could still be in danger."

"What do you need, Laney? You saved my life. I owe you."

Laney pictured Max and Danny. "Does Henry know?"

Maddox nodded. "He's increased security around them at the estate."

"I need to find a way to keep them safe. Danny will have around-the-clock security on the estate. But Max and Kati are my responsibility. And I can't keep them locked up in Dom's bomb shelter forever."

Maddox raised an eyebrow. "Bomb shelter?"

She gave Maddox a small smile. "It's cozier than it sounds."

"Well, you're in luck. It just so happens that I'm looking for a job. My last employer and I have recently... gone our separate ways."

"You want to hang out with a single mom and a four-year-old in the suburbs?"

"Actually, right now that sounds like heaven. And like I said, I owe you. Big."

"Are you sure?"

Maddox nodded. "Yeah. Besides, kids love me."

Laney glanced up at Maddox. He looked like a member of a really, really tough biker gang. Which, she realized, is exactly what she wanted anyone who glanced at Max and Kati to see.

"Thanks, Maddox. It'll just be for a little while until I can figure something else out."

"It'll be a nice change of pace."

"But go see your sister first."

Maddox shored up his shoulders, snapping out a crisp salute. "Yes, General." He winked before turning on his heel and marching off.

Laney shook her head. *General. Great.*

Henry walked up a few seconds later and Cleo popped her head out of the window near Laney.

Henry jumped back. "Um, I guess she's coming with us?"

Laney nodded. "I don't think the local chapter of ASPCA is equipped to deal with her. Besides, she's on our side."

Henry shook his head. "Figured you'd say that. So I arranged for a cage from the local zoo to be delivered to the house, and another to the Baltimore estate."

Laney smiled. "You know me so well."

"Yes, I do. And you're sitting in the back with her."

"No problem," Laney said, opening the back door. She climbed in, and Cleo shifted over to make room.

As Henry pulled out, Cleo placed her head in Laney's lap. Laney absentmindedly ran her hands over the big cat's coat. "Where are we going?"

"Mom's got a house about twenty minutes from here. Yoni and the Witts are going to follow us there."

Laney knew she should be surprised that Victoria had a place nearby, but honestly, her biological mother had ceased to amaze her. If she learned tomorrow that her mother was an alien, she'd probably just nod her head and say okay.

Laney was beginning, though, to realize how truly extensive her mother's resources were. It was a little intimidating.

But it was also comforting. Maybe they *could* win this fight. Actually, with Samyaza dead, maybe they already had.

Henry glanced back at her. "The SIA found something else in the house."

"What?"

"The book that was stolen from Vegas."

"Really?"

Henry nodded, his attention on the road. "It's being shipped to Baltimore."

"You mean the Smithsonian?"

Henry shook his head. "No. I figure if they went to all that trouble to steal it, we need to read it. Fast. Which means me."

Laney felt the weight of responsibility settle back on her shoulders. Whatever Henry found in that book, she hoped it was only an explanation of what had happened. Not a prediction of more danger to come.

Laney stared out the window, watching the Tennessee landscape fly by. The numbness she'd built up during the flight to Tennessee, and maintained during the battle, had begun to wear off. Emptiness rushed in.

Right now, she had nothing else to focus on, nothing to keep her mind occupied. The denial stage was over. Jake was dead. It was like a piece of her was missing.

She let out a trembling breath. He was gone. It didn't seem real. He was so strong. So vital. How could he be gone? And how did people go on when they felt like this?

Victoria had said the chosen always had two protectors: one human, one more than human. Helen had had Castor and Pollux, and Laney was supposed to have Henry and Jake. And now Jake was gone.

Cleo shifted, but kept her head in Laney's lap. Laney rubbed the cat's ears. There was a bond between them now —a bond that Laney couldn't really explain. She wasn't going to let anyone hurt the animal. Not after what Cleo had done to help them.

Cleo let out a little whimper. Laney knew the giant feline missed her mate. Laney lowered her head to the cat's. Tears burned the back of her eyes. "I know it hurts, baby. I know."

Henry pulled off the highway and onto a small country road. Houses were few and far between. Laney focused on the scenery, trying to hold her sadness at bay, at least until she could grieve in private.

Henry turned again, onto a long dirt road. Finally, he pulled up in front of an old estate. Three stories, white with black shutters. Laney let out a little laugh in spite of her grief. "Mom sure does seem to have a type when it comes to houses."

Henry smiled. "Do you realize that's the first time you've called her 'Mom'?"

Laney caught his eyes. "I guess it is."

Another car, a Mercedes, was parked in front of the garage. "Who's that?" Laney asked.

"I'm not sure. Maybe the caretaker. Stay here. I'll go check it out."

Laney nodded, laying her head back against the seat. She knew she should be concerned, but at the moment, she just couldn't work up the energy.

Exhaustion and sadness pulled at her. She closed her

eyes. Maybe if she slept for a little while, the world wouldn't seem as cold or as dark.

Cleo let out a low growl.

Laney's eyes sprang open.

The garage door opened. Henry walked back toward the car, his face pale.

Dread welled up in Laney. She didn't think she could handle any more bad news. She detangled herself from the cat and opened the door.

"Stay, Cleo," she ordered, before closing the door and walking over to Henry. "What's happened? What's wrong?"

Henry shook his head, looking shocked. "It's... I can't believe..."

Laney's uncle stepped out of the shadows of the garage.

Laney looked between Henry and her uncle. "Uncle Patrick? How did you get here?"

Patrick just smiled and stepped aside as another man appeared.

Laney felt the world tilt. She grabbed onto Henry's arm for support.

"Jake?"

Jake walked toward her. Same deep brown eyes, same dark hair, same smile.

Laney stared at him, knowing her eyes were growing larger with every step he took. The man looked like Jake, but she'd seen him die. It couldn't be him.

He stopped when he was a foot away. He reached out a hand.

Laney shrank back. "Who are you?"

"Laney, honey, it's me," he said.

Laney shook her head, stepping back. "No. I saw you die. You're dead."

Her uncle ran to her side. "Laney, I was there, too. And I promise you, it's Jake. It's Jake."

Laney looked at her uncle and then back at the man in front of her. There was a small scar on his forehead—right at the spot where she'd seen him shot. She soaked in his face, every detail, right down to the small crook in his nose where'd he'd broken it when he was twelve.

Her eyes traveled over his body before returning once again to his face. His eyes looked tired, but other than that he was Jake. Her Jake.

Trembling, she stepped forward, putting her hand to his cheek. She gasped as his arms closed around her.

His scent brought tears to her eyes. She pulled him to her, holding him tight. "Jake."

Chapter Ninety-Nine

LANEY REFUSED to let go of Jake's hand. Even when Yoni and the Witts arrived, she would not let him go. They went through the same ritual of disbelief that Laney had—followed by hugs all around. Yet still Laney held on.

She floated between disbelief and dizzying happiness. Jake was here. She clung to his hand, terrified that if she let him go, he'd be gone again, and this would have all been a dream.

They all sat squeezed in the living room now. Everyone wanted to know how any of this was possible. But Laney could tell Jake was tiring. And she was close to her point of exhaustion as well.

She had more reason than anyone to want to know how Jake was there, alive, sitting next to her, but honestly, it could wait. Right now, she was spent, and she didn't want to question her luck. She just wanted to revel in it.

Laney nudged Jake on the shoulder. "Hey there, I could use some sleep."

Jake nodded, his eyelids springing back open. He'd been

fighting sleep since they'd entered the house. "Yeah, me too."

Laney found the two of them an empty bedroom on the second floor. Cleo followed them up and curled up in the corner.

Laney tucked Jake in, and by the time she joined him, he was already asleep. She curled up beside him, content just to listen to him breathe.

But before she knew it, she was opening her eyes. The sun was low in the sky. She must have slept for hours. She checked on Jake. He lay asleep, his breathing normal.

She ran her hand over his hair, and then hugged him tight. How was he here?

It made no sense. He had been dead. She knew that. She was sure of that.

Before, she'd been too exhausted to ask any questions. She'd been too happy just to have him there. But now, she couldn't avoid them.

She'd seen him shot. Even if by some miracle he had survived, he should be, at best, hospitalized. At worst, brain dead. There was no scientific explanation that could make sense of him walking around.

She traced the spot on his forehead where the bullet had entered. There was a small indent there now, but no other sign of trauma. *How?*

She traced over the spot in his arm where he'd been hurt in the car crash. The skin was completely unmarked.

Quietly, she slipped out of bed. Cleo raised her head from where she'd been curled in the corner.

Let's go, girl.

Cleo slipped silently out of the door behind her.

As they stepped into the hallway, Yoni came out of the

room next door. He jumped at the sight of Cleo and Laney. "That cat needs a bell," he muttered.

Laney smiled, but didn't say anything. Her mind was still full of Jake.

Yoni nodded toward her door. "He okay?"

"Somehow, yeah."

"How's that possible?"

"I don't know. He was dead. I know he was." She glanced back at the door and then at Yoni. "I need to go speak with my uncle. Will you stay here? In case Jake wakes up?"

Yoni nodded, with a quick glance at Cleo. "I will, as long as you take your friend with you."

"Deal."

Laney and Cleo headed downstairs. They stopped in the kitchen, where Laney fished a large bowl out of the cupboard. Henry walked in as she was filling it with water. She placed it on the floor. Cleo came over and licked it up greedily.

Patting the cat on the back, Laney turned to Henry. "Have you talked to Uncle Patrick yet?"

Henry shook his head. "I thought I'd wait for you. Ready for some answers?"

"Absolutely."

Together, they headed for the living room. Her uncle sat on the couch, a crossword in his lap. He looked up with a smile. "Jake still sleeping?"

She nodded. "Yeah." She sank down onto the couch next to him.

Patrick wrapped his arms around her. "Thank God you're okay."

Laney let herself relax and take the comfort from her uncle. But the questions about Jake wouldn't leave her. She pushed back. "I'm okay. Just confused. I don't understand how Jake's here. It's just not possible."

"I—" Patrick broke off when Cleo slunk into the living room. "Um, is your new friend going to be okay in here?"

Cleo walked over to Laney, who scratched her behind the ears. "Good girl. Go lie down."

Cleo walked to the corner of the room and curled up.

"She's good." And Laney knew it was true. Cleo wouldn't hurt anyone in this house, not without express permission from Laney.

"How are you doing that without the ring on?" Henry asked.

Laney's hand went to where the ring was hanging from a chain on her neck. "I'm not sure. I think maybe the ring establishes the link, and once established, it's no longer needed."

Turning from the cat, she looked at Patrick. "Well?"

It took Patrick a moment to pull his eyes from the giant leopard. Obviously Cleo's presence had him a little rattled. "Um, I can explain what I saw. But I can't tell you how because, to be honest, I have no idea."

He took a breath, looking between Laney and Henry. "After you two escaped, Victoria told me to hurry. I thought she meant we needed to get to cover. But that's not what she meant. She told me to begin chest compressions. She said we needed to keep his blood flowing."

Patrick shook his head. "I thought she was crazy. The problem obviously wasn't with Jake's heart. But I was in such a state of shock, I didn't argue, I just began the compressions. Then Victoria pulled out a knife."

"A knife?" Henry asked.

Patrick nodded. "She cut her wrist. Then she put her wrist on Jake's wound, her blood mingling with his. I don't know how much time passed, but it was a while. My arms were growing tired, but Victoria warned me not to stop. Around that time, Ralph arrived. And some time before that, the men shooting at us had stopped. I guess they went after you."

Laney nodded, not capable of more than that.

"Ralph took one look at the scene, pushed me out of the way, and started doing the compressions himself," Patrick said.

"And then what? Jake came back?" Henry asked.

"Not right away. The wound, though..." Patrick paused. "It began to close. When that happened, Victoria told Ralph he could stop. That it would be okay. But from that moment until just a couple of hours ago, Jake was in a coma."

"Why didn't you take him to a hospital?" Laney asked, still trying to wrap her mind around what Patrick was saying.

"I wanted to, but Victoria said no. That they wouldn't understand. She said he would be fine, and for some reason, I believed her."

Laney nodded, understanding. Victoria was a riddle wrapped in an enigma, yet somehow, when she spoke, you found yourself believing everything she said.

Patrick continued. "She arranged for a private charter to take us all back to the States. When I contacted the Chandler Group, they told me you were in Tennessee, so I re-routed here. Jake and I disembarked and Victoria continued on to somewhere else. We reached the house only a few minutes before you did."

Laney sat back and stared into space. Victoria had brought Jake back from the dead—with her blood. She struggled with possible logical scenarios. She felt like she was back at the beginning of this mess when she was trying to figure out what Paul and Gideon were.

She blew out a breath. "Okay, so my only thought is 'vampire.' Anybody have anything less supernatural?"

Patrick and Henry didn't say anything for a moment. Then slowly they both shook their heads.

Laney tried not to groan. *Crap.*

Chapter One Hundred

THEY LEFT for the Chandler estate an hour later, when Jake woke. But first, Laney sat with him in the bedroom. Patrick said he hadn't told Jake anything about what had happened during the time he was in a coma. So Laney was the one to break the news to him.

Jake's eyes were large. "Dead? I was *dead*? I mean, I heard you say that when you first got here, but I just thought you, I don't know, misspoke."

"I didn't misspeak. You don't remember anything?"

"Last thing I remember was stepping out of the path in Saqqara. Then I was waking up on a plane with Patrick. Was I really dead?"

Laney nodded. "Yes. It's been three days." If Jake were religious, she'd point out the similarities to another fellow who came back to life after three days, but she was pretty sure that comparison wouldn't be received too well.

"I—" Jake paused. "I don't even know what to say about that."

The door pushed open. Cleo walked in, her tail swishing

behind her. She rubbed against Laney and then Jake before curling up on the bed behind them.

Jake watched the leopard, his eyebrows raised. "Um, have we adopted a cat?"

"I think she's adopted us."

Jake's eyebrows seemed to get even higher.

Laney put up her hands. "I'll figure something out. But she won't hurt you, or anyone. Not without permission."

"You're sure?"

Laney's hand went to the ring around her neck. "Positive."

Jake nodded at it. "How come you're wearing that on a chain and not your finger?"

Laney paused, trying to figure out how to explain her decision. "The power of this thing . . . it's seductive. It would be easy to abuse. I've decided I'm only going to wear it when I need it. But I'll keep it nearby."

Jake leaned down and kissed her forehead. "I think whoever decided you were the ring bearer made a very wise choice." He stood up, pulling Laney with him. "Come on. Let's head for home. Apparently, we have a lot of people to tell I'm not dead."

Laney shook her head as she walked with him out of the room. Every time she thought her life couldn't get stranger...

It took only two hours to get back to Baltimore. Laney held onto Jake the whole ride. They shared the chopper with Yoni, Patrick, and Henry. Mike, Jen, and Jordan had agreed to drive Cleo back—on the condition that she be sedated first.

It was hard, but Laney knew it was for the best. She had faith in her control, but she didn't want to test it while in the air. Or have the Witts test it while they were driving.

By the time the chopper reached Baltimore, it looked like a hundred people were milling around the helipad.

Laney glanced down, knowing they were there to see Jake. She squeezed his hand. "And you thought you didn't have a family. Look down there. That's your family."

Jake squeezed her hand back.

The crowd was quiet when the chopper landed—until Jake opened his door. Then applause broke out. People surged forward to hug Jake, slap him on the back.

Laney kept back, not wanting to get in the way. Her heart wanted to burst with happiness that he was back, but the shadow of Rocky's death kept it from being a perfect moment.

And how exactly did Victoria bring him back?

Jake looked back at her and Laney smiled, banishing the words from her mind. The questions could wait. He reached out his hand.

She walked through the crowd to take it. Right now, there were more important things.

An impromptu party had been set up on the back lawn of the Chandler estate. Everybody from Chandler was there, as well as a bunch of Jake's military buddies. It was a little "Glad you're back—how the hell are you still alive?" party. Everyone was thrilled Jake was here, but Laney caught more than one confused look.

Kati had even come by with Max. But Laney could tell that being out in the open was a little rough for her. She was still suffering aftereffects from the attacks, and her gaze kept straying to Max, who was engaged in some sort of potato-chip-eating contest with Danny. Moxy stood next to them, gobbling up all the misses.

And Maddox was as good as his word. He stayed with them, a tall, scowling bodyguard looming nearby.

Laney pulled Kati aside. She nodded toward Maddox. "You sure you're okay with him?"

Kati nodded, her eyes still on Max. "Yeah. Actually, having him around makes me feel a little better. And Max likes him."

"I'm so sorry for all of this, Kati."

Kati's head whipped back. "Don't you ever say that to me. You are the reason my son and I are alive. You didn't cause any of this, Laney. That's not on you. And as far as I can see, you're doing everything you can to make it right."

Rocky's image floated into her mind. "Yeah, but it doesn't feel like it's enough."

Kati hugged her. "That's because you're not delegating. Other people can take some of the load. It's not all on you."

Laney pulled back. "I know, I know."

"And Rocky wasn't your fault either. She's as independent as you. Her decisions are hers." Kati took a shuddering breath. "And she loved you, just like we loved her."

Laney nodded, but couldn't speak, grief clogging her throat.

Kati squeezed her hand. "Now, if you don't mind, I think I'm going to take Max back to Dom's. He's doing all right, but I'm still not so crazy about crowds."

"Maddox going with you?"

"Absolutely." Kati disappeared into the crowd, before reappearing next to Max and Maddox.

Maddox reached down and picked up Max, then tossed him into the air. Max laughed as Maddox caught him. Apparently, Maddox was good with kids.

She tried not to frown as she watched them leave, along with Danny and Moxy. She hated that Kati was scared. She'd have to figure out a way to make Kati feel safe enough to rejoin her life. It wasn't going to be easy.

Jake walked over and grabbed her hand. "Come dance with me."

Laney smiled. Well, she'd figure all that out later. Right now, she was going to let herself enjoy her time with Jake.

An hour later, Laney, Jake, and Henry found a quiet part of the veranda. Laney and Jake sat next to each other on a lounge. Henry sat across from them.

Laney held Jake's hand, yet again. "Are you sure you feel all right?"

Jake laughed. "Laney, I feel great. To be honest, I feel better than I have in years. All my old aches seem to have disappeared."

Henry shook his head. "And you still don't remember anything?"

"No, nothing between leaving the entrance of the tunnel in Egypt and waking up on the plane." Jake's brow furrowed. "I don't get how Victoria was able to do that. I've never heard of anything like that."

Jake had spoken with Patrick, who'd related Victoria's actions to him. But Jake hadn't been able to shed any more information on what exactly had happened.

Henry gave a little laugh. "Well, hopefully Yoni will get tired of the zombie jokes. Eventually."

Jake groaned. "He keeps telling me that if I get a hankering for brains, to start with the PhDs. Says their brains are tastier." He nudged Laney. "Hey, Earth to Laney."

Laney turned to smile at him. "Sorry. Mind wandering."

"Care to tell us where it's wandering to?" Jake asked.

"Nowhere special. Just thinking about everything." Laney noticed a tall slim black man step out from the house, an attractive woman with pale green eyes next to him. The man cast a bewildered gaze around before spying Laney.

She waved and nudged Jake. "Hey, there's Tom."

Jake glanced over with a smile before standing. "I'll go say hi. You guys can join me after you discuss whatever it is you don't want to discuss in front of me." He gave Laney a kiss on the forehead before he walked off.

"Perceptive bugger, isn't he?" Laney said with a smile.

Henry nodded. "So, what are you thinking?"

"Well, I'm pretty sure Yoni's zombie theory is wrong, but I *have* been thinking about other cases of people coming back from the dead. The only ones I can think of are from the Bible."

"Jesus and Lazarus," Henry said.

Laney nodded. "Yup. But that doesn't seem to apply here. It's as if something in Victoria's blood healed Jake. I think that's why she had Patrick keep his blood pumping. His heart needed to be beating if it was going to work."

"I was thinking the same thing. I mean, I have blood that heals me, but I've never heard of it healing anyone else. And I've run a ton of tests on it. Besides, Mom's not a Fallen or a nephilim."

Laney paused, remembering Amar's words. "But they all seem to know who she is, don't they? Gideon asked you about her. And Amar mentioned her as well. And how does she know all that she knows?"

They both fell quiet. Laney's mind traveled over every mystery involving Victoria, and she was pretty sure Henry had even more questions than she did. Whenever Victoria spoke about the past, it was always as if she had been an eyewitness. And what had Amar meant when he said Victoria played a part in humanity's mortality?

"Do you know who she is?" Laney asked.

Henry shook his head with a sigh. "No. I've wondered, but I'm no closer than you to an answer. The only thing I know is that she's not some mere human, no matter what she says."

"No, she's definitely not." Laney looked over at Henry. "We need some answers."

Henry shook his head. "We can try Mom, but Laney, it would be easier getting blood from a stone."

"There has to be a way." Laney spied her uncle in the crowd. "What about the books?"

"From Ecuador? It's going to take a while to translate them. But I'm going to start working on the one Amar stole first thing."

"No, not those books. The Council books. Flourent had a set, right?"

Henry nodded, his expression thoughtful. "Actually, some of them survived. The bookcase they were stored in was bolted to the wall, which was actually built into the rock face. When the house collapsed, the bookcase was still there. And about half of the books."

"Great."

"I bet they'll have some answers." He glanced sideways at Laney. "But I'll ask Patrick and maybe Jen to go through them."

"Why not me?"

Henry took Laney's hand. "Because I think you need to spend some time with Jake, and maybe focus on figuring out that ring. Let some other people shoulder the burden."

"Delegate." She smiled. "You're the second person to tell me that."

"Mom's not the only thing bothering you, is she?"

Laney sighed, looking over everyone on the veranda, her eyes coming to rest on Jake and Tom. "I want this to be over. I really do. But I don't think it is."

"Why not?"

Her eyes met Henry's. "You, me, and Jake. We're the triad, the three sides of the triangle. Right?"

Henry nodded.

Laney pulled the chain from around her neck, showing Henry the ring face. "What do you see?"

"The Seal of Solomon."

Laney nodded. "Which is *two* triangles. So if we're one triangle, who's in the other?"

Epilogue

The devil's finest trick is to persuade you that he does not exist.

Charles Baudelaire, *Paris Spleen*

GERARD WALKED DOWN THE LONG, white marble hallway. In fact, the whole home was white Carrara marble from floor to ceiling.

Cold and impersonal. Just like its owner, Gerard thought as his footsteps echoed around him.

He was not looking forward to this meeting. He wanted to take a moment to catch his breath. But his presence was already known. Any hesitation would be taken as a sign of weakness.

And that could not happen. Not ever. He knocked.

"Enter."

He stopped in the doorway, waiting for the woman behind the desk to acknowledge him. Elisabeta Roccorio was in her fifties, but she had the shape of a much younger woman. She had dark eyes and dark brown hair, pulled back in a chignon. Her white suit accentuated her ample chest as well as her olive skin tone, a product of her Greek heritage.

A small pair of reading glasses perched on the end of her nose. After a few moments, she removed the glasses and sat back.

Gerard was once again struck by her looks. She was not conventionally attractive. Her nose was too large for her face, her eyes too small and close together. But power radiated from her—and *that* was attractive.

He stepped forward. "I have news from Tennessee."

She gestured for him to stand in front of her desk. "And?"

"You were right. She's stronger than Amar thought."

"I warned him. The ring bearers, they are always stronger than they are given credit for. You knock them down and they get back up, stronger by tenfold. I warned Amar that killing Jake Rogan was a mistake." She eyed him. "You should have stopped him."

Gerard nodded, although he felt anger at the censure. Still, he was smart enough not to let it show beyond the angry flush he could feel climbing his neck. "We've lost our numbers. We'll have to rebuild."

She waved away the words. "Not all of them. Amar and his group were a tiny fiefdom. I still hold the kingdom. And the book? What of it?"

"I'm afraid it was at Amar's home at the time of the attack."

"McPhearson and her people have it?"

Gerard nodded, tensing.

She stared at him.

Gerard felt a bead of sweat roll down his back.

"I'm not happy, Gerard."

"I know. But there is some good news."

Elisabeta's eyes sliced through him. "He finished the translation."

Gerard nodded. "Yes. And you were right. The fifth root race is the key."

Elisabeta smiled, leaning back. "And now you have made me happy again. Even without the book, we are ahead. They won't be able to catch up with us. Not in time at least."

Gerard struggled not to slouch with relief.

Elisabeta looked out the window, her eyes on the canal. A gondola drifted by, its oarsmen looking for a fare. "And to think, all of this rests on the knowledge of a child."

Gerard barely made out the words. But he knew they were not really for him.

She turned back to him, her eyes focused. "Now the real fight begins. Nicely done, Gerard. You are dismissed."

Gerard bowed, careful to back away and not give her his back. She wouldn't like that. "Yes, Samyaza."

Next in The Belial Series

vinci-books.com/belialrecruit

Lou Thomas thought she'd lost everything, but her awakening powers might cost her the one thing she has left: her life.

Turn the page for a free preview…

The Belial Recruit: Chapter One

DETROIT, MICHIGAN

Fifteen-year old Lou Thomas walked down the street, her shoulders hunched against the cold. She knew there were two of them behind her. She'd seen them when she cut through the parking lot of the supermarket five minutes ago.

She hadn't liked the look of them then and she sure didn't like the look of them now that they were following her.

One of them was white, one black, both in their mid-twenties. And they were thin - heroin thin with scruffy beards. They each had old flannel jackets that had seen better days and dark skullcaps.

And although she hadn't gotten too close, the wind had shifted letting her know that one, or probably both of them, were in desperate need of a bath.

Another wind blew against her now. Lou pulled up the collar of her jean jacket, although it didn't help much. She hitched her backpack up on her shoulder. She'd stayed late at her shift at the diner - not that she'd made much extra. People weren't really in a tipping mood these days.

And now these guys are going to take what little I did make, she thought. Anger and resentment ran through her right next to the fear.

She debated what to do. Cutting through the park would be faster and the park would probably be pretty empty with a storm kicking up and it getting close to dark.

She pictured the dark trees and winding paths. The city hadn't been keeping up the park and as a result, the trees and bushes were wildly overgrown creating lots of hiding spots.

A shiver ran through her. *But anyone I run into in there will not be someone I want to chat with.*

She glanced behind - the two men were a little farther back. If she turned the corner quick enough, they might not notice her heading to the park. If she stayed on the streets, though, it would easily take an extra fifteen minutes to get home.

Another wind, stronger this time, blew against her. The chill sliced right through to her bones.

Decision made. Lou picked up the pace, darted around the corner, and leaped over the chain link fence into the park. If she was lucky, they wouldn't realize what she'd done until-

The rattle of the chain link behind her told her she was not lucky tonight. *Shit.*

Moving faster, Lou headed deeper into the park. *Stupid. So stupid. I should have stayed on the road.*

Of course, there wouldn't have been much help there, either. People in this neighborhood didn't exactly leap to one another's defense.

A scuffle sounded behind her. Lou turned her head.

They were closer. Two arms wrapped around her biceps as she collided into someone.

Her head whipped around. "Sorry," she said stepping back.

The two hands held her in place. "Hey beautiful. You can run into me any time."

The man was the Latino version of the other two. Except instead of a flannel jacket, he had on an old dark sweatshirt with the hood up.

Lou's voice turned hard. "Let me go."

"Not yet sweetheart. My friends and I were going to have a little party." He looked up. "Hey guys."

Lou looked behind her. The two guys she'd seen on the street. They'd actually been heading to the park. If she'd stayed on the damned street, she would have been fine.

Fear raced through her. "Get your hands off of me."

He shook her and her head jolted with action. Her backpack slipped down onto her elbow. He yanked it off her and tossed it at one of his friends. "See if there's anything good."

"Let me go," Lou said again, her voice shaking.

"Not until we're done." He smirked, taking a step back while keeping her in his grip. He looked her over. "You're a tiny little thing, aren't you? But that's good. I like tiny. Makes me feel big. Real big."

He pushed her toward the woods. "Come on."

Lou dug in her heels. "I'm not going anywhere with you."

Anger began to replace her fear. At that moment, she was sick of always being scared. Scared at school. Scared at home. Scared just living. And for whatever stupid reason, even though part of her mind yelled at her to just do what he said, she was done with being scared.

And somewhere deep inside of her Lou felt a binding snap loose.

The man holding her reared back with one hand, bringing it toward her face. With a speed that astonished her, Lou reached up and blocked it. Grabbing onto to the man's wrist she twisted it to a ninety-degree angle.

He screeched, dropping to his knees. "Let go bitch."

One of the other men ran at her. Keeping hold of the first guy's wrist she turned and kicked the other guy in the chest.

A crack sounded. He screamed and fell back, holding his side.

Lou's eyes went wide. *Were those his ribs?*

The third guy pulled a switchblade from his pocket, flipping it open.

Lou yanked on the guy she was holding, placing him between her and his knife-wielding friend.

"Tell your friend to get out of here or I'll break your wrist." She twisted his wrist for emphasis.

He yelled. "Get out of here, man."

His friend didn't seem interested in listening. He circled around her and tried to run at her.

Lou was faster.

She twirled her prisoner in between them again and shoved him, turning his wrist - hard. The bone snapped.

He screeched and fell to the ground. The man with the knife tripped over him with a yelp and fell onto his stomach.

The first man scrambled to his feet, cradling his wrist. He backed away from her. "You bitch. You broke my wrist."

The man Lou kicked also got to his feet holding his side. "Get up, Mike." He kicked Mike who was still lying face down. Mike didn't move.

Lou's eyes travelled from the man's ratty sneakers up to

his skullcap. Nothing moved. A dark liquid began to seep from under him onto the path.

Lou took a step back in horror.

"You killed him." The Latino guy stared at her with accusing eyes.

Lou stumbled back from them. "I didn't mean- I didn't - " She looked up into the two men's eyes. Anger burned bright in them and a small dash of fear.

Lou slammed her mouth shut, turned on her heel, and ran.

Grab your copy...
vinci-books.com/belialrecruit

Afterword

FACT OR FICTION?

All of the books in The Belial Series come from facts I've picked up over the years—facts I string together in a way that, I hope, makes for a good story. So here are some of the areas that might be of interest to you. Some are big components of the story and some just passing details. Facts are placed here in no particular order.

Hypatia. Hypatia was an actual woman associated with the Library of Alexandria. She is considered the mother of mathematics and was herself a teacher of mathematics, astronomy, and philosophy. She was killed by a mob sometime around AD 415 or 416. As such, she died before the fire that destroyed the library, so I took a little creative liberty there. She is, however, revered as a progressive thinker, if not the last great thinker of Alexandria.

The Library of Alexandria. The Library of Alexandria is well known, but the details of its demise are not. While multiple sources agree that fire destroyed the famed complex, most differ on who lit the match, and there is some debate as to precisely when it was finally destroyed. I decided to go with the 647 date. The details about its beginning are, however, clear: it was established under Ptolemy's rule in the third century BC. And there is no debate whatsoever as to it being an incredible center of learning in ancient times.

Helen of Troy. There are still questions as to whether Helen was a figment of Homer's imagination or an actual flesh-and-blood woman. What we do know is that the name Helen was known throughout the world, well before Homer wrote of her. There were cults to Helen throughout the Bronze Age and later. And many of those most vocal about her affair with Paris were writing hundreds of years after her life. And seeing as how the city of Troy was once believed to be merely a work of fiction—until, in 1870, the city itself was discovered by Heinrich Schliemann—well, it seems fair that I choose to believe that Helen, too, was real.

All of the information in *The Belial Ring* is accurate when it comes to the historical details of Helen of Troy. Or, should I say, Helen of Sparta. For if Helen was indeed a real person, then she was the heir to the Spartan throne. In the Bronze Age, Spartan rule went through the daughters, not the sons.

Helen did have two brothers named Castor and Pollux. Some say they were twins; others not. Helen was said by some to have been born from an egg. It's been alleged that when she was younger, she was kidnapped by Theseus and then rescued by her brothers.

Was Helen in Egypt during the Trojan War? As explained in *The Belial Ring*, Helen and Paris did stop in Egypt on their way to Troy. And according to the historian Herodotus, a ghost-like doppelganger replaced Helen at this point, and the real Helen never made it to Troy. Instead, she spent the entire war in Egypt.

I used many sources to pull together the information on Helen, but the most helpful was the book *Helen of Troy: Goddess, Princess, Whore* by Bettany Hughes. It is a fascinating account of what Helen's life would have been like, drawing on the historical and archaeological evidence from the Bronze Age. If you're looking for more information on her, I strongly recommend the book.

Übermensch. The Übermensch were an actual part of Hitler's Lebensborn program. In 1932, Hitler began his attempts to create the master race through this program. People with perfect genetic histories were encouraged, or, more accurately, *required*, to reproduce. The result? Forty-two thousand children. Years after the program's initiation, Hitler instituted a six-foot height requirement. Even taller members—those with a height above six foot six—were considered Übermensch. They received a special medal of honor and were automatically promoted to S.S. officer.

The Serapeum in Saqqara. A serapeum is a religious center dedicated to the god Serapis. There are actually a number of serapeums that have been uncovered. In this book, I focus on the Serapeum in Saqqara.

All the information portrayed in *The Belial Ring* about this location is accurate to the best of my ability. The giant sarcophagi are real; they do weigh seventy tons; only three of them have been inscribed; and bones were found in only three of them.

The narrow passages are also real, and it's true that archaeologists can't figure out how exactly the giant tombs were carried into their underground niches.

The Ring of Solomon. The tale about Solomon's son, Menelik, stealing the Ark of the Covenant is rumored to be true.

The Chapel of the Tablet in Aksum, Ethiopia exists and does claim to have held the Ark of the Covenant since the time of Solomon. But Menelik himself was not the one who was supposed to have taken it—but, rather, some other young lords who accompanied him back to his home.

Does the ring exist? That is the question, isn't it? As with many powerful objects from antiquity, its existence is unclear. As is the power it actually conveyed to the user. Solomon was said to have power over animals, the weather, and demons through a ring. Is that true, an exaggeration, or just a myth? I don't know.

The War Scroll. The War Scroll is one of the original seven Dead Sea Scrolls found in Qumran on the West Bank. The Dead Sea Scrolls were all found in sealed pots, and were all written around the first century AD in various languages, most found on papyrus.

The War Scroll (whose formal title is *The War of the Sons of Light Against the Sons of Darkness*) tells of a final apocalyptic battle between the Children and the Sons of Belial. And according to some, that final battle is supposed to occur in Makeda, Israel.

Edgar Cayce. And, of course, many of my story ideas originated with my readings on Edgar Cayce. Edgar Cayce was an incredibly fascinating man. He was a twentieth-century psychic who did health and life readings. Some of those life readings addressed the creation of man, right down to how exactly we appeared on this planet, as well as our early civilizations, particularly the existence of a place known today as Atlantis. And its destruction.

Alchemy. Dr. Hantaro Nagaoka was a Japanese physicist who discovered that if you placed an isotope of mercury under paraffin oil and then bombarded it with one hundred and fifty thousand volts of electricity, you get gold. Yup. He figured out how to actually transmute a metal.

Dogon Tribe. The Dogon people of Mali do indeed exist. Living in West Africa, the Dogon claim to date back thousands of years and today number around one hundred thousand people. They had been largely isolated from modern man until the early twentieth century.

All the information in *The Belial Ring* attributed to them is accurate. They claim to have known about the four moons of Jupiter, the rings of Saturn, and the existence of the star Sirius—as well as the existence of the star Sirius B that orbits it—long before any of those facts were established by modern science.

So how exactly did the Dogon know any of this information? The Dogon claim the origins of their knowledge come from a people who descended from the sky, some time before 3,200 BC. If you have some spare time, look them up. They are truly fascinating.

Animal Experiments. The animal experiments mentioned in the book are also taken from reality. Back in 1959, Dr. Vladimir Demikhov did indeed surgically attach a second head to a living dog. And the dog survived for months. Sick, yes, but real.

In 2003, scientists at Shanghai University did successfully merge human cells with rabbit eggs. The embryos were destroyed after a short time, but the stem cells were harvested. The Mayo Clinic created a pig with human blood, and in Stanford, scientists created mice with human brains. Sometimes fact is stranger than fiction.

Human Immortality. So, were humans ever immortal? Believe it or not, that is not an easy question. The Sumerian King List mentioned in *The Belial Ring* is an actual list that dates to the ancient Sumerians. On the list are dozens of kings, some of whom are reported to have ruled for thousands of years. For example, the list says that Alagar ruled for *thirty-six thousand* years.

Cayce, too, argued that originally humans lived for an extremely long time. So: immortal? Probably not. But early records do suggest the possibility of a much longer life span.

There are, however, snippets from the Bible that suggest the possibility of immortality. But I think I'll save that discussion for a different book.

Vulcan Death Grip. Anyone who has ever watched the original *Star Trek* is familiar with the Vulcan death grip. Dr. Spock could merely grip someone on the side of the neck and knock them out. I always thought that was Hollywood's imagination. Then I went to a weekend seminar with Guro Dan Inosanto.

For those who aren't familiar, Guro Inosanto is one of the most recognizable people in martial arts today. He was also one of Bruce Lee's early students. During the seminar, Guro Inosanto recounted a time when someone had performed the technique on him. Twice. Knocked him out for hours both times.

Guro Inosanto still hasn't figured out how it was done to him. So, does it exist? According to Guro Inosanto, it does. And I'm certainly not going to disagree with him!

Reincarnation Research. The research in reincarnation in *The Belial Ring* is fact. For example, Dr. Ian Stevenson did indeed conduct research that linked a child's birthmarks with injuries from a previous life. And Cayce did do a past life reading for Henry Ford, who, according to Cayce, was alive during the time of Atlantis. Cayce did contend that in his Atlantis life, Henry Ford was an inventor. And all the famous people said to have been proponents of reincarnation really were proponents: including Henry Ford, Mahatma Gandhi, Socrates, Napoleon, and Friedrich Nietzsche.

About the Author

Author, Criminologist, Terrorism Expert, Jeet Kune Do Black Sash, Runner, Dog Lover.

Amazon best-selling author R.D. Brady writes supernatural and science fiction thrillers. Her thrillers include ancient mysteries, unusual facts, non-stop action, and fierce women with heart.

Prior to beginning her writing career, R.D. Brady was a criminologist who specialized in life-course criminology and international terrorism. She's lectured and written numerous academic articles on the genetic influence on criminal behavior, factors that influence terrorist ideology, and delinquent behavior formation.

After visiting counter-terrorism units in Israel, R.D returned home with a sabbatical in front of her and decided to write that book she'd been thinking about. Four years later she left academia with the publication of her first book, *The Belial Stone*, and hasn't looked back.

Acknowledgments

There are a lot of great people who helped make *The Belial Ring* a reality. First and foremost, I'd like to thank all the special critters who have read and re-read multiple drafts of this work. Every week, you helped me iron out the mistakes and find a better way to explain my ideas. I am forever grateful.

Special thanks in particular to Dana Griffin and C.K. Raggio. You guys kept me going by offering support, insight, and the occasional kick in the butt. I couldn't have done it without you.

I'd also like to thank my group of beta readers, who helped make this version of *The Belial Ring* a much cleaner copy. Thank you for reading. And thank you for all your work.

Thanks to my family and friends who have supported my efforts along the way.

Thank you to the people who helped with the editing and cover design. Alexis and Damonza, thank you for all your incredible work. And a special thank-you to David Gatewood for all the time you put in. I am extremely grateful.

Thanks to my favorite beta reader, Elizabeth McCartan. Thank you for reading the first draft and for everything else you do.

To my three little ones who constantly ask me how my books are doing and whether they're done yet. And who occasionally give me some book suggestions for the future. But most importantly, they make me smile and appreciate how good life can be. I can't thank them enough for that.

Thank you to my husband Tae. Thank you for always being there, always supporting me, and always having my back. I never would have had the courage to go down this path without you walking next to me, so my success is without a doubt the result of you being in my life. Thank you.

And finally, thank you to all the readers who have been kind enough to drop me a line and tell me how much you are enjoying the series. I haven't been able to respond directly to all of you, but I have read every note. And they urge me on and give me a little spring in my step. Thank you for taking the time to write. It does mean a lot.